The Trouble With Thieves

Book 1: Return to Averia

Maurice X. Alvarez
&
Ande Li

808 Room·808·Press·

Acknowledgements

My first acknowledgement is to my wife and co-author, Ande Li. without that first drawing in 1988 of a strange man and two girls in a classroom, Kormèr Lezàl would never have been born. Your collaboration on this book and your patience with my brainstorming over the years is worth more than any byline.

A special thanks to our old friend Yury K., the first person to read through all the Kormèr Lezàl stories. The fact that you kept asking for more was an inspiration.

And a huge thanks to author David H. Burton for answering my endless questions about how to self-publish online back in 2010 (aka the dark ages of self-publishing).

And also to our readers, for enjoying our books and spreading the word. Your reviews and feedback are the stuff that keeps us going.

AUTHOR'S NOTE

While Earth (Terran) English is the prevalent language of the Galactic Federation, the denizens of other planets often speak in their native tongues. For the sake of clarity, speech in Elmarian is represented in this text by the use of different quotation marks as in:

<<Elmarian>>
||Averian||
^Halgarin^

PROLOGUE

A pinpoint of golden light pierced darkness deeper than a starless night sky. The spot bloomed into a sparkling cascade, then collapsed back in on itself, like a silent pulse of energy waking from a long slumber. The new pinpoint yawned quietly open into a softly glowing blue portal. Not a friendly pale azure, but an intense, electric cobalt that threatened to swallow whole anything that dared enter its depths. It was a living blue contained inside the edges of the portal: slow and sinuous and hypnotic.

Rectangular and roughly two meters tall, the portal looked particularly door-like, but—like others of its type—it could assume any shape and size, as directed by its user. It almost always hovered about twenty centimeters from the ground, as it did now. And an eight-buttoned tab always protruded slightly from its inner top edge.

This particular portal had been to twelve worlds in three galaxies, not counting the present one. On the solid, gray back side of its frame, it bore the nicks and scratches of its travels, including a thin line about halfway up made by a passing obsidian arrowhead, and a little ding from a grain of space debris colliding into it at 150,000 meters per hour. It had not been mauled by a pack of theropods or taken irrevocably apart by an overeager physicist, as had happened to two of its kind. Not yet, anyway.

Its light washed out through the dark, illuminating a section of polished marble floor that ended at two large ornately crafted doors with twin golden handles.

Kormèr Lezàl stepped out from the portal, the leather soles of his calf-length black boots making almost no noise on the marble floor. Peering through the holes in his silk mask, he scanned what he could see of his surroundings and listened for any sound of alarm. Satisfied that he was alone, he reached up with a black-gloved hand and twisted the tab on the portal. The device shut down instantly, pitching the room back into darkness. By some miracle of physics, for which Kormèr had no explanation, he was left holding not the tab but a crystal cube, an inactive miniature form of the portal itself. This he dropped into the pocket of his long black overcoat.

Kormèr took a moment to let his eyes adjust to the darkness, though he knew exactly where he was. Years of using the portal to break into the palatial home of the interim Duke had instilled in him an almost-innate familiarity with the layout of its rooms. Even now, in complete darkness, he could clearly picture the walls of the antechamber in which he stood. But likewise, his years of experience as a thief had also taught Kormèr the value of being well prepared for the unexpected. Kormèr knew that Duke Bederf would be busy for the next few hours, but the Duchess had a penchant for taking lovers. Kormèr wanted to be ready to defend himself against any overzealous—or perhaps overly jealous—competition.

When he felt his eyes had adjusted enough, he moved to the double doors, twisted the handle and eased one open. He gritted his teeth as the hinge squeaked… unexpectedly. Undaunted, he continued pushing the door open and stepped into the royal bedchamber, even as the bed sheets rustled.

<<Zolt?>> inquired the sweet, groggy voice of the young Duchess Menddilal.

Kormèr rolled his eyes at hearing the name of his competition, one of the Duchess's other lovers. <<No, my sweet,>> he said in a near whisper, closing the door behind him. Then, even lower, he muttered, <<Not Zolt.>>

Bathed in the scant moonlight from the window, Menddilal sat up. <<Light, dim,>> she commanded, and enough light filled the room to reveal its opulence. In Kormèr's eyes, the room paled compared to Menddilal, resplendent even in sleep, a siren whose song was that of silken hair, wide chestnut eyes, delicate yet supple lips, a firm, toned physique and very confident demeanor. She took Kormèr's breath away, though he loved her not at all. And he knew the inverse to be true as well. Their relationship was one of convenience; she got to exert her authority over an admirer, while he got another chance to steal the sparkling tiara that lay on her bedside table, the one prize that had eluded him since his first foray into this bedchamber.

<<Eddrin Ciendd!>> She used the false name he had given her long ago. Then she furrowed her brow at him. <<Just where have you been? It's been weeks since you visited last. >>

Kormèr bowed his head. <<I'm sorry, my sweet. Business called me away. It's been torture without your loving caresses.>> This was not untrue. She had been an exciting lover for nearly two and a half Elmarian years.

<<Excuses are mere words, Eddrin. If I wanted to hear words, I'd be with my husband in council.>>

<<Perhaps I should then take my words and this bauble and slink back…>>

<<Bauble?>> Menddilal's eyes lit up.

<<Did I say bauble?>> He feigned surprise.

<<You did, you silly man.>> She rose from her bed, an ivory sculpture of beauty wrapped in the finest silks from the distant province of Yronl. She stood eye to eye with him as he fished in his pocket for something, anything that would be a distraction for a woman who could have anything, and who probably thought she had everything.

He held up a fist-sized chunk of golden ore that caught the light brilliantly. <<A rare metal from a distant land, precious though most likely a

2

trifle to someone who has as much as you. It is called *pyrite.*>>

Her eyes lit up. <<Why, Eddrin! It's beautiful.>>

<<It's yours, my love.>>

<<And I am yours, my dearest lover,>> she said, breathily. She leaned into him, hands on his chest as they kissed.

Tracing his fingers along her neck, Kormèr teased the thin straps of her silk chemise off her shoulders.

But just as the silk slipped from Menddilal's body, the anteroom doors flew open.

<<Duke!>> The Duchess gasped, shoving Kormèr away from her fearfully. <<Get away from me, you swinish cad!>>

Without hesitation, Kormèr backed to the wall and swept his left hand over the light controls, plunging the room into near darkness. As he danced out of the moonlight coming through the window, his other hand pulled the crystal cube from his coat's pocket. He looked down at the cube in his hand but, until his eyes readjusted to the dark, he couldn't see its one black face, the special switch which activated the portal.

<<Help me, husband!>> cried Menddilal.

<<Face me, coward!>> Duke Bederf stood brazenly blocking the inner doorway, his pear-shaped body silhouetted by the dim light from the hallway. <<I've put up with you breaking into my home for long enough!>>

Kormèr's eyes went wide. *He knew?* he thought, surprised. Then his reasoning replaced the surprise. *With her penchant for affairs? Of course he knew... you silly man.*

He grinned at his own joke, as his fingers calmly and methodically pushed each face of the cube.

Footfalls approached from the hall beyond the antechamber, and the anteroom's lights flared on, revealing two guards at the outer doorway, with more behind them. <<There's no escape for you this time,>> he snarled, as the light washed across Kormèr's waist and legs.

Kormèr turned the cube in his hand and pressed on a face with his thumb. He'd lost track of the turns, and didn't know if he was pressing a new face or one he'd already tried. Relief washed over him as the cube began glowing. He tossed it in the path of the advancing Duke as it transformed into the portal.

Duke Bederf stopped and backed away from this unknown obstacle. <<Guards! Guards!>>

Kormèr spared a longing glance at the tiara, but only for a fraction of a second. Pressing his advantage, he jumped into the portal, twisting the tab on his way, and disappeared from his homeworld.

CHAPTER 1

JERANSY Bolsner simmered in her prison cell. She sat on a cot, her back against a wall, her legs curled with her arms wrapped around her knees. Her bloodshot hazel eyes stared fixedly at the chronometer ensconced in the dark blue obsidian wall, which read, in bright red characters: **February 28, 2289 02:43AM**. She hoped that watching the minutes tick away would distract her from dwelling on her predicament, but the effort proved futile.

Her wavy, dark-brown hair fell around her face as she shut her eyes and let her head droop. She wasn't bothered so much by the fact of being in prison; growing up in Castorbridge, England, prison was one of the guaranteed "firsts" of life, much like the loss of one's first tooth in a brawl or a first mugging. In a city that felt like a prison already, incarceration was practically a vacation. Nearly everyone she knew had been through the prison system once. She knew many *many* more who had been through it more often.

This was her first time, and the experience had shorn her pride. She'd make damn sure she never ended up here again.

In less than an hour, her parents would come to pay her bail and collect her. That was the moment she dreaded most of all. Though they already knew that she had been arrested, they didn't yet know the charge. The thought of her mother's horrified, stricken visage when she found out was almost enough to make Jeransy want to crawl under the filthy, board-thin cot.

"Bloody stinkin' Castorbridge," she muttered. She hated that she'd been born in this city of rabble; hated whoever had duped her grandparents into buying property in it. Though her grandfather used to tell her that it had been different back then. "It held a semblance of hope for better days," he used to say. But Jeransy couldn't see that now, not with every dark corner crammed full of thieves, murderers, drug pushers, hoppers—courtesans, as her grandfather had called them. They avoided the law, and the law ignored them, mostly.

You're sixteen years old, thought some part of her brain, trying to comfort her through reason. *That you've made it this long without being arrested has to count for something.* She knew that it did, that she'd grown up a fairly proper girl amidst the city's chaos. While many of her friends had found strength and a sense of belonging by joining gangs, she had steered clear of such ties. Her parents and grandparents had been role models for her in that regard, encouraging and rewarding her while instilling in her a tough confidence. She raised her head, staring past strands of her hair at memories of nights she'd spent struggling

4

with her maths and science coursework. In Jeransy's mind, education didn't just mean a chance at a decent life, it meant a chance at escaping Castorbridge.

She clenched her fists, thinking of how she had taken one step closer to that independence, only to have it snatched away from her. She had made enough money to move out on her own by running errands and doing special favors for men of money. The apartment hadn't been much, one main room, a kitchen and bathroom. But it had meant everything to her, a doorway to the independence she so desired.

One week, she thought, her brow furrowed. *Only one damn week on my own... Bloody incog! If he hadn't been at the market that day, if he hadn't been so nice...* Her fists and brow relaxed as her head dipped again. *If I hadn't been so stupid.* She might not have guessed that he was an undercover cop, but thinking back over the past week, she had seen signs that the man was too good to be true. She'd been so eager to explore her new independence that she'd ignored the signs and her instincts. The Juvenile Department came down hard on minors for having sex with adults.

And her parents would likely come down hard on her, maybe even force her to give up the apartment. "This is all so bloody stupid," she whispered to herself, her eyes brimming with tears. *And so unfair. I just want a chance to make more of my life. Is that too much to ask for, Castorbridge? Is it, you bloody gaping maw of a city, sucking the life out of every—*

A soft light washed over her suddenly, and she looked up as the air suddenly split open into a glowing blue rectangle that remained hovering in the middle of her cell. A light blue mist swirled in the rectangle's opaque center.

"Chilos! Chilos!" Jeransy's eyes widened as she realized that the shouting had come from this rectangle. She stifled a scream as a man jumped, half-backwards, out of the rectangle and did something that made it vanish. He tensed then, as if startled, his back to her and one gloved fist clenched tightly around something. His other gloved hand slowly reached up and removed a silk cap he'd been wearing, revealing locks of straight, dark hair. He stuffed the silk mask into the pocket of a black coat that came down to his calves. Below the coat, black leather boots wrapped his legs and feet. From her vantage, sitting on the cot, he appeared to be at least two meters tall. His shoulders slouched as his tension ebbed. He stuffed whatever he'd been holding into another pocket.

Then he turned to face her.

Jeransy remained peering at him warily. *What the hell's this now?* she wondered, knowing the strange things that were reportedly done to prisoners. Some of her friends had been injected with unknown substances, sprayed with strange-smelling liquids, forced to share their cells with rocks or other materials. Their families had filed complaints, and investigations had followed. At least, that's what the families had been told. Of course, the police had denied everything, and no evidence had ever surfaced. But the streets were full of stories of others that had reported the same. They and a few of Jeransy's friends had died mysteriously or suffered ailments, rashes, memory loss… Scientific experimentation is what it was. New drugs for this, a new form of psychological therapy for the treatment of that— Well, her parents were coming soon and, if one good thing could be said about that, they wouldn't put up with it. *Of course,* she reasoned anxiously, *a lot can happen between now and 'soon'.*

"*Zu tadded houdabish sinfrandd,*" said the man in a melodic voice, bowing before her.

She stared at him blankly as he casually removed his gloves and stuffed them in his coat pocket. *That sure wasn't English. Cor! They're letting foreign scientists experiment on the prisoners!* She looked him over; clean, pressed white shirt with some kind of fancy collar and black trousers, neatly coifed hair, a trimmed mustache and thin beard around a handsome, kind face. *He's young. Too young, and too well dressed. Maybe he's not a wanker scientist after all.* Her eyes fell on the various jeweled rings adorning his hands. *Them jewels musta cost a bomb. Sure couldn't afford that on a government wage.*

She met his eyes as he smiled and squatted in front of her. Then he pointed to himself. "Kormèr Lezàl."

"There are surveillance cameras. The guards are watching, so…" She couldn't think of what to add. She didn't really expect the guards to do anything should the situation devolve. If it came down to it, she knew how to fight. He might get the better of her, but he wouldn't walk away without some damage.

If he understood her, he gave no indication. After a moment, he repeated the gesture and the words. But Jeransy held her tongue. With her legs still curled in front of her, she had a clear kick-shot at his face if he came at her.

His smile slipped, and he stood, slowly. Looking around the cell again, his eyes stopped on the wall chronometer. He pulled something from his pocket and fastened it on his wrist. He stared at it, then tapped it.

"Hmm." He paced toward the cell door and rested his hand on it. He circled back, tracing a finger along the walls on his way.

She watched him curiously, yet carefully. He seemed normal enough, despite the circumstances of his arrival in her cell. A plus for not taking advantage of the situation and assaulting her. Still, just hours ago, a man that had seemed nice and normal had betrayed Jeransy. She was not about to let that happen again.

He stopped, his eyes staring off toward Jeransy's left, his finger tapping the wall. His head turned toward her with a thoughtful look in his eyes. Apparently reaching some decision, he pulled something from his pocket again and did something she couldn't see. Jeransy jumped as the amazing blue portal opened once again. She stood on the cot as he stepped into the portal with his left leg, his right hand gripping the top edge. "*Ci elàze*," he said to her. Then he swept his free hand from her toward the portal. "*Zu yndest àla.*"

Was he inviting her to go into that thing with him? He'd come from it; presumably it led somewhere else. And judging by his language, it wasn't anywhere near Castorbridge or England. Her subconscious leaped at the idea, and she had to fight the impulse to leap through that magical doorway.

But escape meant becoming a fugitive; she'd never be able to come back to England again. That thought bothered her a lot less than she thought possible. England had let a city like Castorbridge exist; she could do without both. But her parents, she could not do without. While her aborted attempt to move out had been a play at independence from them, she adored them too much to not have them in her life. She couldn't leave them forever, abandon them in this rubbish pile of a city, with them never knowing what had become of her.

Her eyes traced the rectangular outline of the portal. *You can always write to them,* she told herself, *maybe even get them to leave and come to wherever you end up. Think of how much happier you would all be.*

She looked at the man, waiting patiently for her to decide. "Is it nice…" She pointed to the portal. "On the other side?"

He cocked his head slightly, watching her. Then he rested his hand on his chest. "Nice."

Jeransy chuckled mirthlessly. Had he just accidentally repeated the exact word she needed to hear? Did he even know what he was saying? She had no idea. His words made no sense; his being here made no sense. This whole situation made no sense. But it was an opportunity, and Jeransy had never hesitated in the face of an excellent opportunity. She desperately wanted out of her cell, out of Castorbridge, and this man could make it happen.

She pointed to herself, as he had done. "Jeransy Bolsner."

His eyes lit up with unmistakable delight, and he nodded. "Jeransy Bolsner," he repeated. He again swept his hand toward the portal. "*Edra zu.*"

Mum and dad, she thought as she stepped down off the cot, *I'll come back for you, I will. I promise with all my heart.*

With only the slightest hesitation, Jeransy took a deep breath and stepped into freedom.

CHAPTER 2

CECIL Murphy chewed on his lower lip as he scribbled feverishly in a pad that rested atop the overstuffed olive-drab bookbag on his lap. His sandy-brown bob-cut hair hung down the sides of his face and past his brown thick-framed glasses. His black t-shirt sported a quote on the back by Niels Bohr. In white letters, it read: "Prediction is very difficult, especially about the future." On his wrist were three colorful friendship bracelets. He had made them himself, employing braid group algorithms. When solved with the proper keys, they spelled "Cecil".

His father's voice hummed along the periphery of Cecil's awareness, an irritant, much like the drone of the car engine in which he was seated on his way to school. But Cecil's focus didn't waver. He was nearly done with an equation that would produce a sequence of numbers for his new combination lock. If his math was right, the sequence would be the toughest combination to crack by random means.

He added the last variable, then checked his work. "Hah!" he proclaimed, checking his watch. Crafting the equation had taken him two minutes and fifteen seconds. He'd spent the other five minutes and twenty seconds of the 9.85 mile trip from his home opening the ridiculous plastic packaging in which the lock had come.

As the car pulled to the curb in front of St. Yves High School, he set the combination and snapped the lock closed through the small hoops on the twin-zippers on his bookbag. Some of his classmates found it amusing to open his bag from behind and spill his books out onto the floor. This would put an end to that daily event. He spent too much time ordering all the books and materials for his morning classes to have those idiots ruin it every time they crossed his path.

His father started talking again, but Cecil had a new focus now. He peered through his thick glasses at the other children entering the school or otherwise hanging around outside. He didn't see any of the troublemakers about. He opened the car door, hooked his arms through the straps of his hefty bookbag, and got out of the car. He closed the car door, silencing his father's latest excuse for not coming by to see him more often. He'd had enough of that, too. The smell of petrichor drew his eyes to the ground, and he found it was damp; it must've rained during the drive, but Cecil hadn't even noticed.

The whine of the electric window came from behind him, then his dad's voice. "Hey, Cece." Cecil bristled at the nickname. "Remember what I told you to do if those boys come bothering you again."

Cecil didn't turn. "Yeah."

His father's words came to him unbidden: "Pop the leader in the nose with all you've got. You'll get into a little trouble, but once you stand up to them, they'll stop bothering you."

"Sure, dad. See ya later."

Cecil spotted two of his friends, Jeremy and Michael, as they hurried toward him. He knew them primarily from chess club, and while they were not as intelligent as he was, he could at least talk with them at nearly the same intellectual level. It helped that they recognized and admired his superior intellect. They had the added benefit of being lower on the bully totem pole than Cecil, and Cecil understood well enough the value of always having an effective human shield on hand.

"Good morning, Cecil," said Jeremy.

"Hi, Cecil," said Michael. "Todd and the gang are already inside," he added, referring to said bullies, Todd Meyers being the alpha male among them.

Cecil nodded. "Good." If everything worked out, he'd make it through the morning without running into Todd and his groupies. "But I got a lock after yesterday." He walked out ahead of them and wiggled his bookbag to showcase the lock.

"Nice!" said Jeremy. "And six digits is much more than those dummies can count to."

Cecil refrained from pointing to Jeremy that he had ended his statement in a preposition. He'd grown accustomed to such things from these fellows.

"Did you work out the best possible anti-random combination?" asked Michael. Cecil nodded. "Cool! I've only ever done three-digit. But it only took me ten minutes." He added the last with pride, as if he'd accomplished something phenomenal.

Cecil let a smirk slip. "I did the six-digit during part of the car ride here this morning. Two minutes and fifteen seconds." Now that merited a proud boast.

"Wow!" cried the two boys in unison. "Nearly five times faster, but twice as complex!" fawned Michael.

"Much more complex," corrected Jeremy. "It's factorial."

Cecil nodded. Jeremy had always been the brighter of the two. Cecil decided that when he started a company, he'd want Jeremy as his right-hand man.

The three had nearly reached Cecil's locker when a yank from behind stopped Cecil in his tracks. Between that and the weight of his bookbag, he staggered backwards, just managing to stay on his feet.

He spun around and stood face to chin with Todd Meyers. "Why are you always touching me?" he asked, launching the quip he'd come up with last night. "Are you some kind of fag?" He preferred verbal barbs to punches, mostly because he didn't have the arm strength or height to compete with the bullies. But he lacked the speed of wit that came so easily to others. Usually he froze like a deer in the headlights while being bullied, and only came up with a good barb later, after torturing himself with what-ifs for the rest of the day and night.

Cecil glanced at Jeremy and Michael, expecting to see admiring smiles, but they looked appalled and chagrinned by his response. *Cowards. Why shouldn't I use that kind of language? Todd talks like that all the time!*

In the meantime, a collective "Oooh" came from Todd's sycophantic posse. The three other boys stood behind him, leering at Cecil from behind their pack leader. The hubbub in the corridor around them quieted to whispers, and Cecil suddenly felt as if he were boiling in his flannel shirt and jeans.

Todd's grin slipped only a fraction. "Your mom didn't think so last night." Then he looked at Jeremy and Michael. "And yours the night before and yours the night before that!" His eyes lit up. "But they all mentioned that you guys sure seem to be very 'close' friends." He added air-quotes as he said 'close'.

The whispers from the crowd crackled like static in Cecil's ears and through every nerve in his body. But Cecil had spent his one quip and had no follow-up. He stood there shaking with shame and fury, speechless as usual. Fortunately, the warning bell rang, and the crowd dispersed as the other students rushed to get ready for class.

"Come on, guys." Todd waved his admirers along. "Enough time wasted on these dorks. I gotta hit my locker still." Like sheep, they followed him around the corner.

That's right, thought Cecil, taking deep calming breaths as his tension waned. *Go to your locker.*

"That was uncalled for," said Michael.

Cecil rolled his eyes. "Is it ever 'called for'?" Then he turned and trudged the last few steps to his locker. He opened it and took a freshly sharpened pencil from the tin cup of pencils he kept there. Until now, he hadn't been able to keep sharpened pencils in his bookbag, as the tips would snap off when his bag hit the ground.

Boom!

Cecil's lip curled with a barely suppressed smile as he closed his locker door. Things would be different after today.

Teens screamed and ran past Cecil as he, Michael and Jeremy rushed to the scene of the minor explosion. A cloud of white smoke diffused slowly across the ceiling, rising from an open locker with a slightly dented and blackened door. Lying on his back beneath the locker, gripping his mangled right hand and bleeding from several tiny cuts on his face, was Todd Meyers. One of his buddies also sported several of the same tiny cuts on his face, but, like the other two, was otherwise uninjured.

No one would ever trace the homemade explosive back to Cecil. He had heeded his father's advice and punched the bully in the nose, but his way… Cecil-style. And his brilliant coup d'état: when the teachers and principal came to investigate, they would find a do-it-yourself explosives book in Todd's locker. Cecil had secreted it there, along with the explosive, after chess club yesterday afternoon, when no one else was around.

Todd was as good as gone, if not jailed, at least expelled.

CHAPTER 3

ANNDREW Lee listened raptly as her high school economics teacher summarized the cascade of selling that led to the massive market drop of Black Monday. Doctor Grossnov had a way of making the mundane subject immersive, presenting stories from the perspective of people on the stock market floor or in a corporate office setting during key historical events. Anndrew could recount every event as if she'd been there herself.

"And while the market quickly recovered, President Reagan used his executive orders power to establish a Task Force on Market Mechanisms. At its head, Nicholas Fredrick Brady.

"Now, everyone imagine," Grossnov pointed at the classroom door, "in walks Mister Brady to the Oval Office. He shakes hands with the President, Vice President and Secretary of State. President Reagan tells him, 'Mister Brady, welcome aboard. Have you read the ExO?' Mister Brady says he has. 'Great. Now we would like your report to include suggestions on how this can be prevented in the future.' Mister Brady says he understands and expected to have to do this. 'Great,' says President Reagan. 'And you have sixty days.'"

The classroom's PA speaker clicked noisily to life, then hissed softly with background noise. It had been acting up today; breaking up messages and not playing the tone that signaled class-changes.

"*Doctor Grossnov,*"—Anndrew recognized the tinny female voice as the school secretary—"*please report to the principal's office, stat.*"

The classroom PA speaker clicked noisily off.

Anndrew Lee's wide eyes shifted from the PA box to Doctor Grossnov. The man closed his eyes and sighed heavily, then addressed the class.

No, no, no! cried Anndrew in her head. *Class can't be canceled.*

"Apologies, everyone, but it seems you are getting a thirty-minute free period. Class dismissed."

Ugh! Can this day get any worse?

She slung her bag over her shoulder, careful not to snag her long black hair, and trudged out the door with her classmates. More a stomp than a trudge, clad as she was in Doc Martens loafers.

"Thank God," commented Abby, one of her classmates. "I couldn't take five more minutes of that, much less thirty."

"Oh, yeah!" growled Mike. "Now I can cram a little more for my pre-calc test."

Anndrew rolled her eyes. *Really? Does no one else enjoy this class?*

She watched as her classmates dispersed, disappearing through doorways and down corridors like billiard balls into pockets on a pool table. She felt a pang of pity for Doctor Grossnov as she spotted him hesitating, almost steeling himself, outside the school's admin office. Apparently, the rumor was true that the chancellor was coming to examine the books, and it was no secret that the principal couldn't even manage his own checkbook, much less the school finances, without Grossnov's advisement. The Doctor took a deep breath, then let it out as he turned the doorknob and entered.

Me too, Doc. Me too.

That morning, the rumbling and beeping of a garbage truck had awakened Anndrew at six in the morning. Okay, it was New York City and garbage had to be picked up. Then, with only a city block's walk from her house to the subway station and another block from the train station to St. Yves High School, a sudden spring squall had drenched her. *You should've listened to mom and taken the umbrella.* The words came into her head in her older brother's voice, exactly as Danny would have said it. *That's what you get,* he continued, *for swiping my flannel shirt and getting it soaked.*

Okay, she said to him in her thoughts, *you can go now.*

Once at school, Anndrew discovered that Todd Meyers had blown up his locker, which was in the same row as hers. The police had cordoned off the entire corridor while they investigated, so she'd been unable to get the dry spare set of clothes she kept there. She counted herself lucky that at least she hadn't been among the students who had been hit by shrapnel. By that point, she had sensed a pattern to the day.

What next? she sulked, trudging along the corridor. With her next class just under a half-hour away, there was nothing else to do. She shook her head in disgust. *Nothing else to do?* It dawned on her how mundane her life had become. Since the start of sophomore year, her social life had gradually dwindled. She barely saw her old grammar school friends anymore, and they only lived a few subway stops away. As of late, she had only seen the increasingly cramped walls of her room and the never-ending pages of texts she had to read for her classes.

She peered in on a freshman math class and smiled at the memories of her freshman year. New experiences, different faces to get to know, fresh places to explore… What had happened between then and now… in two and a half years? *My god, hasn't even been three years? Junior year really does suck as much as they say.*

Glumly, Anndrew wandered the halls and finally entered the empty classroom where her next scheduled class would take place. She dropped her bag and crossed the room to the windows. The oppressive gray clouds refused to yield, despite the rains. Anndrew opened a window to clear the stifling over-circulated air. A cool breeze washed over her, reminding her that some of her clothes were still damp. She ignored the discomfort and took solace with a deep inhale of the fresh, brisk air.

Outside, a car's horn blared, and a car alarm went off. A deliveryman went by on a bicycle, roster-tails flying off his rear wheel, and a large bag of takeout in the basket on the front of the bike. A large woman walking her small dog stopped at the fire pump across the street. She looked around quickly and walked away without scooping the poop. After a few minutes, the car alarm stopped. Anndrew turned and strode across the dim room to the blackboard. She ran her hand over its smooth, unused black surface. It looked and felt so... plain, boring, just like her. She took up a piece of chalk and scrawled in huge letters: **Boring !!**

She stood back to admire her work. *Lame,* she thought, but shrugged. It had felt good to be the one to mar that perfectly dull board. Only, the more she thought about it, the more she realized that she hadn't marred it, she'd given it purpose. The clean blackboard had been boring because it had not been used, because nothing surrounded it but a lifeless, empty classroom. Now that she'd come, she had breathed life into the classroom and the blackboard!

"Pfft," she said. *Yeah, right. As if you could give anything purpose. You're just as boring as the blackboard.*

A soft light splashed against the dark slate from her left. She turned, half-expecting to find someone standing there with a candle, though she knew no one had entered. Instead, she stared in surprise at a penny-sized spot of light floating in midair a few feet away. The spot silently yawned open into what looked like a blue, rectangular plate of glass. It seemed to be as tall as her and as wide as a doorway. And it was floating. And buzzing. And the buzzing was getting louder.

Anndrew inched toward the light switches on the wall beside the class's doorway. She wanted a better look at this thing, but within a margin of safety. A thump came from the glass. An accented male voice followed, crying out, *"Buomp! Not now! Don't do this now."*

Anndrew rushed to the light switch and flipped on the lights. Even at this new angle, the object looked like nothing more than a softly glowing blue plate of one-inch-thick glass... that floated.

Run! Go get school security, cried her rational self.

But at that same moment, heart pounding anxiously, she instead found herself stepping gingerly toward the glass. She reached out to lay her palm on the smooth-looking surface, then snatched it back with a start when another voice came from the glass. *"Kormèr... Hurry!"* urged a female voice, also laced with an accent.

The male voice replied, *"I know. I know."* A moment later, he added, *"It's clear! Go."*

Anndrew jumped as a young woman rushed out of the glass plate,

14

followed by a man. The man spun before Anndrew could see his face, and did something that made the glass vanish. The horrible buzzing stopped as if a switch had been flipped.

Clad in a skin-tight black turtleneck and matching trousers, the girl stood a few centimeters shorter than Anndrew and had a long, pale face with full lips. Her long dark-brown hair looked wind-tossed, her clothes covered in dust. She took a nervous look around, then lingered on Anndrew.

"Nǐ hǎo," she said.

Anndrew blinked, surprised at hearing properly accented Mandarin from a non-Asian. "Nǐ hǎo."

"Oy, Kayel." The girl nudged the man with her elbow. "We 'ave company. She speaks Chinese, so you'll probably need me to translate." Anndrew now placed her accent as British.

The man turned and faced Anndrew. "I see." He was good-looking, to be sure, about a head taller than Anndrew and lanky, with a slight mustache and perimeter beard. He looked at her over his round-rimmed black sunglasses as they slid curiously down his nose by themselves, revealing eyes as brown as his chestnut hair. With a wry smile, he bowed formally to her. "Whence come you, fair lass?" He straightened, stuffed his hands into the pockets of his black duster and cocked his head to one side as he looked at her.

Stunned, Anndrew thought to herself, *Is this a joke? It must be a pick-on-a-junior day or something. All right. I'll play along.* She grinned impishly and curtsied, her eyes fixed on the man's. "I hail from Hong Kong, sir," she said, in English. "But this is New York, and your vocabulary is off by a few centuries." She looked at the girl. "English is fine, by the way."

"Forgive me if I've offended you," the man said, quickly and with such sincerity that Anndrew felt compelled to apologize.

"Oh, no, it's just… I'm… not offended." *Who is this guy?* she wondered. *No guy's made me fumble for words in a long time.*

"Oh, good." His smile returned. "My name's Kormèr Lezàl, and this is my associate, Jeransy Bolsner."

"'Allo." Jeransy gave Anndrew a curt wave. Then she frowned at the nearest desk and nudged it with her foot. "Huh." She sat in the seat, only from the wrong side, so she fit awkwardly between the desk post and the seat back.

"I'm Anndrew… Lee." She added her last name awkwardly, unused to introducing herself by her full name.

Kormèr gave a quick nod. "A pleasure to meet you."

"So this is 'Noo Yawk'," Jeransy said in an exaggeration of Anndrew's accent. "Why did you pick this place, then?"

Kormèr shrugged. "We were in a hurry; I didn't really have time to think about it. So it was kind of random." Anndrew still couldn't place his accent.

15

Jeransy made an 'O' with her mouth, her eyes wide. "That could've gone badly, especially with how it's been actin' up."

"Yeah." He glanced around the room. "At the end there, I think I was hoping for a repair shop for the portal. Not sure why it brought us here."

"At the end, all I was hoping for was a giant fly swatter."

Kormèr looked at Anndrew. "We accidentally stumbled on a massive hive of huge, omnivorous locusts," he explained, as if that made all the sense in the world.

Anndrew nodded. "Of course."

VVVZZZ. The loud, jarring buzz sounded from somewhere that Anndrew couldn't immediately place, but Kormèr's head whipped around in alarm towards Jeransy.

"Bloody hell!" Jeransy jumped to her feet and squirmed to get her hand around behind her.

"Don't move." Kormèr held her shoulder with one hand and slowly turned her back toward him. "Umm... It's tangled in your hair. Let me just..." Anndrew found the disgusted look on his face priceless as his hands worked behind the girl. He then spun and dashed to the windows, a pair of too-large insect legs and wings wriggling from between his fingers.

Holy cow! she thought. *Huge locust!* She watched Kormèr fling the insect that was nearly the size of his own hand out the window she had left open.

Anndrew shook her head as Kormèr fumbled with the latch to close the window. *That can't have been a real bug. A swarm of those things would've been all over the news.* But St. Yves had an arts department which was well known for producing some highly creative plays with amazing props and stagecraft. These two had to be part of that, though Anndrew didn't remember ever seeing either of them before. And Kormèr seemed too old to be a student. A new teacher? If so, then maybe she should give an arts class a try. Not only did it seem much more entertaining than she'd imagined, but with him as a teacher... Well, there was only one way to find out for sure.

She opened her mouth—

"Wow! Are those actual trees?" Kormèr asked, staring out the window.

Anndrew closed her mouth and blinked. *Okay. Huh?*

"They look real enough." Jeransy joined the man by the windows. Then she grimaced. "Ugh! How ribble!" She looked at Anndrew. "Aren't your viros working?"

Anndrew frowned at her. "My what?"

"Your viros... you know, the machines that control the weather and stuff."

Jeransy seemed to be waiting for an answer. "Are you serious?" asked Anndrew, unable to think of anything better. *Play along!* urged a usually quiet, carefree part of her brain. *It could be fun to join in on the role play.*

Jeransy's eyes went wide. "Oh, no! You're naturalists, aren't you?

Rejecting the viros and all things tech." She pointed at the windows. "How could you stand to live like this?" Out of the corner of her eye, Anndrew saw Kormèr frown at Jeransy, but she wasn't looking at him and didn't notice.

Anndrew sighed and decided to play a slightly antagonistic role, though this had gone on much longer than she really had patience for, so she didn't have to act too much. She gave Jeransy a contemptuous once-over. "Like England's such a sunny place."

Jeransy's brow furrowed. But before she could respond, Kormèr turned and walked toward Anndrew, interposing himself between them. "It's been a pleasure meeting you, but I think it's time we moved on. This was a convenient stop, but we need to be somewhere... else." He fished in his coat pocket with his right hand as his eyes watched Anndrew. "Well, you've already seen this, so no harm, I suppose."

He did something that Anndrew didn't catch, and that blue glass appeared beside him.

Anndrew had almost forgotten how impressive this prop was. She still couldn't figure out how it worked, and like the prop in a magic trick, it irritated her to not know. "What is it?"

Kormèr hesitated, his lips pursed in a moment of silent deliberation. "It's a portal," he said at last, but didn't elaborate any further.

Now under the room's lights, the blue surface didn't look like glass, as she'd originally thought. It didn't reflect the lights of the room, instead appearing to be an opening into an endless blue space. She raised her hand, then stopped and looked up at Kormèr. "May I touch it?"

He frowned. "Um... Sure. But please don't step into it."

Her hand slipped through the surface, the blue swirling like a mist, enveloping her arm. *Whoa!* She swore she could feel the warmth of sunlight on her hand, though she couldn't see anything through the surface. With her arm still in the portal, she peeked behind it. Her arm wasn't there! She used her free hand to feel the back of the portal where she knew her other arm should've been. All she felt was the cold metallic backside of the portal. *Holy cow!* "This thing is real!" she murmured in awe.

"Of course it is!" huffed Jeransy from somewhere behind Anndrew. "Ugh."

"Sorry," Kormèr said to Anndrew in a low voice. "We've had a long day." He turned, then turned back. "Do stay out of the portal, please." Then he turned away again and stepped out of Anndrew's line of sight.

Anndrew heard him speaking with Jeransy a moment later. If Anndrew hadn't been so fascinated by the portal, she might've tried to listen in.

Anndrew cried out as her arm was suddenly forcibly ejected from the portal. It felt as if her arm had been extruded through a shrinking opening.

Kormèr appeared at her side. "What happened?"

Shaking her head, she said, "I don't know. It just pushed my arm out."

She reached out tentatively to touch the blue again, but Kormèr blocked her.

"Best not to," he said. "It's been doing this lately, and I wouldn't want you to get hurt."

Anndrew nodded, letting his gentle touch linger on her arm. "Thanks," she said, and he released her. She held her arm to her chest, massaging it. It actually felt a bit sore. "Do you know what's wrong with it?"

He poked the solid surface with his index finger. "Not really."

"It started after the rock slide while we was hiking on that mountain planet," said Jeransy.

Planet? wondered Anndrew. She glanced from the man to the girl, trying to judge if they were joking or not. They had to be joking, but if the portal proved to be as real as it appeared to be… It certainly was extraordinary, but was it extraterrestrial too?

She stepped around behind the portal and found that the back was not nearly as impressive as the front, just a smooth, glossy gray rectangle. A nickel-sized depression caught her eye. When she looked closer, she found a rectangular hairline groove surrounded it. She touched the depression, even as the saying "curiosity killed the cat" came to her mind. The groove flipped open along one side, revealing a compartment. A small but thick black book slid out from the compartment and into her hand. She fumbled it in her surprise, but managed to keep from dropping it. The cover had gold-lettered writing which, at first made no sense to Anndrew, even making her stomach churn nauseously the longer she looked at it. Suddenly, it resolved into words, as if it had merely been out of focus. It read: *A Guide to Your Portal-Cube.*

She opened the book and flipped quickly through the onion-skin thin pages. An illustration caught her eye, and she flipped back to it. Apparently, another panel lower down contained some adjustable controls. She found this new panel and opened it as well. Just like the writing on the book cover, the contents of the compartment made her head spin as she tried to make sense of what she was seeing. Then a control board came into focus, with dials, switches and gauges.

"Wow!" mouthed Anndrew, watching as smudges on the board turned into letters and numbers before her eyes. But something seemed wrong. She examined the illustration in the guidebook and confirmed her finding: the rock lodged at the corner of the control board did not belong there. She wiggled it, and whipped her hand away as the portal thrummed deeply.

"What was that?" she heard Jeransy ask.

"I'm not sure," said Kormèr. Anndrew heard his footsteps approaching. "Excuse me? What are you doing back there?" He appeared beside the portal and looked down at the open panels. "Uh, what am I looking at?"

"You really don't know?"

He shrugged. "I've never had to do anything back here. The functional part is on the front."

Despite her own warnings, Anndrew was starting to believe that these people were not from the arts department, and perhaps not even from around these parts, so to speak.

"Look here." She pointed to the control panel. "There's a rock stuck there. It might be what's causing the problem with the… the solid… thing."

"Huh. Hey, Jaybee, looks like you were right about the rock slide."

"Bugger," said Jeransy. "Can you fix it?"

"I can try." Kormèr pinched the rock with his fingers and jiggled the rock as Anndrew had done, eliciting the deep thrum from the portal. "Ooh! It doesn't like that."

"It's not alive, is it?" Anndrew asked uncertainly. *Oh, man, if I'm wrong, I'm never going to live the embarrassment down.*

"Sometimes it seems to be." Kormèr tugged on the rock, eliciting another groan from the portal. With a hair-raising scrape, the rock came loose, leaving behind a hole and a flapping bit of what looked like a fabric composed of blue fibers. Kormèr studied the rock, then dropped it into his pocket. He stepped around to the front of the portal, then reported, "Hmm. That didn't fix it."

"We're not stuck here, are we?" asked Jeransy.

"No. Like before, it'll just start working again any minute now." He cleared his throat. "But just to be safe, we should probably head back to my home world until we figure this out."

"That'd be razor!"

Razor? Haven't heard that one before. With Kormèr out of the way, her attention refocused on the open panel. Anndrew chewed her lip, then squatted to study the fibrous flap. With the tip of her finger, she nudged the flap over the hole left by the rock. The flap covered it perfectly, but once she removed her finger, it flopped back down. She sighed. *You're really going to do this, aren't you?* she asked herself, already knowing the answer. She straightened and got her bag from where she'd left it.

She sat cross-legged on the floor behind the portal and took her machine class's tool pouch from her bag. She tore a strip of electrical tape and stuck the end on her wrist. Then she took a few screws and pressed them between her lips as she fetched a screwdriver. She had no idea if this would work, but she had nothing to lose.

"You know," said Kormèr, "your features are very similar to people from the Yronl province on my home world."

"Mmhm." She'd only half heard him as she carefully balanced one screw on the tip of the screwdriver. She touched it gingerly to the fabric. It hadn't shocked Kormèr when he'd touched it, but she couldn't be sure that there wasn't current flowing inside the fabric, and she was about to jab a screw into it. Holding her breath, she pierced the fabric with the screw tip. The portal rumbled.

"Uh, excuse me. Please don't poke around in there anymore, especially not with tools." He squatted beside her. "What're you... Oh. Will that work?"

Anndrew turned the screwdriver and felt the screw bite. "No idea," she murmured out of the corner of her mouth.

He lowered his voice. "This is my only means of getting back to my home and Jeransy back to hers," he explained. "If it breaks, we're stuck."

Until now, all this had seemed unreal to Anndrew. She had had no qualm about poking around because these were just people from somewhere in the world. However, they had gotten here, to New York City, or to this classroom, they could easily just grab a taxi or a plane, and go back. But Kormèr's words suddenly shifted her perspective on it all. Suddenly, this was all real, and a wave of unease came over her at the thought that she might break the portal... more than it was already.

She took the two screws from her lips. "Okay. Before I do anything more, let's test this." She pushed the remaining fabric back into place. "Check the... the front."

Kormèr stood and, a moment later, reported happily, "It's working!"

"Yes!" she heard Jeransy shout.

Anndrew released the fabric. "And now?"

"Oof! It pushed me out, and now it's solid again."

"Stop playing with it." Jeransy came closer. "Just make it work, and let's get out of here."

"Patience, love," said Kormèr. "Remember I said I'd been hoping for a portal repair shop?" He turned his head to look at Anndrew. "It appears the portal brought us right where we needed to be."

"No pressure," said Anndrew, though she grinned. She set another screw. "I thought you said it wasn't alive."

"It isn't, as far as I know. But it reacts to mental commands. So if I think of my home, it'll take me there. If I'm thinking of something nebulous like getting far away and prison,"—he turned and beamed a smile at Jeransy—"it takes me to Castorbridge, England, where I picked up this young lady."

Rain pitter pattered heavily against the window sills.

"Ugh," groaned Jeransy. "It's raining all over the place."

Anndrew set the last screw and covered them all with the strip of electrical tape. As she closed the panel, she looked up and saw Kormèr's gaze locked on the windows.

"Still taken with the trees?" She packed her tools away in her bag.

"Hmm?" he said, absently. "Oh, yes. They just remind me of— Well, never mind." He turned his attention back to the portal. "Oh, you're done!"

Anndrew nodded. "Yep. Moment of truth." When she stepped around the portal, she found Jeransy already there, her arm stuck through the portal's opening.

"It's working," said the Brit.

"Thanks to Anndrew here," said Kormèr.

"Happy to help." Anndrew smiled, pleased that what she'd done had worked. *Look at that,* she mused. *Not such a bad day after all, eh?*

Jeransy nodded at her. "Right, thanks. Okay, let's go."

"Hold on," said Kormèr. "Now that it's stable again, there isn't any rush. Look, that's a calendar on the wall, right?" He looked at Anndrew as if expecting her to confirm. She nodded. "So this is Earth, then?" She nodded again, though that 'this is not real' feeling niggled at the edges of her thoughts. "Excellent! And if I'm reading it right, it's 1987."

"Twentieth century! Three hundred years before my time, then? Bloody hell! No wonder this place is barbaric. Just look at that weather—"

Kormèr cleared his throat, cutting her off. "I'm sure there are very nice sunny days as well. Let's take a day or two to look around this planet."

Jeransy looked up at his eyes, and Anndrew could tell immediately that Jeransy liked him by how she smiled at him. "Alright. It'll be different, I guess, with all these people about." She sat in one of the desk again, this time the right way.

Anndrew looked the device over with the satisfaction of a job well done. The way the portal hovered awed her, and she gently nudged its edge. It glided away from her and slowed to a stop a short distance away. Anndrew approached Kormèr, her eyes still on the portal. "Kormèr?"

"Please." He turned, as if he'd been aware of her the whole time. "My friends call me Kayel."

She smiled. *Aha!* she thought, now making the connection between his initials and what Jeransy had been calling him. *Not Kayel… K-L!* "KL, so maybe this is a dumb question, but what planet are you from that you look exactly like any other human?"

Jeransy extended her palm toward Anndrew, her eyes still on Kormèr. "You see?" She looked at Anndrew. "Not a dumb question."

Kormèr chuckled. "Great, now you're ganging up on me." Then he threw up his hands. "I don't exactly have an explanation. To me, you both look like Elmarians." He looked at Anndrew. "That's my planet, Elmar. And in all my travels, you're the only other people that resemble us so completely."

"That can't be a coincidence," thought Anndrew aloud.

"I can't imagine it is." Kormèr shrugged. "But Elmar is pretty isolated, so it's been quite the mystery."

"So the portal is some advanced tech from Elmar?"

"Nope. Or again, not that I'm aware of. I found it on my world years ago, but this level of tech is beyond anything we have."

Anndrew snapped her fingers. "Oh, speaking of which, I found this in another compartment in the back. It's how I found the control board." She held out the guidebook. "An instruction manual—"

21

Anndrew stopped as the door opened and Cecil Murphy walked in, his face buried in a textbook. He looked up as he passed between Anndrew and Kormèr.

"Look out!" cried Jeransy, too late.

Cecil tripped over Anndrew's bag and toppled through the portal. The text book flew from his hands as he grabbed valiantly for the edges of the portal, dragging it flat onto the floor. On impact, his fingers vanished into the blue mist.

"*Vronjl!*" shouted Kormèr, diving through the portal after the student. The portal sealed. And vanished.

CHAPTER 4

"KORMÈR!" cried the girls at once.

"Bloody hell!" growled Jeransy, staring at the floor where the portal had last been. *This is what we get for ending up on a world with other people,* she thought. But the reproachful thoughts kept her from dwelling on where the portal might have taken Kormèr this time.

"Ditto. I lost track of time and forgot that my next class is starting soon. Usually there's a tone that plays, but the damn PA is broken today."

Jeransy had no idea what the girl was prattling on about. It didn't matter, anyway. Kormèr would return at any moment, and they'd be off again, exploring the universe. Last night she had dined with him on a cliff, overlooking a stunning barren plain that stretched away as far as the eye could see. They had watched the sun set while they ate, finishing their meal by candlelight, with the stars twinkling above them. Having lived all her life in a climate-controlled dome, she had relished the feel of a sun's warmth on her skin during the day, and marveled at the pinpoints of light in the dark night sky. Oh, she had studied all about the stars and seen holo-pics, but she had never been out on a clearer night than that... and never with such wonderful company.

"Where'd the portal go?" asked Anndrew, interrupting Jeransy's pleasant thoughts and reminding her of the perils of jumping recklessly through the portal.

Jeransy shook her head. "I've no idea. Kormèr says it reads your mind, picks the destination from your thoughts." If it didn't have a specific destination from its user, it could easily open into space, or a sun, or the bottom of an ocean, or worse. As wonderful as the portal was, this malfunction as they were trying to escape the swarm had soured her impression of it.

"That's not what I... Wait, can it come back?"

Jeransy studied her. *Why's she sound so worried? Oh! The kid that fell in is probably her friend.* "Of course. Once he's got whoever fell through, Kormèr'll be back. Then we'll be out of your hair."

Anndrew picked up the book the kid had dropped. She placed it on a large table that stood apart from all the other small ones. From historical footage Jeransy had seen, she decided that it had to be the teacher's desk. And the large black horizontal rectangle on the wall behind that desk had to be the... *blackboard.*

23

"He's my classmate." Anndrew opened the cover, then closed it again. She turned toward Jeransy, but didn't look at her. "Sort of."

"Who?" asked Jeransy.

Anndrew looked at her now. "The kid who fell in. His name is Cecil Murphy. He had his nose buried in his chem textbook and didn't see my bag."

"How's he *'sort of'* your classmate? I've never been to a school, but I thought you were all classmates here." *Why are you engaging this girl in conversation?* she chastised herself. *You'll be gone soon, and none of this will matter.*

But this is a unique opportunity, argued the academic in her, feeling perhaps that this was a safe environment for it to emerge and be curious. And Jeransy realized it was right. Here in this foreign city, far in the past, before viros, corrupt police, gangs, Jeransy could relax a little and, as Kormèr had suggested, take some time to learn things that she hadn't previously had access to.

"He's a geek." Anndrew shook her head. "No, it's more than that. He's a snobby dweeb. Doesn't really talk to anyone, like we're all beneath him."

Jeransy nodded as if she understood, though she only understood part of what the girl said. *Don't pretend; you're here to learn.* She shook her head. "What's a *dweeb?*"

Anndrew stared at her. "Huh? Oh, right. It's a person who's studious but with no social skill, so they get picked on a lot."

Jeransy's defenses went up. "Picked on? You mean bullied." Were things just as bad here as in Castorbridge? Or maybe this was just how the downward spiral started, with labels and ostracizing.

Anndrew shrugged. "Yes. I guess it really is bullying."

Bollocks! "There are people just like you where I come from; people who put others down because they try to be better people."

"Whoa!" Anndrew raised her hands, palms toward Jeransy. "You're out of line. I don't pick on him. Others do."

"Do you defend him?"

Anndrew didn't answer immediately. Finally, she shook her head. "I've helped him pick up his books after the others knocked them out of his backpack."

"That's nice, but then you're part of the problem."

Anndrew pursed her lips. "Do you stand up for everyone you see being victimized?"

"Only me family and friends." Jeransy forestalled Anndrew's response with a raised finger. "But things aren't like this where I'm from." She swirled her finger to indicate the classroom and beyond. "You have a chance here. A school like this would be a hunting ground for every criminal in the city. If I could stand up for everyone, you better believe I would." She'd almost lost her train of thought, but that happened when she felt passionately about something. And Jeransy firmly believed that, had more people fought for Castorbridge in the early days, its decline could have been prevented. Her granddad sure thought so. He had been among the protesters back then, but there had been too few of them to make a difference.

"Hmm." Anndrew watched Jeransy. "You're not wrong, and people do rally for the better treatment of others. But Cecil is…different." Jeransy had heard that before. She opened her mouth to retort, but before she could say a word, Anndrew added, "And not in a good way."

Jeransy stared fixedly at her, waiting for her to say more. She rolled her hand in the air impatiently. "Elaborate."

Anndrew looked down at Jeransy's feet, then back up at her face. "Look, I don't know what's happening in his life, but he's not… a nice kid. I've seen him hold doors for people, only to let them go at the last minute to slam into people's faces. He's never thanked me for the two times I helped with his books. Not that I *need* his appreciation," she added quickly. "But it's almost like he thinks he deserves the help." She snapped her fingers. "And that's the general impression he gives off, that he is better than everyone else."

Jeransy nodded. She liked that Anndrew seemed to have helped the boy without an agenda, though she found it hard to believe. She'd grown up with so little of that selflessness around her that it just seemed unlikely, if not impossible. *As impossible as a city without viros? Or a doorway across time and space?* But Jeransy had no retort for Anndrew's last words. She didn't know the boy at all. His behavior seemed to be that of a victim, trying to keep from being noticed. But giving off a vibe of being better than others would not achieve that goal. If anything, it would make things worse… a lot worse.

Anndrew sighed. "Look, we got off on the wrong foot. Let's start over, okay?" She smiled.

Jeransy nodded, her tension easing somewhat. "Sure."

"Hi, my name is Anndrew and I'm a student here in 1987, New York City."

Jeransy stared at her. *I know all this already. Why is she repeating it? Oh! Starting over. She's bloody barmy!*

Anndrew rolled her hand as Jeransy had done a moment ago. "And you are?"

"I am not going to repeat what's already been said." The smile slipped from Anndrew's face and in her eyes, Jeransy read either anger or disappointment. She inhaled, held it, then said, "But I study from my flat… in 2289. I use an alias so that no one can trace the lessons back to me and use them as leverage. I don't have a steady job, but I earn quid any way I can, so long as it's not too dodgy."

Anndrew almost smiled again. "It's nice to meet you. What about Kormèr? He's older, right? Not a student."

Jeransy found this ridiculous, but it was helping to pass the time, even if it didn't stop her from worrying. Where was Kormèr and why was he taking so long to return for her? He'd said something about the portal not always being precise with locations and times. She dreaded the idea that he couldn't get it to come back for her. "Yeah. He says Elmarian years are like four Earth years, so he's around nineteen. I think he's still studying things, though. That hasn't come up in our convos."

"Oh. How long have you known him?"

"Just a week."

Anndrew nodded absently. "Does he always react that way around trees?"

Jeransy smiled wryly. "Funny that, eh? Only 'round real ones, I think."

"As opposed to…"

Jeransy shrugged. "I dunno. Fake ones?"

"Hmm. Fake trees."

Jeransy peered at her. *Is she having a laugh at me?* But Anndrew's eyes had turned to the window, so Jeransy didn't say anything more.

Anndrew looked back at her. "So you speak Mandarin?"

"Of course."

Anndrew tipped her head to the side with curiosity. "I didn't realize it was that prevalent as a second language."

"It's the second global language where I'm from."

"Really? Wow. I would *not* have expected that."

Voices and the shuffle of hundreds of feet came from the open doorway. An almost rhythmic clanking and slamming of metal followed. Jeransy edged away from the door when other people walked past. Most were engaged in conversations, but some glanced in at Jeransy and Anndrew.

Anndrew looked up at a strange disc on the wall which had numbers one through twelve written in black along its circumference, and a black angled stick in the center. "Class time in a few minutes. I hope Kormèr hurries or a lot more people are going to see the portal appear. Are you okay?"

Jeransy had been watching the crowd in the hall as she'd shifted so that Anndrew stood between her and the doorway. Now her eyes snapped over to Anndrew. "Yeah, why?"

"You look tense." Anndrew closed the door, muffling the din beyond.

Jeransy shook her head. The sizeable crowd had rattled her; she didn't like large loud crowds. She felt better with the door closed, but they were still out there, and the room had no other exit. But she would hang-jump from the windows if she had to. "No, I'm fine." *Show no weakness.*

Jeransy stepped backward toward the windows when the door opened and two boys walked in. They nodded curtly at Anndrew, then glanced her way. But rather than come at her, they walked to a far corner and sat in the small desks. Their body language didn't trigger any of Jeransy's alarms; their clothes were neat, their skin clean, their hair styled strangely, but not in any of the typical gang cuts. They talked quietly as they took books and styluses from their bags and put them on the desktops. "They're just proper boys," she mumbled to herself. *This isn't Castorbridge,* she reminded herself.

Two girls walked in, one wearing leopard skin as pants. Her wavy blond hair poofed from her head, as if yelling, "Pull me, tie me to a pole and have your way with the rest of me!"

"Hey, Ali," said Anndrew, unperturbed. "Hey, Pat."

The poufy blond waved daintily, then sat close to the teacher's desk. The other stopped. "Annde! Thank god we got out of that eco class, huh?"

Jeransy saw Anndrew tense at the question, though she had no idea what it meant. Was it a code?

Look out the window and pretend to be relaxed, thought Jeransy. With great reluctance, she turned and stepped closer to the windows until she could keep a watch behind her in the reflection in the glass. She leaned on the sill and looked down. The drop to the ground suggested that the room was on the second floor. She looked for dirt, grass, bushes, anything soft to land on, should the need arise, but she found nothing but concrete. She closed her eyes as more feet shuffled in behind her. If she jumped, she risked injury, and an injured animal didn't last long. She was trapped, and she would have to deal with whatever happened next.

"Annde, watch out!"

Jeransy spun, and her heart leaped at seeing the back of the portal, a small dark compartment open in the middle of the gray metal.

"Oh, don't mind this." Anndrew walked around to the back and placed a black book in the compartment, then slid the panel closed. "It's a prop from the arts department. I think they're putting on some kind of play about aliens invading."

She turned to look at Jeransy. "Right, JB?"

Jeransy did not know what she was talking about. But she did recognize a lie and that Anndrew was covering up the truth for some reason that could be important. "That's right."

The girl faced Jeransy, then smiled. "I didn't know we had an exchange student. Hi, I'm Pat."

Jeransy smiled back. "Julie Boucharde," she said. It didn't matter what the hell she said now. Her ride out of here floated only a few steps away. She walked toward the portal. "I'm part of whatever she said this is." Pat frowned, and though she still smiled, her face looked confused. "It was nice to meet you, but I've got to get back to it. Cheers!" She looked at Anndrew. "Cheers to you too, mate."

Jeransy stepped through the portal.

Whoa! That's some prop! she heard Pat say through the portal. But Jeransy's mind barely registered the sound as it took in the surrounding sights. She stood on what seemed to be a flat, buoyant rock. For as far as she could see, the land consisted of scattered rock masses floating in a sea of clouds. It reminded her of images she'd seen of ice floes floating in the arctic sea before the Slow Melt. The intoxicatingly clear sky seemed so close that Jeransy felt she could touch it if she reached up. The clean brisk air smelled of stone and metal, devoid of anything organic.

Kormèr stood a few meters away, at the edge of the same rock. His back was to her, but now he turned and smiled at her.

"You took your time," she said. "I was getting worried,"

"I'm sorry," said Kormèr. "I tried to send the portal back as quickly as possible."

Jeransy scanned their odd surroundings. The boy was nowhere in sight. "Where's Cecil?"

"Is that the boy's name?"

"Yeah," came Anndrew's voice from behind her. "Cecil Murphy."

"*Buomp,*" mumbled Kormèr.

"You've said that before," whispered Jeransy. "What's it mean?"

Kormèr wrinkled his lips, then whispered back, "Ask me again another time." He stepped past Jeransy toward Anndrew. "Be careful. Both of you. The gravity is weaker here than you're used to, and it's a long way down if you slip between the rocks."

Anndrew's wide eyes looked around as her hands gripped the edges of the portal, her bag hanging from her shoulder, swinging in and out of the portal . "Holy cow!" Her eyes settled on Kormèr. "Is this… Are we on another planet?"

Kormèr took one of her hands in both of his. "Uh, yes. But you should really go back to your world. I don't want to lose another of you."

Anndrew's jaw fell, and she covered her mouth. "Oh, no! Cecil fell through the rocks?"

"No, no. But he's not here… right now. I think he's okay, but I'll need to catch up to him and take him back home."

Anndrew gave Kormèr a look that Jeransy recognized as disbelief. She looked at Jeransy, then back at Kormèr. "I see. You don't want me here."

"Well, it's just that I…" Now he looked at Jeransy. Then sighed. "I was going to say that I travel alone, but obviously that's not true anymore."

Pat's voice came through the portal. *"Annde? Where'd you go? I hear you, but I don't see you."*

Kormèr took Anndrew's hand and turned his body, leading her away from the portal. With his other hand, he reached for the tab at the top of the portal and twisted it. The portal closed.

"KL," said Jeransy, keeping her tone under control. "What're you doing?"

"I couldn't leave it open and risk more people coming through," he said. "Especially not here."

Jeransy nodded. That made sense. "What about her?"

"Yes, KL," said Anndrew, hoisting her bag higher on her shoulder. "What about me?"

Kormèr peered at them both, a half-smile on his lips. "You're doing that again. I feel like I'm going to regret this, but… Anndrew, would you like to join us as we get your friend?"

"If you tell me what really happened to him."

Kormèr nodded. "Fair enough."

Jeransy wanted to scream, "What?!" But she held her tongue. She had hoped for a return to the days before the locust nest, when she'd had Kormèr all to herself. She had to keep reminding herself that he wasn't human, but despite that, she'd grown fond of him and the time they'd spent together. She had hoped that would continue, and that maybe their relationship could grow. He certainly seemed capable, smart and definitely not an incogger. So she didn't want their escapades to end. *But this little hopper's gonna change things… for a bit, anyway. Till we get her friend back. I'll just have to make sure Kormèr stays laser on that, so we get it done fast.*

"When I got here," Kormèr was saying, "I saw the boy flying off. By some stroke of luck, he fell right onto the back of a large bird that was passing."

"A bird large enough to support that boy?" asked Jeransy.

"Yep. They're called Argents. They breed them big here." Kormèr pointed in the direction Jeransy had seen him looking. "They flew off that way before I could catch up."

"Damn," said Anndrew. "But you sound like you know this place."

"I do." He pulled an odd-looking device from his pocket. It had a thick glass screen wrapped in braided copper wire with five brass dials around the edges, two on the left, two on the right, and one on top. Kormèr pushed the top dial and unfolded a short brass antenna. Swinging the device slowly around, he turned and pushed the left and right dials. Data crawled along the glass screen as the device squelched and hissed. "And I have an idea where the bird might be headed."

"Good," said Anndrew. Jeransy couldn't agree more. If he knew this place and where the bird had taken Cecil, they might be done with the two of them before nightfall. "How do we get there?"

"We walk." Kormèr shrugged. "Sorry, but there's no transportation available out here." He hopped over to another rock and helped Jeransy across, then Anndrew.

Jeransy looked into the distance, but couldn't make out anything other than more rocks for as far as she could see. *Bugger. This is not going to be quick.*

CHAPTER 5

SCARED out of his wits, Cecil clung to the huge, squawking bird with all he had in him. He'd lost his bulky backpack, and only a miracle and his tangled hair kept his glasses from slipping off his head. The bird's gyrations and attempts to dislodge him kept him busy enough, however, that his glasses were furthest from his mind at that moment.

He tried to relax, studying the rhythm of the bird's wings. *Between one and three flaps, followed by a long glide,* he managed to calculate, while the motion shoved him from side to side. He adjusted his position and grip accordingly until he found a spot between the wings which didn't jostle him around too much and which, more importantly, didn't seem to interfere with the bird's flight. The bird seemed to approve of this as well. It ceased weaving and settled into its rhythm.

Unable to use his hands to fix his glasses, he pushed his face into the feathery back, jockeying the twisted frames into position. They slid down to the tip of his nose when he picked his face back up, but at least he could now see through them. Overhead stretched the clearest blue sky he'd ever seen. But so much of the bird blocked his forward vision that he could only make out enough of the ground below to know that he was no longer in Manhattan or anywhere in the tri-state area that he'd ever been. Which was impossible. It had only been minutes since he'd tripped; not enough time to get that far away from the city. He should have been seeing either the Atlantic seaboard or streets or greenery with buildings and homes. Instead, the land appeared to be quite barren, with only scattered spots of greenery, and broken up by cloudy fissures.

What the hell happened? The question had been there, in his head, waiting for the right moment to search for an answer.

Cecil had been reading his chemistry text while walking to his next class. He should've known better than to do that, since he'd already run into walls and other things before. But when it came to knowledge, he recognized he had a weakness. His hunger for it eclipsed all else. And this time it had landed him in some impossible nightmare.

It can't be impossible, he reasoned. *You're here. There has to be an explanation that you just aren't aware of yet.* But what could that be? The very last thing he remembered seeing was the face of Anndrew Lee as someone shouted. And a blue thing? Things had happened so fast, but he could swear that there had been something blue right in his way when he tripped. *What did I even trip on?*

Did someone trip me? That didn't make sense. There had been at least two other people in the room besides Lee: the girl that had shouted and one other whose presence he'd caught out of the corner of his eye. He doubted Lee had tripped him; she mostly ignored him, as he did her. The other girl wouldn't have shouted a warning if she'd been the one. Then the other presence, maybe? He ground his teeth, frustrated by not having all the variables he needed to figure this out.

The bird's rhythm changed subtly, and Cecil looked up. He couldn't crane his head up enough to see through his glasses, but something large and blurry lay just ahead. Which brought the question to his mind: *How am I going to get off this stupid bird? Will it ever land?*

The bird pitched upward suddenly, its muscles bunching under Cecil's fingers and loosening his pincer grip. He found himself holding nothing but slick feathers. He slid forward, then down, around the bird's thick neck, managing at the last moment to cling to a cluster of feathers. He cursed, dangling from the bird's neck as it continued its steep climb. Muscles shifted again as the bird leveled out.

Oh no, I'm slipping! Cecil fumbled for a better grasp around the downy neck, but with nothing to grasp around such a wide neck, he ended up losing even more of his hold. Cecil cried out, and the bird squawked at him. Fatigued, Cecil's fingers spasmed, and he fell, screaming.

Back-first, he smashed into something that just as suddenly swallowed him entirely. Stunned by the impact, he felt as if he were floating, legs up over his head. He saw bubbles rising past his head toward beautiful flickering lights beyond his feet. He took a breath… and his eyes went wide as his nose and mouth filled with water. His lungs convulsed and his arms flailed, trying to right him. *I'm drowning!* he thought, in a panic. The impact had disoriented him, and he couldn't tell which direction was up.

Long shadows shattered the flickering light. They grasped his shoulders and pulled him forcefully. He gripped them in return, as he emerged from the water, and tried to push them away, but they held him firmly as he coughed up water.

I'm alive! I'm alive! was all he could think.

As the urge to cough abated, he found that what held him were strangely fuzzy, toned arms. They lifted him bodily out of the water and set him down, shivering and gulping air. He looked to his left and found that he sat beside what looked like a swimming pool. *What the hell is going on? Nothing makes sense! I was in school, then a barren rocky land, and now there's a pool?* His glasses had finally fallen off, so he didn't trust what he was seeing.

He turned back as the arms released him and faded into the blurry background of his vision. He saw that someone stood in front of him, wearing a cowl and some kind of arched backpack. The person crouched and stuffed something into his right hand. Cecil raised his closed hand, recognizing the shape and dimensions of his glasses. With hands that still trembled from his recent scare, Cecil slipped the glasses on and looked at the blur crouched before him. Then he turned the glasses over and tried again.

His eyes went wide as the figure came into focus. He appeared to be a man, almost human, but with feathers for hair on most of his face and head. The birdman's plumage was a white-mottled tan on his back, wings and crown, while his paunch was uniformly beige. A cowl of plumage ran down a thick neck and along broad shoulders. The arched backpack turned out to be wings, folded neatly behind his back. Reluctantly, he took his eyes off the birdman and found, with a glance around, that a crowd had formed around him, a crowd of humanoid birds!

This is clearly not Earth... Another planet then, one of bird people; what's the probability of the existence of a world like this? I must be dreaming. Did I actually fall when I tripped and hit my head, and this is some strange concussion-induced hallucination?

Cecil's eyes snapped back to the crouched male in front of him as pins and needles swept across the inside of his skull. He'd never felt anything like it. He swooned as the sensation caressed his mind, calmed him. Then it dissipated.

||How do you feel?|| asked the birdman in a short set of whistles. Cecil didn't answer right away, his mind busy adjusting to the fact that he'd understood said whistles. And not just these, but also the whistles and chirps that he'd been hearing from the crowd. A second ago, they were just a cacophony of sound. Now he heard... English! Voices wondered if he was okay, and where had he come from, and didn't he know that the baths weren't for humans?

This is unbelievable! He realized that the chirps and whistles were not actually gone, but that he was hearing their translation in his head! His mind was instantly translating a language that he had never heard before! *It must be that tingling I felt. There's no other explanation.* His mind ached for more information. He had to understand.

"You did this. You made me understand you." Cecil pointed at the crowd. "All of you, your language." Who else would have known and spoken to him?

||Your mind is very quick,|| chirped the crouched birdman.

"Where am I?" Cecil looked beyond the crowd at what appeared to be a forest of enormous concrete trees with gleaming metal leaves.

Cecil felt a very brief tingle in his mind again.

||Hmm, yes. You just arrived, I see, quite suddenly at that.|| The birdman paused. ||This city is Birshetland, although it's had other names in the past. You fell from an Argent into a public bath. Quite fortunate for you, as it broke your fall.||

Cecil shook his head. "That's not what I meant. What *planet* is this?"

||This is Frrooweetsee.|| The drawn out chirp apparently did not

translate. ||It is more commonly known as Averia.||

"Huh. That's fitting."

||How so?||

Cecil stared at the birdman. "Ave?" The birdman's large, dark eyes showed no reaction. "The Latin word for bird? Have you heard of the planet Earth?"

The birdman bobbed his head. ||Terra, yes.||

"So you know Terra, but not… Never mind. That's where I'm from."

||Welcome to Averia then, Cecil. My name is Sreet.||

Cecil did not bother to ask how the birdman knew his name. The answer was obvious.

"So you can read my mind and make me understand you. Have you got any trick to dry my clothes?"

Sreet bobbed his head again. ||That I do. But there are much more interesting… tricks. Would you be interested in learning them yourself?||

Cecil eyed the birdman curiously, like a scientist with a new, unique specimen. *A chance to learn whatever the hell the birdman just did?* he thought, his body tensing eagerly. *Hell yeah. But if I wake up and find that this was nothing but a dream, I'm going to be really pissed off.* "Sure," he said, simply.

Sreet stood, then addressed the crowd. ||He is unharmed.|| He offered Cecil a helping hand. Cecil ignored it and stood on his own to emphasize his wellbeing. The crowd dispersed as Sreet made some small motions with his hands, and Cecil felt the discomfort of his wet clothes vanish, his chilled skin warmed by the same action. His hair fluffed, then settled, now also dry.

||If you're ready, please follow me.||

"Where're we going?"

||We are going to an ancient but powerful city called Berdia. There you can learn all you want.||

That was all Cecil needed to hear. To learn was all he wanted.

CHAPTER 6

ANNDREW jumped across a cloudy gap, and immediately pursed her lips, wishing she'd worn boots that morning rather than her loafers. Thirty minutes into the walk, she had felt grit in her shoes. Now, an hour and a half later, she had developed enough of a debris collection in the left one for it to be painful.

"Can we stop a minute, please?" She stopped, removed her shoe, and shook out a few small pebbles and dirt.

"Of course," said Kormèr.

"You need boots," suggested Jeransy.

Looking down and knowing no one would see her reaction, Anndrew rolled her eyes. "Yeah, I was just thinking the same." *Thanks,* she added in silent sarcasm. "How much further is there to go?" She started on her second shoe. She had a hundred other questions for Kormèr, but she imagined that Jeransy had already asked them during their week together, and so she didn't want to make him run through the answers again. At least not so soon. Maybe later. *Definitely later.*

She put the shoe on and stepped up beside Kormèr to watch as he fiddled with that odd device. At first, she thought it was just an electronic compass, but as she watched him use it, she realized it had many more features. He pressed a dial and coordinates reappeared on the glass along with a rough map. This reminded Anndrew of a research paper she had had to write in her sophomore year on something new called global positioning system. He twisted the top dial, and the map zoomed out, revealing the next closest city. "We're not too far from where I think they went. In fact, we should start seeing the outline of the city soon." He squinted into the distance. "That might be it over there." He pointed, and Anndrew thought she could make out a wide grayish blob just on the horizon.

"A city, huh?" said Anndrew.

Kormèr turned back to her. "Yes, why?"

She flashed a tight grin, fueled by a bit of anxiety. "It'll be my first alien city. Should I know anything before we get there? Don't stare? Don't look like I'm trying not to stare? Things like that."

Kormèr smiled, understanding in his expression. "You won't have to worry about any of that. Averians are very understanding and accustomed to off-worlders."

He had told them the planet's name, Averia, along the way, and

Anndrew had immediately started imagining a race of bird-people.

"What are they like?" asked Jeransy.

"The Averians?" asked Kormèr. Without waiting for a reply, he continued. "They're sort of like us, only covered in feathers and with wings."

"Your just taking the piss out of us now."

Kormèr laughed. "I'm doing what?"

Jeransy blushed. "Having a laugh at us. 'Cause Averia is like 'ave', which means bird in Spanish."

Anndrew stared at Jeransy, impressed. *How many languages does she know?*

He shook his head. "No, no. Not at all. That's really how they look. You'll see soon enough."

Anndrew couldn't wait. *I'm about to meet actual aliens! Duh. Kormèr's an actual alien, you dope.*

"By the way," Kormèr continued, "I mentioned that the gravity is weaker here, but the air's thinner, too. If either of you feel dizzy or out of breath, say so and we'll take a break. Are you ready to go on?"

"I am," said Jeransy.

Anndrew nodded. "Same."

"All right then, let's—" Kormèr stopped mid-turn, and peered into the distance. "Hmm." He took a step toward the edge of the rock on which they stood. Anndrew looked off in the same direction, but didn't see anything. She looked back at Jeransy, who looked at her and shrugged.

"*Mran! Hanjlal lnra!*" said Kormèr, in his melodic language. He frowned, then mumbled, "But what are the odds? It can't possibly just be out here, in the open."

"What can't?" asked Jeransy.

Kormèr scratched his chin, then pointed ahead. "Do either of you see a jewel, about the size of my palm, just lying over there?"

"A jewel?" Anndrew looked, but nothing jumped out at her. Could jewels be found just lying around here? This could be promising. "Where, exactly?"

"That rock mass, about halfway across, near the patch of moss."

Jeransy shook her head. "I don't see it."

"Sorry," said Anndrew, feeling disappointed. "Neither do I."

"Interesting." Kormèr dropped the compass into his pocket, then rummaged for something else. "Maybe there are some differences between us after all, and only my Elmarian eyes can see it."

Maybe, thought Anndrew. *Or you're crazy, and I'm a fool for following you.* She felt bad about the unbidden thought immediately. Standing here as she was on some alien planet after stepping through a blue doorway, how could she doubt anything he said? "What's it look like?"

"It's a semi-opaque, dark gray crystal with a cluster of glowing yellow orbs inside." He pulled a four-foot rod from his pocket and aimed it at the rock with the jewel. Anndrew's jaw nearly dropped, seeing as how the rod was many times longer than the pocket was deep. *Maybe I'm the crazy one here.* Kormèr twisted a small knob on the end closest to him, and the rod extended over four times its original length until the tip hit the rock with a sharp rap. Kormèr then poked the jewel with the rod.

"It moved! It's real!" He retracted the rod and slid it lengthwise back into his pocket. "Now the question is: is there a trap? How could there not be, right?"

"Right," said Jeransy. "Who would leave a jewel like that out here without protecting it?"

"Exactly, even if it is invisible to certain species." He fumbled through his pockets once again, this time producing lazy tongs. Kormèr extended the tongs toward the spot where he believed the jewel rested and, with another movement, clamped the tongs closed. Only they didn't close all the way. The tongs scissored closed, drawing the clamped empty space toward Kormèr. Once it came within reach, Kormèr plucked something from the tongs and maneuvered them back into his pocket one-handed. "Remarkable. There it is."

"I still don't see it," said Anndrew. "Oh! But I see the marks on your skin!" *He really is holding something I can't see!*

"Oh yeah," said Jeransy. "How can that be?"

"Its colors are probably off the visible spectrum for humans. I've run into that before."

"Well, color me impressed," said Anndrew.

Kormèr nodded, grinning. "Me too. I've been lucky before, but this is a whole new level of luck." He held it up and looked up through it. "I suppose I should get it appraised. It could just be a fake." He paused, eyes suddenly locked in the distance. "Or maybe someone has just realized they dropped it."

Anndrew followed the direction of his stare. In the distance, a small gray cloud bore down on them.

Kormèr grunted. "Not insects again."

"My pistol, quick!" Jeransy stuffed her hand into one of his coat pockets.

"Don't fire first." Kormèr reached into his other pocket with the hand that held the gem. "They might not be hostile." His hand came back out of his pocket, holding a gnarly stick. He looked at it, then held it toward the cloud. "I hope this still works." Then he cried out, "Shield!"

The air shimmered between them and the cloud. But the shimmer wavered and showed distinct gaps. Through one such gap, Anndrew clearly made out the aerial fleet of insect-like things that made up the cloud. A snap of fire erupted from the attackers and spattered along the shimmering air, setting it aglow.

"Those aren't insects," said Anndrew.

"But they are hostile!" cried Jeransy as she yanked her hand out of

Kormèr's pocket, drawing with it a long-barreled pistol. With careful aim, she fired a single shot at the leading bug-ship. It fell, bounced against a floating rock, and vanished.

Another salvo of needle-like projectiles lit up the shield. Some slipped through the gaps, and Anndrew felt the air whip around her as an attacker passed directly overhead. She yelped and tumbled to the ground as her right leg went numb and gave out under her. She cradled her leg to her chest and grit her teeth against the pain.

"They're magical," she heard Kormèr say. "Just shoot 'em down and they'll vanish." Anndrew saw him jam the gnarly stick into the ground. "And stay behind that. It's not perfect, but it'll offer you some protection."

With a gleeful smile, Jeransy took aim at the swarm flying overhead. "I"—she fired once—"hate"—again—"BUGS!" Another two ships disappeared into thin air.

Kormèr crouched by Anndrew as Jeransy continued to shoot the attacking bug-ships with lethal accuracy. He brushed the hair back from Anndrew's face. "Were you hit?"

"Must've been. My leg hurts like hell," she said through gritted teeth. "Like a cramp, a sprain and pins and needles, all in one."

She took her hands off her leg as Kormèr examined it. "No wound, and your pants are undamaged. Must be a nerve disruptor hit. Probably not even a direct hit, but your leg will be numb for a while." He reached into one of his inner coat pockets and took out a vial of yellowish liquid. "Drink this. Tastes like hell, but it'll at least kill the pain."

Anndrew took the vial but didn't open it. "I actually have a first aid kit in my bag. It has aspirin." She held the vial out to him.

"Aspirin is also a pain reliever," he said, as if reading from a script that only he could see. He took the vial.

"Yep." She removed a small box from her bag. Kormèr whistled when she opened it and showed him its contents; it contained plastic bandages in various shapes and sizes, as well as a roll of gauze and wads of cotton, all neatly arranged. Individually wrapped aspirin tablets sat tucked to one side. She ripped one wrapper open and spilled the two aspirin it contained into her palm. Then she accumulated a wad of saliva in her mouth and used it to swallow the pills.

He nodded approvingly. "Very well prepared."

Womp!

Anndrew jumped at the sudden noise.

Kormèr spun as a buzzing erupted behind him. "The wand is spent. The shield's gone."

Kneeling confidently on one knee behind the stick Kormèr had planted, Jeransy shot efficiently. She fired bolt after bolt in quick succession, blowing the raiders out of the sky. "One suicided on the shield," she said. "Last one…" She aimed and cleanly hit the insect-ship. She watched as it crashed past the fragile clouds. Then she stood, wiped her brow on her sleeve, and walked over to where Kormèr and Anndrew were.

"Is she okay?" Jeransy asked.

"I'll be fine, thanks," said Anndrew. "That was some fine shooting."

"Oh! Cheers, mate," she said, looking surprised. "Should we expect more?" she asked Kormèr.

Kormèr stood and scanned the surrounding skies. "I don't see any more right now, but I have no idea. I've never seen a gem trigger a magical protection spell like that before. If it was even the gem." He shrugged. "Sorry, that was new to me, too."

He looked down at Anndrew. "Can you stand?"

Anndrew flexed her leg and winced as her calf cramped. She still had no feeling below that. "I might be able to stand, but I don't think I can walk yet."

"Alright. Let's take a rest." He gave Anndrew a sympathetic look. "But not too long; I don't want your friend getting too far ahead of us."

Anndrew tried to flex her foot, and her toes almost bent this time. "Okay. We'll see."

"I'll keep watch," said Jeransy, stepping to the edge of the rock and scanning the skies.

"You two work well together," offered Anndrew, looking to better understand their relationship. They'd met just a week ago, but their actions appeared very synchronized. *She keeps her laser gun in his pocket. That has to mean something.*

Flipping his coat behind him, Kormèr sat beside Anndrew. He crossed his stretched out legs and leaned back, supported by his arms. "We do, sometimes. Jeransy reacts well under pressure."

The girl turned her head and flashed Kormèr a smile.

And she likes you, too, realized Anndrew. And Kormèr offered plenty to like, from what Anndrew had seen so far. His good looks, his down-to-earth self-confidence, even his concern for Cecil's well-being despite not knowing him, spoke of a man that could be easy to like.

"So, what's with your pockets?"

He grinned. "They're magical, from this planet, actually. Years ago, when I was last here, I found them and replaced this coat's original pockets with these."

"You 'found' them, eh?" said Jeransy.

Kormèr gave her a sidelong look. "Yes. Why?"

Jeransy chuckled. "Oh, come off it. I've been around enough thieves to know one when I see one."

Kormèr glanced at Anndrew, but she said nothing, trying to read his body language. Was it true?

"With all them rings you've got," continued Jeransy, "the way you dress, the portal and now the pockets... not to mention the ease with which you make stuff up. You're either very rich or a thief."

Anndrew grinned as one of Kormèr's eyebrows went up. "As it happens, I'm both."

"Hah! Knew it."

Kormèr looked at Anndrew again, but she just shrugged. What else could she do? She'd just keep an eye on her belongings and hope that he didn't set his sights on her. It's not like she had anything that could be of value to him, anyway. "Anyway, back to your pockets. They're bottomless or something?"

"As far as I can tell. I've got several things floating around in there. I only have to think of what I want, and I find it."

"That's a fantastic invention! And definitely not 1980s tech. Which begs the question: what year is this?"

Kormèr's face scrunched up. "Wow, that's a good question." He let his face relax. "Last time I was here, it was somewhere around 3780, Terran standard."

Anndrew's head spun. She'd imagined that they were somewhere in the future, but that was a lot more than she'd imagined.

She met his eyes and realized she hadn't said anything. "Um, thanks."

"You're welcome... Thanks for what?"

"Not sugar-coating it. So your portal doesn't just go to different planets, it also crosses time."

Kormèr nodded.

"So obvs," said Jeransy. She pointed at herself. "2289," then at Anndrew, "19— whatever."

Kormèr cleared his throat, and Jeransy turned back to watching the skies.

"What year are you from?" Anndrew asked Kormèr.

"That's a tougher question. Elmar doesn't follow Terran Standard. Not yet, anyway."

"Whatcha mean?" asked Jeransy.

"Elmar is an isolated world in my time. We haven't heard about the Galactic Federation or any other inhabited planets."

"Huh. So we're your aliens, us."

"Yep. So to answer your question—and this is an educated guess—I'd say I'm from somewhere in the 3300s."

Anndrew found it comforting that for Kormèr, this was also the far future. Not as far as for her or Jeransy, per se, but still far.

"How're you doing?" Kormèr asked her.

She wiggled her toes, and her calf didn't cramp. "Much better!" she said, too excited. *Hey, it's my first nerve disruptor!* she chided herself.

"By the way, I'm really sorry for triggering that trap." He held up his hand to stall any platitudes. "It was really careless of me. You could've been hurt." He looked at Anndrew. "If your wound had been any worse, I would never have forgiven myself." He looked about to say more, but held his tongue.

"Apology accepted. But it's unnecessary."

"I've been in tighter situations, KL," said Jeransy. "That how I got my target practice."

Anndrew moved to stand, and Kormèr jumped to his feet. But to his credit, he just stood by with his arms out in case she needed his help. She stood, tested her leg and found it steady enough. "Thanks. I'm good to go."

He nodded and hopped ahead to the next rock, but then turned to wait for her and Jeransy.

"So how'd we end up here, anyway?" asked Anndrew, as she worked up the nerve to make the hop across the cloudy gap. "Jeransy said the portal read destinations from your mind." She made the hop, staggered a bit, but recovered quickly. Her expectation of pain had caused the stagger, rather than any residual weakness in her leg.

"The trees back on Earth reminded me of this place. The portal must've picked up my thoughts and opened here." He shrugged. "I guess."

"Ah! That makes sense. Which reminds me, what's your fascination with trees, anyhow?"

Kormèr smiled with a distant look in his eyes. "Oh, to grow so tall like that! They are quite rare around the universe, in my experience; I've only ever seen them on two other planets. Most planets I've been to only have large shrubbery or other forms of overlarge vegetation. But nothing that defies gravity like that."

"But, there aren't any trees here," said Jeransy.

Kormèr didn't answer right away, but Anndrew couldn't tell if his focus was on the next rock-hop or elsewhere.

"Well," he said at length, "I won't spoil the surprise for you. We should be there in thirty minutes or so, then you'll see the connection."

CHAPTER 7

CECIL stood on a large, round stone platform that jutted out from the uppermost promenade of the city. While the bridge that connected the platform to the city had handrails along the sides, the platform itself did not. Cecil judged the drop off the side to be a nearly quarter-kilometer to the ground. He remained well away from that edge as Sreet negotiated with another birdman.

Other than the precipice, Cecil also remained wary of the Argent that Sreet had procured for his voyage to Berdia. It stood at more than twice Cecil's height and reminded him very much of a giant rock dove. It seemed to watch him with its softball-sized eye, and Cecil wondered at the odds of it being the same one he'd ridden earlier. This one had a harness wrapped around its body, beneath the wings and along its belly.

Sreet finalized the deal and came over to Cecil. ||We're all set.||

Cecil asked, "Is there any other way to get there?"

||The birds are the only allowed transport to Berdia. I can understand your hesitation, but I assure you there is nothing to fear.||

"I'm not afraid. I'm cautious, based on prior experience."

||I didn't mean to ruffle your feathers, young human. Truly, it is a very safe method of transport. You will ride in the harness against the bird's belly. I've been told it is quite exhilarating.||

Cecil didn't care about that. He had never been one for adventure, and if not for his fascination with this planet, this day's events would already have been too much for him.

He approached the bird, which was tethered to the platform, and inspected the harness. Absently, he calculated the risk based on his assessment of the strength of the materials. Satisfied, he nodded to Sreet. "Alright. Let's do this."

Sreet's crest fluffed with satisfaction. ||Very good. The handler will assist you with the harness... yes, there you go.||

The deftness of the handler's taloned fingers impressed Cecil. They strapped him in snuggly without once scratching him. He looked at Sreet, who was watching approvingly, almost eagerly, if Cecil was interpreting the alien body language correctly. Cecil estimated a seventy-eight percent chance that his interpretation could be wrong. What he could be certain of was that Sreet was not riding on a bird himself. "Are you flying the whole way there?"

||Yes. I am among the strongest fliers of my sect, and so I act as the

Birshetland delegate. I have made this trip more times than I can remember.||

The handler disengaged the tether. ||Are you ready?||

Cecil looked out over the edge of the platform, grasped the harness, and nodded. Then he added, "Yes," just in case nodding didn't mean anything to Averians.

The bird's belly muscles tensed against Cecil's back. Then Cecil was pressed firmly into the bird as it took two giant steps and jumped off the platform.

Cecil's stomach lurched, and his brain froze. All he could do was stare stupidly through his thick glasses as he soared over the edge of the city-rock and out over the barren rocky landscape beyond. Even though the glasses were snug against his head, he worried, irrationally, that they would slip off and plummet through the clouds, leaving him myopic in this place that promised so much knowledge. He hoped that fate wouldn't be so cruel to him.

Gradually, the rhythmic *whoosh* of the giant bird's wings relaxed Cecil enough that he could think again. When he remembered to look for Sreet, he found the birdman off to his right, soaring along about twenty meters away. He was surprised the birdman could keep up with the carrier bird, but a quick calculation—based on his best guess at their airspeed—revealed that the Argent had to be traveling below its top speed.

He focused on the floating rock masses below and wondered what kept them afloat. They were much too low in the atmosphere and traveling much too slowly to be in any kind of orbit. There had to be some other explanation. During their walk here, Sreet had mentioned magic existed here. Perhaps some of this magic had been used to set the rocks afloat. He made a mental note to ask Sreet about that later.

His brain switched tracks over to this concept of 'magic'. He had grown up believing that magic was simply a technology so advanced that it defied explanation by a primitive observer. And clearly, the abilities Sreet had demonstrated so far were like magic to Cecil. However, Sreet himself had referred to the practice as magic. Had he been patronizing Cecil? Or had he detected Cecil's eager mind and known that knowledge of the existence of magic would be enough to cajole a friendship out of the boy?

What if he doesn't know the nature of his own abilities? Cecil wondered. *Now that's an intriguing idea.* Had Sreet been born with those abilities? Was it something common to Averians? If so, shouldn't Sreet have had more of a grasp of its underpinnings?

He stopped this inane mental rambling. He still had too many unknowns to formulate anything but wild hypothesis.

With nothing else to do, he busied his mind with computing Zeckendorf representations computed from no less than three Fibonacci numbers. This would be a much more productive use of his time.

Just as Cecil concluded calculating a tenth representation, a large rock ahead demanded his attention. He had noticed it a while ago, when it had been nothing more than a gray blob on the horizon, glinting in the waning sunlight. But until now, he hadn't devoted much attention to it. As the blob grew closer and larger, its majesty overwhelmed Cecil. As Sreet had described, it seemed to radiate a power that rippled over Cecil's skin, vibrated his bones, resonated in his mind. His eyes rolled up until only his whites showed, but still he saw the massive city of Berdia. In seconds he lived the lifetimes of the city's past inhabitants, children, teens, adults... thousands of lifetimes flitting through his mind, slashing, clawing, burning—

||Cecil!||

Cecil fell to his hands and knees onto cold stone, and vomited, his glasses skittering away just in time to avoid the mess. His arms trembled so that he nearly toppled forward into his mess. But Sreet was there holding him, once again saving him from a nasty situation.

||How do you feel?|| asked the birdman as Cecil's trembling subsided.

Cecil said, "Muh." He swallowed another surge of bile. He sat on his legs, but kept his eyes down as his spinning head slowly settled. The feeling reminded him of a time when his dentist gassed him with nitrous oxide to fill a cavity, only five times as intense.

Thankfully, Sreet didn't pressure him and let him take the time to recover. The birdman also handed Cecil his glasses. Cecil couldn't remember what had happened, why he felt this way. *Where the hell even am I?* He slipped the glasses on. The ground seemed to be made of large concentric circles of well-worn stone. Grass grew from cracks in the stone, here and there. Tilting his head back felt as if he were balancing a sack of bricks on it; he had to really focus to keep from letting the inertia pull his head too far back. As his surroundings came into focus, he realized that he was on a stone platform similar to the one from which they had departed Birshetland. Cecil had no recollection of landing or of being unstrapped from the carrier bird, which stood patiently nearby.

Recalling Sreet's question, he tried again. "I'm better now."

||Good! You have passed the trial of Berdia.|| Sreet signaled the carrier bird. The latter turned and, with a short running start, took off, presumably back to Birshetland.

Cecil glared sidelong at Sreet. "You... knew this... was going to happen?" he managed between pants. Presently, he rolled off his knees and onto his butt. The motion sent his head spinning, but his annoyance with Sreet steeled him.

||All who come here go through the trial. It is the city's way of weeding out those who do not belong. That is why the Argents are the only acceptable forms of travel here. Imagine if you had been piloting a mechanical craft; you

certainly would have crashed. | |

That was true enough. Even now, minutes later, Cecil still felt queasy. "I take it that not warning people is part of the ritual."

Sreet inclined his head slightly. | | It is. | |

Feeling better, Cecil looked up, beyond the platform. This city differed from Birshetland. It looked older and darker, almost creepy. The pseudo-trees here were gray rather than white, and they exhibited a higher degree of craftsmanship in their architectural style. Unlike Birshetland, Berdia also appeared to have less of a promenade, and even that seemed to have been added on as an afterthought. In many places, it had crumbled and remained in disrepair.

It then dawned on Cecil why he sensed a creepy vibe: unlike the bustling Birshetland, Berdia was nearly devoid of people. He saw some Averians gliding about, but nowhere near the numbers in Birshetland.

"What's the population here?" he asked.

| | Fifteen or twenty thousand. It is a city devoted to the study of magic; only students and teachers live here now. | |

"Now?"

| | This was our first city. It once held all the Frrooweetsee. At some point, our population became too much for it to support, and we moved outward, founding the other cities. Eventually it was abandoned, left to us sorcerers. It remains a monument to our past. When you are well enough, I will take you to my home tree, the Hovel. | |

"Hovel? That's a strange name for a tree." Cecil stood slowly, testing his legs. But the trembling had subsided.

| | It is the oldest tree in the city, | | sang Sreet, taking Cecil's cue and leading him into the city. | | It was our shelter in the darkest days of our past. There is no more appropriate a name for it. | |

If you say so, thought Cecil. *But you guys really have some questionable naming conventions.*

He had to marvel at the construction. From Sreet's tale, it sounded as if the city had been around for a very long time. Yet, aside from some expected aging, like the cracked, worn stone underfoot and the crumbled promenades, the trees were in remarkably good shape. Either the sorcerers that cared for the city used magic to maintain it, or these Averians were master craftsmen.

The trees grew denser the deeper into the city they walked. Now and then they would pass a shrine or a public bath, all surrounded by idyllic gardens. Cecil equated these to cloisters, serene places for meditation. Sure enough, they soon passed such a garden in which a dozen Averians sat quietly, in deep thought, around a bubbling fountain. In another, an older Averian female lectured five young females. She looked up as they passed and nodded sagely at Sreet. Then she noticed Cecil, and her eyes went wide. She frowned deeply at Sreet. Her students turned to see what had disturbed their teacher so, and they gasped when they saw Cecil.

Cecil was about to ask Sreet about the reactions when his eyes fell upon a massive stone wall just ahead of the next grove. He tipped his head back, following it up and up and up... beyond the tallest of the surrounding trees. It was the most massive tree he had seen so far, over one hundred meters in diameter, by Cecil's best guess. No other trees stood within ninety meters of the Hovel. Instead, elegant, well-tended gardens, complete with fountains and baths, occupied the space. Paths cut through the gardens at regular intervals. The path he and Sreet were on led to an arched entryway set between two of the Hovel's massive support struts, these cleverly designed to resemble roots.

As Sreet led him through the gardens and to the archway, Cecil knew he was really going to enjoy his stay here. He believed this world offered enough new things to occupy his mind for a lifetime. Eagerly, he followed the birdman inside.

CHAPTER 8

KORMÈR fought the urge to dash the last hundred meters to the colossal rock ahead of them. While he longed to set eyes on Birshetland's serene beauty once again, he had mixed feelings about being here again. *I never intended to return,* he thought. *It was supposed to be goodbye forever.* It had certainly been painful enough making the choice to leave, by far the worst time in his young life.

"Blimey! Have we gotta climb that?" Jeransy stared at the steps cut into the stone escarpment that ascended roughly thirty meters to the city ridge.

"Honestly, those didn't exist the last time I was here. I expected to have to scramble up the raw stone. Just take it slowly. Once we get over the top, I'll hail a taxi."

"Really?" said Anndrew. "They have taxis here?"

"They do. I know it's a Terran word, but I didn't realize it was that old. You have them in your time?"

"Yep, and it's probably a century old, even in my time."

"Interesting."

Despite her grumble over the stairs, Jeransy's petite form scampered up the steps, stopping only once to catch her breath. Kormèr let Anndrew go ahead of him to keep an eye on her, but she kept her pace very moderate.

Argents and other birds passed overhead now and then, glancing at the trio before soaring off.

Anndrew stopped and breathed deeply. "I'm trying not to look up anymore." She wiped her brow with her forearm. "Every time I did before, the top wasn't getting any closer."

"Not a bad strategy," said Kormèr. "But we're almost there."

She looked up. "Oh, thank goodness!"

Kormèr smiled. "You did great."

They climbed the last few meters to the ridge, then joined Jeransy in gazing at the view of the Averian capitol, Birshetland. The city extended as far as the eye could see, a fairytale forest of majestic pseudo-trees with their paper-thin metallic leaves. Three layers of platforms connected the trees at different points; Kormèr knew these to be the promenades, which held gardens and public baths, and which provided access to storefronts and gathering spaces for locals and visitors alike.

It had been a long time since Kormèr had viewed the city from a spot like this one. He felt his heart catch in his throat as many memories flooded his mind, the beauty, the tranquility… and Sylvestra. *At last I have returned, my Sylvee. I hope I find you well.*

"This is un-bloody-believable!" said Jeransy in a low voice, as if unwilling to disturb the serenity by being loud. "KL, we've seen some fantastic natural beauty together, but this… I never imagined…" She gasped, and sat heavily on a stone bench.

Kormèr now noticed that an alternating line of benches and perches stretched for several meters to either side of the steps. *Hmm, that's new too.* A humanoid alien sat at the last bench to the left watching the sky, while a humanoid couple talked quietly at the right-most end. A stone pillar with a motion sensor activated when Kormèr swiped his palm over it. A holographic plaque appeared. In various languages, it read: *This Ridge View was donated by Feestoo Trreesoo.* Kormèr could never forget the charismatic taxi pilot that became his personal chauffer during his stay. That the man had donated this wonderful addition to the city pleased him to no end.

"This really is spectacular," said Anndrew. "I understand now what you meant about trees. Just… wow! What am I seeing moving around up there?" She pointed through the trees.

"Averians and taxis, no doubt. They're the only ones allowed to fly around the city."

"Oh! They're *flying* taxis! So that's how we'll get up to those platforms."

"Yep."

"How're we supposed to find where Cecil ended up in this place?" asked Jeransy.

Kormèr frowned. "That's an excellent question, and not one I'd given much thought to. But there are a couple of things to take care of first." He turned his face to the skies, and while he waited, he wondered how much the place had changed since his last visit; it had been… a good number of years, almost one and a half Elmarian. The stairs and ridge view might just be the simplest of the changes he would find. Would he remember the city? Would it remember him?

"Ah, here we go." He spotted an approaching robotic police shuttle. This, at least, had not changed.

The aircar swept down and approached more slowly, stopping two meters away from Kormèr. ||Identification: Kormèr Lezàl,|| sang a tinny voice from a hidden speaker.

Kormèr waved playfully and chirped, ||Confirmed.||

||Didn't we get rid of you?||

Kormèr wrinkled his lips. ||Cute. Who was your programmer?||

The AI ignored his question, but it returned to business. ||You did not register at the port authority on arrival. Your presence has been reported.|| It paused. ||You'll have to clear the two females—||

||Is my word still good here?|| twittered Kormèr.

47

"KL, what're you doing?" asked Jeransy, who hadn't understood any of the exchange.

"One sec, love."

Another pause from the vehicle. | | It is. | | Its mechanical tones sounded almost disappointed.

| | Very well, then. Terran English, please. | |

"Translating."

Kormèr introduced the girls to the vehicle, the latter recording their names and physical details. He concluded with: "They are my traveling companions; I accept full responsibility for them."

A rude flutter came from the speaker. "Information recorded. Have they been inoculated?"

"No."

The robotic vehicle floated closer. "Please approach in an orderly fashion." A panel slid open along its left side and a mechanical arm extended out. A small chrome cylinder protruded from one end.

The girls looked at Kormèr warily, but he urged them on. "It won't hurt."

Anndrew stepped gingerly toward the aircar and watched as the cylinder touched her arm. She winced reflexively when the syringe hissed, but then she smiled. "It hurt a little, but not like a syringe."

Kormèr noticed that Jeransy was not comforted by Anndrew's reaction. She was much less trusting, except perhaps when it came to him. She seemed to trust him almost unquestioningly. Almost.

"It's safe, love," reassured Kormèr. "I've had mine for years."

She nodded, but Kormèr saw her look away when the cylinder hissed against her arm.

"Welcome to Birshetland." The aircar retracted its arm. "Enjoy your stay." It turned gracefully and dashed up and away.

Kormèr smiled at the girls and said, somewhat ruefully, "Sorry about that. I had completely forgotten about the inoculation."

Jeransy shrugged. "It's alright, KL."

"Nonetheless, we've done enough walking. It's time for some pampering." Kormèr raised his hand and watched the sky again. In no time, another aircar swept down and approached, hovering along the ground. Kormèr didn't immediately recognize the white flat-bottom, dome-toped vehicle. But as it drew closer, he spotted the familiar message board on the roof that flashed various symbols in a repeating pattern. One combination of symbols read, "TAXI". The taxi stopped, and the pilot gave them a wave. "High sky, friends," he said, in passable Terran English.

"High sky," said Kormèr, opening the rear door. "After you," he told the girls. He followed them into the taxi and whistled directions to the driver. The taxi lifted smoothly into the air and headed into the city.

Kormèr noticed the absolute silence in the cab as the view out the windows and clear canopy held both girls' attentions. He enjoyed their reactions, their wide eyes and slack jaws as priceless as the most precious gems to his eyes. He'd never traveled via portal with anyone before, mostly because he hadn't wanted to be responsible for anyone else but himself. But the past week with Jeransy, and today with her and Anndrew, had him wondering if he'd been depriving himself of a much better experience by traveling alone.

Recalling the robo-patrol's reaction, his thoughts shifted. *So the city still remembers me,* he thought with amusement. *I guess those were pretty memorable times, and apparently it hasn't been too long since I was last here. I made a lot of friends. A lot of enemies, too.*

He wondered exactly how much time he had skipped by using the portal. Hopefully years and not months. He'd left for very specific reasons, and being back after less than a year or two would be… awkward. *I really should find out before I get into trouble with old friends.*

He gazed out the canopy as the taxi banked high over a promenade. Tourists from various worlds browsed the lively, colorful shops and restaurants along those walkways. Avian children flitted about in the public baths in the center of the streets. Seeing them reminded Kormèr of how mild the weather was, and that he was sweating under his coat.

Sitting at his left, Anndrew turned away from the window. "I thought the view from the ridge was amazing, but this… being in the city is… indescribable."

"It really just keeps getting better and better," said Jeransy. "Where're we off to, by the way?"

"Since I'm assuming the Argent came this way," said Kormèr, "the first thing is to find out if he made it." He looked at Anndrew. "I'll be honest that there's some probability that he wasn't able to hang on to the big carrier bird and fell off between where the portal left us and here."

Anndrew nodded, but said nothing.

"Now, assuming he made it here, there's bound to be news or a report of his undocumented arrival. That police shuttle flagged us as undocumented, too, but they're sort of used to that with me."

"From the last time you were here," said Jeransy.

"Yep. So while I send my feelers out to find this information, we'll need a center of operations. And for that, I have the perfect place."

As if on cue, the pilot announced, "Arriving at the Cheerees Hotel, sir."

"A hotel?" Anndrew's tone sounded detectably sour.

"Not just any hotel," protested Kormèr. "The finest hotel in Birshetland. I lived here for several months. And not to worry; we'll have separate accommodations."

The cab stopped, and as the girls exited, Kormèr removed his coat and fetched a small gem for the driver. The driver looked into the mirror after receiving the fare—and sizable tip. | |Kormèr Lezàl?| |

Kormèr smiled. | |I am. Do you know Feestoo, by any chance?| |

| |Of course I do, sir. He never stops talking about you.| |

| |Tell him I said hello next time you see him.| |

| |I certainly will, sir. He's my boss, you know.| |

| |You don't say! When did this happen?| |

| |Two years ago. He started his own taxi company, he says, just on the fares you paid him.| | He held up the gem. | |I see why now.| |

That explains the donation of the ridge view area! Good for him! | |Wish him luck for me then.| | In the back of his mind, he made note of the fact that at least two years had elapsed since his leaving.

He exited the taxi and joined Anndrew and Jeransy as they strode across the covered platform and through the hotel's wide arched entryway. Clever architects had designed the tall lobby to imitate nature, from archways that looked like smaller tree limbs branching as they rose into an overhead network through which light shined, as if one were staring up at the sky through a forest canopy. Oval chamber entrances sported gold trim, and most of the fixtures looked like polished brass. Ladders and ramps led off to other parts of the hotel. Beyond the reception area, the hotel opened into a vast atrium.

Kormèr's eyes lit up as he looked around, and he felt instantly lighter on his feet. "I hadn't realized how much I'd missed this place until now."

"I'm not being paranoid, right?" asked Jeransy. "People are staring at us."

A passerby, gliding with his female companion across the lobby, whispered to her while pointing at Kormèr.

"Hmm, could be." Kormèr recalled that he'd caused quite a stir midway through his last stay. He'd had to resort to sneaking in and out of the hotel via the service elevators. He did not want a repeat of that. "Let's check in."

"We'll be over here," said Anndrew, pointing as she and Jeransy shuffled toward the atrium. Kormèr nodded. He'd draw less attention solo for now.

Ignoring curious eyes, Kormèr walked to the reception desk. He leaned casually on the counter and crossed his legs.

| |Good afternoon, sir,| | sang the young receptionist. | |And welcome to the Cheerees. How can we help you today?| |

Kormèr smiled. | |Hi. Is Theeseeo here today?| |

| |Yes, sir. He is. Is there a problem with the hotel or staff?| |

| |Oh, no, nothing like that. Please, just let him know that Kormèr Lezàl is here.| |

The young man's eyes went wide. He tapped his screen below the counter and glanced down. | |He'll be right out.| |

| |Thank you.| |

Kormèr turned and watched the girls. They stood a cautious distance from the edge of the walkway, he judged, far enough to keep the vertigo at bay, but close enough to get a sense of the vertical tubular space. Jeransy dared to step closer and pointed upward, probably spying the inverted glass dome that let the natural daylight illuminate the vast space. The lighted walkway spiraled upward only ten more floors, but downward at least fifteen more. Anndrew stepped closer to the edge to look up as well. As she did, Jeransy started when her hand touched the shimmering barrier that prevented non-flying species from tumbling over the edge. Anndrew placed her palm on the barrier, then tapped it with a finger. As if to demonstrate its purpose, an Averian woman stepped past them and leaped into the void, undeterred by the barrier.

Jeransy shrugged, then she turned and walked back to the reception desk. Anndrew followed.

"Is everything alright?" asked Jeransy.

Kormèr nodded. "Yes. I'm just waiting for the manager. Ah, here he comes now."

Theeseeo appeared from his office at the back of the reception area. His light-gray mottled plumage looked the same to Kormèr, though he now had to look up at Kormèr. <<Welcome back to Averia, Kormèr Lezàl!>> he said in formal Elmarian. He'd gone out of his way to learn the language to please Kormèr and his own son, who had been studying it at the time.

||Theeseeo! It's great to see you again.||

Theeseeo's eyes widened. <<You've grown, a lot.>>

||It's been some time,|| Kormèr sang, vaguely, now very curious about exactly how much time had passed. A simple question would have cleared the matter right up, but Theeseeo knew nothing of the portal's existence, nor did he need to.

<<Of course! Forgive my ignorance of such things.>>

||There is nothing to forgive, old friend.||

<<Your room is ready and as you left it.>>

By the gods! Has he been holding my room all this time? ||You always said I'd be back, but I wouldn't have thought...||

<<Come now, it hasn't been *that* long. And you can never keep away from a good thing, you know.>>

||How true.|| Kormèr sighed. ||How is Almp?||

<<My boy is doing very well, thank you.>> His feathers puffed with fatherly pride. <<He's my assistant now, learning the intricacies of management so his old man can retire.>>

||Hah! Old man indeed.|| Kormèr pursed his lips disapprovingly. ||Is he around? I probably wouldn't recognize him anymore.||

<<He's out with his friends today. But he'll be back later. I'm sure he'll hear of your return before I have a chance to tell him.>>

||The way word is spreading around here, I believe it.||

<<Birshetland will not so easily forget Kormèr Lezàl, certainly not in only two years and ten months.>>

So it's been two years and ten months, thought Kormèr. It was just like Theeseeo to be accommodating without even trying. ||You're too kind. But I must ask if you have two extra rooms for my friends? Don't worry if they're not avail—||

||Tut, tut.|| Theeseeo cut him off. ||Not to worry.|| The receptionist passed him a thin sheet of electronic plastic that Kormèr knew as a 'digital flimsy', or simply 'flim', from his home planet. He looked it over, then sang, ||As a matter of fact, there are two empty rooms. We'll just have them provide their biometrics, and they'll be all set.|| He passed the flim to Jeransy with a quick explanation of what to do, then to Anndrew afterward.

When the girls completed the registration process, Theeseeo passed the flim back to the receptionist. ||Excellent! Will you be having your usual selection for dinner?||

Kormèr glanced at the girls out of the corner of his eye, trying to gauge their taste for the unexpected. Well, they were there with him, weren't they? ||I'm not sure, yet. That would depend on my guests.||

"Are you ladies hungry?" he asked them.

"I could eat," said Anndrew.

Jeransy nodded. "But I'd like to wash up first. I can still feel the dust from the locust world everywhere."

"Oh, yes! Same with me. Alright. How about we go to our rooms, we wash up and meet in an hour?"

Both girls agreed.

"An hour it is, then," said Theeseeo, in crisp Terran English. Kormèr wondered if the old birdman hadn't cheated and used an edu-comp to learn that one. As a hotel manager, his fluency with various languages didn't surprise Kormèr. But Theeseeo hadn't been *that* fluent two-plus years ago. "If I may suggest, the weather is especially fine for outdoor dining this evening." Theeseeo paused, all the while looking at Kormèr expectantly. Finally he asked, ||Will there be anything else?||

Kormèr started to twitter something, then stopped and peered at Theeseeo. ||She's here, isn't she?||

Theeseeo nodded. ||She arrived only a moment before you. She's in the lounge.||

Kormèr nodded. ||Many thanks.||

||Enjoy your stay, KL.||

Kormèr turned to the girls as Theeseeo scooted back behind the counter and into his office. "Okay, our rooms are this way." He led them toward a corridor to one side of the lobby.

"You two were sure going on about a lot of things we didn't

understand," said Jeransy.

"Sorry about that," said Kormèr. "Theeseeo's English wasn't that good the last time I was here. Neither was his Elmarian, for that matter. So I got caught up in Song. He surprised me at the end there when he spoke with you."

"The Averian language is called Song?" asked Anndrew. "That's so cool!"

"Yep, Averian Song. It's another one of those names that isn't originally theirs, like Averia isn't the actual name of the planet, but rather, something *in* Song."

"Do you know the real name?"

"Yes. It's…" And he whistled the name, sounding out the syllables as: "*frroo-wee-tseé*".

"That's pretty, but I'll stick to 'Averia'," said Jeransy.

Kormèr chuckled. "Exactly. Most people do, including many locals."

"Anyway, Theeseeo and I were just catching up. I used to go partying with his son."

Jeransy looked at him with a big grin. "Partying? Really?"

"What?" Kormèr couldn't suppress his amusement at the look on her face. "What's that look? I love to dance!"

"Good to know."

"Ah, here we are." He stopped and pointed to a door a little further down on the right. "That's my room, which Theeseeo has actually been holding for me, believe it or not."

"He knew you'd be back," said Anndrew.

"Then he knew something I didn't. Being here is an accident."

"There are no accidents," said Jeransy, as if she were reading something from a distance. "Just opportunities."

Kormèr gave her an approving nod. "I like that. Okay, Annde, this is yours." He flicked a thumb at the door to his left. "And, JB, that's yours over there." Then he showed them how to use the screens beside each door to open the doors and how to get out once inside.

He stepped out of Anndrew's room, followed by Jeransy. "Any questions?"

"Can't think of anything," said Jeransy.

Anndrew shook her head. "Same."

"Alright. Let's start the hour countdown from now." He checked his chrono, which had automatically synchronized to local time. "One hour puts us at six o'clock local time."

"Sounds good," said Anndrew.

Kormèr activated his screen and opened the door. He waved to the girls before shutting the door behind him. Theeseeo hadn't lied; the room looked almost the same, from the nest-bed and dresser set to the small table and extra chairs Kormèr had always kept against a wall for non-Averian company. A wave of calm comfort washed over him, and he suddenly felt as if he'd never left.

He stripped off his clothes and placed them in the refresher set to quick cycle. This wouldn't provide a thorough wash, but it would at least remove the dust and grit of the past day and a half. Then he washed his face and neck in the sink, trimmed his beard stubble and combed his hair.

He stared into the mirror as he waited for the refresher to notify him that it had completed. *What have you gotten yourself into now?* he wondered. Then he shrugged. *Nothing more than the usual, since the portal anyway.* And that was the truth. His life may not have been mundane before the portal, but it certainly had been livelier since. He fleetingly wondered what the con man he'd stolen it from was up to these days. But he really didn't care. The con man had been masquerading as a traveling magician while his partner wandered the audience picking their pockets. Kormèr took issue with the fact that most of the audience consisted of lower-class people who were already struggling to get by. So he and his good friend had taught the charlatan a lesson and cleaned him out. Among the loot, Kormèr had found the portal in its cube form.

He wandered out of the bathroom and opened a closet to find it still stocked with some clothes he'd left behind. Unfortunately, none of them fit him anymore. Some pieces he'd never even worn. However, they stirred his memories, reminding him that Sylvee awaited him.

Ding.

He took his clothes out of the refresher and dressed, leaving his coat hanging in the closet. He wouldn't be needing that now.

Now that his clothes were tidy, the scuffs and dust on his boots stood out. He grabbed a leather brush from a drawer and sat to clean them.

You're stalling, you know. He grunted at the unbidden thought, squeezed the brush tightly in his grip, then tossed it back in the drawer.

He took a deep breath and left his room.

CHAPTER 9

FRESHLY groomed, Kormèr anxiously strolled into the lounge. He hadn't felt this nervous about meeting a woman in a very long time. But Sylvestra was no ordinary woman. And he had left her somewhat unexpectedly. The fact that she was here now, that she had come knowing that he, too, would be here, was promising… or ominous. He couldn't be sure of the reception; she could be here to catch up or, just as easily, to slap him.

He spotted her perched at the bar, and his heart leaped. Until that very moment, Kormèr's presence here on Averia had felt surreal. Seeing Sylvestra, resplendent in her snowy-white plumage, solidified the reality of the moment.

He approached her from the side, not wanting to sneak up on her. She noticed him almost immediately, her glittering black eyes turning to meet his, questioningly. He realized that he probably looked very different from the last time she had seen him, especially with his mustache and beard.

| |Hello, Sylvee.| |

She glanced down at the dozen red hwyiite he offered her, then her eyes widened with recognition.

| |KL!| | She stood and embraced him warmly.

| |It's so good to see you again,| | he sang, wishing the embrace could go on. He then saw an image of himself and the girls on a flimsy on the bar top. Judging by the background, it had to have been the image taken by the robo-patroller.

Kormèr and Sylvestra separated and held each other at arm's length, smiling, studying. He could feel his heart tearing itself to pieces. *Gods, how I love her still!*

| |It's good to see you well.| | She spoke honestly, but with an effort.

Kormèr frowned, reading her mood. | |I went over it so many times and always came to the same conclusion. I had to leave.| |

| |You could've handled it better,| | she twittered, her words biting but mitigated by the passage of time. In that sentence, he knew that he'd done the right thing. She had moved past him at some point during the last few years and had gone on with her life. Things had worked out as well as he could have hoped, given their circumstances.

| |I was younger then, less wise. But even now, I can't imagine how I was brave enough to leave you sleeping that morning. It would have been impossible to say goodbye to you, had you been awake.| |

She smiled and shook her head. | |Still the smooth talker.| |

||I never say anything that isn't true.||

||That's true enough, from what I remember,|| she sang, settling back onto the bar perch and placing the flowers beside the flimsy.

Kormèr grabbed a stool and sat beside her. ||Do I still warrant so much attention?|| he asked, pointing to the image on the flimsy.

||Well, you're not exactly the most welcome person in the city, at least not with the police department. So you raised a red flag again when you didn't register at any port. That goes straight up to the chief of police. And you know how cranky she can get,|| she sang drolly, the light glinting off her badge.

||I remember,|| he sang, chuckling.

||Still using the portal, I take it?||

Kormèr nodded. ||And still getting into trouble with it, as you can see.||

||The two Terran females? I presume the records request will come back empty then?||

||Most likely. Or they might come back showing that they've been deceased for centuries.||

Sylvestra shook her head. ||Well, you vouched for them, and I trust your choice of acquaintance. If you say they won't cause any trouble in my city...||

||They won't.||

||Fair enough.|| She glanced at the photo again. ||You know, I almost didn't recognize you.|| She gestured to his beard. ||And what's that for? It looks painful, like pin feathers coming in!||

||You don't like it? I got tired of shaving constantly.||

She cocked her head to study it. ||It's... different. It makes you look so much older. In fact, many things about you have changed. Just how old are you now?||

||Almost five Elmarian,|| he chirped, basing his age on linear time. Traveling via portal all these years had caused time to lose its linearity. A week on one world; a year on another... Kormèr had lost track of his age several portal hops ago. He found it easier to stick to the linear standard of five Elmarian years. He calculated in his head to the Terran standard that Sylvestra was more familiar with. ||Almost twenty.||

Her eyes went wide with shock. ||That... but how can that be? You were fourteen, and it hasn't even been three years.||

||The mixed blessing of portal travel.|| He sighed. ||I've skipped through time, but time has kept pace with me.||

||It's been almost six years for you!|| She frowned and fixed her eyes on the flimsy. ||This is so strange.||

||What? The portal stuff...||

||No. Well, not entirely. But you've had so much time to... change, to

grow.||

Kormèr realized something about his age was bothering her. But there could be so many reasons. ||You were older than I was then. I've only evened things out, inadvertently.||

||Even then, you were mature beyond your years. Now I must seem like a child to you.||

||Of course not! Is that what bothers you?|| Kormèr resisted the urge to caress her crest feathers. He missed her touch, but he had forfeited his right to it when he left her years ago, and it was her choice to let him get that close again. Maybe later, she would allow it—maybe never again, at all—but certainly not now.

She looked at him and laughed, confusion and sadness entwined in that not so simple sound. ||I don't know what bothers me. Maybe this was a mistake.|| She grabbed the flimsy and stood.

||Sylvee, wait.|| Kormèr stood to follow her, but she stopped him with her nails poised at his chest, just barely touching him.

||No, KL. Please stay. It was very nice seeing you again. Be well.||

He watched her go, not entirely sure why she was leaving or why he wasn't ignoring her last words and going after her. This was not how he'd expected their meeting to go at all.

||Need a drink, friend?|| asked the bartender.

Kormèr turned to him and noticed the flowers still sitting on the bar top. ||Not right now, thank you.|| He grabbed the flowers and headed for his room.

SYLVESTRA leaped away from the entrance to Cheerees, spread her wings and glided, aiming somewhere in between her home and the precinct. Should she go to the office to bury herself in work, or go home to do the same? She couldn't decide. For the moment at least, she ended up doing neither.

She alighted on the upper promenade and did something she rarely did these days, stroll. *Why don't I go for walks more often?* she wondered. Somehow, work just kept her occupied. Not like Birshetland even had a lot of crime. With eighty percent of the population being Averian, and punishments being quite severe, crimes committed by Averians accounted for less than one percent of all crimes. And that was out of an already negligible crime rate.

Freet-See was another matter entirely. Being a port city, many more off-worlders wandered its streets and made it their haven. It also boasted the largest business district on the planet. Shady businessmen frequently made the mistake of thinking that Averia—but more specifically, Freet-See—would make a good place to conduct their illegal activities. More often than not, they quickly discovered the harsh reality. Averia was growing a reputation for swift and tough justice in the Galactic Federation.

Naturally, the police were involved in many aspects of daily Birshettan life, other than crime-fighting. *But is that what keeps me so busy?* wondered Sylvestra. *Or am I just making excuses for not taking the time to relax more often?*

And now, on top of it all, Kormèr's here again.

She took a perch at the border of a decorative garden. The fragrance of its many flowers combined into an intoxicatingly sweet mix. It made Sylvestra think of food and of how she'd imagined that her reunion with Kormèr would result in their dining together.

She sighed and looked across the way to a public bath where several Averian families socialized during their early evening constitutional. Sylvestra recalled the day she'd first met Kormèr at one of the public baths. She imagined the baths would always remind her of that day… of him. Kormèr and his cavalier ways.

No, not cavalier, she reasoned. *He's anything but cavalier. He's… frustrating!*

Maybe so. But it was your idea to go meet him at the hotel today. What did you expect? Her eyes were on the bathers, but her focus was somewhere else. *I didn't know what to expect,* she finally decided. *That's why I had to go meet him. To see him and understand why he was back. The stupid thing is, I still don't know.*

She sighed. Returning to the office was out of the question. She wouldn't get any work done, anyway. She leaped from the perch and headed for home.

Sylvestra heard her house-comm chime through the door as she got to her apartment. She hurried in and rushed to the comm console. The call was from the precinct, specifically from one of her sergeants. The small video window expanded at a touch of her talon. ||Chrreel, here.||

||Chief, we seem to have another unregistered scan,|| chirped the young female. ||We don't have a clear image of him, but we can tell he's Terran. We ran the image and only came back with a two percent match to any of the registered Terrans currently on-planet.||

||Details?|| prompted Sylvestra while checking her mail queue just below the video window on the comm console.

||Male; Caucasian; roughly in his teens; sandy-brown hair; glasses.|| *For an unclear image,* thought Sylvestra, *that's not bad.* The sergeant continued: ||He was first seen when he fell from an Argent into PB-six—||

Sylvestra's crest feathers perked. ||Wait. Did you say he fell from an Argent?||

||That's correct. Just prior to midday, he appeared on cit-cam, falling from above. Another angle caught an Argent passing at that same moment.||

||That was before Lezàl's arrival. Why wasn't this brought to my attention earlier?||

||Sorry, Chief. The Terran was drenched, and it took some time to verify that he wasn't in the scan logs. Lezàl was… easier to flag. Do you think their arrivals are related?||

Sylvestra started to say that there was no sense jumping to conclusions when her eye caught a flash of red reflected in the mirror beside the comm console. She spun around and found a vase with the dozen red hwyiite sitting perfectly in the center of her coffee table. | | I would say that's a very good possibility. | | *Oh! He's such a pain in the tail!*

CHAPTER 10

UPON entering her room, Jeransy immediately stripped off her filthy clothes and headed for the bathroom. It took her a few confused minutes to figure out the controls and to realize that it was actually a water bath and not the sonic showers she was used to. Not that she complained at all after filling the bath and easing her aching muscles into the hot, relaxing water. This was heaven!

Her mind drifted, recollecting the events of the past week. They'd gone from her cell to a planet of islands with spectacular coral formations twisting up out of the water, now home to bird-like creatures. On the island planet, Kormèr had tested the water to make sure it was safe to drink and swim in, and she had actually gone swimming for the first time in her life. Kormèr had called her a natural, as she picked up on his instruction quickly. They'd lain on the pebbly beach, under the afternoon sun, until their clothes dried.

Then it had been off to a small café somewhere to have dinner while listening to live music. Kormèr had picked two such dining locations that they'd alternated between over the week. Except for last night.

Last night, she had dined with Kormèr on a cliff, overlooking a stunning barren plain that stretched away as far as the eye could see. They had watched the sun set while they ate, finishing their meal by candlelight, with the stars twinkling above them.

Having lived all her life in a climate-controlled dome, Jeransy had marveled at the pinpoints of light in the dark sky, and relished the feel of a sun's warmth on her skin. Her studies had taught her about stars, and she'd seen holo-pics of star-filled night skies, but she had never been out on a clearer night than that... and never with such wonderful company.

She had never questioned how he arranged or paid for their meals, but she knew he was a thief, so perhaps it was best that she not know all the details. He had seemed unconcerned about being caught, so she had followed his lead.

She shivered. The water had lost much of its heat, and the cool air of the room chilled her face and shoulders. She sat up out of the water and ran her fingers through her hair. Had she missed something important about a water bath? Her hair still felt a bit greasy. And though she felt relaxed from the bath, she didn't really feel clean. She stood and dried herself off with a towel, assuming that might help. But it did not. Then she noticed the small tray on the counter by the sink. It held a perfumed, paper-wrapped bar of soap, and a little bottle of viscous fragrant liquid. She'd heard of shampoo, but she'd never used it before.

The novelty of the cleaning products kept her busy far longer than she'd planned, so that by the time she was done with the bath, it was just about six. She hated having to put back on her old, dusty clothes, but she had brought nothing else with her. She sniffed her shirt and shrugged. *For now, it'll just have to do,* she thought, as she slid into the stretchy material of her form-fitting trousers.

ANNDREW'S first impulse was to poke around her room. She peeked into all the drawers and closets. She threw open the drapes and found she had a view of the hollow core of the hotel. Suddenly realizing that any Averian could fly right up to her window and peep in, she closed the drapes.

She wished she'd brought a change of clothes. The journey to the city had left her clothes dusty and her skin sticky. She started out washing the grime off of her face, and that alone felt so good that she decided to go for the shower.

When she stepped into that hot, relaxing stream of water, she was glad of the decision. She nearly forgot where she was until she reached for the small complimentary shampoo bottle and found that it read, "Good for medium to oily fur or feathers." Then she laughed. *How crazy life is!* she thought. *Here I am, taking a shower on another planet.*

Upon exiting the shower, Anndrew found an assortment of moisturizers and grooming amenities to suit the variety of species that frequented the hotel. Cheerees was certainly the five-star establishment Kormèr had made it out to be. She now noticed that there was even a compartment in the wall beside the sink with a digital tag above it that read: "Clothes Sanitizer". She glanced at the pile of her clothes sitting on the floor and considered using the device. But without knowing how long it would take to get her clothes back, she opted not to.

Wrapped in a towel, she went to her bag and pulled out a small radio. After a few minutes of trying to tune it to a station, she realized she probably wasn't going to find one. "Duh," she mumbled to herself. "As if a millennia-old radio is going to just work." A section of the headboard suddenly lit up, displaying the time and what looked like a list of music options. She frowned at the display. *That's* serendipitous, she thought, wondering if the headboard had responded to her voice. *Well, if I can figure this thing out, at least I won't have to waste my batteries.*

Anndrew fiddled with the touchscreen controls, passing station after station broadcasting in various other languages, none of which she understood. Finally, she found a station broadcasting in English. Unfortunately, she only understood about eighty-five percent of what was being said. There were entire words and phrases that meant nothing to her or were being used in ways that made no sense.

Eventually, the chatting stopped and music clamored its way out of the speaker. It had some rhythm, but overshadowed by discordant drumbeats and clinks and knocks. She tried to get into it, but eventually gave up and turned the radio off.

I'm out of my element, she realized. *Waaay out.*

Anndrew then realized a buzzing was coming from the door. She touched the screen on the wall beside the door, as Kormèr had demonstrated earlier, and an image appeared of the corridor outside her door. But there was no one there. Messages flashed at the edges of the display in what Anndrew assumed were different languages, but Anndrew ignored them. She glanced at the clock-radio and realized it was ten past six.

She dressed quickly and opened the door. As the display had shown, no one was there. She peeked out to find Kormèr standing at Jeransy's door. He looked at her and smiled. When Jeransy's door opened, he said, "So Theeseeo's plan was for us to eat in my room. But would you two like to go out to eat tonight instead? It'll be much more interesting." Anndrew didn't agree with him on that point, and she was sure Jeransy was thinking the same. But she didn't argue. She was just as eager to see more of this fascinating city.

WHEN Kormèr informed him of the change in plans, Theeseeo insisted they eat at the hotel's rooftop restaurant, and Kormèr obliged him. Aptly called "The Nook", the restaurant sat nestled in a bowl formed by the juncture of two of the hotel-tree's massive branches. A louvered roof covered some of the seating area, but the rest was open air and offered a breathtaking view of the city below and the evening sky. Except for seating that ranged from chairs to perches to other odd configurations, Anndrew found that the restaurant was very much like any on Earth.

A waiter came around after a moment and handed them elaborately decorative plastic-paper menus.

"No holographic menus?" asked Anndrew, surprised by some of the low-tech things she had been seeing. She expected that waiters would be robots this far in the future.

"Oh, no," said Kormèr. "You won't find things like that at any upscale restaurant. These flim menus are convenient and just the right amount of fancy. You'll notice that you can select a language at the top."

Anndrew tapped the spot Kormèr indicated and a list of languages popped open. Fortunately, there weren't too many, and she found "Terran English" halfway down.

"Why is it 'Terran' English?" she asked. "Why not just English?"

Kormèr's eyes grew distant. "You know, that's a great question. I'm not sure. Maybe there's actually another species somewhere that speaks a different English." He shrugged.

"The menu's translated," said Jeransy. "But I've no idea what most of this means. Reduction? Confit? Lumbricus?"

Anndrew perked up at that one. "Some of those are cooking methods. That last one sounds like worms, though."

Kormèr wiggled the menu. "I can go over the menu with you, or I can order for you. It's up to you. I will say that there is nothing on this menu that you won't enjoy." He looked at Anndrew apologetically. "I hope."

Anndrew had her doubts about that, after finding 'lumbricus' listed in at least three dishes. But she had grown up eating chicken feet, snails, frog legs and other Asian delicacies, in addition to the typical American diet of burgers and pizza. *This couldn't be worse than fast-food 'chicken', could it?*

"Surprise me," said Jeransy gamely.

Anndrew stared at the menu, wondering what to do. On the one hand, she didn't want to offend Kormèr by making him think she didn't trust him. On the other hand, she had just met him that morning... *On the other* other *hand,* she thought, *you followed him through a portal and across the surface of another planet for a few hours. And here we are.*

"You pick the appetizer," she said at last. "I'll select my main course."

"As you wish. And drinks?"

Anndrew looked at the list, but nothing looked familiar there at all. "Anything non-alcoholic? Water?"

"Water for me, too," said Jeransy.

"Hmm. I'll get a flight of some of my favorite drinks. You can try them and leave them if you don't like them. How's that?"

A flight? mused Anndrew, as Jeransy agreed. *No pun intended?* "That's fine," she said.

The waiter stopped at the table, and everyone placed their orders.

"So exactly when were you here last?" asked Anndrew.

"It depends who you ask. It's been nearly six Earth years for me. But, for some reason, when the portal opened here, it picked a different time frame. So as far as everyone here is concerned, I've only been gone less than three years."

Jeransy shook her head. "How do you keep that straight?"

Kormèr smiled. "I don't try. Truth be told, I'm not much for revisiting planets. The portal is my doorway to the universe, and I want to see as much of it as I can. I've never consciously thought about it, but I guess, deep down, I view revisiting a place as a waste of time."

"What about the friends you make?" asked Anndrew.

Kormèr sighed. "I miss them sometimes; some more than others. I hadn't realized just how much I missed the ones here until I started seeing everyone again." He paused, his eyes on the table, but clearly seeing past it at some memory. "But Averia was something special. No other planet has influenced my life as much as this one did."

The waiter returned, pushing a shiny bronze cart and accompanied by a portly birdman wearing a white apron. The waiter rolled back the lid, releasing a cloud of steam and revealing the delicacies within. At the sight of the food, Anndrew realized just how famished she was. The portly birdman prepared the first serving for each of them. Anndrew decided he had to be the chef by the very deliberate way he arranged the items on the dishes.

Kormèr savored a morsel and twittered something enthusiastically to the chef, who puffed up his feathers with pride. The birdman replied in a series of noises that reminded Anndrew of a turkey gobble before he returned to the kitchen. Watching him, Anndrew wondered briefly if Averian males showed off tail feathers like turkeys and peacocks. She felt certain that, had he been able to, the chef probably would have, judging from the pleasure in his expression.

"I'm sorry about conversing in Song," said Kormèr, as the waiter dished a bit of each appetizer to each of them. "While they do have English-speaking guests from time to time, I'm afraid most of these folks just aren't fluent enough in it, especially those that don't usually interact directly with guests."

The waiter placed a tray with three small decanters and three inverted cups on the edge of the table. He and the chef said in unison, "Enjoy your meals." Then they hustled off.

"Now that was cheeky," said Jeransy.

Anndrew watched them depart, amused at their chutzpah. Even Kormèr had a big smile on his face. "That was funny." He reached for the drinks tray, flipped the cups over, and poured from a decanter that contained a carbonated yellow liquid.

"I'll try that one," said Jeransy.

Anndrew pointed to a decanter of a blue, milky liquid that reminded her of the portal. She swirled it when Kormèr handed it to her, then took a sip. "Sweet, and... a hint of coconut."

"That's called 'nutria'," said Kormèr. "It's very nutritious, but there're no coconuts here, as far as I know." He raised his glass and twittered something in Song. "It means: 'To the reasons we fly: health, air and sky.'"

"Hear, hear," said Anndrew, and noticed that Jeransy mimicked her, uncertainly, as if she'd never witnessed a toast before. She wondered if toasting somehow went out of style in the future.

"I'm amazed you can even do that," Anndrew continued. "Speak in Song, I mean. If that's the right way to say that. I always assumed birds had hidden tones and such that our whistling just can't reproduce."

"Ah! You shouldn't underestimate your species, you know. Humans are capable of all sorts of sounds. I learned Song from an edu-comp designed by humans, in fact. If we run across one, I'll show you. Languages become second nature."

"Blimey!" said Jeransy, taking her first bite of the appetizers. "This is so good!" She took another bite and rolled her eyes as she chewed.

With that kind of endorsement, Anndrew didn't want to delay any longer. Kormèr had ordered two appetizers, and Jeransy had tried one that resembled green tortellini in a broth. Anndrew spooned one into her mouth and sighed as she bit into the tender morsel. *Bacon pasta,* was the most coherent thought her brain could manage as she chewed. She and Jeransy each served themselves three more, leaving three for Kormèr.

Smiling as he chewed, Kormèr said, "Well, I'm really glad you're enjoying that. And this is just the appetizer."

Anndrew sampled the other appetizer. It had the texture of kiwi, the color of papaya, and tasted like avocado drizzled with citrus.

"What are they?"

Kormèr sucked thoughtfully on a piece of ice. "The orangy one is a local vegetable, and the other one is lumbricus tortellini."

Anndrew nodded. "I figured you'd squeeze an earthworm dish in there. But I'll admit that it was very good."

"It was," said Jeransy, impressing Anndrew with her worldly palate. "I've eaten certain insects before, but never earthworm."

"So, what was different about this planet?" asked Jeransy, as Anndrew served herself another two pieces of the second appetizer.

"Hmm?"

"You said that Averia was special to you, more than other worlds. Why's that?"

"Oh, right. Well, part of it is the amount of time I spent here. I don't remember exactly how long it was, but it was more than anywhere else. And then there were the friends I made. People like Theeseeo, his son and others. They were all very special people who made quite an impression on me."

Anndrew laughed. "I would say *you* made quite an impression on them as well. You've been quite the celebrity since we arrived."

"Notoriety goes both ways. While I helped solve a major jewel heist," he continued, not the least bit modestly, "I ruffled a few feathers along the way."

"Wait, you're a…" Anndrew lowered her voice to a near whisper. "You're a thief *and* you solved a jewel heist?"

"Thanks for the discretion," he said with a grin. "And your question is very valid. I struggled with the same back then. But it was a mystery I just had to solve. And the thief made the mistake of threatening me, which just made me want to solve it more." He paused, still grinning. "After I got over being totally freaked out by him. And finally… we all do crazy things for love."

"Oh?" asked Anndrew, intrigued. *Who does a man like this fall in love with? And do they love him back?*

"Do tell," insisted Jeransy.

Kormèr shook his head. "Too long a story and too sad an ending for an evening like this." He raised his glass again, but this time to point. "Besides, here comes our main course."

Anndrew enjoyed her choice of main course, though she had played it safe and selected a vegetable medley in a curry-like sauce.

When Jeransy tasted her dish, she looked up at Kormèr and said, "This is some kind of insect dish."

"Very good. They're cricket dumplings."

They ate in silence, focusing on enjoying their first meal in many long hours. Despite how hungry she had been at the start of the meal, Anndrew found that between the food and the nutria drink, she felt sated quickly.

When the waiter returned to clear the dishes, he asked, "Would you be interested in dessert or after-dinner drinks?"

"I'm good," said Anndrew.

Jeransy glanced at her, then shook her head. "No, thanks. I'm full."

"Not tonight, thank you," Kormèr told the waiter. "Just the bill, please." The waiter then removed a small electronic device from his vest pocket and passed it to Kormèr. Kormèr reviewed the data on the tiny screen, tapped it once, and passed it back to the waiter.

"How are you paying for all this?" asked Anndrew. She didn't like letting Kormèr pay for the entire meal, but she didn't have much choice. Her money wouldn't be of any use here. "Do you have local money?"

Kormèr looked hurt. "You have little confidence. It so happens Terran girls are a novelty here, and Birshettan men would gladly pay upwards of—" He paused, a grin showing his amusement at their glowers. "Sorry. I'm just kidding. I apparently have a significant amount of credit from my last visit. It's enough to cover this and more."

He stood. "Shall we go for a stroll? Maybe do a little shopping while we're out? I don't fit any of my old clothes."

"What about her classmate?" asked Jeransy. "How long till we find out if he's here?"

"Hopefully there will be some news by morning. I expect—"

"Morning?" Anndrew said, too loudly. She ignored the eyes that turned her way, but she lowered her voice. "I can't be here until morning. My family will start worrying about me if I don't get back home soon."

"You don't have to worry about that," Kormèr said. In a lower voice, he added, "The portal can jump time. You can return to Earth the same moment you left. No one would miss you because, as far as they'd know, you were never gone."

Anndrew mulled this over, the concept mind-bending. "That's just... Could you really be away for days, or even years, and return to the moment you left?"

"That's the way it works."

Anndrew watched Jeransy staring up at the darkening sky. *She's been gone from her home for a week, traveling around with Kormèr. I guess she'll also just pop back to the moment she left when she's ready. But is that what I really want to do?*

You wanted a more exciting day, protested her adventurous side. *Do you really want to go back to classes at school?* The answer to that was a resounding "no".

"Alright," she said. "Until tomorrow then."

"Wonderful! Besides, it's such a beautiful night; we might as well enjoy it."

"The lavatory first, though," said Jeransy.

As Kormèr gave Jeransy directions to the washroom, Anndrew considered going with her. But when Jeransy entered the washroom, Anndrew continued along the hallway and out onto a horse-shoe shaped balcony overlooking the pseudo-forest. Behind her, Kormèr took a deep breath and sighed.

"I can tell you really like it here," said Anndrew, without turning.

"I do. Very much."

"But you can't stay?"

He didn't say anything for a moment. "It's complicated. We all have to go home at some point."

Now Anndrew found herself with nothing to say, her thoughts tangled in their own complicated mess. Despite the conversation at the table moments ago, she still had mixed feelings about staying here for the night.

Kormèr must've noticed something. "Is something wrong?" He stepped up beside her.

Anndrew dropped her eyes. "No." She paused, and he said nothing. "Yes. When we find Cecil, it'll be time for *me* to go home."

"Well, you don't have to leave," he said slowly, perhaps unwillingly, "at least not right away."

Anndrew looked out over the city. "It's like you said: I feel the pull of home. But I also wish I could linger here for a while."

"Oh, I have a lot of experience with those conflicting emotions. But don't dwell on them too much." He pointed, and her eyes followed his arm upward to the wispy white clouds set against the uniformly sapphire background of the dusk-enshrouded sky. "Look at that sky. See how big it is? Life is that way, but some people focus on things that mean nothing and don't see it. Life is *that* grand, *that* limitless."

He rested his hand on her arm. "Besides, somewhere out there is Earth, thirty-eighth century Earth. If you're this far away from home, might as well make the best of it."

The night was cool, and Anndrew allowed herself to lean against Kormèr and share his warmth. "You make it sound so easy."

Kormèr took her hand gently. "I guess. It's not always easy. You have to appreciate those moments when they come, though. And if you're too focused on the hard ones, you're going to miss the easy ones."

"Live for the moment."

"Sort of. I would say, live the moment. Make it yours as much as you can. That's when you truly feel alive."

She relaxed against Kormèr and briefly thought of nothing else but that moment. She suddenly became aware of so many things around her that she had been missing or tuning out only a second earlier; the cool breeze on her skin; the evening-song of birds settling down for the night; the jingling of the metallic leaves; Kormèr's warmth and slow, steady breath.

She took a deep breath and sighed, feeling refreshed and re-energized. Kormèr dropped his hand, and the moment was gone. She turned to face him. "A girl could get used to that." She realized how ambiguous her words must have sounded. But she didn't clarify, letting Kormèr interpret her words as he liked. Either way, it was no less true.

"I'm glad." He smiled, his response just as vague. "Shall we go back in?"

She smiled. "After you, kind Sir."

"You're most kind, gentle Miss."

WHILE the hotel had a shopping mall on one of its floors, Kormèr led the girls out to stores along the promenades, promising a wider variety of offerings, as well as a chance to experience city life. The walkways were busy with Averians and a few other humanoid species, all out for a stroll or merely lounging in the small gardens and baths.

They only had an hour before the stores closed, but they took their time, enjoying the shopping experience, often modeling outfits to each other for opinions on colors, materials and accenting accessories. Jeransy found the process particularly alien, as she was used to a more virtual experience. After years of burglaries, stores had stopped keeping in-house stock and shifted to mirror-like screens that provided live-motion fittings. The only thing lacking from that was the feel of the textures. Jeransy found breathable, durable synthetics that felt similar to those that comprised her current outfit, but better constructed and cut in a more flattering style. They showed off her curves without making her look as though she were soliciting.

She watched Anndrew try on several outfits that she found outlandish, but in the end, the girl chose a couple of unisex-style shirts and trousers in complementary dark hues that she claimed could be mixed and matched comfortably.

Kormèr had all their purchases forwarded to the hotel, a service the stores were more than happy to provide him, even at that hour. The trio then continued their stroll along the promenades.

"So where's the jewelry store that was robbed?" asked Anndrew.

Kormèr cleared his throat noisily and nodded at a couple that passed them, walking in the opposite direction. "Don't say that too loud, love. Averians consider it a touchy point. To answer your question, Chees is actually on our way back to the hotel, one level up." He paused. "Why?"

"Can we swing by?"

Kormèr raised a curious eyebrow. "Sure."

"Fizzy!" said Jeransy, thrilled by the idea of visiting another site from Kormèr's past. She had Anndrew had discussed it while Kormèr had been in a changing room.

"Did you two plan this?" asked Kormèr, playfully.

"Oh, no," said Jeransy, too quickly.

Anndrew grinned. "We're just curious about the site of this 'major' jewel-heist." She said the last in a near whisper.

Kormèr smiled. "I see." He led them to a lift that took them up to the next level of the promenade.

"Plus," continued Anndrew as they stepped out of the lift, "Averians are so into gems, I imagine they must have some amazing specimens."

Kormèr nodded. "That they do. Are you looking for anything in particular?"

"My birthstone."

"I've heard of this custom, gems that go with each month of the year, right?"

Anndrew nodded.

"Interesting. On Elmar we have a similar custom, only it's a color."

"What's your color?" asked Jeransy.

"Red. That's Chees over there." He pointed ahead to a bright storefront.

Kormèr was quiet as they approached the storefront, his eyes wide as they swept across the bright windows. Then he announced, "You two go ahead inside. I'll wait out here."

"What's wrong?" asked Jeransy.

"Nothing. It's just that they might offer me something, gems or a gift or whatever, and I don't want to be put in that position."

"Oh. I'll wait with you," said Jeransy. There really wasn't anything she wanted from the store. Just being here and seeing it satisfied her curiosity.

"I was curious more than anything," said Anndrew, continuing past the jewelry store without stopping. "We don't have to go inside."

Kormèr slowed. "Are you sure? What about your birthstone?"

She shrugged. "It's no big deal."

"What is it?" he asked.

"Hmm? What's what?"

"The gem," Jeransy said, impatiently. *It's like she doesn't speak English sometimes.* "What's your birthstone?"

"Opal. It's a semi-precious, mineraloid stone. Technically, it's more a gel than a stone..."

"Cor!" Jeransy exclaimed, pausing in her step. "I just asked *what* it is. I'm not gormless, mate."

"Sorry." Anndrew laughed. "I have no idea what still exists in your century."

"Well, not a bloody lot. Things haven't been the dog's in donkey's years," Jeransy said humorlessly. "I can't remember when I last had a birthday do, never mind what kind of shiny I should wear on it."

"I see." Anndrew said.

Jeransy shrugged, unsure of why she was even sharing so much. "Whatever. It is what it is."

Kormèr stopped under a glow lamp, fished in his pockets, and finally pulled out a small pouch. He peered inside, and his right eyebrow went up. "Annde, I feel bad about your birthstone."

"That's alright, KL."

"No, really. Just one question: is it okay if it's a little big?"

Anndrew's eyes widened. "You're kidding, right?"

He offered her the pouch. She took it and spilled out a golf ball-sized black gem that seemed to contain flames of vibrant hues: cobalt, emerald, ruby, citrine and amethyst. It shone from within, but shimmered even more in the light from the glowing orbs that illuminated the promenade.

"Wow," said Jeransy, as words seemed to escape Anndrew, who merely stared at the incredible stone.

"It *is* too big, isn't it?"

Anndrew blinked. "Well, you could never make it into jewelry." She eased it back into its pouch and held it out to Kormèr. "It's stunning."

"It's for you."

"What? No, no. It must be worth a fortune."

Kormèr smiled, but kept his hands in his pockets. "Like you said, it's too big to wear, so I can't possibly pawn it. What good is it to a thief, if it can't be sold?"

She shook her head, then finally found her voice. "Thank you."

"You're welcome. Now, put it away. We'll find you a decent gem case for it in the morning."

She nodded, slipping the gem into her pocket.

With a grin, Kormèr turned to Jeransy. "In what month were you born, love?"

Jeransy answered, "May. Why?"

"May," repeated Kormèr. "That would be a… um…" He glanced at Anndrew.

"An emerald," said Anndrew.

"Ah, thanks. I happen to have this necklace… Turn around." When she did, he dropped something around her neck and fastened it under her hair behind her. She looked down and found a rectangular green gem, almost the size of her thumb, surrounded by smaller, brilliant diamonds, all in an ornate white metal setting that dangled from a glittering matching chain around her neck.

"Oh, KL! It's beautiful. I've never seen anything so gorgeous!" She threw her arms around his neck in her joy.

"It's like it was made for you. It brings out the green in your eyes," he said.

Despite the weight of the necklace and gem, Jeransy felt her step was lighter as they continued their walk.

CHAPTER 11

DRESSED in a white smock while his clothes dried, Cecil sat at a stone desk, poring through the pages of a thick book, titled: *The Rise of the Galactic Federation : The First Decade*. Stacked on the corners and edges of the desk were books that Cecil had already speed-read. Stone racks stood like soldiers in formation around him, disappearing into the shadows beyond the circle of light in which he sat.

He had found out that there were no wooden trees on Averia and, therefore, very few paper products. In fact, the inhabitants of Berdia were the only consumers of paper on the planet. These paper products were shipped in from the various Earth colonies, not inexpensively, either. Many books, as a result, were actually printed on the cured hides of creatures that lived on the lower surface of Averia, beneath the floating rocks. The oldest books were putrid-smelling, noxious things; they infused the library with their awful stench. The Averian sorcerers didn't care, given their inferior sense of smell, and Cecil didn't care either. The knowledge they held distracted him beyond caring about such things.

He stopped, removed his glasses, and rubbed vigorously at his eyes. He replaced the glasses, crooked, and continued reading, oblivious of his surroundings and of time. He had a wealth of information around him, just waiting to be absorbed. His mission: to assimilate it all as quickly as he could. He desperately wished for a cup of coffee to help him stay alert and focused.

He heard the *click-clack* of talons on the stone floor of the library before he saw who was approaching.

||You are still here?|| asked a surprised Sreet.

Cecil rose to his feet, wrinkling his nose under his lopsided glasses. He attempted to straighten them, but only worsened their tilt. "Of course."

||It is so late and you've had a long day. I just assumed you'd want to rest.||

"No way. I've learned so much in just a few hours that I can't stop. If I try to rest, I'll just be wasting my time. I mean…" He faltered for the words to express what he had learned, how he felt at that moment. But like a Tao, his enlightenment couldn't be expressed in words. He chose the only path available to him.

"Look at this." He flipped through another large tome to a picture of Earth. "This is Earth, thirty-eighth century Earth! That's eighteen centuries after me. And it's out there." He pointed to the ceiling. "I know about space;

I've known about space and space travel since I was four. But I never knew what eodecs were." He paced excitedly, hands up in the air. "Who in the whole twentieth century would have guessed that travel beyond the speed of light would be so simple once eodecs were discovered? These simple little radiation particles that we'd never known existed until the invention of an FTL particle detector."

Street nodded, but by the way the birdman's wings flicked, Cecil could tell that he didn't care about any of this. He peered at the birdman. "Why'd you bring me here?" he asked, closing the book. "You said I'd be able to learn about the tech you used, not this stuff." He waved a hand dismissively at the books.

Street puffed his chest. ||You're right. But it was magic, not tech.||

"Magic is just technology that isn't yet understood."

||Magic, my dear Cecil, is very real and has nothing to do with technology. It's all in here.|| He tapped his head.

Cecil wondered again if Street truly believed this, or was simply ignorant of the truth. There had to be a technological explanation for magic. He would just have to poke and prod to find the truth. "Were you born with this power?"

||If only it were that easy,|| twittered Street. ||I had to labor for many years as an apprentice before I could cast a spell, just like the others you met earlier.||

Cecil thought about the Caster-level birdmen Street had introduced him to. He hadn't given much thought to the "level" thing then, categorizing the birdmen more as an order of monks. Now it made sense. "How do you learn *magic*?" He couldn't keep the disbelief out of his voice. "I mean, do you have books?"

Street smiled. ||Follow me.||

Cecil followed as Street led him toward the rear of the library.

||Here.|| The birdman pointed to an expanse of stone shelves lined with old smelly tomes. Their color and texture drew Cecil to them immediately; they reminded him of the rare books section of his local library. He reached out to take one, but Street stopped him. ||Not yet, friend. These are for masters. Apprentices must start out slowly.||

"Of course. And build up gradually."

||Correct.|| He pulled a very worn volume from the shelf: *Early Concepts of Thaumaturgy.* ||This is the favorite of most apprentices. It was mine. You'll find it very helpful.||

Cecil took the volume, then looked up at the birdman curiously, his straight sandy-brown hair dangling just above his shoulders. "So why'd you pick me?" He had some idea of why, but wanted to hear it from the birdman.

||Because when you fell into the bath, I sensed you trying to use magic to save yourself. Only you couldn't because you didn't know how. We have

only ever trained Averians here, primarily because we have never found a Terran with untapped power as strong as yours. I thought you should be given a chance.||

Sreet had confirmed his suspicions. While Cecil hadn't suspected magic—and he still didn't—he believed the birdman had recognized his intellect. "Thank you."

||Are you going to stay here any longer? If not, I'll put out the lights.||

"I'm gonna do some more reading. I'll put 'em out when I'm done."

||As you wish.||

"Good night."

||Good night, then.||

Cecil watched the birdman leave, then dove into the book Sreet had given him. If this held the answers to his questions on magic, he wanted to waste no time finding them. Immediately, he grasped the concept of filaments and how they surrounded all living things, supplying energy to them. He tried to apply his knowledge of physics and thermodynamics to the book's concepts, but the only analogs he could think of were the strings of string theory and the cosmological filaments. But neither of those fit the model described in the tome.

The book described the ability to see the filaments at a conceptual level, but with no proper instructions. This frustrated Cecil, and he read faster, hoping to reach some section that described the process in more detail. But he finished the book without finding out more on the topic. He returned to the shelves and found a book titled *Thaumaturgic Concepts II*. The first half of this book focused on spell casting steps, from the *srootee* to the *tep*, which had to do with the motions that gathered energy from the filaments to the release of that energy. The second half seemed to focus on how to position body parts efficiently during the *srootee,* from fingers and toes to crest and tail.

Cecil finished the book and plopped it on top of the others at the edge of the desk. This time, when he visited the shelves, he returned with three books. In the second of those, he finally found what he'd been searching for. Cecil learned to see these filaments, a task not unlike seeing an image in a stereogram. He simply stared into space, then pulled back his focal point until the filaments popped into sight. *That is so ridiculously simple! How have I never been able to do this before? Is it something about this planet? Or maybe it's something about Berdia or the Hovel that makes this possible.*

In the last of the books he'd brought back, Cecil learned to tap those filaments and shape them into configurations of power, or patterns using the physical movements of *srootee.* Once the pattern was complete, the final motion triggered a power surge as the filaments released their energy and cast the spell. This stage was called the *tep.*

Cecil returned the apprentice level books to the racks and came back to the desk with a stack of any books containing *Caster* in the title. *Yes!* he cried in silence, finding that the books finally delved into the details of casting spells. Even the first book had a handful of minor beginner spells, such as pushing and pulling objects across a surface.

At one point, Cecil stopped and looked up and off into the distance. *If only I'd had some of these spells back home. None of the kids would have made fun of me or used me.* Something came to him then. *Maybe, just maybe, there is a way for me to get back home. Then I'll show everyone. I'll demand respect. Yes, that's what I'll do. Nobody will use me or mock me again. I must learn more.*

Dropping his attention back to the words on the page, Cecil continued reading.

CHAPTER 12

IT was nearly eleven o'clock by the time Kormèr and the girls returned to
Cheerees. The girls were dragging their feet a little, and Kormèr felt guilty for
having kept them out so late, especially after the long day they'd had. He, too,
was ready for a good night's sleep.

As they entered the hotel lobby, Kormèr saw Sylvestra rise off a perch
and glide over, landing smoothly, but dramatically, in their path.

||We need to talk, now,|| she warbled. She held up a flim with an
image of a soaked, sandy-haired human boy amidst a crowd of Averians.

"Hey, that's Cecil!" said Anndrew.

"Cecil?" repeated Sylvestra, her eyes glimmering. ||So you know this
human?|| she twittered to Kormèr, accusingly.

"KL, who is this?" asked Jeransy.

Kormèr sighed. So much for a restful night. "Let's not discuss this
here." He glanced at Sylvestra. "To my room?"

Sylvestra scowled at him. ||I should take you to the precinct instead.||
Kormèr raised an eyebrow at this. He had expected her to be angry, but not
this angry. But then her features eased, though more in resignation than
acquiescence. ||Fine.|| And she marched off toward Kormèr's room.

Kormèr watched her go, then looked at the ladies with a grin that he
knew had to look sheepish. "You go on ahead. I'll have some tea delivered."
He headed for the front desk to place his order, and to give himself time to
think. This certainly wasn't the way he imagined the night would end.

"FIRST things first," said Kormèr, once they were all in his room. "Sylvee,
this is Jeransy and Anndrew. Girls, this is a good friend of mine, and the chief
of police of this city, Sylvestra Chrreel."

The girls acknowledged her with a nod.

||Kormèr, they look exhausted,|| chirped Sylvestra. "They don't need
be here," she added in her best Terran English. "My gripe is with you."

"It's up to them if they want to stay," said Kormèr. "But this concerns
them as well. Cecil Murphy, the boy in your photo, is Anndrew's classmate
from twentieth century Earth."

Sylvestra was making some notes on a flimsy, but she stopped at this. "I
think you had better tell whole story." As Kormèr explained the day's events,
she continued making notes. When he finished, she said to the girls, "I not

76

want to be rude. It is easier in my language." To Kormèr, ||Did that make sense? I comprehend it, but don't get much practice speaking it.||

"It's fine."

||Good. Now why in the twelve stones of Steeree didn't you tell me about this earlier? And on top of that, how dare you enter my home... my *life* again after all this time?||

"Hmm. To answer your first question, you walked out before we got to that part." He gave her a knowing look. "Point two, well, you left your flowers behind. Point three, my return here was an..." He almost said "accident" but felt that would've sounded terrible. Instead, he said, "A random draw." He grew serious. "Honestly, Sylvee, I never intended to stir up any trouble."

||Damn you, KL,|| she twittered, more softly. ||You never mean to, but trouble just has a way of stirring up around you.||

"That hurts," he said, sheepishly. "However, this boy falling through the portal *is* my fault, and I accept responsibility for it. I have every intention of finding him, with your help, I hope, and of returning him to Earth."

Sylvestra tapped the flimsy and cycled through various images before showing it to Kormèr once again. ||You will have my full, unofficial cooperation.||

Kormèr looked at the photo. It was of Cecil and an Averian male. He looked back up at Sylvestra. "I'm missing something."

||That male is Sreet, a member of the Hawk Sorcerers. He took Cecil to Berdia. You know we have no jurisdiction there.|| He knew. No one had jurisdiction there.

Kormèr nodded. "I see. So it is up to me then. Any idea why he would take a non-Averian to Berdia?"

||None. Look, KL, maybe I was a little harsh. I don't really mean for you to go there alone.||

"Don't be silly; I have to go alone."

At this both girls were suddenly alert. "Go where?" asked Anndrew. "What's Berdia?"

Kormèr took a moment to fill the girls in on the half of the conversation they were missing, excluding his relationship issues with Sylvestra. Then he added, "Berdia is another city like Birshetland. It's also the home of several sects of magic users. They don't usually allow non-Averians into the city, so this is all very strange."

"But why do you have to go there alone?" asked Jeransy.

Kormèr frowned. "How can I put this? Berdia is... unfriendly, for lack of a better word. These sects have their rules of conduct, so they wouldn't outright harm anyone." He glanced at Sylvestra. "As far as I know."

She shrugged. "There has never been reported incident."

"That's hardly reassuring," said Anndrew.

Kormèr nodded. "Precisely why I can't risk taking anyone else with me. I had a friend there; do you know if Srrcheel is still there?"

| | Yes, | | twittered Sylvestra. | | He did some work for us recently. | |

"Great! Then it's settled."

"No, it isn't," said Jeransy, shaking her head. "You're not going without us."

"I have to agree, Kormèr," added Anndrew. "Unfriendly or not, we're all in this together, and we're safer together. Plus, you're my only ticket home."

Kormèr sighed. "What do you think?" he asked Sylvestra.

| | As Police Chief, I think it's unwise for you to take them. They look to be barely out of adolescence. | | Then her features softened. | | But personally, I'd feel better if you went with someone. And they seem to be as capable of keeping an eye on you as anyone. If I could go with you, you know I would. | |

"I know, and that makes me feel a little better." He thought about it for a moment longer. Other than his friend Srrcheel, Kormèr didn't trust the sorcerers one bit. And he had no defense against magic, if they got into trouble. An image of Jeransy shooting down the magical aircraft popped into his head. *Well, it's not like they're helpless,* he reasoned. "Alright. You can come. But you have to be very careful."

"We will," nodded Jeransy.

"I'll book the passage," offered Sylvestra. "It is least I can do."

"Ah, passage. Of course. We have to be a little official about this, I suppose." He had been planning more of a snatch and run via the portal, but if the sorcerers had some business with Cecil, that would not be a *healthy* maneuver. But getting permission from the Grand Master to enter the city and the Hawk Sorcerer's tree would require a very good reason. "What's my cover story?"

"I do not have one. We can create one now?"

Kormèr nodded. "Simply wanting to visit Srrcheel won't fly, no pun intended."

"Can you bribe someone to let you in?" asked Jeransy.

"Good thinking. But unfortunately not. The sorcerers can create just about anything they want or need."

"You have anything you want to give back?" asked Sylvestra.

Kormèr thought about the pockets of his coat and some of the magical artifacts in them. He'd stolen these from Berdia, but he wasn't about to part with them. "No, nothing… Wait! I don't have anything *on* me, but there is something I stashed it in a secret spot in the Hovel instead of returning it to Srrcheel."

"How that helps?"

"Because unless they've found it, which I doubt, they think I still have it."

She nodded. "That could work. I will start contact."

"Thanks, Sylvee. We'll get ready and head to the port in thirty minutes."

||You're going now?||

"What?" from Jeransy.

"Now?" from Anndrew.

Kormèr was quite exhausted himself. But the thought of Cecil in Berdia gave him a burst of adrenaline. "Unfortunately, we have to go now. I don't trust Cecil in the hands of the sorcerers. The sooner we get him out of there, the better."

Kormèr looked to Sylvestra for some show of support, but she remained quiet. "Bring a change of clothes," he told the girls. "Just in case this doesn't go... quickly."

Anndrew and Jeransy shuffled out of Kormèr's room, but Sylvestra didn't move. ||Do you really think it's that urgent, or are you running away again?||

||I really believe it's that urgent. You know as much as I do how dangerous that place can be. Besides, how can I run, when all I can think about is you, and how much I still love you?||

Sylvestra gave a shrill squawk of irritation and flicked her wings. ||How very like you to say that.|| He merely shrugged. ||If I tell you that I love you too, would that keep you here? Would it make our relationship whole? What do you expect from me?||

Kormèr sighed. ||I don't expect anything from you, Sylvee. Maybe I'm just a silly old romantic, but for years I've felt guilty for running out. This chance opportunity seemed like the perfect one to set things right between us. But it didn't really matter; you had already moved on, so it was really all just about me.||

Sylvestra opened her mouth to say something, then stopped, and it became a sigh instead.

||The stupid thing is,|| sang Kormèr, ||it had all seemed sort of simple in my head. Until I saw you, that is. Then it all became complicated.||

||There we agree,|| sang Sylvestra. ||When I heard you were back, I had all these questions and things I wanted to say to you. But then I saw you... Dammit! I *had* moved on, but of course, part of me still loves you and always will. What we shared was wonderful, and that it was so brief makes it even more precious.||

Kormèr stepped toward her and took her hand in his. ||Say no more, please, my love. I think we are of a like mind in this; we will say our goodbyes, I will take Cecil home and never come—||

Sylvestra leaned in and kissed him. ||I never could resist your quirky sense of melodrama,|| she whispered when they parted.

||Is that what it was?|| he returned, caressing the curve of her brow and nose with his eyes. ||I thought it was my charm and good looks,|| he

joked.

They embraced tightly, drawn together irresistibly by their bond. Despite all their reservations and the circumstances of their separation, they couldn't help giving into the impulse.

||It figures, doesn't it?|| twittered Sylvestra into his neck. ||Now that we have so much to talk about, you have to run off to Berdia.||

||I will be as brief as possible,|| promised Kormèr. They parted again, and he gazed at her beautiful dark eyes. They sparkled with the yellow glow of the room lights, reminding Kormèr of the jewel they had discovered earlier. He reached into his pocket and pulled it out.

||KL! Where did you find that?||

||You're not going to believe this.|| He told her the story. ||I couldn't fence something this amazing.||

||I should hope not.|| Something in her voice made Kormèr pause. She noticed his look and asked, ||You've never heard the children's story of the Tseerleeltrr Stone?||

Kormèr shook his head. ||Must be a local tale. Are you saying this looks like the stone?||

||Remarkably so.||

||Well, tell me the story when I get back. In the meantime, it's yours to do with as you like.||

||Are you bribing me, citizen Lezàl?||

Kormèr put his hand on his chest, feigning shock. ||Oh, no, Chief Chrreel! I wouldn't dare do that. I'm merely turning in property that might be stolen.||

Sylvestra smiled as she took the jewel. ||Of course you are… when Terrans fly.|| She kissed him once again and headed for the door. ||I'll see you at the Argent platform in… you'd better give me forty minutes, just in case the Grand Master plays stubborn.||

||We'll be there.||

When the door closed, Kormèr closed his eyes, smiling blissfully. He sighed deeply, then toppled back onto his bed. He was back, and while he couldn't imagine staying permanently on Averia, he planned to prolong his stay as much as possible, and relish every moment that he could.

SYLVESTRA was waiting for them when they arrived at the city's port. She gnawed on her lower lip as they climbed out of the taxi. ||Everything's set. They've just finished giving the birds their instructions.|| Sylvestra glanced from Jeransy to Anndrew, then back to Kormèr. ||You've told them?||

"Yes, on the taxi ride over, I let them know that it's the only way to get there."

Sylvestra led them through a low, airy building with various closed windows and several tired-looking bird-people, to a circular, open-air platform that looked out past the edge of the city. There, Kormèr and the girls stopped to stare in astonishment at the three huge gray birds that were tethered to the platform. A few Averians ministered to them, feeding and checking the bindings on harnesses that hung from the bellies of the massive birds, their collective cooing like the rumble of an idling motor.

Kormèr gave a short laugh. "They don't seem as big as they used to."

"They're big enough, bigger than you described," remarked Jeransy. "We're flittin' on those?"

"Yes," nodded Sylvestra. "You fly to Berdia. Very safe."

Kormèr noticed the girls didn't seem entirely convinced by Sylvestra's assurance. ||Don't try to help, love. Just move it along as quickly as you can, before they change their minds.|| Part of him thought that wouldn't be a bad idea. Then he wouldn't have to worry about them.

||They're all ready for you, ma'am,|| called one handler.

"It will be fun." Sylvestra stepped up to the birds and waved Kormèr and the girls over.

Kormèr heard Anndrew mumble, "Says her." But he ignored it.

"I'll go first," said Kormèr, stepping up to one bird. A handler helped him climb into the chest-harness and tightened the restraints. Then his legs were hooked to straps where they would be free to dangle, but not so much so that they would drag on the ground. Kormèr double-checked the bindings, and when he was satisfied, turned to the girls and smiled. "Nothing to it."

A handler then led each of the girls to their birds and repeated the process on them. Anndrew was closest to Kormèr, and when the handler had strapped her in, Kormèr heard him whisper, "Takeoff is tough first time. Relax and it be over quickly. Close your eyes might help."

Anndrew nodded. "Thanks. Your English... Terran English is very good."

The Averian smiled at her. "Thank you. We get many tourist here."

"They travel on these birds too?"

He hesitated. "Not really. They usually take sky-hoppers or skippers."

Jeransy's handler whistled shrilly, signaling the all-clear for takeoff.

"Is time," said Anndrew's handler. "Don't be afraid to scream. I heard it helps."

"Scream?" She frowned, then laughed. "Oh! Like on a roller coaster."

The handler seemed confused, but he nodded. "Yes?"

The tethers released and, almost in unison, the birds lurched forward. They sprinted toward the edge of the platform, picking up speed with each step. Kormèr watched the approaching edge, waiting for that sinking feeling in his stomach. While he'd done this before, he didn't think he'd ever get used to that feeling.

And suddenly they were over the edge and gliding.

"Woohoo!" Anndrew hollered into the wind. "Pigeon gliding rocks!"

CHAPTER 13

CECIL put down his cup of hot, fresh coffee and sighed. *That's excellent coffee.* He'd been reading all afternoon and evening, yet he didn't feel one iota of exhaustion. His mind raced with so many new concepts and ideas that it had no room for feeling tired. His body, however, ached from sitting hunched for so many hours. He had stood up now and then to fetch a new book, but the topics in recent books had grown complex and required him to focus more and speed-read less. He'd spent an hour getting through only half of this last book.

He stood and stretched and felt his shirt and jeans constricting and rough. He realized he'd worn them on and off since morning on Earth, and he was tired of them. He immediately swapped them for shorts and a tee shirt before even realizing that he had used a magical spell to do so. Unfortunately, these quickly proved inadequate for the chill in the air. Another cast fitted him with a warm robe. He hugged the long, loose sleeves of the burgundy cloth to himself and felt the chill flow away.

This magical stuff was incredible… limitless! With magic, it seemed he could do almost anything. He had created objects from nothing with a few waves of his hands. He had learned to move up to six objects at the same time with more hand gestures, and not just forward and backward, but also up in the air. After much practice and several bruises, he had even flown around the expansive library like a bird. And when he had tired of flying, he learned how to teleport himself across short distances, like from one end of the library to the other. He had learned the hard way that for the teleport to succeed, he had to have walked or viewed the destination first. He had attempted to teleport a book from the desk to somewhere across the room before seeing the destination. The book had disappeared from the desktop, but when he went looking for it, it was not in the place he had imagined. He tried to locate it magically, but it was nowhere… anywhere. It was a frightening lesson he learned quickly: magic was not to be taken lightly.

He took full advantage of his solitude in the library to test all the spells he could. He created food when he was hungry. When thirsty, coffee, soda or water appeared with a few waves of his hand. When he grew tired of the silence, he conjured a radio and figure out how to make it magically play whatever songs he wanted to hear. He was particularly proud of that spell, as it had taken him several tries to get right.

Not every experiment had yielded roses, however. He'd started a small fire when testing a spell that caused showers of sparks and beams of light to emit from his fingertips. A hastily cast water spell had put out the fire, but it had also flooded the library up to his knees before he could cast a large-scale dry spell that did the job just right.

That last spell had taught him that casting too many spells over a short period of time could drain the filaments of energy. This had the adverse effect of weakening the caster, since the same filaments also supplied his energy. Upon nearly fainting, he'd taken a break from practicing spells and focused on reading.

That had been two hours ago.

He looked at the large tome before him, then marked the page and closed it. In the apprentice books, Cecil had read that the Hawk Sorcerers had six levels: Apprentice, Caster, Enchanter, Sorcerer, Master, and Grand Master. The Caster through Sorcerer levels were each divided into three sub-levels: Initiate, Unfledged and Fledged. Moving between any level required a raising ceremony. Cecil hadn't gone through any ceremony when Sreet had proclaimed him an apprentice. He didn't care much for whatever rituals the birds observed, but he also didn't want to anger Sreet. The birdman had recognized his intellect, after all.

His mind made up, he conjured a locator spell to find Sreet's room and followed the glowing magical arrow through darkened corridors until the arrow vanished before a door.

"Sreet?" Cecil knocked and waited. The door swung open moments later, revealing Sreet squatted amidst a circle of candles in the middle of the small room, his wings tucked behind him.

||Ah, Cecil!|| Sreet looked the youth over, curiously. ||Come in. I was just completing my prayers.||

Cecil entered a small, dim room with odd symbols drawn here and there. A nest-like bed sat tucked into a corner, beside which sat a nightstand with a drawer. Cecil stood just inside the doorway and took in the ascetic decor.

Cecil frowned. "Prayers? With all you can do, you still believe in gods?" Before Sreet could answer, Cecil said, "Oh, I see." He forgot that he'd cast a mind reading spell earlier. Since he'd had no one within range of the spell, he hadn't been sure it worked. Now he knew, as Sreet's thoughts projected themselves into his head. "You revere nature, since it provides the path to your abilities. Interesting, I guess."

||Yes, that's right.||

"Fine," said Cecil just before Sreet asked, ||How is your reading coming along?||

Sreet's eyes widened after a moment, as if he'd finally caught on to what Cecil was doing. ||That's amazing! I've never seen anyone learn that trick so quickly.||

"Mind reading? You've got to be kidding. It's such a simple thing to do."

Cecil performed another small *srootee*, and as he triggered the spell, he said, "Now this took some practice." Street yelped and flapped his wings as he suddenly rose a meter off the ground. Cecil set Street back down gently.

Street hopped up and stood on wobbly knees. | |I knew you would be a quick study, but you… Levitation is a Caster level spell. I told you to stick to the apprentice books.| |

"I did. But there are so few—"

| |So few?| | Street's jaw worked with stunned silence until he managed, | |Just how much did you read?| |

Cecil didn't understand why the birdman seemed so surprised. He had tried his best. Surely no one could read any faster than he had. "Well, it wasn't just reading; I practiced whatever I could. I was just starting the Master level books when I decided to ask you if I should. I mean, do I really have to go through your raising ceremonies?"

Street's wings drooped, his eyes unfocused. *Crap,* thought Cecil. *I think I broke him. Did he or did he not expect me to get that far with the books? It's so hard to read these birdpeople.*

Suddenly, he felt that tingle along his skull that meant someone was trying to read his mind. "Hey!" He threw up a mind-block. "What the hell was that for?"

Street composed himself and crossed his arms. | |I needed to know your intentions before I could tell you something very secret and quite dangerous to me at the moment.| |

"Oh?"

| |We sorcerers are divided into five factions here on Berdia.| |

"Based on what?"

Street waved his hand dismissively as he enumerated the differences. | |Ideology, principles, procedures… All sorts of insignificant nonsense. We are the Falconi Sect, though you might also hear us called the 'Hawk Sorcerers'. We support law enforcement occasionally and have a structured rank-ascension system. The Chichonii Sect don't believe we should interact with outsiders at all, while the Sitachi Sect would choose to live among the general population, if Averian law allowed it.| |

Cecil raised his hand. "Wait. You have all this power, but you are confined to this one city by laws imposed on you by… by the unpowered?" He didn't like that word, but couldn't think of a better one. He almost used 'normals', but that would've implied that the sorcerers were not normal.

Street smiled. | |We call them 'unattuned'. I knew you'd see right to the core of the issue. This is the fault of the Grand Master and his sycophantic masters who bend under these unjust winds.| |

Cecil stuffed his hands into the pockets of his shorts. "Let me guess, you plan to overthrow the masters and take over the Hovel."

| |Something like that. I can't tell you the entire plan just yet, but all the

people you met today are with me in this. And I have established communications with sympathetic members of the Passanseri Sect.||

"So this is more than just about the Hovel."

Sreet didn't answer. ||Where do you stand?|| he asked, instead.

Cecil peered at the birdman as he considered his options. Sreet hadn't told him his rank, but Cecil guessed he couldn't be higher than third level Caster. Any higher and Sreet could have teleported himself and Cecil from Birshetland to the Hovel without resorting to flying with the Argent. To Cecil, that alone raised a red flag. He had glimpsed the basic Master level spells, and thus had some insight into how much more powerful they were than the Caster spells.

Sreet's followers presented several unknown factors in the equation: numbers, ranks and, most importantly, loyalties. Would they truly turn on their masters when the time came? Without more data to form, at a minimum, an educated guess for these factors, he did not like the odds.

"That depends," he said. "What's my role in all this?"

||I meant for you to be proof that our ways are broken. A non-Averian master sorcerer would shake Berdia to its foundations. We have one other non-Averian, but she lacks your aptitude, and certainly your zeal for learning.|| He clenched his fist as he said this. ||But you... you've exceeded my expectations. You've blasted through our ranks, proving that even our regimented structure is meaningless! Even the obstinate Chichonii and Strigi Sects would find themselves without a leg to stand on.

||But more than that, with our numbers and you at our side, the Grand Master would have no choice but to cede his position.||

Is that so? wondered Cecil. *Is he really holding his cards close to the vest here, or is he just another fool idealist?*

"What if he doesn't cede?"

||Then we crush him. You keep studying the master level spells, and I'll get the others to skip ahead as you have. We'll have no problem defeating him and anyone else that stands in our way.||

Sreet seemed so sure of his success, but Cecil still had no way to know for sure. And with all this knowledge he'd gained on the line, he couldn't play those odds. On the other hand, did he truly have to commit himself to Sreet's plan? He could pretend to go along with the plan for now, considering it would likely take Sreet time to put things in motion. In that time, Cecil could continue studying the master tomes. He only had to be careful not to get caught, something he was already very good at.

"Alright. I'm in."

CHAPTER 14

KORMÈR had forgotten that the Argents sometimes dove below the rock and cloud envelope of Averia during the flight to Berdia. Thus, he heard surprised cries from both girls when the giant birds gracefully swooped down through an opening and into the cool darkness below.

"What just happened?" Anndrew's voice carried clearly as the birds settled into a long glide.

"It's faster and more efficient traveling down here," Kormèr said. "Instead of having to follow the curve of the planet, the Argents can mostly glide in a straight line to their destination."

"I see."

"I can't see a thing," said Jeransy. "That's not just me, right?"

"It's not just you," said Anndrew. "But try to look up; you'll see the sky looks like black rock with white marbling where the moonlight illuminates the clouds."

"Oh, yeah." Jeransy sounded less than enthusiastic.

As the three neared Berdia, Kormèr grew more apprehensive over the unknowns that lay ahead. What was happening to Cecil on Berdia? What would they find when they arrived? Kormèr could not even begin to imagine the hardships they might all be in for, much less what Cecil might be experiencing. What worried Kormèr the most was the fact that Sylvestra had never heard of any sect recruiting non-Averians. And rumors suggested that some sects still committed ritual sacrifices, though no evidence existed to support that. Kormèr had certainly not witnessed any such rituals during his visits with Srrcheel, a member of the Hawks.

So what could the sorcerers want with Cecil? The Hawks had been a very strict and highly exclusive sect, selecting only Averians with high magical aptitudes. His stay within the Hovel's walls had been a secret to all there but Srrcheel. Discovery would have meant his expulsion and his friend's severe punishment. Something smelled rotten in the Hovel. Kormèr hoped it wasn't serious. If they had, indeed, used Cecil for some ritual sacrifice, Kormèr would never forgive himself.

Then there was another possibility that he hadn't discussed with Sylvestra. Just because she hadn't heard of any non-Averian recruits didn't mean there couldn't be any. In fact, the first thought to occur to Kormèr was that Cecil had gone to Berdia to learn magic. Just the thought made Kormèr's blood run cold. But he knew from experience that ascension through the ranks was a slow process involving years of study and practice. Fortunately, he had gotten an early start on finding the boy. A mere day in the Hovel would hardly be of consequence.

"Kormèr, this is aces!" yelled Jeransy.

"Glad you like it," Kormèr yelled back. But inside, his worry grew painful. He wished more and more that the girls had not come with him. He had to do some sneaking around to find the object he'd stashed there. Between the risk of getting caught and the simple fact of the false pretense under which they'd come, he would've been much more at ease without them. He had no doubt that they could care for themselves. But this was a new world for both of them, with its own rules and customs. And Berdia was a microcosm onto itself, one that did not take well to strangers or 'the unattuned', as the sorcerers referred to all but themselves.

The Argents ascended through the clouds, and the colossal mass of Berdia appeared, glistening in the silvery splendor of Averia's twin moons, humming and crackling with whispers of long gone civilizations and sacrificed souls. The crumbling ivory rock of the tremendous pseudo-trees menaced the group with its natural formations resembling faces contorted in pain and suffering.

The closer the birds carried them, the more the whispers and formations played tricks on their minds. Shifting patterns of moonlight on the escarpment became ghosts, and the rush of wind beckoned one to release life and plummet to a rocky death.

Kormèr shook his head several times to fend off the seductive onslaught of optical and aural illusions. He had thought that the effect only affected first timers, but perhaps his long absence had diminished his resistance.

Kormèr glanced nervously at the girls. He'd been told that the weak-minded would not stand a chance of surviving the hallucinations. Since the term 'weak-minded' itself hadn't been given with any context, Kormèr simply assumed it included 'young', 'inexperienced', and a general host of other possibilities. He smiled then, seeing that the girls were holding their own well. They seemed fascinated by the sounds and sights all around them, and they even shared a laugh over one shadow Anndrew swore looked like a bunny. *At least I don't have to worry about them being weak-minded,* thought Kormèr, *in any sense of the term. It looks like their banter is actually keeping the worst of it from affecting them. Interesting.* He frowned. *I wish I'd known that years ago.*

Kormèr distracted himself by watching the girls, and before he knew it, the three birds alighted on an ancient, albeit well-maintained platform. It was exactly as Kormèr remembered it, down to the glowing lanterns that encircled the dark stone platform.

"Wow! That was intense!" Anndrew looked over at Kormèr with wide eyes and a big grin. "I wouldn't mind doing that again."

"Now that must be a first," said Kormèr. "My first experience was not as pleasant."

"I wouldn't want to do it again," said Jeransy. "But it wasn't ribble."

Kormèr looked around. "Hmm. No welcoming committee tonight."

"What's that?"

"Well, usually someone is here to assist us and to feed the birds. But it looks like we're on our own. Your legs are going to be—"

Jeransy hit the release and drop from the harness. She stumbled shakily as her stiff chilled muscles reasserted themselves. "Whoa!"

"That." Kormèr planned his drop, since his Argent was near the edge of the platform. "Mind the edge of the platform, please. It's easy to stumble over the side."

Kormèr dropped and let his legs collapse, rolling to his right and away from the edge. He wobbled over to Anndrew just as she hit her release, and helped her to remain standing.

"Thanks," said Anndrew, kicking each of her legs a few times.

Kormèr mimicked the kicks. "My pleasure."

Jeransy chuckled. "You look like you're having a dance, you two."

"Come on over and join us," offered Kormèr. The three of them linked arms and kicked their legs until they could stand steadily.

Kormèr turned to the Argents; the birds watched them expectantly. "I wonder what these guys make of our antics," he said. Then he chirped the return signal. If they were disappointed about not getting fed, they didn't show it. The Argents turned and flew off into the night, back toward Birshetland.

"Hey, how are we supposed to get back?" asked Jeransy.

"If we get a hold of Cecil," said Kormèr, "we'll probably just return to Earth by portal. Otherwise, the carrier birds will be back tomorrow morning."

"Got it."

Someone behind them said, "Hello, KL."

Kormèr recognized the voice immediately, a host of memories rushing back into his consciousness. "Srrcheel!" he half whistled, turning to face his old friend. Srrcheel stood at the bridge that connected the platform to the city rock. He hadn't changed much; he was still the same stocky birdman that Kormèr remembered, though a bit shorter, whereas they'd been the same height years ago. He stood about as tall as Anndrew, with uniform pale brown plumage everywhere except his wings, which had a more mottled white-brown appearance. His eyes glowed with a silvery touch to the large black pupils, his countenance otherwise blank; he seemed neither pleased nor angered at seeing Kormèr.

"It's been a while," said the birdman in Terran English, but spoken with a slight slur.

"Indeed it has," said Kormèr, looking his old friend over. "You look great. I was just thinking that you haven't changed a bit."

"Oh, a bit. But not as much as you have."

"Yeah, so I've been told." Kormèr nodded, wondering why Srrcheel was acting so… cold. During his prior stay on Averia, Kormèr had seduced a wealthy Averian female for a chance to steal a bauble or two. He'd discovered instead that her father was mixed up in corporate misdeeds and that she was Srrcheel's betrothed. He and Srrcheel had worked things out, and by the time Kormèr left Averia, they were mostly back on friendly terms. Or so he'd thought.

"Srrcheel, I'd like you to meet my friends, Jeransy and Anndrew."

"A pleasure," said Srrcheel, though his expression remained unchanged.

"I met Srrcheel during the jewel heist," Kormèr told the girls.

"Still bragging about that, eh?"

"Bragging? It's just a reference point…" He stopped and crossed his arms. "What's really—"

Suddenly, Srrcheel puffed his neck feathers with a hearty laugh. "I'm just ruffling your feathers."

Kormèr pursed his lips. "Very funny."

"That's what you get for being away for almost three years." He looked at Anndrew and Jeransy. "Welcome to Berdia."

"At least you've learned to have some fun," said Kormèr, "even if it is at my expense."

Srrcheel put his hand on his chest, and smiling said: "What do you mean? I was always fun."

Kormèr laughed and put his hand on Srrcheel's shoulder. "Yes, you are, old friend."

Srrcheel clasped Kormèr's other shoulder. "It really is good to see you, KL. Come. Let's head inside."

Kormèr walked alongside him. "I had expected the Grand Master, but I'm glad it was you that met us."

"The Grand Master actually sent me when he heard it was you coming."

"I see. He actually trusts us together?"

"Well, he trusts one of us."

Kormèr nodded. "Smart man. Did he mention why we're here?"

"Something about returning an item."

"Hmm. Let's table that for a more private setting."

"Of course. Did you ever get to walk the grounds before?"

"Not in daylight." Kormèr had mostly portaled directly to and from the Hovel. "But I did come that one night to see Fitzbew."

"Ah, that's right. Personally, I think it's nicer at night. You'll probably notice some changes.

"So, how've you been? You look very well, yourself. Taller. And I like your beard."

"Thanks." Kormèr scratched his bearded chin. "It's a fairly recent addition."

"By the looks of you, more than a few years have passed." During his last visit, Kormèr had trusted only a few people with knowledge of the portal. Srrcheel was one of them. He also knew that Kormèr was a thief.

"Almost six... or so."

Srrcheel made a chittering noise that was just an expression of dismay and had no translation. "Sylvestra won't be too happy about that, I imagine. Have you seen her yet?"

"Yeah. The Grand Master didn't tell you? She arranged our passage here."

"Oh, no. He didn't mention it."

Kormèr took in the landscaping, hoping Srrcheel would drop the topic of Sylvestra. He didn't want to discuss his relationship ordeal with Sylvestra. Not here, at least. Subtle light illuminated the manicured plants and fountains in a variety of colors. Kormèr felt that most of the displays were garish, but he reminded himself that Averians were drawn to shiny things—the gaudier the better. Reminded of gaudy baubles, Kormèr took the lead in changing the topic. "Remember Menddilal?" He'd confided some of his private life to Srrcheel years ago.

Srrcheel nodded. "Yes, the royal girl... duchess?"

"That's right. Well, after being together for so long, the party ended a week ago."

Srrcheel opened his mouth to speak, but Kormèr cut him off. "Yeah, yeah. I know. You told me it was bound to happen. But you should see the loot I picked up while the going was good." He reached into his pocket and pulled out a velvet box that he opened and showed to Srrcheel. Within it was a gleaming gold band with channel-set rainbows of tiny multicolored jewels flanking a four-prong set, five-carat marquis diamond. "Her wedding band," said Kormèr proudly.

Srrcheel gasped, reverting to Song in his awe. ||So shiny! I've never seen anything like it. But after what he must've spent on it, won't the Duke cause problems for you when he finds it's missing?||

"Are you kidding? He didn't spend one *kudot* on the thing. I found out that crooked bastard had it stolen himself."

Srrcheel let out a great guffaw. "Do you ever wonder what's happening there while you're away?"

"Not really." Kormèr shrugged and replaced the box in this pocket. "Remember, I can just go back to the moment I left."

"Ah, that's right! When are you going back?"

"Trying to get rid of me already?" Kormèr nudged Srrcheel's ribs playfully with his elbow. "Honestly, though, I'm not sure."

They came within sight of the Hovel at that moment. Kormèr found that more lighting had been added since the night he'd come. Ground-based lamps illuminated the colossal tree from below, highlighting the artistry of its majestic architecture.

"Oh, my gosh!" cried Anndrew. "That's beautiful!"

Jeransy just gaped.

Kormèr laughed, recalling his own initial reaction.

"Here's something I never thought I would say to you," began Srrcheel. "Kormèr, and ladies, I officially welcome you to the Hovel."

"Thank you," the girls murmured, still awestruck.

The trio followed Srrcheel through a massive archway into an expansive circular foyer. Kormèr looked up at the double-ring of concentric lights, almost as if seeing them for the first time. He remembered having been in this room, but the memory had faded a bit with time. They continued down a wide corridor with several doors on each side. The birdman stopped, opened one door, and beckoned them to enter. A flaming brazier tucked in a corner of the small, square receiving room provided the only illumination. Kormèr took a seat on a chest covered with layers of furs and varicolored tapestries. The girls sat on opposite ends of a brown velvet-covered perch that hung from the ceiling.

Some of the light from the brazier reflected onto the ceiling and reminded Kormèr of the jewel he'd found earlier. "By the way, I found a jewel today that seemed to be protected by a magic spell."

"Found?"

"Actually, yes. I was wondering if you'd be familiar with that kind of thing."

Srrcheel's wings flicked. "Unlikely, but you never know. What did it look like?"

"It was about this big." He approximated the size with his hands. "And translucent, almost dark gray, with glowing yellow occlusions inside."

Srrcheel laughed. "Right. This is your attempt at payback for my little joke earlier, I assume."

Kormèr smiled, uncertain of what Srrcheel meant. "Umm… No, I'm serious. When I picked it up, these flying machines appeared and shot at us."

"They hit me," said Anndrew.

"And I shot 'em down," added Jeransy. "They disappeared once they hit the ground."

Srrcheel waved a hand, then clapped it against his other wrist, and as he pulled the hands apart again, a book appeared between them. He plucked it from the air and quickly flipped through the pages until he found what he was looking for. He turned the book around and held it up for all to see. The left page held an image of the jewel. "Is this what you found?"

"Yes! That's it. What is that?"

"It's a book of children's fairy tales and myths. This one is called the Tseerleeltrr Stone, a mythical stone that supposedly grants its holder tremendous powers." He peered at Kormèr curiously. "And you just found it."

"I said I found something that *looks* like it."

"Where, exactly?"

"Out on the rocks, south of Birshetland. It's the craziest thing; it was just sitting there. But it can't possibly be the real thing. It's probably just someone's idea of a joke."

Srrcheel dog-eared the page in the book and set it aside, but his eyes never left Kormèr, as though he expected to see the stone pop out from one of his pockets. "Where is it?"

"Sylvestra has it." Seeing the glint in Srrcheel's eyes, he added smartly, "Hey, you leave her alone."

||Are you crazy?|| squawked Srrcheel, dropping back into Averian. ||If she sells it, we may never find it again!||

"Take it easy, and stop being rude. Non-Averians here. First of all, Sylvee would never sell it. She's more likely to donate it to a museum than keep it." Srrcheel's wings flicked in mild irritation. "And anyway, I put a tracer on the thing in case I ever needed it back."

Srrcheel eyed Kormèr. "I should have expected you'd do that. Is this all part of why you're here? Do you want something in exchange for the tracking receiver?"

"Actually, no. I'll give you the signal receiver, so long as you promise to leave Sylvee alone."

"I promise," said Srrcheel, reluctantly but sincerely. "I'll requisition the stone for study once it's left her hands."

"Thank you. I trust your word." He gave the birdman a tiny box with a dial and gauge set into one side. Srrcheel carefully pocketed the box as if it were the sacred jewel itself.

"Now," said Srrcheel, settling onto a perch. "As to the reason for your visit."

"Is the room private?"

"Yes."

Kormèr assumed that, at the very least, the Grand Master could probably override any privacy spell. But by the same token, he could probably also just read Kormèr's mind and take whatever information he wanted. He hadn't done that on Kormèr's last visit, as far as Kormèr knew, so Kormèr figured the chances were slim he'd do it tonight. "I'm looking for someone, a young Terran named Cecil Murphy. I was told he was brought here by another sorcerer named Sreet."

Srrcheel's crest feathers rose slightly. "Oh, him. Yes, he's here."

"Is that a ruffled crest I sense there, old friend?"

"Well," he lowered his voice, "I'm not one to easily get jealous, but not only is the Terran—"

Srrcheel stopped when Kormèr raised his hand. "Sorry to interrupt, but since when is that allowed?"

"Oh, the ban on non-Averians entering our ranks was lifted a year ago. But he's only the second exception we've had."

Kormèr shook his head, scowling. "Wait, I was just referring to the ban on bringing non-Averians to Berdia. Are you saying he's actually been made an apprentice?"

"Not exactly. There are procedures, and interviews that usually take place…"

"Usually?" Kormèr didn't like the sound of that.

Srrcheel inhaled deeply and held it. "You know there are things I can't talk about. The situation with Sreet is one of them."

Kormèr threw up his hands, then let them slap down on his lap. He noticed Anndrew's head pop up, but didn't look over. "I don't care about Sreet. I'm interested in Cecil."

Srrcheel tipped his head to one side. "How do *you* know the Terran boy, anyway?"

"He's my classmate," murmured Anndrew. Kormèr stole a glance her way and noticed her eyelids drooping.

"They're from twentieth-century Earth," added Kormèr. "He shouldn't be here, much less learning anything."

"What would you like to see happen?" Srrcheel asked, noncommittally.

Kormèr's mind raced, though he found it increasingly difficult to keep his fears from clouding his judgment. He had to find out how much the boy had learned, and he had to plan how to get him to forget it all before taking him back home.

"That's a good question." Kormèr watched Anndrew nod in and out of sleep. "And one not easily answered."

Jeransy's usually alert eyes were still open, but they were far from alert. He calculated that sending them off to rest would be the best way to keep them out of harm's way while he plotted. "Listen, our rides left and won't be back until mid-morning. Do you have a room for my friends?"

"Of course. And for you, too. The Grand Master asked that you be brought to see him in the morning."

"Err. I see," said Kormèr, not liking the idea much. He should have expected it, of course. "Just me?"

"He only asked for you."

"I see."

"Have you eaten?"

Kormèr couldn't help but smile. *Srrcheel, ever the host, even in my youthful impertinent days.* "Yeah, back in town. Thanks."

"Alright. Follow me." Srrcheel showed them to their rooms. Before leaving Birshetland, Kormèr had asked the girls to pick a few of the articles of clothing they'd purchased, and he'd placed them in his coat pockets. He handed these to them, then bid them a good night.

"Have a minute?" Kormèr asked Srrcheel, opening the door to his room.

"Sure."

The room was completely dark when Kormèr entered it, but the faintly musty, papery smell felt comforting and familiar. "Is this the same room I stayed in last time?" he asked, ignoring the dresser with the lamp that he knew was nearby as he walked in a few paces. Srrcheel lit the lamp, and the room glowed in the magical candlelight.

"Yes, it is. I'm amazed you remember. You must've spent only a few minutes in here before you started snooping around."

"Ha, ha." Kormèr sat on the bed while Srrcheel took a perch by the dresser. As before, aside from the perch, bed and dresser, the room had no other furnishings. "So what's new, dude? How're your studies?"

"You are talking to an Unfledged Enchanter," beamed the birdman.

Kormèr didn't know exactly what that meant. But Srrcheel had only just made Initiate Caster level during Kormèr's last visit, so this had to be a higher level. "No kidding! Congratulations. How many steps away from Master is that?"

"Technically five. There're two Sorcerer levels and then, after a long study period, Master. Of course, there's only one true Master, the others are just minor Masters."

"Of course. Still, it's great to see you progressing."

Srrcheel nodded, then grinned. "I know I said it before, but it's good to see you again, KL."

"It's great to see you too, old friend. I wish I were here under better circumstances."

"So, how did this Terran end up here?"

Kormèr sighed. "I screwed up. He accidentally fell through the portal."

Srrcheel shook his head. "You used to be more careful."

"Hey, I still am. No one else—besides you and a couple of others—has ever learned about the portal." He rolled his eyes. "Well, except for Sylvestra. And Jeransy and Annde, of course."

"And the boy."

Kormèr pursed his lips. "Yeah, and the boy... Cecil."

"Right, Cecil. So how'd Sylvee take your coming back after six years?"

Kormèr shrugged. "I guess it could've been worse. She was surprised, for sure. Aside from helping me recover Cecil, I don't think she wants anything to do with me."

"When have I heard that before?" Srrcheel said wryly. Kormèr knew he was referring to the days of the jewel heist, during which Sylvee had considered him a suspect. "I couldn't believe when I heard that you two had actually started dating."

"Believe me, I was as amazed as you."

"What are your plans, then? If you stay, there would still be that pesky marriage prohibition to deal with, unless you're not planning to make an honest woman of her."

"To the sub-surface with that stupid law!" Kormèr abhorred the ridiculous Averian law that prevented Averians from marrying offworlders. Then more calmly, "I honestly don't know, old friend." He leaned forward, elbows on his knees. "The truth is, a woman like Sylvee doesn't come along every day. I've never loved anyone the way I love her. But she's already moved on, so maybe I should just let her go."

Srrcheel's eyes went wide. "Wow! The indefatigable Kormèr giving up the chase? I never thought I'd see the day." Srrcheel sighed, looking more wistful. "I felt the same after Syrree. But I got over it."

Kormèr looked up hopefully. "You found someone."

"No, I gave up looking. My point is, you need to be fair to both of you. You both deserve happiness. However, you have a certain… wanderlust, and this will never feel like home to you. Just as she would never feel at home anywhere else in the universe."

"I know." He shook his head. When he spoke again, his voice was soft, listless: "I need time to consider my options. Which would be easier if I didn't have the more pressing matter of Cecil. As I started telling you, he stumbled through the portal and ended up here. I've got to get him back to Earth."

"That might not be so easy. But why not leave him be?"

Kormèr frowned. "I can't do that. It's my carelessness that got him here; I've got to make up for that."

"I think he's happy here." Srrcheel rolled his eyes. "We're not, but he is."

"That's my biggest concern. Srrcheel, I can't take him back to Earth with knowledge of the future, and even less of magic; he's young and irresponsible."

"He hasn't been taught properly, either," grumbled the birdman.

This intrigued Kormèr. He didn't know much about the ways of the Hawk Sorcerers. Any insight proved interesting. "Taught? I thought you said he was reading history texts."

Srrcheel shifted restlessly on the perch. "KL, things are in bad shape here. Grand Master Fitzbew is old and his council is in their dotage… They don't have the same control over the young ones as they used to. Sreet skipped all the usual procedures to get Cecil here, then let the boy loose in the library."

Tightness gripped Kormèr's stomach. "Exactly how much has the boy learned?"

"I was returning a book to the library a few hours ago and saw him, unsupervised, perusing the Initiate Sorcerer spell books."

Kormèr's heart stopped. "He is more powerful than you?"

Srrcheel simply nodded.

Kormèr fell back onto the bed. *Damn! Damn! Damn! And he's only been here a day. What am I going to do now?*

Kormèr sat back up, slowly, resting on his elbows. "Can he be made to forget?"

"Only the Grand Master has the power to do that. Without proper provocation, I don't think he'll do it. And I doubt your reasons qualify as proper provocation."

"Dammit, Srrcheel! Something's got to be done."

"I know. I just don't know what *can* be done."

"Hasn't Fitzbew been told of this blatant lack of protocol? Isn't that reason enough for him to put a stop to what's happening?"

"Only a few know Cecil is even here. Sreet has some followers, and they're mostly the only ones that know. A few others, like myself, have just stumbled onto it. And you'd better believe I complained. But the Grand Master dismissed all my concerns. He says there's no harm in the boy's enthusiasm. The boy can be taught the proper disciplines later." Srrcheel shook his head. "I don't think he believes the boy is absorbing what he is reading. His aptitude for learning is really unprecedented."

Kormèr snorted. "I can't believe this." He stood and paced the short length of the room. *Why is this happening to me?* He reached the window, looked through the sagging panes into darkness as murky as the pitch that haunted his thoughts at the moment, turned and continued pacing. "I've had the stupid portal for so many years, always so careful with it, and this is what I get for it."

"You should rest. You're tired, and so am I. In the morning, you'll see the Grand Master, and maybe you'll be able to convince him. You have a way of talking people into doing things they wouldn't normally do."

Kormèr laughed at this.

"We'll be able to think of something, I'm sure."

Kormèr shook his head. "I don't—"

"KL, the boy needs sleep as well. An evening will do no harm."

Reluctantly, Kormèr nodded. "You're right. It's been a long... long day." He chuckled. "This is my third planet today. I started the day being chased by a killer swarm of bugs and topped it off with Cecil ending up here. What happened to the good old days when I was simply a jewel heist suspect?"

Srrcheel smiled. "You've grown up... and so have your problems. Sleep well."

"You too. I'll see you in the morning."

Kormèr stared absently at the door, contemplating Srrcheel's parting words. *He's not wrong. But what am I supposed to do now?* He stepped to the dresser, put out the lamp, and remained standing in complete darkness. *I can't wait till morning, old friend. I won't be sleeping this evening anyhow, knowing what I now know. I'll be in worse shape for it in the morning, but right now I've got to relax and think.*

His senses heightened in the dark. He listened to the little sounds that filtered through the walls and from his own body, smelled the familiar, old masonry and the mustiness of the unused room, felt the chill of the night air in his nose and face. He felt the tension vibrating through the muscles in his arms and legs, tightening his chest around his rapidly beating heart. He pushed away the sounds and smells, and focused on his breathing: in to contain the tension, and out to release it with his exhalation. Slowly, he settled down on the floor, his legs crossed.

When he felt ready, his focus shifted to the issue at hand: *I must return Cecil Murphy to Earth.* A trickle of anxiety accompanied this, and he focused on it: *Cecil Murphy has learned magic and cannot return to Earth with this knowledge.*

Why? he asked, playing devil's advocate with himself. *Because he is not supposed to have knowledge of magic or of Averia… or of the future. With such knowledge, he could alter future events. But more than that, he is undisciplined in using magic, and there is the potential for abuse on a planet where no one else knows magic and therefore cannot discipline him.*

Maybe not. What if he is as responsible as I am, and he can be trusted?

I have no way of knowing how responsible he might be, and I can't sit around and watch him for the rest of his life.

With this fresh, objective perspective, he was ready to focus on solutions.

There definitely isn't a simple solution. Regardless of what Srrcheel had said, Kormèr hadn't given up on the idea of convincing Grand Master Fitzbew to wipe the knowledge from Cecil's mind. He was sure he could persuade Fitzbew somehow. While Kormèr was not looking forward to the meeting at all, it would at least present him the opportunity to put this solution in motion.

Well, that's one solution. Two or three backup plans would be nice now.

A second came almost immediately. *There always hypnosis, I guess. I don't know if such a thing really works. But even if it does, how would I hypnotize him? I'd have to find him first.* The Hovel was too expansive to begin a random search. Ideally, Kormèr would have used his portal, but all the nests had been magically shielded after his last visit.

After a few minutes with no new ideas, he shrugged. *Well, one incomplete backup plan is better than none.*

Now, for my next task: recover the magic glasses I hid years ago. He had to maintain the cover story under which he'd been granted permission to come to Berdia. And that meant finding his way back to the spot he'd hidden the glasses. Kormèr had discovered a maze of secret passages behind the walls of the Hovel. Ever curious, he'd followed them around to witness Srrcheel's first ascension ceremony. He'd also found Fitzbew's room. With that in mind, he decided the former plan of convincing Fitzbew was the best to pursue, no matter how distasteful it promised to be.

Kormèr opened his eyes, now adjusted to the darkness. He could see the doorway outlined in the very faint light from the corridor outside the room. In moonlight filtering in through the window, he could just make out the dresser and with the lamp on top and the light-colored sheets of the bed... and the small orb that floated between the bed and the wall. *Damn, a magic eye,* he thought, and he turned away slowly, as if he hadn't seen it. *Someone wants to watch what I'm up to. Fitzbew wouldn't resort to this; it's got to be someone else. But who else would care? Well, I can't wander around with that watching me.*

Kormèr stood, his limbs refreshed, and saw the eye flinch. But it's owner must've felt sufficiently concealed by the darkness to remain in the open by the bedside. *Brazen,* thought Kormèr, *but amateurish.* He walked around the bed, appearing as if he neither suspected nor saw anything. He folded the top of the sheets back, sat on the edge of the bed, and stretched. Then he lifted the sheets as if he were simply slipping under them. But with a swift yank, he sent the top sheet cascading over the orb. He whirled around and bunched the sheet below the eye so it could not slip out. He considered smashing it, but decided not to, assuming it would take longer for the caster to dispel it before casting another one.

Instead, he tied it to a finial on a corner of the bed frame. Another might come, but whoever wanted to monitor him would need time to recast the spell. Kormèr could get a lot done in that time.

CHAPTER 15

FOR the third time since trying to get some sleep, Cecil urinated out one of the four arched entrances of the Hovel. He'd set a motion-sensing spell in place to warn him if someone approached while he was occupied. *Of all the things Sreet showed me, a bathroom apparently slipped his mind,* Cecil thought with annoyance. *Bird-brain.* He rolled his eyes. *I probably had too much coffee, too.* He'd considered casting a drying spell on his bladder or teleporting the urine from his bladder, but images of all the things that could go wrong stayed his hand. He still made too many mistakes and didn't trust casting on himself that way.

He completed what he hoped was his final bio-break and started the walk back to his room. He had to climb three ladders to reach his room on the fourth floor, each set at a forty-five degree angle. The library was on the seventh floor, and he'd nearly fallen off a ladder getting back up there after his second bio-break. That's when he had moved his studies to his room. Between the double-long day and the energy-drain from all his casting, he felt absolutely exhausted. He'd read that the more a sorcerer cast, the greater his endurance became, but clearly not in one night.

An empathy spell he'd cast earlier triggered as a wave of anxiety washed over him, nearly knocking him over.

"Are you saying he's been made an apprentice?" The faint voice came from nearby, and Cecil realized immediately that the language used was not a translated one, heard as whistles and understood in his head, but actual English! Cecil knew that there were other humans on Averia, but he'd believed he was the only one currently in the Hovel. That there was another intrigued him.

He tuned down the empathy spell and listened, but heard nothing more. He cast a small sound-amplification spell, and adjusted the volume until two conversing voices filtered through. He followed the voices until he reached the room from which they came. The room had a privacy screen in place which muffled the voices. Had it not been for the empathy spell, Cecil wouldn't have heard anything. *I think I know a spell or two that can breach this privacy screen, but I'm too damn tired to cast it. But maybe...* He turned up both the empathy and amplification spells until the strong emotions combined with the voices carried through the privacy screen. He made out two voices, both male. And then a third one chimed in. *"He's my classmate."*

It took a moment to place the voice, and when he finally did, Cecil's mind reeled. What was *she* doing there? *Anndrew Lee?* And who were the other two? He *had* to find out.

Cecil turned up the empathy spell, hoping that the cause of the anxiety behind the voices would reveal itself. Instead, waves of exhaustion overwhelmed him, and he crumpled to the ground. His concentration failed, and various active spells, many of which he didn't even realize were still active, dissipated. *Whoa! Someone in there is as exhausted as I am.* He shook his head. *And I've gotta keep better track of what spells stay active. Those must've all been draining me this whole time.* When he felt capable, he stood, using the wall to steady himself. He marched in place to get his circulation going, hoping the effort would give him back enough energy for a few more minor spells, useful ones that wouldn't tax the filaments much more.

The door suddenly opened. Thinking fast, Cecil made himself invisible. He watched as four people exited the room, two males and two females, one of which was Anndrew. Both girls looked thoroughly exhausted, and even the tall human man looked very tired. The Averian he'd maybe met before; he could see the differences between the birdfolk, colors and spots and such, but recognition of individuals still eluded him. As the group walked away from him along the corridor, he chanced a cast of a mind-reading spell. While not a very minor spell, the energy requirement wasn't too great.

Anndrew was so tired, he'd gain nothing from her. But what of the human man? Cecil reached out to the man's mind and found it completely open to scrutiny. *Kormèr Lezàl, huh? And he's not from Earth, but from a planet called Elmar. Fascinating! He looks like any other Earth-human. Let's see why you were all talking about me. He feels guilty… because my being here is his fault? And he wants to take me back?* Like the pieces of a puzzle, dots connected in Cecil's brain. *Could the man and the other girl have been the other ones in the classroom with Anndrew when I fell into this world?* Before he could glean any more information, everyone disappeared down another corridor, and the spell dissipated. The invisibility wore off, leaving Cecil standing alone in the corridor. Knowing enough, but still curious, Cecil followed the group up to the fourth floor.

Peering carefully around a corner, he watched while the birdman showed the girls to their rooms and then joined Kormèr in his. When the door closed, Cecil shuffled quietly to the closed door and pressed his ear against it. But not a sound came through. He cursed the privacy the doors provided. He took a deep breath and ran through the various spells he'd read about. There had been a scrying-eye spell, and because of the way it worked, it could possibly circumvent the privacy screens. But Cecil couldn't recall the spell's exact *srootee.*

Walking as fast as his long legs allowed, Cecil hurried to the library. He skimmed across the shelf where he remembered the book had been and pulled it out when he found it, a third level Caster book. He flipped the pages haphazardly, not caring if he damaged the ancient book. Ah, there it was, and the energy requirement was not *too* high. Memorizing the pattern with a single run through, he set all things out of his mind and patiently cast the spell. Something about the *srootee* jumped out at Cecil, a peculiarity he'd noticed with some of the higher level spells, but until now hadn't really thought about it. *Still not the time,* he told himself, focusing on completing the spell. His muscles fatigued and his head feeling as if it were pushing through a dense fog, he performed the *tep*.

Exhausted, he dropped into his old seat at the stone desk, and slumped over the desktop. He craned his neck back and smiled at the fruits of his effort; inches away from his face, a crystal ball floated over the desktop. Within its smooth surface, an image of a dark room with the Elmarian man sitting motionless on the floor. Connected by magic to the crystal ball, a crystal "eye" floated in Lezàl's room. Cecil pushed himself up onto his elbows. *Oh, dammit! The sorcerer is gone. What could they have been talking about?* After a few minutes of watching Kormèr sitting on the floor, he wondered: *What the hell is he doing?* He hated not knowing and felt frustrated at not having a way to find out; as far as he knew, the mind-reading spell could not be effectively cast over distances or through the enchanted walls of the nests. All he could do for now was watch.

||Ah, there you are,|| sang Sreet's familiar voice. ||I just came from your room— What're you doing?||

Doesn't this guy ever sleep? wondered Cecil, annoyed by the birdman's constant presence.

"I'm watching this Elmarian," he said, pointing to the image in the ball. He looked up at the birdman.

||An Elmarian? Why would you watch—|| Sreet stepped closer to get a better look through the ball—and gasped. ||By all that's sacred! That's Kormèr Lezàl!||

"Yeah. You know him?"

||Not personally. But he was here a few years ago. He ruffled a lot of feathers at the time.||

"I read his mind. He's here with one of my classmates from Earth, and another female. He wants to take me back."

||I see.|| Sreet said nothing for a moment, his eyes watching the image in the ball. ||Do you *want* to go back?||

"No! Of course not." He almost added, *What a stupid question!* But he held his tongue. He didn't much care about Sreet's plans, but they provided a means to an end for him, with that end being his study of magic. So instead he added what he assumed Sreet would want to hear. "You've given me a purpose here, and I want to see it fulfilled." It sounded terribly corny—and even insincere—to him, but Sreet smiled. "I'll have to tell this Lezàl that I refuse to go."

||And if he doesn't accept your answer?||

Cecil hesitated. *I hadn't considered that. Why wouldn't this guy accept my answer?*

Just to appease his own guilt over bringing me here? Hmm. It sounds ridiculous, but...
"Does it matter? He has no magic." Cecil shrugged. "If he insists, I'll just show him how serious I am about staying."

||Very good. I've been summoned by the Grand Master. Most likely he's learned about your being here and wants to discuss your continued studies.||

Cecil wrinkled his nose at the birdman. "That's ambiguous. What do you mean by that?"

||It means I'm not sure what he wants or what his reaction will be. The tone of the message revealed nothing.||

"Go, then. Find out." *Leave me alone.*

||Yes.|| Sreet patted Cecil on the shoulder. ||I'm on my way now.||

Cecil turned back to the crystal ball and found Kormèr still sitting on the floor. *How long can he stay that way? Is he asleep— Whoa!*

Cecil drew the eye back reflexively as Kormèr suddenly stood. *Easy, Cecil. The room is dark; he won't spot the eye.* Cecil held his breath as Kormèr walked directly towards the eye, then turned and folded down the sheets.

He looks normal enough, thought Cecil, as Kormèr sat on the bed. *Still can't believe he's from another planet. Unless it's an Earth colony or something. I'd love to talk to him and ask—*

The image blanked suddenly. Cecil turned it this way and that, but he couldn't restore the image. *What the hell happened? It went so fast.* Frustrated, he dispelled the eye and set about casting another. Head spinning, he triggered the spell. He curled his lip, fighting to stay awake just long enough— The room was empty. "Fu—" Cecil toppled onto the floor.

CHAPTER 16

KORMÈR faced the wall of his room beside the dresser. Somewhere on the wall was a mechanical release that would open a secret door. Finding the release had become habit his last time here. *When I was shorter!* he reasoned. He slid his hand down thirty centimeters and pushed. A meter-tall section of the wall swung silently open. He grabbed the lamp off the dresser, ducked and stepped into complete darkness. He stepped to the right, and the secret door clicked closed behind him. With a light touch, he turned the lamp up to its dimmest setting, just enough to see the narrow space in which he stood. It had been years since he'd had traversed these hidden corridors. Did he still remember his way around?

He couldn't imagine why the passages existed or that the Averians of old had built such narrow corridors, without leaving room for their wingspans. A reason must have existed long ago, now as forgotten as the passages themselves. Were the sorcerers even aware of their existence? He had never run into anyone else within them.

To add to the mystery of the corridors, each room had an interface mounted on this side of the wall that could be used to see inside the rooms. Kormèr stopped and tapped one to glowing life. This technology seemed so out of place in this ancient magical tree that all the old questions came back to him as he wiped decades of dust from the screen. Who had built these corridors? Why? Who had placed these screens here?

The screen activated, the display split into four quadrants, each with a different view of the room on the other side of the wall. *Whoops,* thought Kormèr, seeing Anndrew peeking out her room's door into the hall. Fortunately, she was dressed, but he deactivated the screen anyway, and continued down the dim passage.

A smile teased his lips as he thought about the familiar faces he'd seen so far. Sylvestra in particular, Srrcheel and Theeseeo, all good old friends. And he had to admit that it was fun being here with Jeransy, and Anndrew too, as unexpected as that had been. *It would've been better if I hadn't needed to creep around back here,* he thought, feeling some bitterness about this forced trip to Berdia. On the one hand, he felt bad for Cecil, but on the other… *That klutzy kid is like a storm cloud over everything.*

He paused at a T-intersection. *Was it a right here, or a left?* He turned left.

He had met so many others… To be fair, he always befriended some inhabitants on the planets he visited, bonding with them on many levels. But there were few of those he considered 'true friends', unlike those he'd made on Averia. Theeseeo and his extraordinary courtesy; Srrcheel and his formal, unconditional friendship—which Kormèr had betrayed so thoroughly and yet had been so readily forgiven; Sylvestra, the only woman he had ever so selflessly loved. Sure, she had been the chief of police, and he had not only been younger than her, but also a person of interest, yet she had been willing to give him the benefit of the doubt and a chance to prove his innocence. He had loved her long before becoming a suspect and went out of his way every chance he got to prove himself to her, something he had never done for anyone else.

The passage widened, triggering more memories. *Yes! I know exactly where I am now.*

He followed the wall on the right until he found a familiar rivet. *This is it!* Knowing where he was, he turned and stepped toward the opposite wall until the light illuminated a horizontal crack that bisected the wall. A small silk bundle sat tucked into the crack. Setting the lamp down, he removed the bundle from the crack and folded back the silk, revealing a pair of round-framed sunglasses. He couldn't stop the smiling as he flicked the legs open. They were small for his face, but they still worked. As he put them on, the darkness vanished. He saw the room as if completely lit, his footprints in the thick dust, the small pile of crumbled rock below the crack.

Night-vision had been one of Srrcheel's first spells, and he had wanted to show Kormèr how well he cast it. So he had created the magical glasses for Kormèr. Later, he had been scolded for revealing secrets and had asked Kormèr to return the glasses. Kormèr's smile slipped into a frown at the memory of his own awful behavior; he'd instead handed Srrcheel a similar pair of glasses and hidden the real ones here. He had left Averia months later in such emotional turmoil that he'd forgotten the glasses. He never thought he'd see them again.

Kormèr slipped the silk wrap and the lamp into his coat pocket and continued along the corridor. He tiptoed down stairs when he came to them, and stopped halfway down when he came across a familiar door. *The old artifacts room!* he remembered, reaching for the release that would open the secret doorway. Then, reminding himself why he was there, he curbed his larcenous instinct and continued down.

Kormèr cursed himself for not having asked Srrcheel where Cecil's room was located. It would've been so much easier if he'd been able to sneak into the boy's room from the secret passages and… do whatever he was going to do, which was still nebulous in his head. The only clear plan still rested on enlisting the Grand Master's help, something Kormèr was dreading. He didn't fear Fitzbew; the old birdman was not an unreasonable birdman; in fact, he'd been quite gracious about Kormèr's intrusions into the Hovel. But he was very political, and the actions of politics were driven by forces that defied reason. And more often than not, those forces were money and power.

Kormèr stopped. *This is it, I think.* He removed the glasses and activated the interface. Two of the four panels were dark, no doubt where the pickups had failed or been disabled. But one of the two functioning panels clearly displayed the room's occupant, old Grand Master Fitzbew. *Wow! He's aged a lot in two and a half years.* Fitzbew was speaking with someone that was out of view of the pickups. Kormèr raised the volume and listened.

||I will not have my position threatened by that Terran child,|| twittered Fitzbew angrily. ||By all that's sacred, he's not even properly trained!|| He shook his head. ||How could you have let this happen?|| he warbled.

||Deepest apologies, Grand Master,|| chirped the other. ||I left him reading the history texts for only a moment. I had no idea he'd find the spell tomes.||

||A moment? He's reached the Master level tomes. He could hardly have done that in a moment.||

Kormèr cursed silently. *Good gods! Cecil's reached the master level spells? And all Fitzbew's concerned about is his position. Big surprise.*

||So what am I to do with him?|| chirped the other.

||I don't know, and I don't care. You brought him here,|| *—So it's Sreet,* thought Kormèr—|you get rid of him.||

||Yes, Master. What about Lezàl?||

||Ah, yes, the Elmarian thief.|| Kormèr winced. ||Another headache returned to our enchanted halls by this Murphy boy.||

||Yes, Master. And Cecil is aware of Lezàl's intentions. Lezàl is here to take the boy back to Earth because his coming here was an accident.||

Kormèr's breath caught in his throat. *The magic eye! It must've been Cecil's. He probably heard my entire conversation with Srrcheel. So much for your pretense, my love,* thought Kormèr, recalling Sylvestra's plan. *We should've known better than to imagine we could pull a con on the sorcerers.*

Feeling a chill spreading through his body, Kormèr forced himself to continue listening.

||You should have no trouble getting rid of the child then,|| sang Fitzbew. ||Give him to Lezàl.||

||Can we just let him go after all he's learned?||

||Not on our planet, certainly. But on Earth, who cares?|| The casual disregard of the words stunned Kormèr. Fitzbew had to have lost his mind.

||But—||

||But nothing!|| And suddenly Fitzbew was his old commanding self. ||Don't argue with me. Get rid of the boy, I don't give a damn how! Destroy him, if you have to! Just get him off… this… planet!|| He hacked a terrible cough for a moment, then collected himself. ||Dismissed.||

||Thank you, Master,|| chirped Sreet, and the door creaked open, then

slammed shut.

Kormèr reached to deactivate the interface, when Fitzbew spoke again. ||Decided to move our meeting up, have you, Lezàl?|| Kormèr's eyes went wide. *Oh, buomp!*

SREET considered what to tell Cecil as he walked to the Terran's room. The Grand Master had reacted exactly as Sreet had expected. *The old fool! So enamored with his position and entrenched in the old ways that he can't see the stagnation and oppression.*

He knocked on the door to Cecil's room, then again after a moment, but there was no reply. He tried the latch and found it unlocked. Inside, once again, he found the room empty and practically unused. *Heavens! It's the middle of the night! Doesn't this child sleep?*

Sreet closed the door and headed for the library, certain that he'd find the boy there. He admired the boy's zeal; he remembered his own days as an apprentice and how eager he had been to please his master and achieve his first raising ceremony. Even as an Initiate Caster, he had seen the cracks in the dogma, though they had been easy to overlook as he acclimated to the new demands of his level. But by the time he'd reached Fledged Caster, Sreet could no longer ignore or write-off the number of issues he had with the "religion" of the sorcerers. As a recruiter, he had interaction with the outside world but also with the other sorcerer sects. That was when he'd learned the endemic nature of the sorcerer dogma; every sect shared the appearance of freedom to choose their rules and path, but when looked at closely, they all fell into the same inflexible mold.

Thanks to Cecil, the ingredients had fallen into place to fracture that mold, if not destroy it entirely. Then the Berdian sorcerers would truly be free.

As he'd expected, he found Cecil passed out on the floor in the library, a small puddle of drool had leaked from his mouth onto the floor. Sreet saved a magic tome that had likely tumbled with Cecil and lain millimeters away from the puddle. He then shook Cecil's shoulder. ||Cecil.||

Cecil sat up, his eyes still closed. "I'm awake," he said, then rubbed the drool from his face with his sleeve. He half-opened one eye, and from beneath a heavy eyelid, looked up at Sreet. "Oh, it's you." He climbed onto the bench and rubbed his eyes.

||You really need to sleep,|| sang Sreet. Then he added: ||And to stop casting. You've seriously depleted the filaments around you.||

Cecil ignored him, his gaze shifting to the crystal ball on the table. The last time Sreet had seen it, it held the image of Kormèr Lezàl. Now it only reflected a distorted view of the room. "So what did the Grand Master have to say?"

Sreet didn't sugarcoat the message. ||He told me to get rid of you, not

106

just from Berdia, but from Averia entirely.|| He saw Cecil's fists clench. ||He wants you gone.||

"How dare he?!" growled Cecil, standing. He turned his back on Sreet and paced furiously between the stacks. "Just because he's powerful, he thinks he can dictate *my* life. *I'm so sick of it!*"

Sreet waited a moment then chittered, ||I know exactly how you feel. It's how many of us have felt for some time. But we don't have the numbers to do anything about it. He has the other masters and years of experience.||

Cecil stopped pacing and faced Sreet. "What reason did he give?"

||Pretty much the one I'd expected: that you would quickly outrank him, and he doesn't want to give up his position to a—||

"To a mere Terran," finished Cecil.

||Well, yes.|| *Among other reasons*, thought Sreet. *But this one should be enough to motivate you.*

Cecil grew quiet, his wide eyes distant and unfocused. Sreet recoiled as waves of anger from Cecil buffeted his heightened empathy. He could see Cecil drawing power from the nearly depleted filaments around him. ||I know you want revenge,|| Sreet twittered quickly, before Cecil could act on his thoughts, ||but I have a plan that would help us take down all the sorcerers who support the Grand Master. Then *you* could be Grand Master.||

"I don't *want* to be Grand Master!" he hissed, surprising Sreet. He thought that all of the boy's rapid progress had been driven by a desire to take control. "Don't you understand that?"

Sreet truly did not. He had once, in his youth, but not any longer. Magic was a means to an end, and that end was freedom through power. ||That's fine. If you don't want the position, we can form a ruling council instead.|| That had actually been his ultimate plan: to form a council of members from the different sects. That unity would have more power behind it than all the members of any one sect alone.

Cecil studied Sreet in silence. Then he shook his head. "I'm grateful for you bringing me here and showing me all this, but while I sympathize with your cause, your plans don't interest me."

Sreet felt disheartened by this. ||I see. So you just want… to learn more? Is that it?||

Cecil nodded. "Now you get it."

Perhaps not all was lost. ||Maybe we can find a middle ground.|| *And if not,* he thought, glancing at the crystal ball, *I can think of an alternative.*

Cecil watched him for a moment. "Alright. Let's negotiate."

CHAPTER 17

KORMÈR deactivated the interface as he shook his head. *I guess I should've known better than to spy on Fitzbew.* He dropped the night-vision glasses in his pocket and hit the release for the secret door.

||While I did not intend to move our meeting up, I'm glad of it,|| chirped Kormèr, ducking through the short doorway and into the spartan room. It was larger than most nests Kormèr had ever seen in the Hovel, with enough space for a large marble desk and several perches covered in gray velvet. The usual magical lamps lit the room; these hung along the walls from black, wrought iron hangers. Wearing his usual colorful robe, Fitzbew stood near his desk, rolling up a parchment and sliding it onto the shelf of a wooden bookcase. As he turned away from it to look at Kormèr, the bookcase vanished.

Kormèr bowed his head slightly at the old birdman. He left the secret door ajar, just in case, but Fitzbew immediately crushed any hope Kormèr had of using it as an escape route. Fitzbew stared at the opening, motioned with his fingers, and the doorway filled with stone, leaving the door trapped forever in an open position. ||That's the end of that.|| He looked at Kormèr. ||It's very dangerous to snoop about like that.||

||I can imagine,|| twittered Kormèr.

Fitzbew scowled. ||I recall you were more polite as a youngling, though no less intrepid.||

||I assure you, Master Fitzbew, that I am as polite as ever.|| He glanced at the door. ||I apologize for my… intrepidness. In my zeal to deal with my situation, I forgot my place.||

||You forgot your place many times before this. I tolerated your intrusions here because you were a youngling, and I thought it might be good for Srrcheel's training to associate with an unattuned.||

||Thank you for that,|| chirruped Kormèr, sincerely. ||I still value my friendship with Srrcheel greatly.||

||As do I. It was you that removed Srrcheel's greatest distraction, his betrothed.||

Kormèr held his tongue. Perhaps Fitzbew was more competent than Kormèr had assumed.

||After that incident,|| continued the Master, ||he devoted himself fully to his studies, and he has excelled.||

||Of that, I am glad.|| Kormèr wondered where all this was going.

||But the opposite could easily have happened, had Srrcheel mourned her loss too greatly instead.||

Fitzbew grinned, and Kormèr thought it was one of the nastiest things he'd ever seen. ||That's the gamble, isn't it? Just as you gamble each time you set foot in the Hovel.||

Kormèr almost argued that he was only gambling with his own life when he did that, but technically, that was untrue. He had been endangering Srrcheel as well. Having this pointed out to him made him cringe inside. Here he was trying to make up for being careless with Cecil, when he'd been just as careless all along. And only now was he realizing it.

Fitzbew let out a low wheezy rumble, and Kormèr realized the birdman was chuckling. ||I don't need magic to know what you're thinking,|| Fitzbew chirped smugly.

||You are as keen as you are powerful, Master Fitzbew,|| chirped Kormèr. ||But that was then. Tonight I've come on a different gamble. And let me thank you for granting our request to come on such short notice.||

||Hmm. I honestly believed you had actually returned out of contrition for keeping the night-vision glasses. It's a shame that you have the Chief of Police mixed up in your deceit now.||

||She didn't know.|| A lie, but one Kormèr delivered deftly. ||I lied to her as well.||

||As you say,|| sang Fitzbew.

Kormèr wondered if the birdman really believed him or if he was simply willing to accept Kormèr's lie. *Another 'you owe me one', courtesy of Fitzbew.* Kormèr nodded; at least now he understood where he stood with Fitzbew. ||Very well. As you know the reason for my visit tonight, I only ask for your intentions on the matter.||

||Come now; don't play stupid. You overheard enough of my conversation with Sreet to know my answer. Take the boy back to his world.||

Kormèr nodded. ||Thank you. May I ask a favor?|| Fitzbew waited. ||Would you please wipe his mind of all he learned here?|| Fitzbew's crest feathers fluffed slightly, but he said nothing. ||The reason I ask is that the Terrans are all unattuned, as you say. Taking him back as he is would leave him in a very powerful position.||

Fitzbew warbled something that Kormèr didn't catch. He then twittered, ||It can't be done.||

Kormèr's heart sank into his stomach. ||Oh. A magical limitation, or for the reasons you stated to Sreet?||

Fitzbew's crest feathers rose in anger as he peered at Kormèr from the corners of his black eyes. Instantly, he appeared at Kormèr's side. He grabbed Kormèr's arm tightly, and the room vanished.

<<What!?>> Kormèr reeled at the sudden blackness around him.

Fitzbew glowed in a soft golden light, still gripping Kormèr's arm.

||This is a private place, but it will only last a few moments,|| explained Fitzbew. Kormèr stopped struggling against the birdman's iron-grip, convinced that if Fitzbew had wanted to hurt him, Kormèr would've been powerless to stop him.

||I'm listening.||

||There are matters afoot in the Hovel that the council... that *I* am powerless to stop,|| sang Fitzbew. ||Sreet is unaware of these matters, but he too is plotting something which I haven't been able to decipher. And I believe that Cecil Murphy is a pawn in his plot.

||I have read in the journals of Grand Masters long past that, at one time, there were forces on Averia that could be called upon to control these situations. But that knowledge has been lost.||

||Has Cecil really become that powerful?|| asked Kormèr. He recognized that he sounded somewhat single-minded, but then again, that was his primary concern.

||He is beyond the point in his learning at which mind-wipes are easy to perform. But a conclave of senior Masters have their tricks too. It can be done.||

Kormèr nodded. ||Alright. Now *I* don't need magic to know that a condition is coming.||

Fitzbew grinned again, but there was no malice in it. There was only an old tired birdman. ||The conclave process to perform this mind wipe would leave me in a very vulnerable position. Without knowing which of my peers I can trust, I can't convene the conclave.||

Kormèr nodded. ||I understand. I wish it were otherwise, but I do understand. Why are you trusting me with this, after all the sneaking around I've done?||

||Because despite all that, I know you are a good man, Lezàl. I remember how you risked facing me to offer a good word on Srrcheel's behalf. I followed what you did in Birshetland, not the jewel heist but the whole incident with the Theesl family. And Srrcheel is like you. This is why I wanted him to ascend the ranks quickly. I knew he would be a loyal peer who might one day succeed me.||

Kormèr's eyes were wide with surprise. ||You've had this all planned out for years!||

||Of course. I knew I would have to name a successor at some point; for all our power, we have no control over our mortality.||

||What were these forces you read about? Is it something that can be found? I'm pretty good at that, you know.||

Fitzbew smiled. ||They were Averians, as far as I can tell. A special breed, black from crest to talon.||

||Black feathers? I've never seen that. Are there any clues where they

can be found?||

||A few. I will gather what I know and have it ready for you in the morning. We've been in here too long already; it's about to fade.||

||But how much time do I have? If Cecil continues to hit the books...||

||I will stall him for as long as I can. In fact,|| that malicious grin returned, ||I will send him on a tour of the other Berdian factions in the morning. Sreet will be his guide.||

||I guess I have no choice then,|| chirped Kormèr. ||I will await your notes and begin the search as quickly as I can.||

Fitzbew nodded. ||If you can find them, I will gladly convene the conclave and wipe the boy's mind. Maybe these mysterious forces will set everything right themselves.||

||That sounds too good to be true, frankly. But I'll take whatever I can get.||

The darkness vanished, and they were back in Fitzbew's room. Fitzbew released Kormèr and stepped back to lean on his desk. He then continued speaking as if nothing at all unusual had occurred. ||I will have my notes delivered to you in the morning, as I said. I think it might be prudent for now if you were to exit as you entered.|| The stone vanished from the formerly secret doorway.

Kormèr looked from the reopened doorway to Fitzbew with a smirk. ||For what it's worth, I don't think anyone else knows of those passages. I've never seen footprints other than my own in there.||

||They are blocked to magic, so I believe you are correct. Nonetheless, I won't tolerate a second entrance to my room. I'll reseal it behind you.||

Kormèr nodded. ||Of course. Thank you for your time, Master Fitzbew. I hope the next time we meet, it will be to both our benefits.||

||You are an optimist, Lezàl.||

Kormèr ducked back into the passage, and the doorway sealed with stone as promised, plunging Kormèr into darkness. He put the glasses back on and returned to his room. The magic eye was gone from his sheets, and no other seemed to have taken its place. However, the door to his room stood ajar.

Kormèr peered out into the hall before opening it fully, but found no one there. That's when he noticed that the doors to the girls' rooms were also ajar. He cursed silently, already expecting the worst. Kormèr raced to Anndrew's room and found it empty. He checked Jeransy's room and found a broken dresser drawer and shattered lamp, but not Jeransy. They were gone! And their disappearance smelled of Cecil or Sreet.

Cursing the moment he'd allowed the girls to come here with him, Kormèr dashed back to his room, into the secret passage and down to the artifacts room. Boxes layered thick with dust stood stacked about the room, looking as if no one had disturbed them since the last time he was here.

With no idea where to find the girls, he was in for a long, exhausting night. And with a high risk of running into Cecil or Sreet, he had to be prepared to use whatever he could find. He dove into the boxes, hoping that, if he found something useful, it wouldn't be too old to work.

SITTING at the foot of her bed, Sylvestra yawned, tired from a night of fitful sleep. She hadn't even had time to dream, waking numerous times to check her messages for any word from Kormèr. Not that she was really worried about him being there. With Fitzbew's official approval, Kormèr and the girls would be welcome guests. And Kormèr knew well enough how to handle himself around the sorcerers. They also hadn't discussed having him message her, although that had been their habit years ago. *Another one of those things that has probably slipped his mind over his six years away*, she thought, still feeling a little bitterness about his extended absence.

She pushed that aside. What truly nagged at her was why Sreet had picked the Murphy boy at all. Sylvestra had heard rumors of the sorcerers opening their doors to a tiny number of non-Averian recruits.

She frowned. *When do I get to go to Berdia?* she wondered, a bit jealously.

Then she sighed. *Okay, girl. Your lack of sleep is bringing out your worst emotions. It's a bath, then nutri-caf morning.*

She stood and stretched, then walked to the refresher and stepped into the bath. The cool cleansing water felt wonderful and finished the job of waking her up. Memories suddenly came to her of Kormèr using the bath. While he had eventually grown accustomed to the cooler water temperature, they'd had to compromise at first, just a bit warmer than she liked and just a bit cooler than he liked. That had been their first negotiation as a couple.

Gods, we were so young.

She dunked her head, then tipped back and to each side, dipping each of her wings. Then she just hunched there, chest-deep in the water. She didn't want to get out of the bath today, which was rare for her, as she hated feeling waterlogged. Reluctantly, she stepped out and into the gentle breeze of the automatic airstream. As she dried, she looked at herself in the wall mirror and then ran a de-sheathing wand over herself, breaking up the keratin tips of some of her new pin feathers. When the airstream shut off, she straightened some feathers that were out of place and plucked some loose ones. Satisfied, she returned to her bedroom and clipped on her belt-sash before checking for messages again.

Still nothing. This is going to be a long day.

As she clipped her stun gun to her belt, she sensed a subtle shift in the air pressure at her back. *Someone's here!* Whirling around, she lashed out with her foot and connected, sending a light brown blur sprawling onto the floor. She aimed the stunner and fired, but the beam warped around the birdman and dissipated into the floor. She spread her wings and used the inertia to pounce on the invader, pinning him to the floor. But as she fumbled to unclip the binders from her belt, an invisible force shoved her back.

Sorcerer! she realized instantly, as she backpedaled awkwardly to keep from falling. She spread her wings again, pressing them to the wall behind her to steady herself, then fired the stunner again and again as the birdman got to his feet. The beam still did nothing but warp around him. She compressed her wings and darted forward, stunner still firing to keep him distracted.

But he raised a flaming hand between them and chirped, | |Stop!| |

That's when she recognized him. *Sreet!* | |You have some nerve breaking into my home!| |

| |Drop the stunner,| | he commanded.

She hesitated, but realized the futility of resisting a sorcerer. She folded her wings and bent to place the stunner on the floor. *He can't be this stupid. What's he playing at?* | |There will be repercussions for this. You must know that.| |

The corner of his mouth curled slightly. | |I'm counting on at least one outcome. But I don't have time for small talk right now.| |

He cast, and her home vanished.

CHAPTER 18

KNOCKING stirred Anndrew from her sleep. She lifted her head and listened. Had she actually heard knocking in her sleep, or had it been a dream?

Knock-knock-knock.

Not a dream, she thought, sitting up. She'd been so tired that she hadn't turned off the lamp or even made it under the covers before falling asleep. She yawned as she walked to the door. *I wonder how long Elmarians sleep. If it's just a few hours, I hope Kormèr understands I need more sleep than that.*

She opened the door and yelped as two floating, green basketball-sized eyeballs with arms shoved their way into the room and surrounded her. Their scaly green arms and hands held very long, very lethal-looking swords. One nudged her from behind while the other waved its hand, beckoning her out of the room

She spotted two others at Jeransy's door. As the door opened, she yelled, "Jeransy, look out!"

The creatures charged into the room. Something shattered like glass. The sounds of a struggle followed with thuds and thunks. One of Anndrew's escorts zipped to Jeransy's door and rapped it's sword against the doorjamb. The noises stopped, and Jeransy scooted out of the room, pursued by her two eyeball creatures. Breathing heavily, she looked at Anndrew and shrugged. "Not much to fight with in the room. But thanks for the warning."

The eyes led them down to a dim foul-smelling room where an Averian male stood waiting. Without a word, the birdman cast a spell that lifted their arms over their heads and bound them to a wall. Then he left them in the care of the eyeballs.

"I wonder who that knob was," said Jeransy, dangling by her wrists only a couple of meters away.

"Could be the Grand Master, for all we know." Anndrew watched the eyeballs circle the room. "God, those things are freakish."

But Jeransy was distracted, prodding the manacles with her fingers and wriggling her wrists. Finally, she stopped. "I can't find the bloody lock on these things," she said.

"I don't think there is one. Especially if they're magical."

"Well, that's just pants."

Anndrew didn't know what that meant, but she figured it wasn't a good thing. "Yep."

"Oy," shouted Jeransy at an eyeball. "You got ears and a mouth to go with your arms?"

But it didn't react.

"I guess not," said Anndrew.

Jeransy tapped her foot restlessly. "Sod it all. Nothing we can do but wait for Kormèr to settle things, I guess." She kicked her foot angrily at nothing, and ended up swinging on the bindings. "It really narks me to wait for help."

To Anndrew, the wait felt like more than an hour, maybe closer to two. Her shoulders ached and her legs felt wooden from standing for so long. But her gaze almost never wavered from the eyeballs that still kept guard over them. They had fascinated and terrified her long enough that she'd stopped questioning why eyeballs should have arms.

A section of wall across from the girls swung open suddenly. A dark ball or disc shot out of the opening and struck an eyeball. The eyeball vanished in a puff of white, its sword clattering to the ground. Jeransy ducked her head as another object flew out of the opening right at her. With amazing precision, it exploded on the bindings, and they too vanished in a puff. Jeransy dropped shakily to her feet.

Wearing round-rimmed sunglasses, Kormèr ducked into the room through the opening and took up the fallen sword. "Hi, there." He beamed them a quick smile, then spun just in time to parry a blow from one of the three remaining eyes. "Sorry I'm late. Are you both okay?"

"They didn't hurt us." Jeransy looked at Anndrew, who affirmed with a nod. Then her eyes slid up to Anndrew's bindings. "Got any more of those things you threw?"

Holding the large sword two-handed, Kormèr parried a high thrust and riposted, only to be parried. "One sec, love." He feinted a low thrust, swung up and cleaved an eye in half. Both halves fell to the ground with a wet *plop*.

"I've got two pellets left." Kormèr fished in his pocket as the remaining two eyeballs moved in to attack.

Jeransy pinned the wrist of the fallen eye-half with her foot and grabbed its sword.

Anndrew cringed as an eyeball rushed toward her, its sword tip barely a meter away. It suddenly vanished in a white puff, its sword clattering to the ground at her feet. In the next moment, she felt a breeze on her wrists, and her arms flopped to her sides.

As she massaged her wrists, Anndrew watched Kormèr engage the last eyeball. Jeransy flanked it and cut off its sword arm.

Suddenly, the halves on the ground regenerated their missing halves and rejoined the fight, both brandishing fresh weapons.

"Look out!" Anndrew reached for the sword by her feet.

Jeransy spun just in time to parry aside a thrust. "Ow! Those scrawny arms are bloody strong."

Kormèr slashed another in half, and in moments, those halves had also regenerated. Even the arm Jeransy had severed regenerated into a whole new combatant.

"*Buomp!*" spat Kormèr, backing toward a wall.

"We have to get out of here," said Anndrew.

Kormèr nodded. "My thoughts exactly." As the eyes moved to surround him, he skewered two together and hurled them, together with his sword, into a third.

Waving her sword menacingly, Anndrew sidled toward Kormèr as he activated the portal. She hurried through, only to step into near darkness. Jeransy appeared beside her, awash in the faint blue glow of the portal.

Kormèr rushed in, spun and quickly shut the portal down, plunging them into complete darkness.

"Umm, where are we?" asked Anndrew.

"Sylvee's apartment," said Kormèr, slowly. "Only, we're not alone."

"How d'you know?" asked Jeransy.

"I'll explain in a moment." He whistled. "Damn! The lights aren't working."

Footsteps and the *whoosh* of fabric and air came from where Kormèr had been standing.

"Kormèr, what's happening?" asked Jeransy.

"Just looking for a light."

"Sounds like more than that," mumbled Anndrew.

"Having some trouble, that's all. Aha! The dagger glows. They must be light sensitive."

"Who?"

"Our uninvited guests." More sound of movement, then Kormèr announced: "I found a light. Cover your eyes." Anndrew shut her eyes tightly as Kormèr muttered, "Activate."

Nothing happened.

"Ugh. Reverse!"

Even with her eyes shut tightly, Anndrew had to cover them with her hand to block out the intense brilliance that manifested around her.

The intensity of the light quickly dropped to a warm glow. Anndrew risked a peek and found Kormèr grimacing, his head turned away from his outstretched arm, which brandished a short stick. She remembered he'd used a similar stick after he triggered the trap on the invisible jewel. *They're actual magic wands!* she realized. A glow faded from the stick's tip as she watched it. In his other hand, he held a beautiful black dagger with exquisite filigree detailing along the blade.

"Bloody hell!" cried Jeransy, blinking back tears.

Squinting into the waning brilliance, Kormèr asked, "Are you okay, love?"

"I'll be fine, just… Cor! That was bright!"

"Sorry. I had no time to warn you." He looked at the stick, then dropped it into his pocket. "There were more magical creatures here."

Anndrew shivered at the thought of more of those eyeballs around her in the dark. She saw a few seats, perches, a coffee table on a shag rug and other furnishings. But no creatures. "Where'd they go?"

"The light banished them. What I'd like to know is how they knew to ambush us here."

They all spun, as whistling came from behind them. An Averian stood there, surrounded by several minions, gruesome creatures with large eyes and razor-claws at the ends of thin, gnarled fingers. Anndrew recognized him immediately. But what the hell was he doing in Sylvestra's apartment? "That's the guy that trapped us at the Hovel."

"Sreet," said Kormèr.

The birdman's wings flicked, and he sang a quick series of whistles.

"Translate, please," said Kormèr.

The birdman rolled his dark eyes, then made a few quick motions with his hands. ||Honestly, I assumed you understood Averian Song. What did Sylvestra see in you?||

Anndrew realized immediately that the words she heard were in her head and not actually the sounds coming from Sreet. He had spoken in Averian Song. She glanced at Jeransy, but the girl's furrowed gaze was fixed on Sreet. *If her eyes could shoot daggers…* thought Anndrew.

||Oh, I understand you well enough,|| chittered Kormèr. ||Where's Sylvee?||

||She's fine, and she will remain so as long as you do what I ask.||

Oh, no! thought Anndrew. *He's kidnapped Sylvestra too!* She watched Kormèr, his grip on the dagger flexing as he clenched it tensely. She wondered if he intended to fight the sorcerer. *Considering what they can do, can he actually win in a one-on-one fight?* She readied herself to jump in and support him in any way she could, if it came down to it.

Kormèr didn't lower the dagger. ||I'm listening.||

||Find Cecil Murphy and take him home.||

||Find him?|| The arm that held the dagger wavered. ||He's at the Hovel.||

||Cecil is no longer in Berdia. He disappeared a short while ago.||

||I doubt that a Terran child just walked away right from under all your wings. It's more likely that you're stalling me until Cecil becomes too powerful for me to take him home.||

Sreet frowned. ||You'll have to take my word that this is not the case. Not that you have a choice really.||

Kormèr lowered the dagger. ||You slick-feathered capon. You kidnapped the girls knowing that I'd come for them. But you couldn't have expected me to best your eye-creatures. How did you know we'd come here?||

||You're resourceful, but you're also predictable. I had sent some *guests,* as you said, to your hotel room too. I won't be needing them any longer.|| He drew his hands apart, then clapped them together.

Kormèr said nothing for a moment, his eyes watching Sreet. Anndrew wished she could peek into his thoughts. If Cecil had learned enough magic to escape the sorcerers, what hope did Sreet have of Kormèr catching him and returning him to Earth? Unless this was a ploy to get Kormèr out of the way for something more sinister. Or maybe both? This situation had suddenly grown wildly out of control. She'd talk with Kormèr later and try to convince him that maybe Cecil was no longer worth this much effort. It pained her to even think that way, to imagine that he'd effectively just disappear from Earth, and no one but her would ever know why or how. But she didn't want to see Kormèr or Jeransy get hurt over the kid.

||I'll do your dirty work, sorcerer.|| Kormèr's lip curled with distaste as he said it. ||But let Sylvee go.||

||No. She's... extra incentive.|| Kormèr started to protest, but Sreet cut him off. ||She won't be harmed. The quicker you handle Cecil, the sooner I'll release her. And don't bother trying to use your portal to rescue her; I've sealed her prison magically, and bespelled you so that your portal won't work for at least a day or so.||

Anndrew heard Kormèr's teeth grind. ||You've thought of everything, haven't you? Everything except how to do the job that Fitzbew gave you. I know it was *your* job to get rid of the kid.||

Sreet's wings flicked, and the birdman tensed. ||How could you know that?|| Anndrew had seen that body language before, but only now did she link it to irritation.

||You said it yourself: I'm resourceful. The old man is afraid of Cecil unseating him. He told you to get rid of him no matter how.||

||How... Well, that... that's no concern of yours,|| growled Sreet, clearly flustered by Kormèr's knowledge. ||It's your job now.||

||Why can't you just find him using magic?||

||He has... shielded himself to magic, to put it simply.||

||I see. So what am I supposed to do once I find him? I'm not confronting him with what he's learned.|| Anndrew was happy to hear Kormèr say that.

||Take this crystal.|| Sreet held out a slim, clear crystal. ||It will offer you some protection against him, should you need it. At least long enough for you to shove him back to his planet through your portal.|| When Kormèr hesitated, Sreet made an exasperated noise. ||Oh, just take it. If I wanted to harm you, I'd hardly resort to such juvenile tactics.||

||Like kidnapping?|| Kormèr stepped forward. Sreet's nasty minions

moved closer to their master at Kormèr's approach. But they cringed back when Kormèr flicked the dagger at his side. He took the crystal and stepped back. | |So, how am I supposed to find him if you can't? I don't even know the limits of your magic. I mean, could Cecil have transported himself to another planet?| |

Sreet shook his head. | |No, no. Even the Fitzbew can't— that is, the Grand Master doesn't have the power to do something like that.| |

Anndrew hadn't considered that Cecil could now teleport. She supposed it was good news that he was still on Averia... somewhere.

| |So how far *can* Cecil teleport?| | asked Kormèr.

Sreet hesitated. | |Well, at his level, he can go quite far, but only if he's familiar with the destination, and if he has enough eleron.| |

| |Eleron... That sounds familiar. What is it?| |

| |An ore that enhances our spell casting. There are deposits all over Averia. That might be a good starting point for your search. Otherwise, he's limited to teleporting to locations he can see.| |

| |That's a lot of ground to cover. We're going to need transportation.| |

Sreet shrugged. | |You'll have to make do on your own for that.| |

| |Can't you use a little magic or something?| |

| |Now you're just goading me. I'm sure you know that's forbidden.| |

Kormèr slipped a hand into his pocket. | |Of course. Then I'll have to be resourceful.| | He produced a tile of carpet from his pocket. "Ladies, if you would please kneel on this and hold on to an edge." The tile extended into a large flat carpet.

Whoa! Could this really be a magic carpet? wondered Anndrew, as she and Jeransy stepped onto it. They kneeled and grasped the edges.

| |Where did you get that?| | asked Sreet, and Anndrew confirmed her body-language hypothesis as his wingtips flicked.

Kormèr did not answer. Instead, he pulled what looked like a black pancake from his pocket and tossed it at the wall. The pancake stuck to the wall, then enlarged, forming a large hole through which Birshetland glittered in the early morning sunlight.

Sreet's crest feathers fluffed. | |Who gave you these items?! I demand you tell me!| |

| |You're not in a position to demand anything more, sorcerer.| | Kormèr kneeled on the carpet between the girls, grabbed the tassels, and the carpet lifted smoothly off the floor. "Don't worry, the carpet won't let you fall." The carpet sped forward, and as it darted through the hole, Kormèr snagged a black flap along the hole's edge, and the pancake came away in his hand. Anndrew looked back and saw the wall of Sylvestra's apartment was whole once again. *Awesome! A portable hole!*

Then her gaze traveled down and down... She gasped and turned her head back around, but the carpet was not very large. Wherever she looked, she had views of the open sky above and plummeting drops below. Despite Kormèr's assurance that the carpet would keep them from falling, Anndrew's stomach gurgled anxiously wherever she looked. This was worse than her voyage on the Argent, where she had at least been strapped in.

"This is stonking, KL!" Jeransy was smiling, so Anndrew assumed that 'stonking' meant she was enjoying the ride. But then she noticed that Jeransy's eyes were closed.

"Hah! You have your eyes closed," said Anndrew.

"Spot on!" Jeransy laughed, and her humor relieved some of Anndrew's tension. Even Kormèr smiled as he manipulated the carpet's tassels.

Anndrew closed her eyes so she could say what she wanted to say without losing focus. "Listen, Kormèr, I don't want to see either of you get hurt, so if Cecil has really become too powerful, maybe we should just leave him or find some other way to stop him." She opened her eyes and focused on the side of Kormèr's face, the sharp bend of his beard along his jaw, how the leg of the sunglasses sat over his ear… Anything but the vast open space at her left. Still, she didn't miss their soaring past the edge of the Birshetland rock.

"Don't worry," he said. "We're not going after him alone. Things got complicated a lot faster than I imagined possible. You heard the conversation with Sreet, so you know that Cecil's been learning magic."

"Srrcheel said that Sreet had skipped the normal process," said Jeransy.

"That's right. So I met with Grand Master Fitzbew last night… sort of by accident. Anyway, he really wants Cecil gone from Averia. So I negotiated with him, and we have a plan. He was supposed to give me some notes this morning, but that's obviously not happening now. He was also supposed to stall Cecil's learning. Speaking of which, what are his study habits like?"

Anndrew shrugged. "He was smart. I don't think he studied much, or even needed to. Sometimes I'd hear him bragging about photographic memory, but I never believed it."

"If photographic memory means what I think it does, he definitely has it. In the hours Cecil had with the books, he learned more magic than Srrcheel has learned in years, practically enough to unseat the Grand Master."

"That's why you're not in a rush to take him back home," said Jeransy.

"Exactly. He'd be a danger to himself and everyone around him. And then we have Sreet. What do you think of his demands?"

"Me?" asked Jeransy.

"Both of you. I'd like your thoughts."

Anndrew shook her head. "I'm really not sure. He seemed very sure of himself, but I couldn't tell if it was an act or not."

"Right," said Jeransy. "You seemed to surprise him some, but otherwise, he was there acting like he had all the aces. Yet, he kidnapped Sylvestra, the knob! Makes me think he's not so powerful, resorting to kidnapping. And how'd he get away with crossing the rozzers like that?"

"Sorry," said Kormèr, "I'm not sure what 'crossing the rozzers' means? Is that the police?"

"That's right."

"Ah. Yeah, he's made a big mistake doing that. I just hope he's not desperate enough to harm her. The police and the other sorcerer sects would eliminate the Hawk Sorcerers if they dared to go too far. And I think you're both right about Sreet. He either he doesn't want the kid found, or he really can't find him."

Jeransy shook her head. "How's that, now? If he doesn't want Cecil found, why'd he ask you to find him?"

"He could be stalling. Think about it; with Cecil able to teleport around the planet, this task is monumental. And Sreet was unwilling to give us any magical help. But all that aside, I'm actually inclined toward the other theory. If I'm right, and Sreet *can't* find Cecil, he might think that I have a good chance of doing it, based on my track record."

"Can you?" asked Anndrew.

Kormèr said nothing for a moment. Then he chuckled nervously. "I honestly don't know. Solving the jewel heist was really a team effort; it was the media that pinned it all on me. But I'll do now the same thing I did back then: I'll give it my best shot."

"Wait, I thought we *weren't* going after Cecil."

"We're not. We'll just take some time to locate him, and by then, my portal should be working again. I'll update Fitzbew and see if we can pick up the plan from where we left off. Or maybe—call me optimistic—maybe he'll actually help, considering the circumstances."

They'd been flying with the sunrise to their right. Now Kormèr banked the carpet gradually into the sunrise.

"Where are we going?" asked Anndrew.

"Well, we need transportation… something with sensors."

"Won't the carpet do?"

"No. It'll revert to its tile form in a little while."

"While we're flying?!" asked Anndrew.

"No." Kormèr chuckled. "It lands first. That's why I'm pushing the carpet's top speed. I'm trying to get as far as we can before it stops. After that, we'll only have enough charge for one more ride."

"So, *where* are we going?" asked Jeransy, repeating Anndrew's question.

"Hmm? Oh! The name of the city is Freet-See."

"That tells me a bloody lot."

"You'll just have to wait. At this speed, we should get there by tomorrow afternoon."

CHAPTER 19

WEARING a brown T-shirt that read: "'Ignorance is never better than knowledge' -- Enrico Fermi", Cecil sat at a makeshift desk, under a canopy tent, on one rock of the barren Averian landscape. He turned the page of the master level tome he'd taken from the Hovel. Then he squeezed his eyes close and pinched the bridge of his nose, lifting his glasses on his thumb and index finger to massage his irritated skin. He always removed his glasses before going to bed, giving his nose a rest. But the various times he'd passed out since arriving here had been while still wearing the glasses, and he felt it. He took the glasses off and set them on the desktop beside the tome. Everything further than five inches from his face was blurry. His dad had thought it funny once to say, "Well, Cece, when you were about to be born, they gave you the choice between brains and eyes, and you chose brains."

I miss mom, he thought, and wondered what his parents thought of his sudden disappearance. He knew that it had happened centuries ago, that both his parents were long dead. But he still wondered if they'd searched for him, put his photo on milk cartons… How long had it taken them before they'd given up? Had they held a little funeral for him, with an empty casket? *From a psychology perspective, that would've been an interesting study to watch over,* he reasoned.

Of course, he also knew very well that he'd obviously skipped forward in time to be here. And that skip had occurred instantaneously, not via cryo-sleep or time dilation. Combined with the fact that some magic-like form of science existed… A day ago, he would have argued vehemently that traveling backwards in time was a physical impossibility. But today, it fell well within the realm of possibility. And if he could do that, then theoretically, he could return to the moment he left, and no one would be the wiser.

He stood, stretched, then performed a small *srootee* which caused a plate with a scrambled egg on toast to appear on the desktop beside the tome. He'd taken a break from casting since arriving there, and he could see the energy slowly building back up in the filaments. He scooped up the plate, took a bite of the sandwich and sighed. He felt his own energy returning as well, particularly after the teleport here had left him drained enough to pass out again. Without Sreet to wake him, he'd slept all morning, lying on the rock with his arm for a pillow. It had been one of the best sleeps of his life.

Carrying the plate, he walked to the edge of the tent and stared out at the bright, blurry landscape. Though he couldn't see it clearly right now without his glasses, the massive rock of Berdia floated out there, perhaps only five kilometers away. Mere hours ago he had listened to Sreet's tiresome plans. They sounded fairly well thought out, but for Sreet and his like-minded cohorts. Such things as Sreet had in mind were beneath Cecil. Knowledge formed the foundation of his ambition, his desire for it the very fuel that burned as hot as the sun when he was denied it. But then Sreet had made his alternate offer, one that seemed very reasonable. And so Cecil had agreed and teleported from the Hovel to the Argent platform, and from there to here, where he'd passed out.

Cecil breathed in the warm air and sighed again, unable to imagine more perfect weather. He looked up at the bright sky, the sun burning brightly at its summit. Watching that fiery ball sitting up there, so high, he felt he could do anything he wanted without having to worry about anyone standing in his way. *I can be just like that sun, burning my way to the top, to wherever I want to go.*

He finished his egg sandwich and turned back to the tome on the desk as he chewed. The layout and style of the sorcerer tomes belied the fact that they'd likely been compiled by one or more sorcerers ages ago. Though he hadn't come across it in any of the books he'd read, Cecil assumed that such history was probably taught to the Averian students during their tedious progression through the ranks.

Also missing, he now realized, was any mention of how to create new spells. *Can it be that the tomes contain the only spells possible? No,* he thought. *There has to be more to being a sorcerer than just memorizing someone else's spells. There's got to be some creativity, some way to combine spells or parts of them.*

He recalled that the *srootee* for the magic eye spell had sparked his interest when he'd cast it. Something about its structure suggested that it might be a combination of two spells. He went over the motions in his head, recognizing that the first portion resembled a conjuration spell, but for something very specific. A small motion followed that didn't appear to have any function of its own, and then came the rest of the spell. And now that he pulled it apart, Cecil recognized that the last portion of the pattern was a spell on its own. A scrying spell. That had to be it. The small motion between the two spells had to be a concatenator, merging the two spells together into a larger spell. In this case, the first part conjured the crystal ball linked to a scrying eye. *Now this has promise!*

He sat back down, slipped on his glasses and flipped through the tome looking for other spells with the same concatenator pattern in them. He found several easily. In fact, many of the master-level spells consisted of other combined spells. They also had other components in the patterns that Cecil hadn't noticed before. He dove into the challenge of deciphering these new components, with no reference to start from, finding it akin to cryptography. After more than an hour, he believed he had found the reason for them.

Cecil stood and walked to the edge of the rock, facing a larger, flat rock. He produced granules of eleron from a dimensional pocket he'd created. He'd read that these granules warped reality to reduce the energy draw on the filaments and caster alike. Again, the scientist in him discarded this reality-warping stuff as more sorcerer mumbo-jumbo; there had to be an explanation grounded in science. But as long as it worked as advertised, Cecil didn't really care… for the moment. He would, of course, want to find out eventually.

One teensy spell prepared the granules, dissolving them and creating an ephemeral honeycomb of energy in the air. Cecil then traced the patterns of two spells in the air, one of food creation and the other of enlargement, and added the concatenator between them. A huge mound of food appeared on the flat rock and immediately collapsed from the weight, some of it tumbling over the edge and through the clouds.

Cecil stared with an open-mouthed grin. *It worked!* A simple set of spells, but they had worked together flawlessly. Of course, he'd have to adjust the output of the enlargement spell in order to control the amount of food created. And that's what he believed the other components did. He could almost picture where in the pattern to insert the controller, though he'd have to perform some trial and error to get it right. But dammit, it had worked! What couldn't he do now?

Teleport myself to Earth, that's what. I've got to find a way to get to Earth, this new Earth, with its miracle leaps in science and technology. My old world holds nothing for me anymore. I can't teleport that far, unfortunately. But there has to be another way.

Wait! There are other humans here. How did they get here? By starship, of course! I have to get myself a starship. I'll see about renting one tomorrow.

The plan made sense in his mind, like a mathematical equation. But something nagged him, a missing variable in the equation. *The Hawk Sorcerers,* he realized, and the imbalance in the equation abated. As a hole, they represented an unknown entity. They had very little to offer him aside from the tomes of their library that he hadn't yet read. He would have ignored the sorcerers themselves, only borrowing the tomes as needed and bringing them back—after all, he didn't believe in interfering with anyone else's learning either.

But the Grand Master had made it abundantly clear that he wanted Cecil gone from Averia; this was a threat that risked enforcement at any moment. And it would devastate Cecil to lose access to those tomes; who knew how many secrets the highest level tomes held? Maybe he'd even find the link to technology that he firmly believed had to be there. But the threat of them made Cecil feel the way Todd Meyers made him feel, small and helpless. And he could not abide by that. Like he had done to Todd, he had to hurt the Hawks somehow, gain enough leverage over them that they'd leave him alone. With that thought, the equation balanced.

Once I deal with the Hawks, I'll return to Earth. And no one there will stand in my way ever again.

Chapter 20

THE sun had set with a dazzling show of colors. The sight lifted Kormèr's spirits; he'd had too much quiet time during this voyage to dwell on Cecil, Sreet and Sylvestra, all of whom weighed heavily on his mind. The twilight show had left him in awe of the grand beauty of nature. *How can our tiny problems seem so insurmountable compared to that?* he wondered. He was glad he'd decided to travel above the rocks. As with the Argents, he'd had the choice to shave some time off the trip by traveling below them. But he didn't trust his hastily obtained knowledge that far.

He'd found the carpet tile with a hand-written document clipped to it that explained its use. Apparently it had been a sorcerer candidate's raising experiment, much like Srrcheel's nightvision glasses. Kormèr had only had a minute to skim the document before stuffing the tile in his pocket, along with the myriad other artifacts he'd stolen from the Hovel. With such a rudimentary understanding of the magic carpet, he had decided not to risk flying below the rocks. If it discharged before he could get it topside, they would have to land in the Forbidden Lands, and no Averian in his right mind would come to their rescue—if there was anything left of them to rescue.

The girls had grown comfortable enough with the carpet's safety features to give in to their exhaustion. They'd slept through most of the smooth trip, Jeransy snuggled under Kormèr's coat, and Anndrew wrapped in a large beach towel Kormèr had in his coat's pocket.

As twilight faded to dusk, the carpet's tassels rumbled in Kormèr's hands, signaling that the carpet's charge was nearly spent. Kormèr put his hand on Anndrew's shoulder until she half-opened her bleary eyes. "Time to wake, love.". She nodded and closed her eyes. "We'll be landing soon," he added, to make sure she didn't fall back asleep. "You'll need to be awake for that."

"I will," she mumbled.

Kormèr repeated the process with Jeransy. "Morning," she said with a grin, growing alert almost immediately, shifting up onto her knees and gripping the edge of the carpet.

He smiled at her joke. "Good morning." He realized this was probably the sixth time he'd said those words to her. Part of him recognized that this should not have been significant. Except that it was. He hadn't had a living person share six consecutive morning—or even wakings, in this case— with him in nearly six years. Not since just after Sylvestra—

125

The tassels rumbled a final warning, and the carpet descended. Anndrew sat cross-legged as the carpet settled onto a floating rock. They stepped off the carpet, and it reverted to its tile form.

Anndrew yawned. "Wow! I really needed that nap."

"The trip was amazing, though." Jeransy handed Kormèr back his coat and then stretched.

"You should've seen the sunset." Kormèr examined the carpet tile, wondering how he would know when it was ready to continue. The instruction sheet had indicated it had three charges, with each lasting between twenty and twenty-four hours, depending on use. But it hadn't included the rest time between charges. He shrugged, stuffed the tile in his coat pocket and pulled out a flashlight.

He then pulled several wands from his pockets and used the flashlight to read the inscription on the side of each one. It would get cooler overnight, and while the girls had additional clothes in his pockets, he wanted to get a fire going. Unfortunately, the rocky surface of Averia provided little in the way of kindling or other material to burn. So he hoped to get lucky and find a wand that cast magical fire.

Not this stack. He handed the wands to Jeransy and pulled another bunch from his pocket. Finally, he spotted one whose inscription read: *Ring of fire.* He handed it to Anndrew. "I'll take those back," he said to Jeransy, and stuffed all the others back in his pocket.

"How'd you get all these magic items?" But the look on Anndrew's face said she knew exactly how he'd gotten them.

"I found a storage room with a note that read, 'Kormèr, anything here could help you with Cecil. Take as needed.' How could I turn that down?"

Anndrew nodded. "I suppose it also read: 'This message will self-destruct in three… two… one'. Then, poof! And left no trace."

"That's it exactly," he said with a big smile. He stepped clear of the girls, trusting the magic only so far, and pointed the wand at the ground. "Ring of fire!" Nothing happened. He cleared his throat. "Fire ring." Three concentric rings of thin tubular flames sprang from the rock. Each flame burned mostly blue except for a tongue of yellow at the tip. The fire didn't provide much illumination, but what it lacked there. it made up for in heat. Satisfied, Kormèr slipped the wand into his inner coat pocket, a standard pocket, so it wouldn't get mixed back in with the others.

"We're camping here, are we?" asked Jeransy.

"We are. The carpet needs to recharge, and we skipped lunch."

"Umm…" Anndrew looked around anxiously. "What if we have to… you know… nature calls?"

"Bio breaks?" asked Jeransy. "That's easy; just find a cozy spot and squat." She put her hand out toward Kormèr. "Supplies, please."

He pulled a roll of toilet paper and some wet-wipes from his pocket and

126

offered them to her. "We've been using these up for a week. We'll have to ration what's left until I can resupply, so use only as much as you really need."

"Aren't we a boy scout?" teased Anndrew as Jeransy took the items and wandered off behind an outcrop.

Kormèr shrugged. "I think I know what that means: I try to be prepared for any eventuality."

"That makes those pockets invaluable. Do they get heavy with all you've got in them?"

"Not at all."

"Cool. So how far before we reach where we're headed?"

Kormèr pulled his multi-function device from his pocket and activated the map. "At a guess, I think we're only a few hours from Freet-See. But we have to wait for the carpet to recharge, so we might get there by noon tomorrow. That's pretty much what I expected."

Anndrew looked at the map. "I remember that." She pointed to a dark band across the displayed surface of Averia. "Lots of air turbulence."

"It's called the Great Western Rift."

"I didn't want to say anything, but I thought for sure we'd go down. Like, crash."

"Bloody hell!" cried Jeransy from behind the outcrop, startling Kormèr. But then she added. "I did, too!"

Kormèr thought to himself, *Me, too.* He'd held onto those tassels so hard he thought they were going to tear off in his hands. Fortunately, the carpet's enchantment had kept them from falling off as it tossed about, nearly out of control. "That was tougher to navigate over than I'd thought. I've never crossed it on a carpet before." He shrugged. "It's a piece of pie in a skip."

"Piece of cake," said Anndrew.

"Hmm. So it's as easy as pie, and a piece of cake, but not easy as cake or piece of pie. What does the pastry have to do with whether or not something is difficult?"

Anndrew laughed. "I don't know. English has a lot of funny old sayings like that. Their origins are lost to time."

"What is the Rift, exactly?" asked Jeransy.

Kormèr put the device away and waved his hands near the fire. Gripping the tassels for so long, his fingertips had chilled and were taking too long to warm back up.

"I asked about it years ago," he said, "but no one had a definite answer. It's just an area completely devoid of the floating rocks. Hot winds vent through, displacing the rocks, or something. I'm not sure where the winds come from or even why they pick that area to come up through instead of just… all over the place."

But the rift was far behind them now. With the ground solid beneath his feet and the last light of day vanishing, Kormèr felt the warmth of the fire relax his aching muscles.

"Oh, I almost forgot to try this." Kormèr pulled the cube from his pocket. He pushed the black face, and the cube glowed. Immediately, the glow faded, and the cube remained inert. "Damn! Sreet wasn't bluffing about keeping me on a leash."

"How much longer will the spell last?" asked Anndrew.

Kormèr sighed. "He said a day, so I guess until morning. At least, it'll be ready in case the carpet runs out of charge before we get there. Is anyone hungry?"

Anndrew shrugged. "A bit."

"Yes," said Jeransy.

"Okay. Let's see what I've got here." He rummaged through his pockets and produced one of the many foil-wrapped, freeze-dried ship-rations that he still carried from six years ago. But he'd once put his chrono in his coat pocket, and when he'd removed it days later, it had displayed the date and time when he'd pocketed it. He'd experimented a bit and found that time seemed to freeze in the pockets. In any case, he and Jeransy had been eating these occasionally over the past week, with no ill effects.

He glanced sidelong at Anndrew as he held up a foil-wrapped bundle. She wrinkled her nose. "More lumbricus?"

"No, but these things tend to be tasteless, however nutritious."

She held out her hand. "I don't care. So long as it's food, I'm fine."

"Next," said Jeransy, returning with the remaining toiletries.

Kormèr prepared their meals while Anndrew took her turn behind the outcrop. He activated the heating mechanism in the foil-wrap and set each bundle out on the rock with eating utensils.

Jeransy didn't wait for the foil to cool before she dug into her meal. Watching her eat, Kormèr wanted to do the same, but he waited for Anndrew to return. Fortunately, by then the bundle had cooled to a palatable warmth.

As they ate, Kormèr noticed Jeransy looking up at the stars. Anndrew must've also noticed her silent focused vigil and followed her eyes upward, remarking: "Oh, wow! Two moons?"

Kormèr looked up. Averia's two moons almost overlapped, one further out than the other. "In five nights, they'll be celebrating Cheerretee here." He looked at the girls. "That's what Averians call the full eclipse of the far moon by the near moon. Legend has it that the Averians once lived on the surface below this, in actual trees. But one day something happened: the sky went dark and their tree-homes died. Seeing the faint light in the sky above, they came up here in time to see the moons overlap, and this was an omen of good fortune for them."

"That's brill!" said Jeransy. "I've never seen any moon so clearly, and never two."

"They have names," said Kormèr. "But I don't remember them

anymore."

"We call ours Luna."

Jeransy looked at her. "Really? I'd only ever heard it called Moon."

Anndrew nodded. "It's a Latin name, for moon."

"Oh, that's why. I've heard of Latin, but no one knows anything about it anymore."

As the girls discussed the ongoing presence of Latin in English, Kormèr turned his eyes back up to the moons. Nearly three years ago, he'd missed the general Cheerretee celebrations. He'd been at the Hovel instead, illicitly witnessing the private ceremony that the Hawk Sorcerers held on the same night. The overlapping of the moons brought about a surge of power strong enough that, when coupled with the proper rituals, allowed a sorcerer to perform at peak ability. They held their annual raising ceremonies on that night, and candidates who were ready would ascend ranks.

Did Cecil know about this phenomenon? Even if he didn't, Kormèr assumed he would sense the increased energy. And with his knowledge and lack of discipline, Cecil could become a significant danger to everyone around him on that night. Kormèr had to get to him before then... before Cecil realized the potential of his power.

"Well, not bad, that," said Jeransy, picking up the empty foil wraps. She nudged Anndrew. "Watch this." She stacked the foil on the ground, pulled one of the thin cords embedded in the foil, and stepped back. In seconds, the foil dissolved completely.

"Wow!" said Anndrew. "What's it made of?"

Jeransy shrugged. "Dunno. I just find it fun, is all."

"We have tons of aluminum cans in my time; too bad they aren't made of whatever that was."

Kormèr stood and shook out the large towel that Anndrew had used as a blanket earlier. Handing it back to her, he said, "You can cover yourself with that again, if you like."

"Haven't you got sleeping bags in those pockets?" asked Anndrew.

By Anndrew's grin, Kormèr figured she'd meant the question as a joke, but he truly felt bad that he couldn't offer her something better to sleep on. "I'm sorry, but no. We've actually been roughing it for the past week. Besides the towel, the best I can offer you are some rolled up sheets to rest your heads on." He took these from his pockets and gave them to the girls.

"That'll do for me." Jeransy unfurled a length of it to wrap her upper body, leaving just enough to still have padding for her head.

Anndrew set the beach towel down, then did the same as Jeransy with her sheet. "What about you?" she asked Kormèr.

Kormèr scraped up some of the bushy moss growing on the rocks and gathered it into a small pile. "A natural pillow for me."

"Are you sure? You can take the towel back, and I'll just lie on the ground."

"No, no. Honestly, I'm fine." He lay down and let his head rest on the moss, unsure of what to expect. But he'd slept with nothing but his arm for a pillow before, and the moss proved to be just cushy enough.

As the chatter between the girls gradually quieted to a hush, he gazed up at the stars this time and thought about the time he'd spent up there on a spaceship. It had been a means to an end, getting him here to Averia from the Terran system. But he hadn't enjoyed the experience very much. He preferred to have his feet solidly on the ground... and the ground solidly on a planet's surface. The irony in that thought, considering Averia's floating surface, was not lost on him.

Though he tried to fight it, his thoughts invariably turned to Cecil. Still, he refused to focus on them, letting his brain run through what-ifs while drowsiness nibbled at the edges of his consciousness. The weight of the day slowly drained from his body, leaving behind nothing but aches and exhaustion. And more thoughts and worries about Cecil. *This is going to be a long, painful night.*

As he was about to roll onto his side and try to sleep, Anndrew appeared over him, wrapped in her towel, glowing a soft blue in the dying firelight. A glance at Jeransy showed her to be fast asleep.

"Hi," he whispered. "Did you need something?" She smiled, and he sat up. "What's up?"

She kneeled in front of him, not answering right away. "I don't mean to be forward..." she started, dropping her wrap from around her shoulders.

"Wait." He recognized the searching look in her eyes, and alarms chimed in his head. "Before you say anything—"

She didn't speak, closing the distance between them without warning and pressing her lips to his. In the chilly night air, she felt warm and welcoming, but he tried to keep his mind focused elsewhere: on Jeransy, Cecil, Terran baseball... anything but Anndrew Lee's kiss.

"Wow," he murmured, leaning back to reclaim his space. He wasn't sure what to say, how to stop her advances without insulting her, but he had to think of something soon, before she kissed him again. She leaned towards him again, but he stopped her gently with a hand on her shoulder. "I'm sorry. We can't... *I* can't do this."

Anndrew sat back on her heels and stared. "You mean 'can't do this *now*'? Or, like, never?" Her shoulders slumped. "Or, just not with me?"

"It's nothing to do with you," he blurted. "You're amazing... beautiful, wonderful." And he wasn't exaggerating. Both she and Jeransy were all those things, and more. And perhaps under other circumstances... But not here. He glanced at Jeransy out of the corner of his eye to make sure that she was still asleep, but it was about more than simply choosing between the girls, if such a thing were even possible. Here, his heart and mind belonged to one woman, even if that relationship had ended long ago.

"But…" she prompted, a little impatiently.

He couldn't think of anything witty or charming to say, so he spoke truthfully. "But this feels wrong to me. I've tried to earn your confidence and trust, and this feels like a betrayal, like I'd be taking advantage of you." He didn't like how that sounded, even to himself, but he couldn't find better words.

"You wouldn't be," muttered Anndrew, getting to her feet. "But thanks." Her voice sounded disappointed, but not despairing, to Kormèr's relief. "Thanks for being honest."

"You deserve an honest answer," he said. "You shouldn't ever settle for anything less."

"Getting honesty from a thief, huh." She picked up the towel from the ground.

"Even a thief can tell the truth, from time to time," he said, smiling.

"Yeah, I suppose you're right. It's just harder to tell when it happens." Kormèr raised an eyebrow inquisitively, but she didn't elaborate. "Good night, Kormèr. Sleep well."

He watched her return to her makeshift bed next to Jeransy. *That could've gone better. We'll see how things go in the morning.* He closed his eyes, now so tired that he barely felt the soreness that had pained him earlier. Gone, too, were his worries about Cecil, as he finally fell asleep.

JERANSY had missed the sunset, but she very much wanted to see the sunrise on Averia. She woke up to find the sky brightening, that morning twilight that she'd read about but never witnessed until she'd met Kormèr. Now she couldn't get enough of them. This would be her fifth, and she remembered every one.

She stood, double-wrapped the sheet around her, and sat atop a tall outcrop facing the brightest spot in the sky. Although she had enjoyed sharing the sunrises with Kormèr, her one regret was that her parents couldn't be here to see them with her. They deserved a break from their lives, and she knew they would love traveling to all these exotic worlds as much as she did.

Obviously, she could have asked Kormèr to send the portal to her flat and allow her parents to come with them, but she hadn't. During one of her early conversations with him about the portal, he'd mentioned that he could count the number of people that knew about portal travel on two hands.

"It's too tempting to misuse it," he'd said. "Even I have to watch how I use it. Believe me, there are a few things in my past I'd love to go back and change."

"I don't understand," she'd said. "Why don't you?"

"Because… where do you stop? You change your past, maybe fix the past mistakes of your loved ones, and then? They ask you to fix their loved ones' mistakes, or maybe some event that adversely affected them or their town. And then, what if the changes you make only make things worse? Do you have to stop yourself? Can you?" He shook his head. "I don't ever want to have to find out. The past makes us who we are today. There might be regrets, but I'm happy with who *I* am despite them… or maybe thanks to them. So the fewer that know about the portal, the better."

Sitting here now, watching the sun crest over the horizon, she almost understood what he'd meant. She knew that he deeply regretted letting Cecil end up here; even when he wasn't voicing it, she could see the concern eat at him. And yet, because of his mistake, they were all here, together, flying on carrier birds, magic carpets, meeting sorcerers… *Meeting up with old flings,* she added, a mite jealously—she couldn't help but fancy him a bit. How less rich would their lives have been had that mistake not happened?

Jeransy looked to her right as she heard the crunch of footsteps.

Also wrapped in a sheet, Anndrew stepped up beside the outcrop, her eyes on the horizon. "Wow," she said. "I've seen some sunrises, but that's something else."

Jeransy glanced back and saw Kormèr was still asleep. She turned back to the sunrise with that pang of jealous animosity she still held toward Anndrew. She knew it hadn't been the girl's fault or intent to insert herself into their lives, but she couldn't help feeling that way. Anndrew had become the ever-present reminder that the good thing she and Kormèr had shared, had changed.

She also fixed the portal, she reminded herself. *Yeah, alright. She's not all that bad.*

"It's ace, that," Jeransy finally said, in response to Anndrew's comment.

"This may be the last time I'll see it."

Jeransy looked at her, the girl's face bright in those first rays of sunlight. "Why d'ya think that?"

"Well, as soon as we find Cecil, I'll be on my way back home too."

Yay! thought Jeransy. Then she felt bad for the girl. Anndrew wouldn't get to travel with Kormèr anymore and visit any other beautiful worlds. She'd have to go back to that rubbish rainy Earth with no viros. *Still's got to be better than Castorbridge,* she reasoned. "You never know," she said.

"No. It's probably for the best. I'll have some glorious memories… And I'll be alright with that."

Something in her tone didn't sound as alright as Anndrew made it out to be, but Jeransy didn't press her. *If she wants to go home, that's her choice. Why should I care, anyway?*

Behind them, Kormèr yawned audibly. "Good morning," he called.

"Morning." Jeransy carefully stepped down from the outcrop.

Anndrew turned slowly. "Good morning."

Kormèr stood and stretched. "Looks like another beautiful sunny day," he said, as he slapped his coat to shake off dust and dirt.

"Does it ever rain here?" asked Jeransy.

Kormèr slipped back into his coat. "Occasionally. Maybe once a week, or so."

"Amazing. Back home, if there isn't a squall at least once a day, everyone gets their Alans in a twist."

"Let's see if this works yet." Kormèr tested the cube. Once again it glowed, but stayed a cube.

"Guess not," said Jeransy. "More carpeting then, is it?"

"It looks that way." He pulled out the carpet tile along with a crumpled sheet of paper. He studied both before saying, "It looks like it's recharged. We can head out after breakfast."

Kormèr found some rations that satisfied their breakfast palates, Jeransy preferring sweet waffles with syrup and cinnamon, while Kormèr and Anndrew went for a more savory melange of eggs with diced potatoes and onions. They ate quickly, and in silence, enjoying the sunrise. This was fine with Jeransy, as she was eager to see Freet-See.

"What's Freet-See like?" she asked once they were on their way.

Kormèr smiled, and Jeransy could see in his expression that he was seeing the city in his head. "Oh, it's… amazing. It's dense; nothing like Berdia or even Birshetland. It's the only spaceport on the planet, so the architecture is a mix of pseudo-trees and off-world buildings. There's the spaceport itself, a financial center, housing, shopping, diverse restaurants that serve cuisines from all over the Galactic Federation… It's totally awesome, as an old Terran friend used to say."

"What's your favorite city?" asked Anndrew. "Birshetland or Freet-See?"

"Hmm. Freet-See was the first city I ever saw when the ship I was on landed here—"

"You didn't portal here?" asked Jeransy. All this time, she'd been thinking he just portaled everywhere.

"Not that time. I arrived by space ship with a group of Terran entrepreneurs. They had a new spacecraft landing system they were trying to market."

"So… favorite city?" prompted Anndrew.

Kormèr chuckled. "Right. Birshetland. I spent months there, so it holds a special place in my heart."

"Aww."

"And nothing at all to do with a certain lady friend, I'll bet," teased Jeransy.

He blushed a bit as he smiled and said, "Well, maybe that, too."

"How much farther till we get there?"

Kormèr looked down at his chrono. "Probably under five hours."

"I wish I'd brought my playing cards," said Anndrew. "Not that the wavy carpet would work as a tabletop."

"Sorry," said Kormèr. "I know the landscape isn't that exciting out here, but Freet-See will make up for it."

Jeransy watched the landscape. She studied the different shapes of the rocks, the patterns of moss growth and spots where the rocks appeared to cluster together by size. After a while, she looked up and realized she was dizzy. *This is peaceful, but really boring,* she thought. *I'm bloody going barmy here.*

"I spy with my little eye," said Anndrew, "something green."

"The spotting game?" said Jeransy, recognizing the words. She hadn't heard them since she was nine.

"Yeah."

"Is it moss?"

"It's moss."

"Oh, I'll go. I spy with my little eye… something white."

Anndrew looked around. "Is it a cloud?"

"'Tis."

When Anndrew didn't continue the game, Jeransy looked at her. "I think I'm done with that," said Anndrew. "There isn't much else to see."

Jeransy nodded. "Yeah. Alright." They'd spent more time on the carpet yesterday, but they'd spent most of it sleeping. Now that they had rested, the prospect of another three hours seemed endless.

"Let's try this," said Kormèr. "How about we each ask a question of each other, and we can answer any way we like? Then the others have to guess if you're lying or not."

"Oh, I know this game," said Anndrew.

"I don't get it," said Jeransy.

"You've never played this game?"

Jeransy shook her head. "We don't play games where I'm from. Can't gather in groups larger than three or you'll attract the watchers. Don't want them noticing you."

Anndrew stared at her, appearing to be uncertain of what to say. Then her eyes narrowed. "You're already playing, aren't you? Liar."

"I had you, I did!"

Anndrew smiled. "You did. I'll get you back."

"We'll see. I can spot 'em a mile off."

They played this game for what seemed like only a short while. But when Jeransy checked her watch, she found that two hours had passed in a blink.

"It's your turn, KL," said Anndrew.

But he didn't answer, his gaze locked in the distance.

Jeransy looked ahead and spotted a massive flat shape against the horizon. "Is that it?"

"Yes," he said, slowly.

"Is that a black cloud?" asked Anndrew.

"It seems that way, doesn't it?"

As they drew closer, the black cloud grew and stretched across the sky.

The last leg of the trip passed in silence as the trio watched the city grow, their focus riveted on the spectacle of the billowing black smoke. The carpet climbed to get over the city ridgeline. But the beautiful city of Kormèr's memory was not what welcomed the trio as they soared over the ridge. Smoke enveloped half of the city, poured from blackened burning structures and rubble alike. Dozens of vehicles and smaller drones hovered and zipped about, fires quenched in their wake with what looked like wave blasters to Jeransy. But there were so many fires!

"Wow!" said Anndrew. "What the hell happened here?"

"Whatever it was," muttered Kormèr, his face ashen, "it was bad. This place was beautiful."

Kormèr jumped, as if shocked. "Whoops! Our transport has reached its limit."

Kormèr angled the carpet away from the destruction. The air currents blew the smoke away from the half of the city that remained intact. In eerie counterpoint, the sun shone brightly on that half as if nothing at all was happening only meters away.

Spent, the carpet settled to the ground by a wide road on which a handful of strange vehicles sat empty and abandoned, their doors left open. The carpet remained just long enough for its passengers to disembark. Then it shrank and vanished.

A few hundred meters off to her right, Jeransy saw crowds staring at the unfolding horror or helping survivors that came running or plummeting out of the black to collapse into waiting arms and medical help. In fact, she spotted hastily cordoned areas where people tended to others, Averian, human and alien alike. Some were blackened and bleeding, others covered in soot and ash; some screamed, some cried, and others just lay there, motionless. No one had even noticed the trio flying in on a magic carpet.

Jeransy had seen a lot of death and violence in her fifteen years; but this amount of suffering was more than she could bear. She turned her eyes away in time to catch Anndrew wiping a tear.

"Is there anything we can do?" asked Anndrew.

Kormèr stood, nearly transfixed. Only his eyes moved, roving the wall of black smoke. "No," he said, his voice strained. "They've got this. Let's go." He turned and stepped onto a moving pedestrian walkway. This carried them along at ground-level, away from the disaster and deeper into the city. "See the yellow glow on the walkway?" he said after a moment. "Put your right foot on it. It'll automatically shift us over to that other walkway... now." They transitioned smoothly onto another parallel walkway that turned and climbed gradually through the complex architecture of the city. More walkways branched away toward different buildings and trees.

"These walkways are usually swarming with non-flying offworlders," said Kormèr. Now the walkways were almost deserted. News screens bordering the walkway flickered to life at their approach and flickered off once they were past. Other massive displays on the sides of buildings and trees remained on. All displayed a dizzying array of layered images of the burning city as commentators discussed the catastrophe in several languages.

Kormèr directed them onto a side walkway, and in moments, they rode into the lobby of a tall building. Stepping on a red glow on the walkway brought them to a stop. They hopped off and walked to a wall screen. Kormèr tapped the wall, and a soothing female voice asked, *"Welcome, Kormèr Lezàl. How may I help you?"*

"Personnel directory," instructed Kormèr. "Search. Jeremy Tailor."

The screen flashed, and Kormèr read the information it displayed. "Oh, good. He's still here."

"You do not currently have an appointment with Mister Tailor. Would you like to make an—"

"No, thank you," he interrupted, beckoning the girls to follow as he walked off. "This is one of the Terrans I flew here with," he said, stopping at a bank of lifts. "He'll be surprised to see me."

The lift door opened to a bright lobby with a gray marble-floored reception area. Floor-to-ceiling windows made up the far wall and afforded a spectacular view of the city. A human woman, neatly dressed in a slim jacket and knee-length skirt, turned away from the window as they stepped off the lift.

"Oh," she said, stepping back to the reception desk. She looked down at the desk, then up at Kormèr. "Good afternoon, Mister Lezàl. Would you like to make an appointment with Mister Tailor?"

Kormèr walked up to the desk. "Good afternoon, Penelope."

He knows her too? wondered Jeransy, then noticed the electronic nameplate on the counter.

"Jeremy and I are old friends," he continued. "But he doesn't know I'm in town, and I'd like to surprise him."

"You are *that* Kormèr Lezàl?" she asked, studying Kormèr's face. "I'm sorry, but he has mentioned you." She looked down at her desk again. "Your ident is a match, but—"

"I'm older. It's an Elmarian thing. So his office is… that one?" Kormèr pointed to a bright room with frosted glass walls.

"Yes, but—"

"Is he in a meeting?"

"Mister Lezàl, I need to—"

Jeransy followed as Kormèr walked toward the office door.

136

"Mister Lezàl, you can't just…" The woman tried uselessly to block Kormèr's path, but he ignored her protests and pushed open the office door.

Much as Penelope had been doing, a man stood by the office window, staring outside. He turned at the commotion. "Excuse me." He moved toward his desk.

Jeransy felt a rush of adrenaline as his movements triggered her danger-sense. She stepped up beside Kormèr and quickly sized the man up: he seemed to be around Anndrew's height, burly with a slight ash-brown handlebar mustache and wavy shoulder-length hair. And he wore glasses.

"I'm sorry, Mr. Tailor," apologized Penelope. "He says he's—"

Kormèr cut her off, saying, "I'd like to re-equip my D2-X8 with grav-repulsor suspension, and I heard you were the man to see."

The man peered curiously over his glasses at Kormèr for a long moment, then his face contorted into mixed expressions of surprise and great joy. "Kormèr Lezàl?" Kormèr smiled broadly. "You sonovagun!" The man walked around his desk to Kormèr, taking long, eager strides and engulfed him in a powerful hug. Over Kormèr's shoulder, "It's alright, Penelope, thank you." He stepped back to look Kormèr over as the woman left, and Anndrew stepped in. "How the hell've you been?"

"Well, you know how it is in my business: always take, take, take." They both laughed. "These are my companions," continued Kormèr, "Jeransy Bolsner and Anndrew Lee. Ladies, meet the man who revolutionized vertical landings, Jeremy Tailor."

"You're still collecting beautiful works of art, I see," Jeremy remarked, none too quietly. "It's nice to meet you both," he said to the girls. "Please, have a seat." He directed them all to a couch at the far end of his office, then took a seat across from them. "Penelope will be in shortly with refreshments, I'm sure. So, how do you like the new spread, kid?" He waved his hand around the room.

"Very nice," said Kormèr. "And congratulations, Mister Director."

"All thanks to you." To the girls, "Ladies, if you ever want to go places," he pointed at Kormèr, "that's the man to see. 'Cause behind all that wit and greed"—Kormèr gave him a disapproving glare—"you'll find a good friend."

"A friend who's willing to forgive and forget when an old friend calls him greedy," smiled Kormèr.

"Ambitious, then," Jeremy smiled back. "Look at you, kid. You look great, older… taller. What are you now, almost two meters tall?"

"Almost. A little over one-meter-eighty, last I checked. You look great yourself. Nice suit." He reached over and playfully brushed the grayish fabric of Jeremy's lapel.

"Ah, baloney. Sitting behind a desk for two years has made me soft." He sat back as Penelope returned with a small tray of drinks and sweets, and he patted his stomach. "And Penelope here is no help in that area. She's scheming with my wife to get me on a diet, I just know it." He gave Penelope a playful wink.

"Wife?" Kormèr's eyes went wide.

"A year and a half now. You've been away for a while, friend." To Penelope, "Thank you, Pen. Shut the door on your way out, would you?"

"How are the rest of the guys, Kit, Roke…?"

"Continuing the business. A few are back on Earth working on new developments. Kit's head of operations there. Mack's heading one of our branches on Beldar 2." He nodded. "Business has really taken off."

"That's wonderful! Congratulations."

"Thanks. You might have recognized the building's AI on the way in, too."

Kormèr took a moment before saying, "Stardust?" Jeremy nodded. "I thought the voice sounded familiar."

"I couldn't let that ol' gal just sit in a museum. I have her to thank as much as you."

A moment of quiet paused passed as Kormèr and Jeremy smiled at each other. Jeransy could almost see the silent exchange of old memories between them. She felt a bit jealous, wishing that she could have been part of those memories, that she could have met Kormèr when he was just around her age and seen him in action.

Jeremy broke the silence. "It's really great seeing you again, kid. You left so suddenly… I mean, you did say goodbye, but I didn't think you'd *really* go."

Kormèr nodded. "I had to get back home. You know how it goes."

"With you, yeah. The mystery kid." To the girls, "He was always popping up when you least expected it, then disappearing before you knew it."

Jeransy nodded, no doubt in her mind that it was true. Did this guy know about the portal? It didn't sound like it.

"I've settled down some."

Jeremy glanced at the girls, then back at Kormèr. "No offense, kid. But I don't believe it for a moment."

"I always knew you were smarter than you looked," teased Kormèr.

"Oh-ho! Listen to you," laughed Jeremy.

Kormèr tipped his head toward the large window behind Jeremy's desk, through which the thick black smoke was visible. "I guess I could've come at a better time. What happened? I only caught blips from the news feeds. Did a ship explode or something?"

Jeremy turned to look, instinctively. "No, there are safeguards against that." He stood and walked to the window. Kormèr and the girls followed him. "Early this morning, I got word that someone had been asking around for a ship. Now when I say asking, I mean demanding, to the point that it got on the CAB, you know, the citywide alert system. He wouldn't give any information; he just demanded a ship be given to him or else. He was an unknown persona, so of course, his request was denied all around. I reported him to the authorities; I'm sure others did too.

"So a few hours ago, he stood on top of that building over there," Jeremy pointed to a smaller, cylindrical building, "and... I don't know how, but somehow he destroyed half the city. Just like that." He snapped his fingers. "Thank goodness my guys have all checked in, and are all okay, but Freet-See..." He shook his head despairingly.

"He did all that, by himself?" asked Kormèr, horrified.

Anndrew asked, "What'd he look like?"

"He was only a kid, for cryin' out loud. Can you believe that?" Jeremy tapped the window and luminescent shapes appeared in the glass. He manipulated them, and a new image overlaid a two meter square section of the view. In the image, the city was still intact, and Jeransy saw the incongruent beauty of the architecture that Kormèr had described. The superimposition of this archival footage over the thick black smoke visible around the edges of the overlay shocked Jeransy.

Glancing next to her, she saw Kormèr and Anndrew watching in stunned silence, just as transfixed and horrified by the wanton ruination as she was.

Jeremy traced a square around the top of the cylindrical building, then swept his hands apart, zooming the image in toward that spot. "That's him. Like I said, just a— What's the matter?"

Kormèr had paled. "That kid is a little friend of ours that we've been chasing for just over two days now."

"Friend?" cried Jeremy, clearly missing Kormèr's sarcasm. "You had better judgment once."

"His being here is all a horrible accident. He's been to the Hovel," said Kormèr, gravely.

Jeremy's eyes opened wide. "Cris... he coulda killed us all."

Kormèr shook his head. "I don't think so... Maybe. He's so out of control; I just don't know anymore."

"And he's your friend?"

"Actually," grumbled Anndrew, "he's my classmate."

"Long story," explained Kormèr at Jeremy's confused stare. "We've been after him ever since he fell through my portal by accident."

So he knows about the portal! realized Jeransy.

Jeremy stared at him. "By accident? Most people just fall and break a leg. Only *you* would have an accident like this. Well, I hope you catch him... before he destroys the whole damn planet!"

"That's the plan. But we need a ship," said Kormèr, quickly.

"Oh, no! Not you too." Jeremy dropped into his desk chair, hands on

139

his forehead. "Aww, hell. Fine," he said from below his hands after a moment. He swiped a finger across his smooth desktop and it lit up, though Jeransy couldn't see the display clearly from her angle. "They won't like it— Jees, you never got a license, did you?"

Kormèr shook his head. "No pilot implant either, so I need manual controls. And scanners."

"I suppose you want it to travel through time too?" quipped Jeremy. Kormèr's eyes went wide. "No, I'm just kidding, but manual isn't standard anymore. Here's one; no AI. Atmospheric only?"

"That's fine," said Kormèr.

Jeremy deftly manipulated the data on his desktop with his fingertips. Jeransy moved closer and saw a schematic of the ship appear with specifications and cost. "I'll sign it out for you."

"Thanks, Jer. I'll owe you for this."

Jeremy called the ship an "RV with customizations" as he walked them down to the hangar. Kormèr seemed to understand the reference, but Jeransy did not. "I changed it after you told me about your magic carpet voyage," Jeremy had said. "Figured you'd want a comfortable place to wash up and rest." Jeransy understood *that* very well; she suddenly liked Jeremy a bit more.

The ship turned out to be a lot larger than she'd expected. It looked like a squashed egg with wings, sleek and electric-blue. Inside, it had a central corridor with three individual bunk rooms, a shared washroom, and a mess. Jeransy found some terms amusing, such as "head" for the lavatory and "mess" for the kitchen space.

Jeremy showed them to the cockpit last. Looking very self assured, Kormèr eased himself into the floating pilot's seat. He tapped a screen, and the bridge lit up with new lights as other screens came to life. "Pre-flight check," he said, as he watched as the various systems self-test.

Jeransy sat in the co-pilot's seat, which bobbed up and down for a moment as it adjusted to her weight. She looked in awe at the advanced controls. Anndrew sat behind her, keeping her hands on her lap, far from the complicated panels around her.

"Are you sure you know how to fly this?" Standing at the cockpit entrance, Jeremy's posture seemed tense.

"Jer, I flew your ship here part of the way from Io."

"Yeah, but there've been some changes…" He ran fingers through his hair. "Forget it. Good luck, and for crissake, try keeping it in one piece."

"Last call before take-off," announced Kormèr, loudly.

"Yeah, okay, bye," said Jeremy, taking the hint.

"I'll be back soon. Don't worry."

"Nice meeting you," called the ladies after Jeremy, as he turned to leave.

"Likewise," said Jeremy, then disappeared into the corridor. Seconds later, a red square on one of the panels blinked, then turned green.

140

"Reading hatch closed," said Kormèr, as he tapped another screen. "Departure clearance requested. Now, flight controls are… ah, here. Good. Not all that different from last time."

Jeransy felt almost no movement as Kormèr eased the craft out of the bay and onto the specified area of the pad, where he waited for the port controller to clear them. He announced everything as he did it, which Jeransy appreciated. She liked understanding what was happening.

"Of course," said Kormèr, tapping a screen. "There are clearance delays because of the… because of Cecil."

"What's the plan?" asked Anndrew.

"Sreet mentioned that the sorcerers use an ore called eleron when casting spells, and that ore is found around Averia. That's one of the reasons I wanted a ship; I figured we could use the ship's computer to identify deposits and quickly hit each one. But I also did a little research in Jeremy's office and found out that eleron is a very low-frequency radioactive substance. If Cecil is carrying the stuff on him, we might also detect him with the ship's sensors."

He stood and bent over the station at which Anndrew was sitting. "This is the nav console, but I think…" He tapped the screen and opened an overlay. "Aha, perfect. This is sensors. Now we just set what we're looking for, refine it… Once we get going, with any luck, we'll start getting hits from eleron sites. I see a list of three known quarries already."

Boop.

Kormèr returned to the pilot's seat and checked a display. "We're cleared for takeoff. Here we go." Jeransy watched the port drop out of sight on the forward screen, replaced by a smoky blue sky. Kormèr eased the ship up, retracted the landing gear and angled for clearer skies.

"There's a blip on the screen here," said Anndrew almost immediately.

"Tap it," said Kormèr. "That should pass me the information…"

"I get a menu."

"Or that."

"Sending to pilot," said Anndrew.

Kormèr pointed at a screen just as it flashed with new information. "Acknowledged. We'll be clear of Freet-See air space in three, two and…" He paused for a moment. "Here we go." He increased thrust, and they shot across the landscape.

After thirty minutes, Kormèr announced: "The blip matches one of the quarries on the list." The ship turned and set down on a large rock. "I'm going to take a closer look. You can stay here."

"Isn't the radiation dangerous?" asked Anndrew.

"It's VLF, so not very dangerous or even the Averians would be affected."

"I'm sorry… what's VLF?"

"Very low frequency." He put his palms up in front of him. "I'm no expert on what that means, but the text said that brief exposure isn't harmful. I'll be quick."

"I wonder if this ship has one of those learning computers that Kormèr mentioned," said Anndrew, "when he talked about learning the Averian language."

Jeransy nodded. "That would be great!"

"I'd learn Spanish so I can test out of it for the rest of high school. You know a few different languages yourself, don't you?"

"Three or four, but not very well."

"Still, that's very impressive. Are they required for school?"

Jeransy shook her head. "We don't have schools like you, remember? They're on the net, and you take 'em when you can. My 'rents make me study daily."

"Oh, that's very good."

"Defs. I'm not at all complaining. I like me studies. They're my ticket out of my city. Well, they were before…"

"Before Kormèr?"

"Yeah, for now." She turned to the navigation screen. If she looked at Anndrew, she'd have to think about the end of her journeys with Kormèr. But seeing the blinking dots and concentric rings of the nav screen distracted her just enough.

Fortunately, Kormèr entered the cockpit and sat back down in his seat. He looked at each of them. "Cecil was here, I think. There are signs of recent excavation, and I assume the sorcerers would use the quarries closer to Berdia before coming this far out." He flicked a hand at the nav screen. "In any case, sensors aren't picking up VLF outside of the quarries and Berdia itself. So unless Cecil is on the other side of the planet where the sensors can't reach, it might not have been him."

"Supposing we find Cecil," began Jeransy, "what've you got in mind to do?"

Kormèr mused on the question momentarily. "I'm not really sure. Fitzbew and I had planned on making him forget everything that's happened, but that avenue might be shut now. Thanks to Sreet, I missed my appointment with Fitzbew. But putting that aside, it required Cecil to be accessible, which he no longer is. My second option had been hypnosis, but even if I could get close enough to him, he'd have to be willing to be hypnotized for it to work."

"I wouldn't trust hypnosis," said Anndrew. "That's considered quackery." At the blank stares, she added, "Medical nonsense. It doesn't really work the way most people think."

Jeransy nodded. "That's true in my time as well. But I'll tell you what, I've seen people brainwashed into doing horrible things. Maybe we can use it the other way."

"Maybe," said Kormèr. "Unfortunately, our best option right now is to do as Sreet wants, which is frustrating since I blame him fully for this mess. Helping him is the last thing I want to do. But with Cecil as powerful as he is, we need the sorcerers to deal with him." He sighed. "We'll see. If either of you think of anything else, I'm always open to suggestions."

Kormèr paused, eyes locked in the distance out the cockpit window. "I'm starved. How about you?"

"Famished," said Jeransy. "Those little teacakes we had at Jeremy's were good, but scanty."

"Agreed," said Anndrew. "With everything going on in Freet-See, we forgot about lunch."

"I'm sorry about that. We can eat on board."

"I hope the ship has more than rations aboard, though."

"I'm sure there's some good food here. I survived on burgers and vegetables for days last time. Afterward, we can spend the night here rather than going back to the hotel. Is that alright with you?"

"Out here?" protested Jeransy.

"Well, in the ship, but yes. I'll seal the hatch and put up shields. We'll be safe. And the beds in the quarters are cozy."

"I'm fine with that," said Anndrew.

He tapped some screens, then stood. "The ship's secure. Let's eat."

CHAPTER 21

AN insect flew out of Freet-See across the bright Averian sky. Born aboard a starship amidst a shipment of organic material, she had fed and mated, then escaped her metal confines and gone in search of a place to start her nest. The metal and stone city in which she'd found herself had seemed idyllic at first. She'd tested a few locations that seemed suitable, but numerous predators had chased her away every time. She'd finally made it to an open space devoid of predators, but also devoid of suitable nesting sites. The dry, sun-baked rocks offered little in the way of protection or sustenance for her eggs.

Tired and hungry, she spotted darker patches on the rocks. She descended to investigate and found them to be organic, moist and with nooks that would hold her eggs safely. With no other apparent competition or predators out here, her children would thrive.

A euphoric feeling suddenly teased her antennae. It came from one of the nooks, and she felt compelled to investigate. She stepped down into the nook, eagerly searching for the source of the feeling. Suddenly, the stems pressed in around her. She tried to turn, this way and that, but she couldn't move. She couldn't even back up. The euphoria intensified until she didn't care that she was trapped, or that she was slowly being digested.

Sinking deeper into the carnivorous moss, her antennae twitched reflexively at a sudden change in the air a short distance away. At any other time, she would have flown away to avoid the abrupt disturbance, and the looming figure that emerged from it, but she no longer had the strength, or the will.

CECIL Murphy stumbled blindly, his foot landing painfully on an uneven patch of rock covered by thick, verdant moss. He immediately fell to his knees and hands, just barely stopping his head from hitting the ground. His mouth moved, but he couldn't talk. He could barely think, with one question repeating in his head: *What have I done?*

One entire half of the city had burned with a few simple waves of his hand, two spells joined hastily and unattenuated in a moment of anger and frustration.

No less than what they deserved! came this new thought, surprising him.

No! It's not what I meant to do.

Isn't it? They denied us a ship! At every turn, and for no good reason, they kept us from going home.

Cecil shook his head. *No good reason? Surely they had reasons… They told me their reasons, and they made sense, even if they weren't what I wanted to hear.*

You fool! They stood in your way just because they could, because they had power over you. And you let them.

No.

You had the chance to stop at the first one…

No!

…and take whatever ship you wanted.

No! No!

But Todd Meyers will always be bigger than you, and you'll never stand up to him toe-to-toe.

Cecil had learned early in his dealings with bullies that screaming into his pillow helped him release his anger. He imagined that screaming louder would help even more, and even if it didn't, maybe it would drown the voices in his head. Using magic to augment his voice, he shouted: "*NOOOOO!*"

The air shot from his mouth in ebony torrents, splattering onto the rock like thick tar. He watched in amazed horror as every last breath left his lungs this way. Drained and exhausted, he collapsed, gasping as darkness closed in around him. The pool of tar inflated like a balloon, rising from the ground and taking on a strange. Two angry almond-shaped slits opened, and red eyes stared at him. Then he passed out.

CONSCIOUSNESS came with a dizzying brightness, and Cecil squeeze his eyes tightly, immediately forgetting the dream he'd been having. The sun felt warm, but not hot. He wasn't even sweating.

Oh crap! How long have I been lying in the sun?! He sat up and gingerly tested his skin for sun burns. Thankfully, and much to his surprise, he hadn't burned. He squinted up at the blue sky; the sun had dipped toward the horizon. *Another future marvel, or something about this planet's atmosphere blocks the harmful UV rays. Is there anything about this future not to love?*

Whatever the reason, it took the edge off the residual anger and frustration he'd felt over Freet-See. *There will be other opportunities,* he thought. *I can probably just book passage on a transport, or whatever they call it these days. I would just need to steal whatever passes for currency—*

He froze at the crunch of gravel behind him. Slowly, he turned, and the memory of the moving tar rushed back to him. A creature of pure darkness lay sphinx-like on the rock.

Oh, my freaking god!

Its eyes glowed red beneath four enormous horns rooted to its head, two curving upward and two to the sides. The creature's black pelt seemed to absorb the sunlight as it lay there. It brought its thick tail into the light, and

145

Cecil saw that it terminated in a flesh-covered ball the size of a basketball pocked with long bony spikes.

It looked at Cecil and yawned, saliva dripping from dagger-like fangs. Then it settled its massive head back down onto its massive front paws. Its coat confused Cecil's eyes, sometimes looking like fur and other times reminding him of the slick tar he'd vomited earlier. The creature terrified him and yet… and yet he hadn't run screaming for his life. He didn't feel as if he were in any danger from this beast. But more than that, he felt a connection to it. The pieces worked themselves out in his head, a small logic puzzle requiring a tiny intuitive leap.

"You came from me," he said to the beast. "You're like a familiar spirit."

The beast regarded him, then groaned and set its head down on its front legs, these ending in large clawed paws.

I have a pet! he thought. Then he amended: *I made a pet. I guess I should name him.* The story of Prince Rupert came to mind, and he considered calling the beast Boy after Rupert's dog. But that just didn't seem to fit this creature. "Your name is Spot," he told the beast.

The beast's naturally furrowed brows rose as he regarded Cecil again, and Cecil sensed its acknowledgement. Perhaps mirroring his own hunger, Cecil also sensed Spot's hunger.

"Hmm. What do you eat?"

Spot clacked its fangs together, and Cecil sensed it would eat anything. So he conjured a heap of random food items, as he had done the day before. Spot stood and stretched languidly. It was taller at the shoulder than Cecil's 5 feet 9 inches, and easily twice as long from nose to tail. *Sheesh! How much of that stuff did I vomit?* Spot leaped to the other rock and sniffed the various foodstuffs, then tore voraciously into it.

Filled with Spot's satisfaction, Cecil conjured himself a big burger with ketchup, mustard, lettuce, tomato and pickles. He despised onions and didn't care much for cheese. He frowned at a French fry he found poking out of one side of the bun. *I didn't conjure that.* He plucked it out and ate it. *But I won't complain.* He took a huge bite of the burger and sighed.

"How about dinner and a show?" he said to Spot, and immediately felt good about having someone to talk to again. He set the burger down on a conjured plate and cast a scrying spell. Only this one didn't create an eye on the other side of the crystal ball. He realized that the glass eye had simply served as an anchor for the source of input. But the same could be done with air. He grinned as the crystal ball displayed a live image of Freet-See. He took another bite of the burger, then maneuvered the view along streets and walkways.

He'd been both amazed and disappointed by the city: this distant-future metropolis had him marveling at the advances in technology, yet certain things that he'd expected to be replaced by advanced tech still existed or hadn't reached the level of advancement he'd imagined. Manual non-robotic labor still existed; he hardly saw any holographic display screens; most disappointing of all, matter transportation didn't seem to exist. He understood the physical and computational complexities of the process, not to mention the moral and ethical ones that came with the potential for cloning, but he had expected that such things would've been worked this far into the future.

Cecil breathed a sigh of relief when the space port came into view. It showed some signs of damage from his outburst, and the ships all seemed to be grounded, but it appeared mostly intact. If he'd destroyed the port, he would've been stuck on the planet for much longer than he wanted.

He realized that his real disappointment on Freet-See had been with himself. His petulant outburst was an embarrassing testament to that. He had begged and pleaded for a ship like a fool, and then thrown a tantrum when he hadn't gotten his way. But now, he knew he was better than that. He didn't need to ask for anything. He could easily have anything he wanted.

He watched curiously as a small ship appeared from a hangar and hovered out onto a platform. This represented yet another area where Cecil had expected technology to replace organics: ship piloting. He could hardly believe when they'd asked him to show a pilot license before they could give him a ship. *How difficult can it really be?* he wondered. *It's got to be mostly computer-controlled.* He dove the view through the ship's hull and into the cockpit to see what exactly a pilot had to do.

And he nearly spit out the mouthful of burger. "Lezàl!" he sputtered. "They gave *him* a ship!"

He cranked up the audio and listened as Kormèr talked about eleron and how the ship's sensors could detect it. Cecil considered it almost lucky that, due to his miscalculation in Freet-See, he'd spent the entire load he'd picked up. Now he'd have to find a way to mine and carry eleron without it divulging his location. He could always keep the stuff stashed in a dimensional pocket that he'd created in his clothes. Even knowing of the pocket's existence, nothing in this dimension could detect its contents. As for the quarries: using magic, Cecil could obtain large amounts of ore in seconds and be long gone before Lezàl could catch him.

Lezàl had also mentioned Sreet. The birdman had told him about eleron, too. *Why would Sreet do that? He knows Lezàl is looking for me... Maybe he wants Lezàl to find me, but why? If he wants Lezàl out of the way, he can easily deal with the man himself... Of course he can, but he wants me to do it... like a test. He wants me to best Lezàl.*

He watched intently as they located a quarry, and chuckled when they admitted not knowing what VLF was. He followed Lezàl outside as the man inspected the quarry, the same quarry Cecil had used just before heading to Freet-See.

It then came as no surprise to hear Lezàl say that he'd been working with Fitzbew. Cecil knew that Fitzbew had ordered him banished from the Hovel, but he hadn't known that they could erase his memories, or that such a thing was even possible. This new knowledge became a factor in his decision to leave the planet and return to Earth. He knew there had to be a more knowledge stashed somewhere in the Hovel, secrets too dangerous to store openly in the general stacks of the library. Before he left Averia, he had to get his hands on those secrets. He would have to return to the Hovel. And that meant he would have to deal with Fitzbew. Perhaps if he could gain the mind wipe knowledge first, he'd use it on the old bastard. That would be justice!

The last he heard Lezàl say was something about putting up shields. *Now there's a technology that seemed impossible in the 80s, but that they solved— Hey!* The crystal ball blanked. He tried to wiggle the source, but found nothing there to wiggle. The shield had severed the connection.

Technology had interfered with magic!

Although he had inadvertently proven Cecil's theory that magic and technology were somehow related, Lezàl was seriously getting on Cecil's nerves.

Cecil removed his glasses and rubbed his eyes. He then squinted at the thick rims and fat wad of tape that held the bridge together. Someday, when he had more time, he'd do something about his eyesight. He still hesitated to alter his body with spells, but he couldn't, of all things, remain a blind sorcerer. He put the glasses back on, crooked, and focused on his next steps.

First he had to return to the Hovel and find any hidden tomes or scrolls. That would require careful planning. He felt capable of fending off two or three masters, but doubted he could handle more than that, yet. Throw in Fitzbew, and that number quickly dropped to maybe one. He put the logistics of that aside for the moment.

After that, he'd return to Earth, with—or without, depending on how step one went—the Hovel's most arcane knowledge. Home at last, he would catch up with all the latest tech, advances in mathematics, medicine… he might even consider enrolling in school and continuing his education. This far into the future, he imagined that humanity had evolved to be much more tolerant and educated than they'd been in the twentieth century.

Then he could decide whether or not to work on the problem of returning to the twentieth century, where he could be a god. He'd told Sreet that he didn't want to be a grand master, and while that was still true, his reasons had changed. Then, he'd simply still been interested in nothing but learning. But the accumulation of knowledge had to have a goal, something greater than the betterment of the individual. It had to be the betterment of society by those individuals capable of wielding great knowledge. Why else would fate have given him this great gift, if not to reshape society as he believed it should be? Once he demonstrated his power and intellect, the leaders of the world would bow to him.

That was his three-step plan, and he would succeed!

Spot's huge form flowed almost silently behind Cecil, where it settled onto the ground. Without even thinking, Cecil leaned back against it.

"Did you enjoy your dinner?" asked Cecil. The monster growled, and Cecil seemed satisfied with the response. "Good. Now it's time for me to plan. Step one…"

CHAPTER 22

KORMÈR stepped out of the portal and glanced left and right along the Hovel's corridor. No sorcerers were about. He sealed the portal, took a moment to orient himself—the doors all looked the same and had no visible markings to differentiate them. *This was my room,* he thought, pushing open the door and peering inside to confirm, *so the girls' rooms must be those.* He crossed the hall and opened a door. Sure enough, the meager belongings Anndrew had brought with her to the Hovel lay neatly stacked at the edge of the nest-bed. He smiled, suspecting that Srrcheel had been the one to arrange them that way. Kormèr stuffed them into his pockets, slid out and into Jeransy's room where he repeated the process. He then returned to his room and sat on the edge of the bed.

Moments later, the door opened. Silhouetted in the doorway stood Srrcheel. "I figured you'd be back."

"I hadn't intended to leave so abruptly. But we ran into some trouble and had to make a hasty departure."

The lamp glowed to life as Srrcheel closed the door. "What kind of trouble?"

"The Sreet kind. He kidnapped the girls and held them at sword point in one of those little cells downstairs."

Srrcheel's crest feathers rose. "What?"

"You heard it, buddy. Had them guarded by these floating green eyeball things. And he disabled my portal for a day."

Srrcheel's wings flicked irritably. "How dare he?!"

"That's not the last of it. He's got Sylvee too. Won't release her until I find Cecil."

"By all the gods! Come with me." Srrcheel made for the door.

"Whoa! Where are we going?"

"To see Grand Master Fitzbew. We have to tell him."

Kormèr remained sitting. "You tell him. I've already spoken with him and... well, there's not much he's willing to do right now." Kormèr didn't want to get into Fitzbew's troubles with Srrcheel. Fitzbew had revealed his issues in confidence, and Kormèr would not break that trust, even with Srrcheel.

Srrcheel's feathers fluffed in disbelief. "I seriously doubt that. He mustn't know all the details. He wouldn't let something like this go."

"You're probably right." This could be the perfect excuse for Fitzbew to deal with Sreet. He could even make an example of Sreet to force the other troublemakers to fall in line. But Kormèr had no time to waste with political games. "And I really hope Fitzbew finally takes this seriously. Sreet should be banished to the Forbidden Lands for this fiasco, or worse."

Srrcheel stopped and regarded Kormèr. "Worse?"

"You haven't heard?" Kormèr nodded. "Fitzbew must know by now; I'm sure law enforcement has contacted the Grand Masters already, even if the media is keeping this quiet for now."

"KL, what are you going on about?"

Kormèr breathed and let it out slowly. "Cecil decided yesterday morning that he wanted a starship. When he didn't get one, he destroyed half of Freet-See."

Srrcheel balled his fists in rage, then sighed and plopped down beside Kormèr. "I can't believe— Tell me he at least let the people evacuate first."

Kormèr shook his head. "Not a soul. Jeremy showed me the footage. It's terrible there right now, old friend."

"Why aren't we being deployed? We should be out there providing assistance, support... something! What are we here for, if not to help in times like these, especially when it's our fault?"

Kormèr always admired his old friend's earnest resolve and readiness to offer his help, for the good of all. "You know you can count on my vote for Grand Master, for what it's worth."

Srrcheel stood, walked toward the door, then turned to face Kormèr. "I need to speak to the Grand Master now and see if I can find out what's going on. I really hope he's preparing a support team for Freet-See and maybe just hasn't let the news trickle down. And hopefully a cell for Sreet, as well."

"You do what you have to do," said Kormèr, "and I'll do the same."

Srrcheel peered at Kormèr. "I hope you're not seriously considering going after Cecil."

Kormèr said nothing, just stared blankly at Srrcheel.

"You *are* crazy."

"There are other concerns besides me..."

"Yes, Sylvestra." Srrcheel threw up his hands. "Look, Kormèr, I'll worry about finding and freeing her. I'm sure the Grand Master will force Sreet to reveal her whereabouts. If he doesn't," again his crest feathers ruffled, "I will." And Kormèr had no doubt that he would. "You stay as far away from that boy as you can. Like I said, the Grand Master will probably have us hunt him down and deal with him in our own way. I'm sure Fitzbew doesn't want this to be any more of a public relations nightmare than it already is."

"Right, 'cause that's important," Kormèr murmured through gritted teeth.

Srrcheel looked at him evenly. "KL, I *do* care about the loss of life."

Kormèr calmed himself. "I know. I'm sorry. I didn't mean you; that was a dig at Fitzbew. It's just that this has gotten so out of hand. Sometimes I wish I could go back and undo it."

They were silent for a moment. Srrcheel held out his hand, palm up. "Well, why not?"

"You mean use the portal to go back and stop Cecil from falling through?" Kormèr had had this same thought so many times before that he knew exactly what Srrcheel meant. His own foster father, Yunzen Lezàl, had died at the hands of an intruder in their home when Kormèr was only two and a quarter Elmarian years old. He would give anything to go back and stop that from happening.

Srrcheel nodded. "Can't be done... and to be honest, I'm not really willing to try again. I did once, as a test, and what I tried to change happened anyway, if in a slightly different way." He didn't mention the fact that he now had multiple memories of the same event, and he couldn't tell which one had actually happened. "Which makes sense. What if I stop Cecil from falling through the portal? Then I'd never have had a reason to stop him to begin with, so he falls through anyway. It just gets crazy complicated."

Srrcheel's wings flicked. "Yes, yes. I get it. I can understand the filament principle behind magic. But one minute listening to your time travel nonsense, and I'm lost."

Kormèr sighed. "Sometimes I think I don't understand it either. I just go with the flow." He turned to look out the window. "I should be getting back to the girls. With that lunatic out there, I don't want to leave them for too long."

"And I've got to get to the Grand Master."

They both stood, and Srrcheel dimmed the light as he opened the door. Kormèr walked with Srrcheel into the corridor.

"Good luck, old friend," said Kormèr, clasping the birdman's shoulder. "And be careful. Sreet might be just as crazy, you know."

"Thanks for the warning. Be careful yourself." As Srrcheel started down the hall, Kormèr watched him go, wondering if or when he'd see the birdman again. He hoped the next time would be under better circumstances. He opened the portal and returned to the ship.

There, he set each of the girl's bundles on the mess table and keyed messages to alert them when they left their rooms. Assuming the girls hadn't slept comfortably out on the rocks the previous night, he expected them to sleep a while longer. He had gotten up before dawn to make the trip to the Hovel, but he almost wished he'd also stayed in bed. He wasn't tired, but staying in bed would've been preferable to facing the challenges of the day.

He sighed and strolled to the cockpit. The lights flickered on as he stepped in. He'd left the forward screen off, so the diffuse lighting and the instrumentation gave the cockpit a cozy, if claustrophobic, ambiance.

Kormèr sat in the pilot's seat and brought up a status list of the ship's various systems. *How many times did I watch Roke and Kit do this,* he wondered, *never imagining I'd be doing it for myself one day?*

"Hmm," he said aloud.

"Something wrong?" asked Jeransy from behind him.

He turned and smiled at her. "Good morning."

Jeransy stepped up beside him wearing blue jeans and a white shirt with its sleeves rolled up, her hair up in a bun. "Morning. And thanks for the stuff I left at the Hovel. How'd you get it?"

"I portaled over this morning."

She smiled and nudged him with her elbow. "Cheeky, you, sneaking back there."

"I also had to let Srrcheel know why we left. He didn't know… about any of it."

She sat in the co-pilot's seat. "What? Not even Freet-See?"

Kormèr shook his head. "I'll admit that I'm more than a little disappointed at the sorcerers."

"Disappointed? They're a bloody gormless lot of knob jockeys, them!"

Kormèr didn't understand a lot of Jeransy's colloquialisms, but he got enough of this one, and a smile burst past all his worries. "That… that's pretty accurate."

"Honestly, though!" she continued, still indignant. "What the hell are the sorcerers even here for if they're not going to protect the people?"

"Srrcheel said almost the same thing."

"Wish I'd been awake enough to know him better. Sounds like a good bloke."

"He's definitely a diamond among stones," said Kormèr, glancing back at the anomaly he'd left on the screen when Jeransy walked in. He tapped the screen and traced several lines, their function and status immediately appearing at his touch.

"So, what's the matter there?" asked Jeransy. "You had grunted as I came in."

"I'm checking the systems for a power leak," said Kormèr after a pause. "We lost some energy on the shields last night, and there aren't any records of animals or the like bumping into them."

"What d'ya think it could be?" she asked, activating the forward viewscreen. The cabin immediately filled with bright, early morning sunlight.

"Probably a frayed wire or some loose insulation, though I can't seem to find it."

"Is it a problem?"

"Not really. We're up to full now, and there's no more loss being detected. I was just curious why it happened at all." He cocked his head, hearing distant tinny music. "Do you hear—" He cringed as distorted sound blasted from the ship's internal communications system.

"Sorry," called Anndrew from the aft cabin once the noise had stopped. *Oh! She's also awake,* he thought, his ears still ringing. "What was that?"

"Annde's trying to connect her radio into the ship's comm system," explained Jeransy. "'Tis too bloody quiet in here, in case you hadn't noticed."

"Good idea," Kormèr said, unwilling to stop anything that was obviously bringing the girls together.

The music blasted again, then dropped to an acceptable level. Kormèr didn't think Jeremy would mind the minor upgrade to the ship; it could even be the next 'big thing' in starship technology.

"Alright, try not to go outside if you don't have to, just in case there is more to this shield issue. I've decided that I still need some proper sleep. I'll be in my cabin if you need me." He stood and disappeared through the doorway.

Jeremy had provided them with a very comfortable ship. He'd also included a few extras that he hadn't mentioned, though he had to have known that Kormèr would discover them. These included two, port and starboard laser lances, hidden top and belly dual particle cannons, short-range missile rack and a top-of-the-line tracking system for each weapon. In fact, the ship's programming contained an entire primary routine devoted to weapons control, something which Kormèr understood was not very common, especially for an atmospheric-only vessel. *I may not exactly know what I'm up against with Cecil, but I'm armed to the teeth.*

Music flowed through the comm system as Kormèr passed Anndrew, the latter still fiddling with cables and connections. He smiled approvingly at her for both the music and the camaraderie with Jeransy. As he stepped into his cabin, he briefly wondered how she figured out all these different systems with such ease. He guessed she just had a knack for it.

Against the far wall was his bed, covers still disorderly from the previous night's fitful sleep. *Trinket, this place could use a bot's touch*, he thought, longing for his little robotic servant. The idea of portaling back home, even if for only a few moments, tempted him. But he decided against it. He had too much on his mind to take home with him.

Kormèr sat on the edge of the bed and sighed. He then looked himself over, and his brows curled disapprovingly. *These clothes need washing, and I need a shower.* Kormèr undressed and dumped everything but his coat into the refresher, realizing too late that he didn't have a private head in his room. *That was stupid. I could've used the refresher feed in the head. Now I've only got my coat to wear to get to the shower.* While Elmarians had little issue with nudity, Kormèr understood that other species did take offense. *Oh, well. It'll have to do.*

Kormèr donned his coat, peeked along the ship's corridor from his door, and seeing Anndrew had finished and vacated the corridor, scooted into the head unseen.

"HOW do you figure this stuff out?" asked Jeransy, as Anndrew capped the wires and wrapped them with electrical tape she'd found in one of the maintenance bins.

Anndrew shrugged. "Wiring and stuff like that just makes sense when I see it. I probably get it from Dan, my brother; he's an electrical engineer. We used to take things apart together and try to make other things from spare parts." *Funny that I never noticed how much I actually enjoy doing this.*

"It'd be cracking if we could rig volume and station control from the bridge."

Anndrew tucked the wires away and stared at the radio sitting there against the wall. "That's probably a bit beyond my amateur skills," she said. "I don't want to damage the ship. This tap was easy; all the parts were already there except for the radio itself." Anndrew stood and mulled over what she'd just said. "Actually, you might be onto something. Let's look at the ship's menus and see if we can find where this feed actually goes."

"Do you have any brothers or sisters?" Anndrew asked Jeransy as they browsed through menus and schematics on the cockpit screens.

"It's just me," said Jeransy. "And that's alright. I couldn't imagine worrying over a younger brother or sister. Or having any more people worrying about me. Now that me grans are gone, it's just me and my parents."

"The way you talk about your hometown, it doesn't sound like a great place."

"It's a right shite-hole, is what it is."

Anndrew cringed inwardly, hoping she hadn't touched on too sour a subject. "Oh."

"That's why I want out. It's why I left with Kormèr."

If Kormèr was right and the portal had chosen her classroom to appear in so that Anndrew could fix it, Anndrew now wondered why the portal had opened to Jeransy's location. The girl didn't seem to have the skills for repairs, if the portal had even needed repairs at that time. Jeransy had said that the damage likely occurred during her travel time with Kormèr. So if the portal hadn't needed anything, had it sensed that Jeransy needed… 'repairing', so to speak? Or had it brought Kormèr to her for his sake?

Or maybe it's all random, and we're all just anthropomorphizing a simple machine. Ping-ing-ing.

The sound came over the cockpit speakers, startling Anndrew.

"Oh, hell."

Anndrew turned. "What happened?"

"I accidentally switched something on."

Anndrew recognized the image on the display from the night before. She stood and tapped the blip on the screen as she'd seen Kormèr do. A popup box appeared alongside it: "Eleron…" She glanced at Jeransy. "Go get Kormèr, fast."

Jeransy bolted from the cockpit as Anndrew continued reading the information in the box, location, distance, VLF readings in kilohertz.

Kormèr dashed in and flashed her a smile before glancing at the sensor display. "It's a quarry." Then he spun past her, took the pilot's seat and fired up the engines as Jeransy entered the cockpit.

"Strap in, ladies," said Kormèr.

Anndrew sat and watched the forward screen as the ground dropped away slowly, then blurred when Kormèr pushed the throttle controls. In only minutes, the ship overshot the quarry.

"Whoops," said Kormèr, guiding the ship through a graceful deceleration loop back to the site. He settled it gently to the ground. Then, with a few deft taps and swipes, Kormèr brought an image of the quarry up on the main screen. He magnified the image, then his hands balled into fists.

"Buomp!" Kormèr slumped into his seat. "We missed him again. He must've teleported in and out in a matter of minutes. Not even active sensors set at maximum can pick him up."

"How do you know it was him?" asked Anndrew.

He pointed to another smaller image superimposed over the main screen. Anndrew couldn't make heads or tails of the fluctuating colors. "By the amount of exposed seam," he said. "At least that's what the display shows. Someone recently removed a large amount of eleron from here, but there's no residue or sign of it having been mined. That means it was taken magically." He paused, his brow furrowed. "Of course, it could just as easily have been Berdian sorcerers preparing for Cheerretee."

"But such a large amount shouldn't be too hard to spot if we fly around," suggested Jeransy.

"True, but he could be anywhere on the planet. Even in this ship, a search like that could take a day. I'd hate to lose a day on the small odds that we'd cross his path. I have to imagine that a load that large, if he was the one that mined it, means he's got something big planned." He paused, drumming his fingers on his knee thoughtfully.

"Kormèr?" Anndrew had a question that she hated to ask, hated that it had even entered her thoughts. And she knew she'd hate it more once it left her mouth. "I'm starting to think that, even if we manage to return Cecil to Earth, he'll never be anything but a threat. God only knows how many people he hates after being picked on and abused for years."

"I must agree." Kormèr spoke slowly, the conflict inside him clear on his face. "Srrcheel said the sorcerers had their own ways of dealing with him." He shook his head. "I have no idea what that involves. With their reputation, they might want to… well, to kill him." His voice trailed at the end of the sentence.

Anndrew thought about that for several moments. He'd hit on her question. "What if that's the only way?"

"I can't accept that," he said sharply. "There has to be a way to reason with him or make him forget. Once we find him, we'll have more of an idea what we're dealing with. Until then, I'm not willing to rule anything out."

Anndrew nodded, hoping Kormèr was right. She would surely never sleep comfortably knowing that Cecil could, at any time, remember his magic and come after her for bringing him back to Earth. But at the same time, she would never be able to live with herself if he was killed for being nothing more than an extremely intelligent, albeit socially inept, kid.

"I've never had to kill anyone while I was robbing them," Kormèr continued, softly. "Or otherwise. I'd like to keep my record clean. But you've reminded me of that jewel I rescued from a life of boredom when we first arrived." He reached into his coat pocket and pulled out his funny compass. He read something from the display and typed it into one of his screens. "Please tap that new orange blip on your screen," he told Anndrew.

"Done," she said, tapping it and sending to pilot once again.

"Thanks. It's time to get that beauty back." The ship lifted off, then tore after the new blip on the scanner.

Anndrew was confused. "Didn't you give the… uh.. box… tracker thingy to Srrcheel?"

"Despite my better judgment," said Kormèr. "I like Srrcheel and all, but Averians tend to get crazy over gems, and this gem seems to be particularly interesting."

"What's so special about it?" asked Jeransy.

"I don't know exactly, but everyone I've mentioned it to thinks it's special. Srrcheel thinks it grants its owner powers." He looked over at her. "I didn't feel any different while I had it, but I'm going to take the chance that they're right. We're going to need everything we can get our hands on right now."

"Here we are," said Kormèr. Anndrew looked out the forward screen, but saw nothing except for sky and clouds. "We're high over Birshetland. There isn't a lot of air ship traffic out this way, so eventually we'll get noticed and someone will investigate why we're sitting here. But for a few hours at least, I've focused passive sensors on the museum, recording all movement in and around the tree." He typed on the keypad, and floor plans of the tree's interior appeared on the screen. "In a little while, I'll review that data and figure out a good way in and out."

"You're going to steal it?" asked Jeransy.

"Of course, love. Ideally I'd ask Sylvee to get it back, but she's still MIA. And I can't just knock on the museum door and ask them to hand over the most valuable jewel they have ever seen because I need it to save the planet." She shrugged. "Yes, okay, I could do that. But I don't have that kind of reputation around here. Besides, it was too easy to get the first time."

"Oh, was it really?" said Anndrew, pointing at her leg.

Kormèr grimaced. "A *little* easy. This time, it'll be much more fun." He stood. "Let's have some lunch. The ship will fly itself and alert us if any authorities come out to see us." As they left the cockpit, he added, "While we eat, I'll bring up all the info the ship's got on the jewel, so we can hopefully figure out what we can do with it."

CECIL'S arms flailed in a panic as his surroundings swam around him. This was the furthest he'd teleported himself in a single port, and either the effort or the distance left him dizzy. Fortunately, he was very familiar with the Hovel's library. After only a moment, the ill effect subsided.

He produced a basketball-sized quantity of eleron ore from his dimensional pocket and set it to levitate before him. And he began to cast.

Despite all the casting he'd done so far, seeing the glowing filaments appear in the air still awed him. The ghostly golden strands tickled his fingertips as he shaped them into the configurations of power. He worked the *srootee* carefully, making sure to get all the concatenators right on this new spell, a spell he had crafted himself over the past day. He estimated that this spell would take a few minutes to cast, but its effect would be instant.

At the proper moment, just before the main spell completed, a second spell spun the eleron cluster into a dense disk that gradually thinned and spread until it encompassed the entire vast room. It stopped spinning and dropped, coating everything in the room in a fine dust. Goosebumps prickled all over Cecil's body with anticipation as he looped his pinky around a filament and pulled. The spell activated.

A massive pulse of energy ballooned outward from the great library. It encompassed the whole tree in a second, and collapsed just as suddenly. In its wake, every magical tome, parchment and scroll vanished.

Awed by his own greatness, Cecil stared across the empty racks. It had worked! Everything was gone!

Alarmed twittering filled the room, then instantly drowned in a rumbling that vibrated through the floor. The stone racks crumbled into rubble around him, leaving him standing exposed and facing a furious Fitzbew, surrounded by a small mob of sorcerers.

Crap, thought Cecil. *I should've dealt with Fitzbew first.*

| |What have you done?| | sang Fitzbew in a low warble.

"Ask Sreet," said Cecil, in a masterful riposte. This would lay the blame for Cecil's actions on that bastard Sreet. He quickly cast a teleport spell to return him to the rock from which he'd ported in. He activated it, but nothing happened.

||Not so fast, little Terran,|| warbled Fitzbew, as another group of dark-robed sorcerers appeared around the room. ||You have our property, and we mean to get it back.||

If they can teleport within the Hovel... Cecil glanced up, cast, and vanished from the library. He popped into Sreet's room and immediately cast a quick spell. An image of the Hovel appeared in the air with red highlights showing all the stores of eleron within the tree. One load was right there in Sreet's room. Just as Cecil found the magically hidden stash, the door exploded off its hinges. Before the splinters even hit the ground, Cecil was off again. He hopped around within the massive tree, using the eleron stores as targets, bypassing the limitation of only porting to places he'd seen before. In this way, he easily stayed one step ahead of the mob. He imagined he had to be losing some pursuers with each port, since the younger ones wouldn't be able to port to places they hadn't already been. Of course, that would leave him with the more dangerous ones to deal with, if he found himself trapped. He just had to keep his lead on the mob.

Only one pursuer could track him anywhere he went: Grand Master Fitzbew. Cecil popped into a large observatory-like room at the uppermost level of the Hovel, the last store of eleron in the old stone tree. Fitzbew appeared on his heels and instantly launched pulses of blue energy at him. They coruscated harmlessly over a clear hemispherical barrier that formed between Cecil and the elder birdman, a trick Cecil had learned while testing various spells against Lezàl's ship the other night. Fitzbew gaped, visibly surprised, and Cecil reveled in the birdman's shock.

"Cute trick, blocking my teleports out," said Cecil. "Too bad you didn't think to do the same within."

||There are more tricks where that came from.|| Faster than Cecil could react, a flash of white arced around behind him and exploded, tossing him like a rag doll a dozen meters forward. Instantly, columns of fire lanced toward him. But Cecil recovered quickly, reasserting his shield. The lances ricocheted away, searing every surface they touched. Incessant percussive blasts slammed into his shield, pushing Cecil back toward the wall, three meters at a time, until it seemed they would crush him against it. Heat and a bright red glow alerted Cecil to the truth. He glanced back to see that the stone wall was glowing red hot, almost liquefying. And Cecil was being driven back right into it.

While hopping from room to room within the Hovel, Cecil had prepped a spell, linking the various loads of eleron for maximum casting power. He had left the spell primed, holding it reserve as a last resort. If the teleport-block lifted and he could just flee, the spell energy would simply dissipate. But Cecil realized he had run out of options. While he was more powerful than Fitzbew, he had neither the experience nor the stores of energy that the old birdman had. If Cecil didn't act now, he would die at Fitzbew's hands, and all his efforts would have been wasted.

He triggered the spell.

KORMÈR sat on the floor of his cabin, back straight, legs crossed and hands resting on his knees. He focused on his breathing, keeping his mind and body deeply relaxed. He had the plan all worked out: he would proceed the old-fashioned way and break into the museum without the portal. His insides tingled excitedly at the thought, and he allowed the feeling to pass through him, expelling it out a grounding point he had made through which such disruptive feelings could exit. He needed to be as calm and as focused as possible for what was to follow.

From studying the data the ship had collected over the past five hours, Kormèr had gleaned that the upper three stories of the museum rarely had anyone in them. He assumed they were used as storage. His plan hinged on entering through one of the three openings from the rooftop into the uppermost floor. Like the Cheerees Hotel, the museum had a central atrium to provide natural illumination during the day. Unlike the floors at the Cheerees, which were all the same size, the museum floors grew larger by closing off the atrium as they descended. The museum curators had suspended the Tseerleeltrr stone across the narrowest atrium gap on the second floor. Kormèr had easily found images of it all over the planetary network, resplendent in the light filtering down from the atrium's dome.

A soft chime sounded from his chrono sitting on the bedside table. Slowly, he unfolded his legs and stood. He'd left his black clothes neatly laid out on the bed. Moving slowly, deliberately, he dressed himself, including his black silk mask. Kormèr slid into his coat and produced his night-vision glasses from his pocket. He slipped them on and stepped out of his room.

The girls' voices carried to him from the mess as he passed. He stuck his head in through the hatchway and announced, "It's time. I'll be moving the ship."

Without a word, they followed him to the cockpit. Switching off all exterior lighting, he guided the yacht down over Birshetland and set it to hover just above the pseudo-tree that housed the museum. The Birshetland police would respond at any moment to the unauthorized ship in their airspace, so Kormèr had set the autopilot to fly off after he left. He'd then exit the museum and rendezvous with the ship and the girls at the city's western escarpment.

"I'll be back before you know it." Kormèr hoped his words would ease their concern. Then he headed for the side hatch. The hatch door opened, and the night chill hit him, the breeze whipping his coat around him. He tensed to jump onto a branch, when Jeransy's call made him stop. Her voice carried more than worry in its tone.

"What is it?" he asked, sealing the hatch and racing back to the cockpit.

"Something huge on active sensors," said Anndrew, turning in her seat excitedly to face Kormèr. "At Berdia."

Kormèr expanded the display, and more detail appeared. "Buomp! That's at the Hovel!" He dropped into the pilot's seat and disabled the autopilot.

The engines screamed as the ship dashed away toward the Hovel.

CHAPTER 23

KORMÈR fought off Berdia's Mesmer-effect, using the ship's speed to close the distance and punch through before it could distract him or force him to lose focus and crash. He didn't need to fight all that much, however, as he and the girls stared at the growing image on the forward viewscreen in disbelief. Fires burned and smoke billowed from the darkness where the Hovel had stood. Even the lighted gardens on the grounds around the old tree were dark.

Kormèr set the ship down on the same platform where Srrcheel had met them just days before. There was no one to greet them this time. "Stay here," he said as he grabbed the laser pistol from its recharger and stormed out and down the boarding ramp.

"Wait!" called Jeransy behind him, but he couldn't wait. He had to find out if Sylvestra and Srrcheel had been in the tree during the attack.

Beyond the platform, the landscaped gardens sat shrouded in near darkness. Still wearing his night-vision glasses, he saw debris scattered everywhere. He skirted large chunks of branches and walls, leaped over hedges, and trudged through smashed fountains along the way. The clearing where the Hovel had stood now held only acres of rubble. Of the Hovel, only a few floors remained, jagged walls glowing eerily through clouds of smoke and dust as fires blazed within.

Sorcerers from other sects were doing what they could to sort through the debris. Kormèr wasn't sure if they were searching for survivors or for salvage; he wouldn't put the latter past the lot of them. But when they saw him, they nodded solemnly and didn't try to stop him. An older birdwoman approached him.

||You are Kormèr Lezàl, correct?|| she asked.

||Yes. What happened here?||

The birdwoman shook her head slowly. ||Multiple explosions from within. It's… it's so horrible.|| Her song broke as she wept.

||Is anyone alive in there? Can you find them magically?||

She composed herself enough to answer. ||We only arrived minutes ago. We are creating search and rescue teams now. Would you like to join one?||

||Sure.|| But Kormèr knew full well he wouldn't wait around for them. ||Let me know when you're all set up. I'll be inside.||

||It's too dangerous!|| she called after him, but he was not about to

162

just stand around when one or more of his friends could be alive. He took a foil package from his pocket and tore it open, revealing a moist white cloth. He positioned it carefully over his nose and mouth, and it automatically molded itself to the contours of his face. One deep breath activated the filter.

Flames from scattered fires lit the way as Kormèr made his way over heaps of rubble. His head swam with memories of this grand, awe-inspiring place, and his heart grew heavy knowing that it was gone forever. He kept moving forward, motivated by the hope that he would find survivors in the devastation. And if one of the survivors happened to be Cecil, well... he'd think about that when the time came. In the meantime, he hadn't come across anyone, living or dead, which was odd given the magnitude of destruction.

He passed through a doorway and into a corridor with a rickety stairwell and several blocked doorways. Trusting ancient architecture, he chanced the stairs. With his night-vision glasses to aid him, he picked his way up the stairs with little effort. As he reached the second flight, Jeransy's voice carried up to him.

"KL, where'd you go?"

"JB, stay down there. It's too dangerous to come up." She didn't answer.

At the top of the stairwell, the floor had collapsed. But a room to the left seemed to connect around the gap. The ceiling had collapsed, and the items in the room had caught fire, leaving the floor littered with rubble and ashes and the blackened brazier that had fallen and set the room ablaze.

Kormèr stepped through a shattered opening in the scorched wall and into the next room from which he exited back into the corridor. Kormèr continued on and up another flight of stairs toward the nests. He found that nothing remained of these, as if the entire section of the tree had been blasted away. The remaining walls had crumbled, exposing the once-secret passages behind them.

A tremendous chunk of rubble suddenly dropped from above and crashed through the floor only meters ahead of Kormèr. Kormèr fell backward as the stone floor crumpled beneath his feet. He scrambled back on elbows and heels, away from the abyss that opened. He looked up instinctively, but he was sure no one had pushed the stone down. Other pieces of stone looked to be on the verge of collapse. *Maybe the birdwoman was right. I'm taking a big risk—*

He stopped, his ears straining to identify a sudden new sound. *Was that a moan? But from where?* With all the openings, it could have come from anywhere. Kormèr focused on his hearing, filtering out the crackling of the fires and the shifting of stone, until he again heard the sound. *Yes! There it is again. It's distant, but clearly there!* He listened again. It came from a secret passage, which now lay exposed.

Kormèr scrambled over a mound of debris toward the opening. *Someone's alive back here.* He darted through the narrow corridor, over gaping crevices, until he spotted an Averian pinned under several sections of collapsed wall. He recognized the plumage at once.

"Srrcheel!" Kormèr struggled to remove the large chunks of debris that covered his friend, now bloodied and pale, wings folded unnaturally.

"Kormèr," mumbled the birdman when Kormèr kneeled beside him, "you still... have the glasses. I knew you'd kept them... you bum."

Kormèr ripped the filter mask off his face. "Hang on, old friend."

The birdman raised his hand to stop him. "It's too late, KL."

"Stop talking nonsense," said Kormèr, too loud.

Shaking his head, Srrcheel smiled grimly. "You think I'd be lying here... if I were well enough to heal myself?"

"I don't know, you'd do anything for attention," Kormèr quipped to distract the birdman, while attempting to push aside the large rock that pinned Srrcheel's legs. "Do you know if there are others?"

"No. Cecil came... in the night. Caught us by... surprise. Fitzbew trapped him inside. But something... went wrong. At least my fellows went quickly." He gestured weakly to some scattered mounds of blackened ash that Kormèr had noticed throughout his search effort. Kormèr swallowed with the realization that the mounds were all that remained of the sorcerers of the Hovel. Srrcheel continued: "These pieces of wall... saved me, briefly anyway."

"What about Sylvestra?"

"I never found her. She wasn't here... that I know for sure."

Kormèr's heart lifted, briefly. But if Sreet had not brought her to the Hovel, where was she? He focused his attention back on Srrcheel. "We brought a ship, with supplies. If I can get you back—"

"Don't waste your... time." Srrcheel's energy was visibly fading.

Kormèr turned as steps crunched behind him. Anndrew and Jeransy stepped through the broken wall, both wearing headlamps. Upon seeing Srrcheel, Jeransy's delicate features tightened, and Anndrew gave a sharp cry. They both rushed over.

"I told you to stay in the ship," he admonished, his voice a little shakier than he liked. "This place is falling apart."

"Tough," said Jeransy, kneeling beside Srrcheel. Anndrew stood behind her.

"Good." Srrcheel paused, his breathing sporadic for a moment. "You brought your friends."

"Why?" asked Kormèr, not looking directly at anyone lest they should see the tears welling in his eyes.

Srrcheel did not bother to answer. Instead, he reached into a pocket in his blood-soaked robe and brought out a thin crystal of eleron suspended from a chain.

"If we sorcerers could not stop him... you will fail, as well... unless..."

He winced, his face grimacing. Clutching the eleron pendant, his hand rose and pointed to Jeransy. "Jeransy, I empower you with the knowledge of the gauntlet." Strain filled the birdman's eyes as he traced patterns in the air. The eleron glowed for a moment, and when the glow faded, it had diminished in size.

Kormèr watched Jeransy suddenly recoil, as though in intense pain. Her hands balled into fists, and she flopped onto her side in a dead faint.

"That's one... I invented for a raising." Srrcheel's voice was just above a whisper. "Use it well."

Srrcheel's hand swung around to point at Anndrew. "You, Anndrew, I—" He winced again, and when he opened his eyes, death loomed in his wide pupils. "I empower you with mastery of the flame." Again he motioned with his hands until Anndrew clutched her head, her mouth open in a silent cry.

"Stop it," hissed Kormèr in Srrcheel's ear. "You can use all this to save yourself!"

His breathing ragged, Srrcheel focused his eyes on Kormèr, and to Kormèr watched his features relax. "Kormèr Lezàl, my dearest friend... I give to you—" His eyes closed as he inhaled. In barely a whisper, he said, "*Everything.*" Srrcheel's eyes flew open, and his hands clasped around Kormèr's head with surprising strength. The chain with the eleron crystal fell around Kormèr's neck, the chunk of eleron glowing brilliantly. The space between Kormèr and Srrcheel warped around the light, holding the two locked together for only seconds. Then the birdman's eyes glazed, and his hands released Kormèr and dropped lifelessly at his sides.

Kormèr fell back against the wall, convulsing. Memories flashed through his mind like tiny explosions of images, sound and voices. Collections of *srrotees* tumbled like flood waters, filling every corner and crevice of his mind, so many wonderful and lethal abilities crammed into every little space... he tried to sort it all out... put this here, that there, this, that, too much, too fast! His mind reeled in shock. Then succumbed to darkness.

"KORMÈR." Jeransy's worried voice echoed in his head. He thought he heard himself respond, his own voice sounding weak and distant. Then her voice cleared. "Are you alright?"

"I think so," he said. *Why wouldn't I be alright?* he wondered. *Why does my head feel like I've had an entire bottle of—* Srrcheel! The memories returned sluggishly, as if wading through thick mud to reach his consciousness. *What did you do to me, old bird?*

He opened his eyes to find Jeransy cradling his head in her lap, and Anndrew keeping a worried vigil over her shoulder. But his eyes couldn't focus, as fine glowing strands crisscrossed his sight, blurring everything.

Filaments. The word came unbidden, and it took him a moment to connect it to what he was seeing. He closed his eyes again, taking quick breaths to fight a spinning nausea that threatened to overwhelm him. "I just need a moment, love," he said, his eyes still closed. "How long was I out?"

"Around five minutes," said Anndrew.

"How are you two doing?"

"A bit dizzy," said Jeransy.

"Like I just got over a nasty headache," said Anndrew.

Kormèr put a hand to his head. "Yeah, I feel both of those." *Sit up*, he told himself. "Alright. Here we go." He opened his eyes and lifted himself slowly. The action felt like an unfamiliar experience to him, as if he had never before sat up straight.

His surroundings swam into focus.

"Srrcheel." He clambered on hands and knees over to the body of the birdman, then steadied himself against the wall as his head spun.

"He died while he was... holding you," said Anndrew.

"Yes, I think I remember." Kormèr struggled with the memory, clouded by the tumult in his head and the depth of his grief.

"What'd he cast on us?" asked Jeransy. Kormèr turned his head to look at her. She stared at the length of her slender arms, clenching and unclenching her hands, as if she expected something to happen to them.

"I'm not sure," said Kormèr. He turned back to Srrcheel and gingerly got to his feet. "There's nothing more we can do for him. You should go back outside and wait for me. I'll be along in a few minutes."

"But we—"

"Please," he said sternly. "I need to do this alone."

"Alright," said Jeransy. "But we'll be right outside."

"That'll be fine. Thanks."

Kormèr stared at Srrcheel's body as their footsteps receded. He cradled the sliver of eleron crystal that remained on the necklace that Srrcheel had dropped around his neck. And as he did, he remembered Srrcheel's last words. Though the birdman hadn't spoken them, Kormèr heard them clearly in his head. "*Get Cecil for me, KL.*"

The words were so unlike Srrcheel that his uttering them at all was like a clarion call for Kormèr. If this peaceful, gentle and forgiving being had found it in himself to make such an appeal... Kormèr's nausea vanished. Holding the crystal around his neck tightly, he said, "The rules have changed."

He hated leaving Srrcheel there, but there was nothing he could do. The stone that had pinned him was much too heavy for Kormèr to push aside. And even if he could, the effort wouldn't help Srrcheel anymore. *He's not there,* he told himself. *That's just the shell he had been wearing.*

He turned and continued wandering around the more stable areas of the Hovel in the hopes of finding other survivors. It was a testament to the solid construction that any part of the structure was still standing. *What a phenomenal loss this is. All the history in these crumbling walls lost. What has stood for centuries, destroyed by such a petty creature.* He shook his head. No words could express the loss properly enough.

And all the people. Kormèr found many piles of ash and a few crushed bodies, some appearing gnawed on, with slashed flesh and bite marks on bones. Along the way, Kormèr raided any intact storerooms, chests and cabinets, taking anything that looked even remotely magical. After all, no one here would ever need them again. And the other sorcerers of Berdia would likely scavenge them, anyway.

As Kormèr worked his way back out of the ruins, he ran into the female sorcerer he had met earlier. Apparently, the Berdian sorcerers had finally begun their search and rescue efforts. He saw several others working behind her, using magic to lift and move debris. They each had a brightly glowing sphere hovering over their shoulders.

||There you are,|| she sang. ||It was very risky rushing in here like that.||

||The risk was mine to take,|| he sang as pleasantly as he could manage under the circumstances.

She peered at him, then nodded. ||So it was. Did you find anyone alive?||

Kormèr nodded. ||Yes. I found my good friend. Unfortunately, he succumbed to his injuries .||

The birdwoman surprised him by clasping his shoulder. ||I am truly sorry for your loss, Mister Lezàl.||

Kormèr looked at her as if for the first time. ||Thank you. You can call me Kormèr.||

She lowered her hand from his shoulder. ||I'm Sylveena, of the Sitachi sect. All of us here are Sitachi.||

||Very nice to meet you, Sylveena. Your tree is the Lacuna, isn't it?||

||Yes, it is,|| she sang, with surprise in her tone.

||I have only heard good things about your sect.||

||Thank you. Are you and your friends still interested in helping with our search?||

Kormèr hadn't found anyone, but that didn't mean there couldn't be some still alive under the rubble. ||Sure. We'll do what we can. My friends don't understand Averian Song, though.||

Sylveena smiled. ||That's okay. We have translation spells. We'll also cast some protection spells on you… if you don't mind. They'll keep you safe from falls and collapses.||

||Hmm. I guess I'm okay with that. But my friends will have to decide for themselves.||

||Of course. Your glasses, where did you get them?||

Kormèr tensed, worried she would try to collect them from him. ||They were a gift from my friend, from his first raising ceremony.||

| | I see. He really was a good friend. | |

Kormèr sigh. | | Yes, he was. | |

They worked through the night, sifting through tons of rubble. Sadly, they only found bodies, many of which were mere charred remains or piles of ash. Kormèr kept his eye on the other sorcerers, making sure that they didn't steal anything. But true to what he'd heard about the good-natured Sitachi, they took nothing for themselves. Instead, they gathered all the magical artifacts they found into a clearing that they had made roughly fifty meters from the foot of the Hovel. All Averian remains were also teleported there. By early morning, the search halted. Magical probes could find no further signs of life in the ruins.

Everyone gathered at the edge of the clearing, and Sylveena sang: | | There are no words for this, because this is a tragedy we never imagined possible. Each sect has its differences in culture, opinion, and perspective. But in the end, we are all sorcerers, and more importantly, we are all Averians… | | She looked at Kormèr. | | And highly honored guests. May this song lift our hearts. | |

She paused, then sang: | | Return brothers and sisters to the sun, the wind and the rain, to the air that we breathe with every breath we take. We will hear your song of hope and cheer, as you feel no more pain, no more fear. We will see you in the clouds above, and in twittered words of love. One day, we will soar alongside you; until then, we will listen for your song. | |

The remains were vaporized magically, in the custom of all the sorcerer sects.

You guys were weird, thought Kormèr, by way of his own eulogy, *but nobody's perfect, and you didn't deserve to die this way. Wherever you are, I hope you're all better off.*

Throughout the search and the brief ceremony, Kormèr had memories suddenly flash into his consciousness. Images, smells and textures seemed to trigger these memories randomly. Just now, the faint scent of sulfur and vanilla triggered the memory of a spell pattern—a *srootee.* He'd heard this word before, but the pattern of motions to cast the spell? That was not his memory; none of them were. *Srrcheel, is this your doing? Did you give me your memories?* He found the very idea intriguing but highly concerning. Srrcheel had obviously never done anything like that before; it seemed to be a very onetime thing to do. Had he been aware of any repercussions? *Should I be aware of any side effects? What if these memories replace my own over time?*

"Kormèr." Jeransy nudged him with her elbow.

This new discovery had him so distracted that he hadn't realized Sylveena was speaking to him.

| | Oh, yes. I'm sorry, I was— | |

| | No need to apologize, | | she sang. | | I understand. We are done here for now. We'll be returning to Lacuna. We'll return over the next few weeks

168

to clean up and restore the gardens, and to set some automated maintenance in place.||

||My friend would've liked that.||

Sylveena smiled. ||What was his name? Does he have family to be notified?||

||Srrcheel Froo-kee. No, no family that I know of.||

She nodded. ||I will petition that these gardens be renamed the Froo-kee Gardens, as his legacy.||

||He would've *really* liked that. Thank you so much.||

||Well, it'll be up for a vote and may not happen, but I will try for at least a portion. Now, if there's nothing else, I really need to rest.||

"How long will the translation spell last?" asked Anndrew.

||It will dispel as soon as you leave Berdia.||

"Oh. Okay." She sounded a little disappointed.

"It was nice having it while we worked," said Jeransy. "Thanks for that. And nice meeting you."

||It has been a great pleasure meeting you, Sylveena,|| sang Kormèr. The memory-flashes were coming quicker and becoming very distracting. ||I am glad for this chance to have gotten to know your sect.||

||You're always welcome at Lacuna, Kormèr,|| she sang, as she took a few steps back. ||We have no issue with visits from honored offworlders.||

||Who is your Grand Master?|| he asked.

She smiled at him again. ||I am. High sky, Kormèr Lezàl.|| She turned, unfurled her wings and flew off, leaving Kormèr alone with the girls.

"She was cool!" said Anndrew.

"Yes, amazing. Too bad Srrcheel wasn't a member of her sect instead." *He'd probably still be alive,* he thought. "I wish I could do more." Kormèr stared wide-eyed at the ruins.

"You've done a lot, considering you didn't really like these guys," said Anndrew.

Kormèr shrugged. "I take death very seriously. Actually, there's one last victim here that hasn't been accounted for." He pointed at the ruined pseudo-tree. "The Hovel. I may not know much about its history, but it deserves a memorial, I think. Whoa!"

A rapid series of flashes overcame Kormèr, and he staggered, bumping Jeransy.

She grabbed his arm to steady him. "What's wrong, KL?"

"Memories," he muttered. "Srrcheel's, specifically. I think he gave me a bunch of his memories." As before, the flashes were of a spell pattern, but only one, an enchantment... to protect the ruin from scavengers and... a recorded message to anyone who came within range. *Well, that's oddly convenient.*

"Is that what he did to us, too?" asked Anndrew.

169

"I'm not really sure. Maybe." He could picture the whole pattern in his head; it didn't appear very complicated. But would it work for him? *Why would Srrcheel have given me these memories if I couldn't use them?* "I'm going to try something… or I'm going to look very silly for trying. It's probably best if you stay here."

He walked back to the foot of the Hovel and through the one remaining archway that the Sitachi had cleared of debris. The receiving hall had fully collapsed under the weight of the floors above, but a member of the rescue party had magically carved a passage and steps through the pancaked floors. Kormèr climbed these to the top of the central rubble pile. There he worked through the pattern of a spell, moving his fingers, arms and hands as directed by the memory. But nothing happened when he finished.

<<Of course that didn't work,>> he mumbled to himself in Elmarian. Then he snapped his fingers. <<Maybe an artifact!>>

He focused on the properties of the spell he wanted, reached into his coat pocket and found three wands and a stone tile the size of his hand. Based on the inscriptions on the wands, he tossed two back into his pocket outright. But that left him with one wand and the tile. <<What am I supposed to do with you?>> he asked the tile. It gave him no answer.

Kormèr nearly dropped the tile when a series of three memories flashed through his mind. One showed a similar tile being placed on the ground and the other two were of sorcerers casting spells on the tiles. In one memory, he could clearly see the tile and a glowing red glyph on it.

Kormèr set the tile down on the rubble. Immediately, the wand felt lighter in his hand, and based on the pattern he'd just tried, he felt he knew what to do. As he traced the glyph he'd seen in the memory with the wand, he recited what he knew of the history of the Hovel, of the Hawk Sorcerers, and of the greatness that the destroyed pseudo-tree once held.

Though there was little left to steal, Kormèr added a warning to trespassers of certain injury if they attempted setting foot on the site. It was no idle threat, for part of the spell contained a ward that would cause trespassers to feel terribly weak for days after crossing a threshold. Kormèr intended no cruelty, but he wanted the place respected, honored… Srrcheel would have wanted it that way.

When Kormèr finished the recording, he traced a loop with the wand. The wand pulled his hand down until its tip pointed at the stone tile, and a faint white spot formed and sizzled over the glyph. The time had come to set the threshold. Kormèr retraced his steps to the entrance, wand and spot tracing a glowing, sparking line behind him. He walked past the arch and around the entire base of the ruined tree until he closed the line. The line pulsed and shot upward, leaving behind a shimmering transparent wall around the ruin.

The wand dissolved.

"Was that it?" asked Anndrew, her voice low and sluggish. She and Jeransy both looked exhausted.

"Yes, I think so." He wanted to do more, but he too felt exhausted and out of ideas on what more could be done. Not even the bright sunrise could lighten the heaviness in his heart. "Let's go back to the ship. We'll just spend the night here and figure out our next steps after a good night's— after some rest."

MOONLIT darkness.

Scuffling of feet and claws on stone.

A sudden flare of blue-white light.

In the magical fire's light, Cecil and his creature, Spot.

Cecil staggered and fell on his rear, arms behind him, uselessly trying to cushion the impact. His spine jarred all the way to his neck, and he dropped painfully to his back. His fingers clawed the stone in frustration as spots filled his vision. "Aaaggghh!" he cried, angry at the weariness that overcame him like no other he'd ever experienced. He had used a good amount of energy to wreck the Hovel, and now he had to rest. *Okay, no more casting for a while.*

Spot nuzzled him, worried.

"I'm fine, just tired..." But with those words, exhaustion overcame him.

Cecil opened his eyes to a gray twilight sky. *Dammit, I passed out.* Grunting with effort, he lifted himself up onto his elbows and looked down at his burned and tattered robe.

"Stupid sorcerers!" Cecil spat. He regretted having had to destroy the Hovel; after all, there had to have been Averians like him there, deeply interested in study. But what truly bothered him was how badly he had overestimated his own capabilities. If not for his quick thinking, he would not have escaped Fitzbew's trap. As it was, his magical shield had barely helped him survive the explosions he had triggered. He had been tossed around like a rag doll, and buried in a heap of debris, barely conscious. It had taken him at least ten minutes to muster up the energy to teleport away.

Spot growled in sympathy. Cecil looked over at his creature, not too pleased that it had simply stood by instead of rescuing Cecil from the debris. Cecil pushed himself the rest of the way up to a seated position.

"They ruined two-thirds of my plans. Even Sreet died before I could get to him." He sighed. "But at least I'm free of them. Now that they're out of the way, there's no one to stop me." That thought gave him strength, and he stood, slowly. Once again on his feet, he closed his eyes and breathed deeply of the crisp morning air. When he opened his eyes, they sparkled with renewed vigor. "Without the sorcerers backing him, this Lezàl is an annoyance easily dealt with. And Lee... well, once she sees how powerful I've become, she'll come to my side."

He imagined himself relaxing in an enormous room, books lining the walls from floor to high ceiling and Lezàl in a cage hanging overhead like a trophy. Todd Meyers would be Cecil's foot rest. To Cecil's left, Anndrew Lee on her knees, head bowed, handing him a book while the Bolsner girl fanned him with a large Argent feather. All of this was now his for the taking.

"No one can stand in my way!" he cried out into the darkness.

Spot growled/laughed.

"Yes, my pet. In *our* way."

As his euphoria ebbed, his stomach growled. "It's time for me to eat."

Cecil tested a small conjuration spell, and a plate appeared with an apple on it. Instantly he was nauseous. "Damn! I guess this'll have to do for now."

He bent over to pick up the apple, then stopped.

Something's not right. His wide eyes scanned the darkness, but the uneasiness he felt did not come from his immediate surroundings. *No, it's not here.* He searched further with his mind. *It's at the Hovel!* he thought, sensing a disturbance in the magical ether. *But I made sure there was no one left alive, dammit. My crystal ball—*

He reached into a fold in his robes and produced the transparent sphere from the pocket dimension. The spell to activate it was a small one, and he began tracing the pattern. As he completed the spell, the ball glowed blindingly and emitted streams of searing light that encircled Cecil's head. Cecil screamed, his mind exploding with pain and the vision of one man who now had a protection spell around him. "LEZAAAAAL!"

CHAPTER 24

KOO-RREE Freesewee swept down and landed gracefully in front of the Birshetland Police station. A few officers standing by the front door stood at easy attention as he entered. Almost as one, they greeted him. ||Good morning, Captain.|| One added, ||Welcome back, sir.||

||Good morning, everyone.|| He went inside, where the process repeated itself as he made his way to his office. After a week of mandatory leave at the resort city of To-Weetsa-Woo, he was glad to be back. Not that he hadn't enjoyed the time off, but he missed the bustle of the station and the work itself. Birshetland might not be Freet-See, where he'd started his career, but it had opened its doors to more and more offworld business over the years. And handling that kind of traffic fit squarely in his gizzard.

He passed Chief Sylvestra's office, a little disappointed that she had her privacy screen up. She would know he was back, of course, but he wanted to check in with her anyway, in case she had anything for him to jump on immediately. Especially considering the disaster at Freet-See. He'd wanted to cut his leave short when he saw the media footage, but unless the Chief specifically recalled him, he was mandated to complete his time off.

Now back in his office, the first thing he did was check in on the investigation on AvoNet. The global police network wouldn't have every detail, but it would certainly have more than the public media. He almost couldn't believe what he found. *A Terran sorcerer!* That had certainly been withheld from the public media. Such a thing would have caused a major panic in every city around the planet.

How could a Terran know magic? he wondered. He'd never heard of Terran sorcerers before. If they could also have sorcerers, then what other species couldn't? That could be very problematic. He found a note that Berdia had been contacted. The head of the Sitachi sect had jumped at the opportunity, and Fitzbew of the Falconi sect had responded with his usual calm aplomb. That eased some of Freesewee's tension; he wouldn't want to deal with a rogue sorcerer without their support.

Strangely, the Terran didn't show as having registered on arrival at Freet-See. That happened occasionally; he'd had some ideas on how to cut it down, but had been transferred before he could propose them. It pained him to see his former city in such a mess, when it might have easily been prevented.

With nothing more to learn about that investigation, he flagged it so that it would alert him of any updates, then closed the file.

Switching tracks, he opened his mailbox and grunted at seeing over eight hundred new messages. He pushed that aside, and focused instead on the task list he'd left himself before signing off a week ago.

Aha! The duty schedule for the next three months. He flicked the file from his desktop to his wall and reviewed the schedule. This schedule included mechanical and non-mechanical personnel. He had three patrol bots in the shop for repair at the moment. That left eight in operation and two in reserve, which for a city the size of Birshetland, was enough. He had five of his Averian staff going on holiday next month and six the month after. The office would be fully staffed for the last month on the schedule.

||Approve,|| he twittered, and the large display flashed a pastel green, then cleared.

Freesewee turned back to his task list and closed the first item. He grunted as the second one appeared. It read: *Read your damn emails!*

With a deep breath, he reopened his inbox and started on the emails. After a few hours, which included a few interruptions from his sergeants reporting in, he'd reached the end of the emails.

That wasn't so bad, he thought, checking the task off on his list. The next task appeared: *Go eat something.*

He chuckled. *I know myself too well.*

He checked the time, and it actually was time for lunch. Freesewee usually brought lunch from home and ate in his office. But as much as he'd enjoyed the relaxing atmosphere of To-Weetsa-Woo, the restaurant fare there didn't compare to that of his favorite haunt here in Birshetland. It was a small place downtown, but they made the second best mealworm crumble he'd ever had. His mother still made the best, of course.

||Ring the Chief,|| he called into the air, figuring he'd ask Sylvestra if he could pick her up anything… or perhaps if she would like to join him. She occasionally took him up on his offer to bring her back a drink or a dessert. But she rarely ate lunch out of her office.

The comm chimed softly several times. ||Discontinue ring. I'll just stop by.|| He stood and headed out of his office. Her office was next to his, but between the privacy screen and her not having stopped in to see him, he hadn't wanted to bother her.

Out in the hall, Freesewee found that Sylvestra still had the privacy screen up. He swept his hand over the sensor next to her office door and waited a moment before repeating the gesture. Then he rapped on the door and chirped, ||Chief? It's Freesewee.|| But there was no answer.

Concerned, he turned from the door and stared into the distance, trying to think of where the Chief might be. His stare returned to the corridor in which he stood in time to see the department go-for passing.

||Srreedee, hold up,|| called Freesewee. The youngster stopped.

||Yessir.||

Freesewee approached him. | | Have you seen the Chief today? | |

| | No, sir. She hasn't been in all day as far as I know. I don't know if she left word, but I can find out. | |

| | Do that, please. I'll be in my office. | | Freesewee turned and left the youngster scooting along his way. He returned to his office but could not relax.

It was unlike Sylvestra to take time off without warning, even if she was ill, which Freesewee had learned of her, was very irregular. The more he thought about it, the more he grew worried.

She had been uncharacteristically distracted the day Kormèr Lezàl had been spotted entering the city. Freesewee had tried to intercept the report of Lezàl's arrival, but Sylvestra had had strict instructions in place to have any sighting of Lezàl reported to her immediately. She had disappeared for several hours after that, but she'd turned up at her home later in the evening.

Freesewee knew there was some kind of history between Sylvestra and Lezàl. Freesewee had been transferred from Freet-See shortly before the jewel heist three years ago. He'd arrived and gotten acquainted with the Birshetland department in the midst of all the chaos that the heist had caused. He'd also been present when Lezàl had solved the case. There had been much resentment from those involved, and though Freesewee had only been at the periphery of the case, that bias against the Elmarian had rubbed off on him.

Freesewee's subsequent promotion to captain had been a great honor, but one that had come with a not-so-small price. He had found himself in the awkward position of having to quash the department's grumbles as Sylvestra continued spending time with Lezàl. The two were seen together frequently, dining or at the theater or museums... even at each other's residences. It was obvious that they'd been having an intimate relationship. Freesewee had had enough respect for Sylvestra, and for himself, to only broach the topic with her once. She had thanked him for his concern, and that had been that.

Then one day, seven or eight months later, Lezàl had simply vanished.

Freesewee had grown closer to the Chief in that time as well, and he could see that she was grieving. But she'd hidden it well. Sylvestra had busied herself with work, and Freesewee had found himself falling for her. But their relationship, though beyond strictly professional, had remained very platonic. They occasionally dined together, or went to a show or even worked late at each other's homes when a case called for it. But neither had ever made a move to take their friendship to the next level. Which was fine with Freesewee. He was perfectly happy spending time with the wonderful woman. He would continue to do so and hope that someday, perhaps, they would grow to be something more.

But now Lezàl was back, and things were uncertain. Why was he back? Where had he been these past three years? And more importantly, what were his plans for Sylvestra?

But the pressing issue now was, where had *she* disappeared to?

Srreedee returned quickly. ||No word, sir. No one in the department's seen or heard from her for three days.||

||Thank you.|| But his mind was elsewhere now. *Three days?! With me away and after what's happened at Freet-See?*

||Can I get anything else for you, sir?||

||Hmm. No, that'll be all.|| The boy left. Freesewee called Sylvestra's personal comm, then her home line. But she answered neither.

Something's seriously wrong. He walked out onto the precinct floor and signaled for everyone's attention.

||I don't care why no one mentioned to me this morning that the Chief's been missing for three days,|| he chirped. ||But if that happens again, there will be hell to pay.|| He pointed at his sergeants and lieutenants, and signaled them to follow as he walked to a sit room. When they'd all gathered, he closed the door.

||Sir, I—|| began one of the sergeants, but Freesewee cut her off.

||What do we know, folks?||

They all looked at each other, their body language showing their unease. Sergeant Tseeo, the most veteran of the group, spoke up first. ||Sir, she didn't leave any word. She had the privacy screen up, and we... well, we assumed she was working on something big.||

||That would've been a fine excuse, if not for three things: I was on leave; Lezàl is in town; and Freet-See.|| He stressed the last point. ||Have you seen the footage on AvoNet?|| They all had.

||We need to be better, folks. I *know* you're better than this. Lieutenant K'swee.||

||Captain?||

||I want you and your partner on surveillance outside of the Chief's flat.||

||Yessir.|| She left the room.

||Sergeant Tseeo, get all staff and bots on alert for any sign of her.|| He pointed at the Sergeant. ||No media, understand?||

||Yes, sir. What about Lezàl?||

Freesewee knew that Tseeo also had some history with Lezàl. In fact, Tseeo's poor choices in dealing with Lezàl had cost him the promotion to captain. ||You have your task, Sergeant.||

||Right, sir.|| And he was off.

||The rest of you, find out what you can about what the Chief was last working on. I want a full account of the last day anyone saw her. That includes video footage... anything. And Sergeant, make the Cheerees part of your search route. If you end up around Lezàl's room, ask him if knows anything and if he wouldn't mind coming down to the station to answer some questions.||

||Just like that, sir?|| asked the sergeant, subtly asking for permission to be more aggressive. The problem was, Lezàl's mere presence on Averia hardly counted as a justifiable cause.

||Just like that.||

Freesewee returned to his office and went through his mail once more, hoping he'd merely missed some note from Sylvestra in the volume. He then overrode the lock on her office door and searched her office for any clues, disabling the privacy screen along the way.

Freesewee ached to be out in the field, to be doing more. But he had to wait for his teams to report in. He busied himself by calling some of the places Sylvestra frequented: her favorite eatery; common friends and family; other people and places that the precinct staff wouldn't know much about, but that he was familiar with. Many hours passed before Freesewee received the answer he had been hoping not to receive. But his efforts turned up nothing.

||Captain?||

Freesewee looked up. ||Ah, Sergeant, come in. What've you found?||

The Sergeant entered the office, activated her data pad and swiped it up onto the wall display. ||No one has found any sign of the Chief. We found Kormèr Lezàl, however. Word is he is traveling around in a rented mini-yacht with two Terran females, Jeransy Bolsner and Anndrew Lee. All three were tagged by robo-patrol four days ago—that alert was sent to the Chief—and all were unregistered at any port.||

Freesewee shook his head at this news. *How does he keep doing that?* he wondered, angrily.

With a few deft strokes, the Sergeant moved chunks of data from her pad onto the display. ||A bartender and surveillance footage place Lezàl with the Chief at the Cheerees Hotel, also four days ago. Shortly after, the Chief visited the Foosee Museum, where she donated a rare gemstone for their collection.|| She checked her notes. ||We have a record of the Chief arranging passage for Lezàl and the two females to Berdia, and eyewitnesses that saw him leave by carrier bird in the middle of the night. That was just over three days ago. The last person to see the Chief was her doorman as she returned home that same night. Her badge is in her flat, and records show it's been there for three days.||

||I see.|| So there was nothing to tie Lezàl to Sylvestra's disappearance. His leaving Birshetland the night she vanished closed that avenue, more or less. But there were questions that this raised as well. Why was Sylvestra arranging passage for Lezàl and his companions to Berdia? Why in the middle of the night and with such urgency? What the hell was Lezàl doing back here, anyway? Considering the Terran sorcerer, the link between the Chief, Lezàl and Berdia troubled Freesewee deeply.

||Thank you, Sergeant,|| sang Freesewee.

||There may be more, sir.|| She cleared the display, dumping all the contents into a case folder. Then she highlighted another case folder. ||We had a report of a Terran falling into one of the public baths. Since this happens now and then, no one thought much about it.||

||Who is the Terran?||

||He was unregistered.||

Freesewee's crest feathers perked. ||Go on.|| His song sounded calmer to him than his racing pulse felt.

||When word of this got to the Chief, she got very agitated. She asked for the enhanced cit-cam footage and images, and then met with Lezàl again at the Cheerees. After that, she returned here to book Lezàl's passage to Berdia.||

Freesewee nodded perfunctorily. ||Play the footage, please.||

||I can't, sir. The file is locked.||

Freesewee drummed his fingers on the desk. He had privileged access to Sylvestra's private case files, just as she could access his. But did he want to open this in front of the sergeant? He decided to do just that. He'd been fostering a sense of trust with his direct reports, and this situation called for just that.

He keyed the file to open, and the sergeant stood by as he looked through its contents. He read through the short report of the Terran boy falling from the sky into a public bath. Sylvestra had added a few follow-up notes. One was an identification of the man that had rescued the boy and later taken him to Berdia. A sorcerer-recruiter for the Hawk Sorcerers named Sreet! Another was a brief explanation of why she was using precinct funds to send Lezàl to Berdia after the boy and a link to the receipt. And there the follow-ups ended. How Lezàl had gotten to Freet-See was a mystery, which was no surprise. Freesewee recalled that three years ago, it had been the same way. Somehow, Lezàl always came and went without the port authority's knowledge.

Freesewee ran the cit-cam footage, and in his shock missed the chance to pause when the clip focused on the Terran. He replayed the footage, and this time paused it at just the right moment. He split the screen and played the footage from the Freet-See disaster.

||By all that's sacred!|| The Sergeant's crest feathers tensed. ||It's the same Terran! He's a sorcerer.||

||And once again, Lezàl seems to be in the center of it all.|| *But this time, I'm here to keep Sylvestra from taking any heat.* ||I want a location on Lezàl's ship—||

An officer stopped outside the office door, waving through the glass partition until Freesewee waved her in. ||Sir, a mini-yacht was recorded operating illegally over Birshetland airspace last night. It's registered to Kormèr Lezàl.||

Yes! You've finally given us cause, Lezàl. | |Where is it now?| | Freesewee grabbed the data and adding it to the case file.

| |It flew off eastward.| |

| |Thank you.| | *That means either Freet-See or Berdia.* To the sergeant, he sang, | |Find Tseeo. I want each of you to select two squads of twenty each, day shift, night shift... include anyone with combat training. I'll prep a command team for the frigate.| | He'd have to inform the Mayor of the operation, but he felt confident he would have no problem getting authorization.

| |Yessir. What's the target?| |

| |Lezàl's ship.| |

CHAPTER 25

KORMÈR stared at the ceiling of his cabin as easy instrumental tunes played through the comm speakers. He felt little better for his fitful six-hour rest. *Too many good people have died,* he thought, his hands clenched into fists. *And all by Cecil's hand.* He shook his head, slowly, overwhelmed by the idea of this stupid kid having such power that even the sorcerers could not stop him. *Just like Srrcheel had warned... Poor Srrcheel.* His eyes watered at the memory of the birdman. *He was such a great guy, and a wonderful friend.*

And it's my damn fault he's dead! I brought Cecil to Averia!

But not to Berdia, argued some other, more logical side of him.

Does it matter? he returned. *If I leave a knife out and someone steals it and uses it to hurt someone, it's still my fault for leaving the knife out.*

The argument sounded weak, even to him. There had been a series of failures that had aligned perfectly to allow the situation to get to this point. Some of those failures came from Cecil himself, or at least from his life experiences. *Why couldn't someone like Jeremy or Srrcheel have fallen through my portal instead? Good folk with good intentions.*

He wiped his eyes. *This what-if nonsense is getting me nowhere. I need to think clearly.*

Srrcheel had given him a gift, a mass of knowledge delivered in haste and now a tangled mess inside Kormèr's head. *I have to sort through all this if I'm going to keep my promise to Srrcheel. I just hope it's enough to stop Cecil. It's got to be enough. But if the Hawks failed to stop him...* Kormèr pushed away that thought. He didn't like to dwell on negative possibilities; thoughts like that led nowhere.

He took a deep breath and got up from the bed. *Speaking of failures...* He recalled his failure to cast the enchantment spell over the Hovel. He thought he had followed the *srootee* exactly. He tried it again, amazed at how the pattern came to him so clearly as he went through the motions. He completed the pattern, but once again, nothing happened.

I must be missing something— From the corner of his eyes he saw something shimmer, but when he looked, it was gone. *There has to be more to casting a spell than just these patterns; after all, what prevents someone from just making these motions by accident and triggering a spell?*

He blinked and again the shimmer caught his eye, but once again, it vanished when he looked for it. But this time, the shimmer triggered a memory: he remembered seeing shimmering threads when he'd regained consciousness, after Srrcheel gave him his memories. *That's right! Filaments,* he thought, drawing on some of Srrcheel's memories that explained the eerie effect. *They power the spells.* He let his eyes relax, instead of trying to focus on the filaments, as if he were merely daydreaming and staring off into space. The filaments wavered in and out of his vision, but he kept at it until he successfully held them in sight. The vast number of them fascinated him, as they sparkled with energy all around him. Many filaments even flowed through him, and even through the walls of the ship.

He practiced bringing them in and out of focus until it almost became natural.

Once he was comfortable with that, Kormèr next focused on touching and bending the ephemeral filaments. He tried this for twenty minutes before finally succeeding. He began with *twanging* one and seeing its effect on the surrounding ones. Then he pulled two filaments together and "felt" the bump in energy that their joining produced, like a buzz at his fingertips.

Something in the jumbled knowledge in his head told Kormèr that there were novice spells that only required two filaments to cast. Even if that were true, he either couldn't think of any, or more likely, he didn't have access to them. This rang true the moment it occurred to him. *All this knowledge was rammed into my mind… There's probably some kind of blockage. Probably my subconscious mind just has to process it all, to tease apart the tangle of data and make sense of it. Hopefully sooner rather than later.* He found irony in the fact that most of the spells that came easily to him involved multiple filaments being folded into complex patterns.

Impatience filled Kormèr with angst, and he lost sight of the filaments again. He had been at it for over an hour now and needed a moment to calm himself.

I will understand this process completely before tonight, he told himself. *But I should take a break for now.* He left his room and made himself a sandwich in the mess's galley. He took a bite and walked to the cockpit where he found the girls playing one of the onboard video games. "Hi," he said. "I made a sandwich for myself. Have you eaten?"

"We just finished around ten minutes ago," said Jeransy.

"Great. I've been figuring out more about what I can do, what Srrcheel gifted me, and it's made me realize I need to practice."

"You're not alone," said Anndrew. "But we don't have a lot of room in here. I've been trying a few things, but I'm afraid to damage the ship."

"Hmm. I have an idea."

FREESEWEE stood at the Captain's station aboard the police frigate, on video conference with his counterpart at the Freet-See police department, the police chief and the city's mayor. Freesewee had reached out to the Captain there to fill in any gaps they had in their investigation into the disaster. He'd discovered in the process that the department had been hit hard by the conflagration: twenty-six officers injured and twenty-two lost, many Freesewee's former brothers in the force.

| |Captain,| | sang the Mayor, | |I'll be honest with you: we're short-handed and swamped with rescue and relief efforts. We have even resorted to fast-tracking senior academy students. They may not be front-line ready, but they'll free up those that are. A few recent retirees have also volunteered to assist. In short, I grant you full autonomy to conduct your investigation and pursue in my city.| |

| |Thank you, sir. I would gladly loan you as many of my team as you think you'd need to effectively supplement your numbers.| |

| |That is very generous of you. I'll let you work those details out with the Chief and the Captain. Signing off.| | The Mayor's image vanished from the display.

| |We could use twenty officers,| | sang the Chief, | |if you can spare them.| |

That would be nearly half of his team, but he had confidence that he could still apprehend Lezàl. And it was thanks to the Chief that he'd been transferred to Birshetland. | |They're yours. I can have them there within an hour or two, depending on whether we get through to the Hovel in the next thirty minutes.| |

The Captain looked away from the camera for a moment and said something inaudible. Then he turned back. | |I must go. Let me know when you arrive, and I'll have someone meet your team.| | Freesewee nodded, and the Captain vanished from the feed.

| |What's your plan?| | asked Freesewee's old Chief.

| |The plan had been to locate Lezàl's ship and arrest him. But his transponder's gone dark.| |

The Chief frowned. | |Dark? How's that possible?| |

| |It shouldn't be. But nav-sat logs show that it stopped transmitting a few days ago.| |

| |Hmm. That reminds me of a case I worked years ago where pirates used broadcast radio emissions to illegally jam transponders.| |

| |I remember that. We studied that case at the academy. That's when they pulled the old radio receivers from ships. Well, if that's what he's done, that's a second felony to charge him with.

| |In any case, as I mentioned before, Freet-See cit-cams captured footage of Lezàl riding the walkways and visiting his acquaintance, Jeremy Tailor. The records you shared show that Mister Tailor provided him the mini-yacht, so he's a person of interest.| |

| |That makes sense. And if he registered a flight plan, even without the transponder—| |

| |Well, that's the other problem. No flight plan.| |

The Chief nodded. | |That's not illegal, unfortunately.| | Freesewee recalled that the Chief had been advocating for that for years with no success. ||So no response from the Hovel yet? That's out of character for Fitzbew.||

||It is. But it's more than that: we're not even getting an ACK signal. It's as if their comms are offline. That's why I've set our flight path to pass within a few klicks of Berdia.|| Though Berdia had no official police force, it was designated as having its own jurisdiction, so Freesewee couldn't simply go there without notice, even if he was chasing a fugitive.

||Sir,|| began the pilot, ||we are within sight of Berdia.||

||Hold one sec, Chief,|| sang Freesewee. Then he ordered, ||On screen, please.|| At last, they'd have some answers. The forward screen shifted, and the Berdia city-island appeared, glowing in the waning light of sunset. Freesewee peered at the image; something didn't seem right. ||Magnify.||

Gasps filled the bridge as the destruction that had befallen the ancient tree appeared on the screen.

Had the old fools finally done themselves in? wondered Freesewee, shocked and saddened by the loss of the historic tree. *Or was it more of the Terran sorcerer's doing?*

||Koo-rree, what is it?|| asked the Chief.

||It's the Hovel, Chief. It's been destroyed.||

||By the gods!||

Aside from Fitzbew, there was one other Grand Master on Berdia with whom the police had equitable dealings. Freesewee turned to the communications officer. ||Contact Grand Master Sylveena. We'll see if she—||

Before he could finish, a voice penetrated his mind. In Averian, it seemed to be telling a story of some kind. He glanced around the command center of the frigate and realized by the baffled expressions of his crew that they, too, were hearing the voice. He focused on the voice and recognized the story as a brief history of the Hovel and the Hawk Sorcerers.

A stunned silence filled the command center after the story ended. The Chief broke the quiet, twittering, ||I'll leave you to it. Fill me in later.||

||Of course.||

As the comm screen went dark, the image on the forward screen shifted again, revealing a ship parked on Berdia's north western landing pad. ||Sir,|| chirped the sensor specialist, ||that mini-yacht matches the description of the one registered to Lezàl.||

||Get me Sylveena, or any Grand Master, on comms, fast!|| *It seems we'll get to Freet-See later than expected after all.*

"HAVE you ladies figured out what you can do?" asked Kormèr, finishing his sandwich as he walked with the girls across the bridge from the landing platform. He used his trusty multi-function device to scan ahead, hoping that no one would come out this way for a while. He'd determined that the open air on Berdia was the safest place to practice, as long as there weren't any nosy sorcerers about. He didn't want to have to explain how an Elmarian and two Terrans suddenly had magic abilities.

"Srrcheel called it 'the Gauntlet'," said Jeransy. She concentrated for a moment. Suddenly, her right forearm and hand appeared to morph into a flexible silver gauntlet. "Wow! It's getting easier to invoke!"

"Ah! Gauntlet, like a glove," said Kormèr. "I was thinking of the expression 'run the gauntlet'. That's cool. What's it do?"

"It gives my hand extra strength." She picked up a small rock and cracked it to pieces in her silvered-palm. "And I can shoot different kinds of energy from the fingertips." To demonstrate, a golden beam *zapped* from her index finger and narrowly missed a chunk of debris a few meters away. Jeransy smiled, blushing. "I need a bit of target practice, I'd venture."

"That's why we're out here."

"Oh, and since it's really in my mind, it can't be damaged... as far as I can tell. I'm sorry, KL, but I put a right nasty dent in the mess table earlier."

Kormèr smiled. "No worries, love. What about you, Annde?"

Anndrew held up her right hand, and a tiny purplish flame suddenly burned over her up-turned palm. "I can conjure up flames and fires with different properties." She changed the flames subtly, as she spoke, from cobalt blue to pale yellow, to warm red. The flame slowly dimmed, then suddenly flared violently. Anndrew snapped her hand closed, extinguishing it instantly. "Whoa."

Kormèr's brow rose in surprise. "I'm glad we're not inside the ship."

"Yeah. Regulating the intensity takes a lot of focus, but it's getting easier too. The flames can have either destructive or healing qualities. I imagine that with a lot of practice, I can duplicate what Cecil did at Freet-See... something I hope I'll never have to use. So what about you?"

"I'm not sure of everything I have. Areas of my mind are still in... shock, I guess, from the data transfer. I think Srrcheel somehow gave me all his knowledge of magic."

"Wow!" said Jeransy. "That's a cracking gift!"

"It is." He nodded solemnly, thinking of its great cost. "But it's so much information that I can't figure it all out. When I concentrate, I can see these amazing filaments." He brought them into focus, then let them fade away. "They're like thick golden strings all around us, and they kind of sparkle with energy. I have the knowledge of how to weave these filaments into configurations of power, and these become spells." He paused as he focused back on the girls. "That's a big start, but it's one thing to know *how* to cast a spell. It's another thing to know *what* to cast."

"Like a recipe book," suggested Anndrew.

Kormèr nodded. "I like that: 'recipe book'. I have an entire library of all the recipe books that Srrcheel had memorized, but I can't access them. Or maybe I just don't know how; maybe Averian brains store information differently than Elmarians, and I just need to understand what that is." He shook his head. "I just don't know."

"But you used spells at the Hovel," said Jeransy. "Where did you get those recipes?"

"Actually, I used a wand." Kormèr shrugged. "I tried to cast a spell, but I didn't know what I was doing, so it didn't work. Now I know just enough, but again only about *how* to cast. There are some recipes that are easy to access and easy to cast. I've been using those to practice. There are wards, like protection spells against different things."

"That's pretty useful," said Anndrew.

"Yeah. I just wish there was a single ward for everything. It's as if you have to know what you'll need, which I can't imagine is practical. Besides the wards, I also have a powerful mind-shield, which I think resists magic of all kinds… but I'd rather be sure of that before putting it to the test. That one's got a complex pattern, so I haven't even attempted it yet."

"Pattern?"

"That's the actual Terran English word for the series of movements needed to cast a spell, the 'recipe' in your simile. Some spells, like the wards and shields, stay active, using a trickle of power to keep running. For example, here's a spell I practiced earlier that's still active."

Kormèr focused on his cup and willed it to move across the table toward Anndrew, then back.

"Telekinesis!" said Anndrew. "Cool!"

"And telepathy," he projected to their minds. *"Did that work?"* he asked, never having tried it on a person before.

Jeransy's eyes were wide, and she nodded slowly. "Blimey! That's weird, hearing your voice in me head."

"Can you hear ours in return?" asked Anndrew.

It suddenly occurred to Kormèr that this spell could get awkward. "Well, um, it has an empathic component, so I can sense feelings and emotions in others." He considered not saying more, but he also wanted to be honest with the girls. *Trust is not easy to earn, but very easy to lose,* his father once told him. "I think I can also read minds… to an extent." At their wide-eyed look he added, "Believe me, I would never pry without first asking. I respect your privacy." The girls smiled uneasily, so he went on, changing the topic. "There are several other abilities, but they're not as useful or interesting."

"Can't you just track Cecil down with your telepathy?" asked Anndrew.

Kormèr grunted. "That sure would make things easy, wouldn't it? Unfortunately, no. I tried, but it seems he's got a block up that prevents me from locating him." He rubbed his temples. "A rather painful block, too. Maybe, as I remember more, I'll find some way of getting around that."

"What about teleportation?" asked Jeransy. "That's how Cecil is getting around without a ship, right?"

"That's right. Actually, that's one ability I'm not sure of. I'm also afraid to try it… I mean, if I don't have full control of it, I might end up in a wall or something." He chuckled sarcastically. "That wouldn't be much fun. Sreet said that you are limited to places you have previously visited. I guess I'll have to try it at some point, but I'm not ready to test that just yet.

"One option that's now open to us is visiting the Sitachi sect. The Hawks were the oldest and largest of the sorcerer groups here, but the Sitachi might be willing to help us, particularly after last night's efforts."

"You don't sound too sure," said Anndrew, and Kormèr realized he had allowed his own doubts to filter into his voice.

Kormèr sighed. "They are all unknown entities. I knew the Hawks and how to deal with them, for the most part. And even then, I didn't like dealing with them. These other sects… They might be easier to deal with, after all, Sylveena seemed very nice. But they might also be worse. We just don't have a lot of time."

A thought struck him then, and he quickly checked his chrono. "Two nights left till Cheerretee," he mumbled aloud.

"Till what?" asked Jeransy. "Oh, that festival you had mentioned?"

Kormèr looked up, realizing he had spoken aloud. "Yes. But there's more to that festival than I let on. I never thought five days would go so fast and with so little progress." And he told them of the danger the planet faced if Cecil was not dealt with by Cheerretee.

"How powerful are we talking about?" asked an appalled Anndrew.

"*If* he figures out how to harness the power boost…" Kormèr sighed. "I honestly have no idea. It's not one of the things Srrcheel and I ever discussed."

There was silence for several moments, and in those moments a new spell trickled into Kormèr's consciousness. "Huh. A new spell."

He traced the short pattern and cast the spell. The girls' startled expressions told him it had worked, though he saw no change himself.

"Did you teleport?" asked Jeransy.

"No. I'm still here, just invisible." He ended the spell.

"That might come in handy." Anndrew's words triggered Kormèr's suppressed doubts to suddenly resurface.

Kormèr shook his head. "This is ridiculous. Cecil is so far ahead of us." He tapped his palm with his fist. "That settles it; we need the help of the Berdian sorcerers. I wish I'd realized that earlier. I'm sure I can convince at least Sylveena that Cecil is as much a threat to them as he was to the Hovel. And maybe with her help, we can convince the others."

"I think that's a good idea," said Anndrew.

Jeransy seemed unsure, but she nodded.

186

"Then that's what we'll do. Once we're back aboard, I'll contact Sylveena and set it up. In the meantime, we need to practice our abilities until we've mastered them." He scanned the area once again with his multi-function device. "There's still no one around, so let's get started."

They practiced for several hours, with Kormèr frequently stopping to scan the area. As the sun set, however, he thought it might be time to stop. "I think we should stop for now. We've been lucky not to attract any attention during the day, but I don't want to push our luck here. I also don't want to overstay our welcome. Let's break for dinner and I'll contact Sylveena."

Kormèr joined the girls around the mess table. "Alright, Sylveena agreed to meet. But she wants to discuss the situation with us first."

"Discuss?" Jeransy threw up her hands. "What's there to bloody discuss? Cecil's destroyed half a city and a tree of sorcerers who should have been powerful enough to stop him."

Anndrew nodded. "It's like everyone has their head in the sand. What's so hard about deciding to be helpful?"

"It might be political," said Kormèr. "But I don't really know. I guess we'll find out; I set up a meeting with her for an hour from now."

"Are we all going?" asked Jeransy.

"If you'd like."

"I definitely would like. I wouldn't mind seeing the inside of another one of these old trees."

Kormèr put his fork down. "I hear beeping." He stood and rushed to the cockpit. A red status bar blinked on one of the pilot screens. Kormèr sat as the girls rushed in behind him and took their stations. "That's odd. Autopilot is offline," he said.

The comm panel announced a new message, and Kormèr tapped it and Sylveena's voice played over the comm. //*I'm sorry, Kormèr, but the police have charges against you that I cannot ignore. Please comply with their requests.*//

"Police? Well, I guess our meeting is off."

"Um, we might have a situation here," said Anndrew.

Kormèr turned. She slid her chair back, giving him a clear view of the sensor screen. Numerous blue icons dispersed around the central green icon representing the ship. The blue color identified the icons as law enforcement.

Kormèr switched the forward screen to display a collage of views from the various external cameras. Surrounding the ship, a large group of armed Averians maintained themselves afloat, in formation, with their graceful wings. A bright spotlight illuminated the Averians and the entire platform from a craft that hovered just above them, an Averian police frigate, its insignia, though shrouded in shadows, still familiar to Kormèr as being that of Birshetland. Kormèr did not doubt for one minute that the vessel had every one of its bristling weapons trained on his ship.

"Yes, our meeting is definitely off."

CHAPTER 26

||*THIS* is *Birshetland Police,*|| chirped the comm. ||*Kormèr Lezàl, please acknowledge.*||

Jeransy watched Kormèr stare blankly at the image on the screen, and she wondered what he was thinking. To her left, Anndrew watched the sensor display for a moment, then turned and looked at her for a moment before looking toward Kormèr.

"Let's see what they want." Kormèr opened a channel and put it up on the screen. Immediately, an Averian appeared in an overlay on the screen.

||Hello. I'm Kormèr Lezàl. With whom do I have the pleasure of speaking?||

Still able to understand Averian, Jeransy grinned at his suave politeness.

||Kormèr Lezàl, this is Captain Freesewee of the Birshetland police. My men are here to escort you and your two companions back to the station to be questioned on the disappearance of Chief Sylvestra Chrreel, on the illegal intrusion into Birshetland airspace and on the illegal interference with your ship's transponder. You are not under arrest yet, but any attempt at escape or show of force will be dealt with harshly.||

||I believe you, Captain. I have no intention of giving you such a cause. I humbly accede to your orders.||

||Good,|| tweeted the birdman. ||You are to slave your ship's controls to mine. Upon arrival at the station, you will come out of the craft with your hands in full view.||

||As you wish.|| Kormèr tapped his controls. ||Done. The ship is at your disposal.||

||Very good. Now, please lower your boarding ramp. My men will board the craft and take it to the impound for safekeeping until you we are done.||

||But you...|| Kormèr frowned at the screen. ||Of course. I assume we will ride aboard your ship.||

||That is correct.||

||We'll be right out.|| Kormèr flicked off the comm and turned to the ladies.

"He lied!" said Anndrew.

"Your time must really be a dreamland," said Jeransy. "Police always lie."

Kormèr waved his hand. "Things aren't that bad. All we have to do is explain our situation. We shouldn't have to lie; we haven't done anything wrong. Although I'd leave out the part about wanting to steal the jewel from the museum. We were just there to ask for it back, of course."

"What if they don't believe you?" asked Jeransy.

Anndrew backed her with a nod. "Yeah. You've mentioned that they don't particularly like you."

Kormèr hesitated. "For now it looks like our goals are somewhat aligned. They want to find Sylvestra, and so do we. Together, hopefully we can do it faster. And once I tell them about Cecil, maybe we can get their help with that as well."

Jeransy peered at Anndrew, and saw her nod. She looked back at Kormèr, but said nothing. She didn't agree with his optimism. But he knew this planet and its ways better than she did. She trusted him to know what he was doing.

Kormèr stood. "Let's meet our guests. Keep your hands visible, by the way. Police get jumpy when they can't see your hands."

Eight armed and uniformed officers mat them at the base of the boarding ramp. Four of the officers marched up the ramp and into the ship. The other four escorted the trio aboard the frigate and locked each in separate holding cells. The cell walls were simply bars, so Jeransy could see Kormèr and Anndrew. but Kormèr said nothing, and so Jeransy followed his lead and kept her mouth shut. Thankfully, Anndrew did the same.

Her watch showed that the trip took less than an hour, but sitting there with nothing to do, she felt it had to have been longer. They led Kormèr away first, then Anndrew. Finally, the one remaining officer opened her cell and sang something.

"Sorry, I don't understand." She suddenly missed the translation spell dearly, but it would've worn off when they left Berdia.

"You, come with me," said the officer.

She walked in front of him as he directed her. They stopped once, for her to surrender the few personal effects she carried on her, and then once again in a room with a table, some perches and a chair.

"Sit, please." The officer placed the chair behind the table, straddling a perch that was bolted to the floor. When she sat, he walked back to wait by the door.

Jeransy didn't like this at all, finding the procedure all too familiar. In a panic, she wondered if Earth and Averia shared their criminals' records. If they did, would her minor infraction have survived this long? *Don't be daft,* she told herself, quelling the thought. *Who would even imagine that I'm that Jeransy Bolsner?*

She nodded off twice while she waited. Between the late hour and the emotional stress of the past day, she felt drained. Between the quick naps, it occurred to her that she hadn't been getting nearly enough sleep since coming to Averia.

After more than an hour of waiting, the door opened and two Averian men entered. Jeransy was immediately alert. One birdman sat to her left, at the other end of the perch that ran under her chair. The other stood on the perch across the table from her. He reached up and touched the badge on his belt-sash. Jeransy immediately picked out the small camera lens inset in the badge.

"Hello, Miss Jeransy Bolsner." He spoke in very clear English, with only a slight whistle to his sibilants. "I apologize for the wait."

Jeransy just nodded once, not wanting to appear too congenial. But the birdman's fluency with English impressed her.

"I'm Captain Freesewee and this," he nodded toward the birdman at her side, "is Mister Trreessleet, a lawyer appointed to you. I understand you are from Earth, and that you're a minor, and for those reasons the lawyer will be present throughout the questioning; I would not like to break the process with which you are accustomed."

"Thanks." She honestly couldn't care less whether a lawyer was present or not; as far as she was concerned, the lot of them were just as corrupt as the judges, at least back home.

"Miss Bolsner, I want you to understand that you are not under arrest at the moment. However, we need your cooperation for a case we're investigating. Everything we say, including this, is being recorded and can be admitted as evidence should there be such a need."

He hadn't asked anything, so Jeransy said nothing.

The Captain watched her a moment, then his eyes flicked to the lawyer and back. "Do you understand?"

"Yeah."

"Good." He tapped the table top and flipped an image around so that it faced Jeransy. It was an image of Kormèr at Freet-See. "Do you know this man?"

"You know I do."

"It's just for the record. What's his name?"

"Kormèr." The Captain waited, and Jeransy rolled her eyes. "Kormèr Lezàl."

"Right. And how do you know Mister Lezàl?"

Kormèr had said to be honest, and despite her better judgment, Jeransy fumbled for an answer. *I can't bloody tell him that Kormèr broke me out of jail!* "He's my friend," she said quickly, hoping he wouldn't press her for more.

"How long have you known him?"

"A few weeks."

"Just a few weeks? Did you meet here, on Averia?"

Where's he going with this? "No."

"So you traveled here with him?"

Uh oh. "Yes." She cringed inwardly as she said that, anticipating the next

190

question.

"Are you aware that Galactic Federation law requires all new arrivals at any planet to register immediately with the local authority?"

Answering honestly, Jeransy said, "I had no idea. This is my first time away from home."

The Captain smiled at her. "That explains it." He produced another image. "Who is she?"

"That's Anndrew Lee."

"Thank you. She is also from Earth, yes?"

"Yeah but from—" *Bloody hell! Almost said she's from a different time.*

"From?"

Thinking quickly, she said, "From a different city."

"Hmm. And how long have you known her?"

"Where's this going?" asked Jeransy. "How's this helping your investigation?"

"Miss Bolsner, I'm just trying to establish the relationship between the three of you. Believe me when I say that this will help both of us a great deal."

"That doesn't make sense. What's our relationship got to do with your case?"

The Captain watched her. Then he produced another image. "Do you know this woman?"

"Yeah. That's the Chief of Police. Umm… Sylvestra."

"You met her at the Hotel Cheerees."

"That's right."

"When was the last time you saw her?"

Now Jeransy understood where this questioning was going. The Captain had to be investigating Sylvestra's kidnapping. "Three or four days ago. She saw us off to Berdia."

"Because of this young man?" Another image appeared on the display, this time of Cecil atop the tower in Freet-See.

"So you know about him." She realized how daft that sounded the moment she said it. "I mean, of course you do, after Freet-See."

"What do you know about this boy?"

"That's Cecil Murphy. He's also from… Earth."

"Did he come with you, Miss Lee and Mister Lezàl?"

"No." She'd responded without thinking, but technically, she hadn't lied. Cecil had come on his own.

"So why did Chief Chrreel arrange passage for the three of you to pursue the boy to the Hovel?"

Jeransy doubted Kormèr's honesty extended to revealing the portal. She tried to think of a reason that didn't involve Cecil's tumble through the portal, but she couldn't. And after almost a minute, she knew that any answer she gave would sound made up. "I really can't say."

Freesewee stared at her for a few seconds, then sighed. "Miss Bolsner, you, Anndrew Lee and Kormèr Lezàl are all under suspicion in the disappearance of the Chief of police. If you don't answer my questions, you're only hurting yourself."

"I believe I am answering your questions, am I right?" She looked to the lawyer.

Mister Trreessleet had been sitting staring at his hands, which rested on his large belly. Realizing Jeransy was finally speaking to him, he looked up, cleared his throat and said, "Yes, yes. Of course you are."

"We'll skip that question for now," sighed Freesewee. "To the best of your knowledge, what is Chief Chrreel's relationship to Mister Lezàl?"

Jeransy had been wondering about that herself. "Hang on." She turned to Mister Trreessleet, and lowered her voice to a whisper. "I can guess what their relationship is, but I can't be sure if I'm right."

"Then you don't know, do you?"

"Thanks." She addressed Freesewee. "I don't know."

"Are you certain?"

"I can only speculate, and speculation isn't fact." The lawyer nodded to support her statement, then slowly his eyes dropped to his hands again.

"Has Lezàl ever spoken harshly about—"

"Look, the only thing I can tell you about Kormèr and Sylvestra is that he cares for her. As for her disappearance, we've nothing to do with it. In fact, we were trying to find her ourselves when you stopped us."

"So you have some idea where she might be?"

"A sorcerer named Sreet kidnapped her."

The Captain looked very surprised. "Why would he do that?"

"To force Kormèr to find the boy."

"Where is this Sreet now?"

Jeransy shrugged. "Dunno. He was from the Hovel."

Freesewee nodded. "Are you aware that the Hovel has been destroyed?"

"Yes." The haunting memories came back to her. "We arrived just after it happened."

"For what purpose?" asked the Captain.

"Kormèr had a friend there. So we helped with the search for survivors, but there weren't any. Cecil Murphy is really the one you should be after. It's all 'is fault."

The Captain leaned forward, appearing suddenly interested in what Jeransy had to say. "Tell me, do you know what happened there?"

Now even the lawyer seemed to lose his interest in his hands.

Jeransy struggled against her instinct to hold back and not say anything more. She'd already said so much... But Kormèr's instructions repeated in her head, and she trusted him. "Well, 'tis a long story, but..."

192

ANNDREW sat waiting for several hours before her interrogators showed. She'd watched a few cop shows over the years and figured this was an intimidation technique, and that someone was probably watching her through the large mirror on the wall to her right. She smiled at the mirror and waved. There had to be someone back there. There always was in the movies.

If intimidation truly was the goal, then it was failing miserably. Exhaustion had its grip on her and wouldn't allow any other feelings to take hold. Even her guard had slouched at his post by the door after the first hour.

"Can I get some water, please?" she asked after she caught herself drifting off.

The guard nodded, then chirped into the device on his wrist. Minutes later, a young officer entered, carrying a tray with two glasses. One had clear water, and the other looked like the blue milky nutria drink that she'd had a few nights ago at the restaurant. The guard took the latter, and the young officer passed her the one with plain water.

"Thank you," she said, taking the glass and gulping the water down. The young officer took her empty glass and left the guard still sipping his drink.

A few minutes later, two Averians entered the room. One was the Captain from the ship that had captured them; she recognized him from the feathers that fanned down from his cheeks like sideburns. The Captain introduced the other Averian as a lawyer.

"Miss Lee, what exactly is your association with Mister Lezàl?" asked the Captain.

Anndrew looked up from Kormèr's image on the tabletop. "We are friends."

"Yes, but how do you know him?"

"Well, we met on Earth. I've been traveling with him since." She intentionally kept that answer as simple as possible. Kormèr had said to cooperate, but the portal wasn't relevant to the facts.

"I see. And how did you come to be on Averia?"

Anndrew cringed. *So much for the portal not being relevant. How do I explain this?* "Heh, that's a long story. One of my classmates from Earth accidentally got transported here."

"Accidentally?" asked Freesewee. "I'd love to hear that story."

Of course you would, she thought. "Kormèr felt it was his fault for being careless with some… equipment that caused the accident to occur. So we came here to help him get back."

The Captain brought up Cecil's image on the tabletop. "Is this your classmate?"

Anndrew nodded. "Yes, that's Cecil Murphy… unfortunately."

"Why unfortunately?"

She couldn't take her eyes off the maniacal look on Cecil's face in the photo. "Because of what he was doing there." She looked up at the Captain. "Because of Freet-See."

"Do you know magic, Miss Lee?"

I do now, she thought. *But you don't need to know that.* Instead, she deflected. "Terrans don't know magic, Captain."

The Captain stabbed the image of Cecil with a finger. "This one clearly does. How is that?"

Anndrew was silent, thinking furiously. *Do I tell them he's been to Berdia and learned magic? He's got to know already.*

"I'll tell you why," said Freesewee, surprising her, "because he's learned sorcery from the Berdians."

Anndrew nodded. "Yes. He was very studious back home; he must've found magic very easy to learn."

The Captain drummed his fingers on the tabletop. "How exactly did Mister Lezàl expect to find your classmate?"

"The first person he talked to was the Chief of Police, Sylvestra."

"This was at the Cheerees Hotel."

"That's right," said Anndrew, surprised. Then it dawned on her that he was probably comparing her story to someone else's, Jeransy's or Kormèr's maybe. Or perhaps he was saving Kormèr for last and pumping her and Jeransy for information first. That's what she would've done.

"To the best of your knowledge, what is Kormèr's relationship with Sylvestra?"

Anndrew responded honestly. "He explained to me that they'd dated a few years back, and now are just very close friends. That's really all I know."

The Captain nodded. "So you went to Berdia after the boy with help from Sylvestra and found it destroyed."

"Yes... I mean, no."

"Which is it, Miss Lee? Yes or no?"

"Yes, we went there, but no, it wasn't destroyed yet." This was stupid. Freesewee appeared to have a good amount of information; lying or holding back didn't seem like a good idea. She decided to tell as much of the truth as she felt comfortable with. "Let me tell you what happened."

| |I remember you,| | sang one of Kormèr's two guards as she held open the door to the interrogation room. | |You were just a youngling. I didn't think Elmarians aged this fast.| |

| |We usually don't.| | Kormèr couldn't tell where the birdwoman was headed with her comment or whether or not she was a fan. | |What's your name, officer?| |

| |Lieutenant K'swee.| |

Kormèr sat at the table facing the doorway through which he'd just entered and folded his hands on the tabletop. The other guard stood in the doorway, pointedly ignoring them both. | | It's nice to meet you, Lieutenant. | |

| | Do you know where the Chief is? | | she asked in a whisper.

Kormèr looked up into her eyes. | | I wish I did. I would've been there rescuing her. | |

| | I believe you. I just wish you'd— | |

| | Everyone out! | |

Kormèr looked to the door as the guard stepped aside and Sergeant Chreel Tseeo strutted into the room, followed by a burly officer. The Lieutenant backed away, then headed for the door. Kormèr's hopes for a diplomatic exchange went out the door with her.

Without a word, the burly one moved to stand behind Kormèr as Tseeo closed the door.

| | Hello, Sergeant Tseeo, | | chirped Kormèr, politely, but inside he swore various times in Elmarian. This would not go well.

Tseeo had been one of the officers who, three years earlier, had been investigating the jewel heist Kormèr had solved. The case would have promoted him to Captain. But his own high-handedness had cost him the case, and by solving it, Kormèr had robbed him of the promotion. Tseeo had never liked Kormèr, and after that, the birdman had done whatever he could, within the law, to make Kormèr's life difficult. Kormèr had little hope that time had healed old wounds.

| | It's been a while, hasn't it? | | twittered Kormèr.

The Sergeant grinned victoriously. | | Not long enough, Lezàl. But I knew one day I'd have you sitting right there. | |

| | Right here? How prodigious of you. | |

| | Shut up, you worthless pile of droppings. | |

| | Come now; that's just rude. At least I have the decency of calling you *Sergeant*. | | Kormèr drew out the title, knowing it would irk the birdman.

A sharp blow to the side of his head by Burly knocked Kormèr out of his seat and onto the floor. Kormèr glared at the smirking birdman, fire in his eyes. *This is not the time, Lezàl. Control. Your chance will come.*

| | Get up, Lezàl, | | chirped Tseeo, impassively.

Kormèr got up from the floor and repositioned himself in the seat. | | Is it standard procedure to mistreat suspects whether they are guilty or not? | |

| | Oh, you're guilty. This time we have at least two charges to hang on you. | |

Two charges? Wondered Kormèr. He figured one had to be hovering the ship over the museum. He didn't think that would go unnoticed. But he hadn't counted on such a fast response, nor had he counted on Birshetland's police to come looking for him outside of the city.

Tseeo stared at him for several moments, then looked away, and only then did he seem to regain his composure, as if the mere sight of Kormèr stirred anger in him. Then: ||Where is Sylvestra?||

||That's presumptuous,|| warbled Kormèr.

Tseeo turned to face him. ||No. We know you met her at the Cheerees, twice.||

||She was welcoming me back to the city… A little more warmly than you have.||

Chreel ignored the jibe. ||Later that night, you were seen with her at the Argent port.||

||That's right. Should I be impressed that you know this? It was all aboveboard.||

||The way I figure it, you circled back and kidnapped her from her home.||

Kormèr sniffed condescendingly. ||After your screwups three years ago; I don't understand how Sylvee still tolerates your incompetence.|| Anticipating Burly striking him again, Kormèr made a small motion with his hands, nudging Burly's mind in another direction. The big birdman promptly smacked himself hard.

||What the hell was that?|| asked Tseeo, looking quickly at Burly.

||Ticks,|| chirped Kormèr before the other could answer. ||Anyway, as I was saying… had you been doing your job instead of sitting on your downy rump, you would have found that at the time of the kidnapping, my companions and I were in Berdia.||

||Is that so?|| asked Tseeo. ||Do you have alibis?||

Kormèr realized he was at an impasse; the carrier birds themselves were trained animals with no real intelligence. The handlers could surely testify to the fact that Kormèr and the girls had left on the birds, but wouldn't the police have already questioned them? Would they have lied? Why? And of course the Hawk Sorcerers were all dead, leaving no alibis. ||Regretfully, no. The Hovel was destroyed—||

||Conveniently, wouldn't you say?||

||What? Are you kidding? You must really be—||

||Who else could have—*would* have been capable of it? We found the upgrades on your ship, the weapons you used to destroy the Hovel.||

||I'm sure you'll also find that the ship's logs will have no record of the weapons being used.||

||You sabotaged the transponder, something that's supposed to be impossible to do. I'm sure you could've scrubbed the logs as easily.||

That's got to be the other charge, Kormèr realized. *But I didn't mess with the transponder. Why do they think I did?* ||So you only investigate the things that support your crazy notions. This was your problem three years ago, Sergeant.||

||Careful, Lezàl.|| Tseeo's eyes burned holes through Kormèr.

But Kormèr wasn't intimidated by him. ||Investigate, man! You'll find that the damage was all magical, not caused by chemicals or energy weapons.||

Tseeo slammed a hand on the table. ||We can't investigate. No one can get close enough to the place.|| Kormèr swore quietly, remembering the protection spell he had placed over the ruins. ||Besides,|| continued Tseeo, ||I believe the contents of your pockets are enough evidence against you.||

Kormèr was shocked. How had they found anything in the pockets? Someone had to be thinking of an item or… or the idea of an item. *Someone must've expected to find magical artifacts and found magical artifacts. Dammit. I should've hidden the coat on the ship.*

||Let's see if I have this straight. You kidnapped Sylvestra and went to Berdia thinking you could hide her in some abandoned area of the old tree. Some unlucky sorcerer saw you and, afraid their magic would catch you, you destroyed them all and stole all their magical artifacts. Where am I wrong?||

||Where aren't you wrong? You're a fool if that's what you believe, because somewhere out there, Sylvestra is still being held captive while you're wasting time badgering me.||

||Where is she, Lezàl?||

||I always knew you'd invent something to arrest me. But this? You fat, old, jealous bastard.|| Kormèr's neck hairs prickled, warning him of the approaching blow.

Kormèr swirled out of his seat and stood eye-to-eye with Burly, whose arm stood frozen where he had raised it. He warbled, ||If you hit me one more time I'll—||

||You'll what, Lezàl?|| chirped Tseeo, loudly. ||You'll what? Throw him in a cell. It's going to be his new home from now on anyway.||

As Burly led him out of the room, Tseeo chirped, ||You're a stupid man to resist me, Lezàl. I'll get where you're hiding her if I have to torture you to do it.||

||I might be stupid, but I've met Argents are smarter than you, Tseeo.||

With that, Burly shoved Kormèr through the door and toward the holding cells.

||Three years ago, the media wrote that Kormèr Lezàl can do anything.|| Burly shoved Kormèr into a cell. ||Let's see if you can break out of jail.|| He locked the cell and posted three guards by the door, all facing the cell.

Kormèr knew that many officers in the precinct disliked him, but he felt that he might have been able to get someone to listen, anyone except Tseeo. *My choice of words could've been better too, but it's not like it would've made a bit of difference with Tseeo. The Sergeant would never have listened anyway.*

And what he desperately needed now were allies. He needed a voice who could call on all the sorcerers of Berdia to get off their asses and handle Cecil.

While he wanted nothing more than to see Sylvee free and safe, Kormèr knew no one on Averia would ever be safe with that Terran menace running around.

Kormèr glanced out his barred window. He couldn't be sure, but it appeared to be early morning. *Two days left until Cheerretee, and I'm stuck in here.*

Kormèr slumped onto the rough cot in the cell. *C'mon brain; get over your stupid trauma and give me access to Srrcheel's spells!* He closed his eyes and focused on his breathing. He needed to calm himself from the botched interrogation.

But try as he might, he just couldn't relax. The interrogation played in a loop in his head, frustrating him with the various fruitless and pointless directions it could have taken. After two hours, he got off the cot and paced across his cell and back, trying to look casual instead of desperate to just be moving.

"Don't you bloody touch me!" Jeransy's voice snapped him out of his reverie. "I can walk on my own, ya bloomin' rozzers. Liars, the lot of ya. Saying we wasn't arrested." Then she came into view, being led by two guards down the corridor of cells.

"Kormèr," she said, seeing him.

He ran to the bars and reached out to her, if only to convey reassurance through a simple touch. But the guards immediately reacted and clubbed his arm with the side edges of their hands. He only touched Jeransy's fingertips before he had to pull his arm back. His arm throbbed. He wanted to massage it, but stubbornly refused to let the guards see that they'd hurt him.

Fury raged through him.

"We'll be out of here soon," he telepathed to her. *"I promise."*

She glanced at him and nodded, before her escorts led her away.

CHAPTER 27

FREESEWEE stopped in his office to prepare some new questions for Lezàl based on the information he'd gotten from his interrogations of the two Terran females. Though he had told them that they were not under arrest, he had them placed in cells until he could corroborate their data with Lezàl. The two Terrans still represented a mystery insofar as the lack of data on them in the Galactic Federation database. The same had been true of Lezàl three years earlier. But having two more turn up in Freesewee's city, and in Lezàl's company, established a pattern the Captain could not ignore. He would not allow Birshetland to become known as a safe haven for the undocumented.

On top of that, these girls were mixed up with Lezàl and whatever he was up to. Freesewee originally believed that Lezàl had coerced them or perhaps even deluded them into following him from Earth and partaking in whatever he was up to. But from their interrogations, they appeared to be genuinely following him of their own volition. And if that turned out to be true, they stood to face charges of complicity. Their fate rested in Lezàl's answers now.

Freesewee yawned. He'd been awake just over twenty-four hours now. He'd pulled all-nighters before, but never just back from a vacation. *Was I really just on vacation? I don't even remember it anymore.*

He reviewed the new questions, then headed to the room where Lezàl was waiting. He'd kept the man waiting long enough. On arriving, however, he found the room empty. He turned to face the officers, whose desks were outside the room. | |Where's Lezàl?| |

The nearest officer answered. | |He's in a cell, sir.| |

| |Oh. Do me a favor and bring him here. I'm ready to interrogate him.| |

| |But, sir, Sergeant Tseeo already interrogated him.| |

It took a moment for that to sink in. Considering that the focus of the investigation was the missing Chief, protocol dictated that the Captain perform, or at a minimum, be present for the interrogations. | |What? By whose order?| |

The officer shrugged. | |I don't know, sir.| |

Freesewee fumed. | |Where is Tseeo?| |

| |He was on his way to your office to deliver his report.| |

Freesewee rushed back to his office, but Tseeo wasn't there. A light blinked on the desktop, indicating that data had been added. He tapped it, and the case file opened onto the wall display. A new folder blinked for his attention. He opened the folder and read the two summary lines of the report: //*Prisoner was uncooperative. Had him incarcerated pending further questioning or confession.*//

He then played the attached recording of the interrogation, his hands clenching tighter and tighter the more he watched. ||The stupid moron!|| he chirped when the recording ended. Freesewee closed the file and stormed out the door and to the desk floor. ||Tseeo!|| Activity in the area stopped immediately as all eyes turned to Freesewee, no doubt startled at seeing him so angry.

||Sir, he's left the building,|| managed one officer.

||Thank you. Do me a favor: find what cells Lezàl and his companions are in, and bring them to my office.|| He wanted to add an order to have Tseeo found and brought back, but he wouldn't do that to a Sergeant in front of all the others. That conversation would be a private matter inside a sound-proof room.

||Yessir.||

SLUMPED over on the cot, Kormèr felt the weight of time heavy on his shoulders. Between that and his exhaustion, he wanted to just collapse onto the ratty pillow and have a good sleep. He'd been in the cell for six hours; every minute was one less that he had to find Sylvestra and stop Cecil. The only thing this downtime provided was a chance to work on accessing the spells locked in his head, but he hadn't even been able to do that yet.

Focusing on his breathing once again, he found it easier now to slow his heart, to let the tension flow from his tight muscles. A memory came to him in a flash, Srrcheel's master showing him a special relaxation technique. Kormèr followed the master's instruction, turned his mind inward until he could no longer feel the pressure of the cot beneath him or hear the whir of the air vent or smell the mustiness of the cell. The constraints of the material world seemed to just fall away, leaving him fascinated by the lightness of being that suffused through him. He had meditated before, but never had he achieved such a high state of consciousness.

"By the gods! Finally!" The voice touched Kormèr's saddened heart with joyous, silvery familiarity.

"Srrcheel?" asked Kormèr, though the words he heard were not words in themselves, but rather like images or feelings that conveyed specific meanings.

"Yes, it's me."

"What? But how? I can't see you."

"I think I can fix that."

Ripples of light split the darkness that Kormèr's senses defined as "straight ahead", though there didn't seem to be any actual directionality in this mind-space. The ripples steadied, and Kormèr gasped at the scintillating aura that surrounded the grinning image of Srrcheel. He smiled and his wings flicked proudly. "How's that for a trick?"

Kormèr's first reaction almost snapped him back to reality, where his material body sat in a cage. But the warm and sincere emotions he felt from the aura helped him stay.

"It is you! I'm... beyond confused. Are you a memory, a ghost... something else?"

"I feel like me. But to be completely honest, I don't really know. The spell I cast should only have transferred my memories to you. Of course, I've never had to do that before. I sort of made the spell up just in case someone happened by while I was waiting to die. I knew you'd come by once you heard the news, and I counted on the most extreme probability that whoever came by would run into you."

"Instead of saving yourself? Again, why? What would that have accomplished?" Kormèr wanted to wave his hands and arms at the irrationality of what Srrcheel had done, and felt frustrated that he didn't have arms or hands to wave.

"Because I was too badly injured! You needed the knowledge right away to help with Cecil. I was going to need months of recovery, if I even recovered. The spell was triggered to transfer to you when someone came close enough." He shrugged, and his wing tips shrugged too. "I don't know; maybe that's where the spell went wrong."

"Or went right. You're here, and alive— well, kind of alive, you crafty specter."

Srrcheel's aura seemed pensive, though at the moment Kormèr was not sure if he saw it in the aura itself or felt it. Then he felt understanding from it. "At first I was floating in darkness, thinking that if that was death, it left very much to be desired."

"I would imagine so."

"After a while, I thought maybe I wasn't dead. Only I didn't have a body any longer, or at least not one I was aware of. I tried to will my hands to move, to touch each other, but there was nothing. It wasn't that I *couldn't* move, like paralysis, but that there was just nothing to move. It was very frustrating for a while, but then I started getting input from you: sights and sounds. And I finally realized that I was inside your headspace. The problem was, I had no way of communicating with you. So I did the next best thing. I fed you memories, like messages, trying to get you to understand or just giving you what you needed at the time."

"This is absolutely fascinating," said Kormèr.

"I agree. But there are more pressing matters that deserve our attention."

"Very true, old ghost."

"Can we dispense with the adjectives?"

"As you wish, O great spirit in my head." Kormèr sensed frustration from the aura and answered with mirth.

Srrcheel sighed. "This is going to be tougher than I thought,"

"I think I can get used to it, my transparent counterpart."

"Anyway," said Srrcheel, as if that would wipe the slate clean. "I know you understand the gravity of the situation."

Kormèr put aside his teasing. "Yes, quite well."

"Then you also understand that you've got to get out of this blasted cell."

"The thought had crossed my mind," said Kormèr, sardonically.

"Yes, well, have you got any ideas?"

"A few, but which is the best?"

"Present them to me," Srrcheel said.

"Well, first, I'd like to try—"

"No, no. Use the rest of your mind. Imagine you're prowling through someone's home and you can't say anything to your partner."

"I never have a partner; I work alone."

"Oh, for... Just imagine!"

Kormèr suppressed laughing at Srrcheel's growing frustration. Quickly subduing his silliness, Kormèr did as Srrcheel told him; he presented all the different plans he had for escaping in one quick burst of thought.

"You see," said Srrcheel, "it's much faster that way."

"Very keen of you, old apparition."

"Now," continued Srrcheel, ignoring Kormèr's deliberate images, "You've got some interesting stuff here."

"Won't I need more eleron to do this stuff?"

"Not really. The eleron acts as an amplifier for the spells, but isn't entirely necessary. It's mostly used by initiates to help them along. The higher ups don't use it at all."

"Hopefully, Cecil won't figure that out. He appears to still be using it."

"Excellent. I take it you've been trying to capture him that way?"

"Trying."

"Well, as for your various plans, I think you'd be better off going with—" The aura seemed to fade suddenly, and Kormèr intercepted feelings of a distant awareness. "Your body," Srrcheel said, urgently. "Go!"

Kormèr raced back into his body... and toppled sideways on the cot, his rubbery limbs slow to respond. He blinked against the brightness as his eyes snapped open. When he could focus again, he found two of the guards standing over him, inside the cell.

||What the hell's wrong with him?|| chirped one guard.

||Nothing's wrong with me.|| Kormèr sat up slowly, so as not to arouse aggression from the guards. He chuckled. ||I guess I fell asleep.||

||With your eyes open?|| questioned the second guard.

||Don't you know that's the way Elmarians sleep?|| Kormèr hoped that, like most Averians, these were not well traveled and wouldn't know he was lying.

||No kidding?||

||No kidding.|| A glance out the window told him the sun had to be overhead; nearly noon. *That chat with Srrcheel took longer than it seemed to.*

||Well, we just wanted to make sure you were all right,|| explained the first guard, as they both backed toward the cell door.

||Can't you stay?|| Kormèr pouted. ||I don't get much company these days.||

The guards laughed. ||Tell you what, you bring the snacks and drinks, and we'll join you for the party.||

||Oh, you want a party?|| Kormèr stood and faced the window. ||I'll just hop out through the window here and go get the snacks and drinks then. Be back soon.||

They laughed again. ||As much as we'd love to see you—||

Before the guard could finish his sentence, Kormèr reached for the window and vanished, using an invisibility spell.

||What the—|| All three guards rushed into the cell, their plumage compressed tensely. Still invisible, Kormèr slipped behind them, put them to sleep with another spell, then locked the cell door.

That seemed to have worked well enough, old ghost, he thought, wondering if Srrcheel could hear his thoughts without his being in deep meditation. But if Srrcheel heard him, he didn't respond. Without waiting for a reply, Kormèr cast two more spells: one an illusion that would make it appear as if he were still in the cell and one that made the guards invisible. The illusion would fade within the hour. The invisibility would dissolve as soon as the guards woke up. Kormèr hoped that would buy him enough time to rescue one or both of the girls… and his coat. Refreshed with renewed purpose, he headed in the direction he had seen Jeransy go.

JERANSY waited patiently in her cell, her mind busily running through different escape scenarios. Most involved using the Gauntlet to knock out the guard that stood vigilantly outside her cell, and cut through the bars. Beyond that, she'd improvise as she made her way outside. Once there, all the plans grew more nebulous as the variables became too unknowable. And somewhere along the way, she would rescue Kormèr from his cell. She'd leave it up to Anndrew to free herself… maybe.

However, Kormèr had told her that he would get them out. She didn't want to mess up his plans, so she waited. But as the hours ticked away, she couldn't help wishing he would hurry; this cell… *any* cell, made her skin crawl.

The doorway at the left end of the corridor opened, drawing her and her guard's attention. *Kormèr?* she wondered. But it was just another guard who strode up and engaged her guard in conversation. The latter seemed surprised by the newcomer, but suddenly he laughed, pat the newcomer on the back and, still laughing, walked away. The new guard watched the other disappear through the doorway. He then turned to look at Jeransy.

"Hello, my love," he said in Kormèr's voice. "They've treated you well, I hope."

Jeransy gaped.

"Lovely tonsils." He unlocked the cell door.

Jeransy closed her mouth. "You've learned a few tricks, you cheeky bum."

"And more. But I'll tell you later." He opened the cell door, made a few elaborate movements with his hands, and vanished. "Now we're both invisible. Let's get out of here."

"Where to?"

"The ship first."

"What about Anndrew?" she asked, certain that Kormèr wouldn't leave her behind.

"I'll have to come back for her. I don't know exactly where she is. Besides, magic is proving to be very draining. Let's get back to the ship for a bit of recharging."

She suddenly smelled ozone and electronics as their surroundings changed into the darkened corridor of the mini-yacht. Disoriented, Jeransy steadied herself against the wall. *That must've been a teleport! That was aces!*

"Shush," he said to her mind. *"We're not out of the woods yet. Stay here. I'll be right back."*

A moment later, a sudden thump came from the direction of the cockpit, and Kormèr appeared in the doorway. He came scurrying back to Jeransy's side and telepathed, *"There was only one guard up front, but I want to check for bugs before we make any noise. You're visible now, by the way."*

Can you hear my thoughts? thought Jeransy.

"Sit down here, if you want," Kormèr continued without acknowledgment. *"Would you like something to drink or eat? Don't answer, just nod or shake your head,"* he said at her pause. She nodded and made the motions of drinking from a glass. Kormèr scurried soundlessly toward the mess and soon returned with a cup of water and a pack of dry rations.

"I'll be back." He motioned with his hands, the air folded around him, and he was gone. Jeransy had just finished the rations when he reappeared, this time wearing his coat. He stumbled and dropped at her side, his back to the wall. *"Whew. That's an exhausting spell."*

She tapped her ear and waved her palm around, hoping he'd understand her silent question: *Where are the bugs?*

He nodded after a moment, then stood and beckoned her to follow him. In the cockpit, Jeransy only glanced at the Averian officer slumped in the pilot's seat as she joined Kormèr at the sensor station. There, the screen displayed a diagram of the ship, complete with several pulsing pinpoints. He indicated each one, then drew the laser pistol from his pocket and, using a fine beam, shot at one corner of the forward display. Something there sizzled and sparked briefly. Immediately, one pinpoint vanished from the display.

Jeransy opened a compartment beneath the copilot's station, revealing a storage case with a single pistol and three fully charged clips. She took the pistol and pointed at the sensor screen, then at both of them. *We'll do it together.*

Kormèr smiled and nodded. Then they went to work.

An hour later, Kormèr and Jeransy slumped beside each other on the floor of the central corridor.

Kormèr sighed. "That was a lot more exhausting than it looked. But then again, I don't think I've slept since yesterday afternoon."

"Why'd we use pistols?" Jeransy laid her pistol on the floor and massaged her tight shoulder. "It was hard to aim at those teeny buggers."

Kormèr turned and got onto his knees behind her, then massaged her shoulders. "They're silent, especially at the low setting. If we'd used our fingers, it would have been too noisy. This way, it might be a while before the police notice their bugs aren't working."

He yawned, then got to his feet, to Jeransy's chagrin; she'd been enjoying that massage.

"I'm going to take a fifteen minute nap before I go get Annde," he said. "I've left passive sensors on to warn us if anyone comes near the ship. And our friend in the cockpit will be out for at least another hour." He looked into her eyes. "You should rest too. We're probably going to need it before we get out of this."

"Right. Wake me when you get up if I'm not already up."

"Will do."

CHAPTER 28

SYLVESTRA woke up in darkness, dizzy and disoriented. Her stomach felt like an empty pit and her tongue like damp sandpaper.

Dammit, she thought. *I passed out again. Third time in the last*—she checked her chrono—*two hours. That's not good.* Sreet or his minions had been bringing her food and drink at first, but no one had come by for two days. If she didn't get out of here soon, there might come a time when she would slip off to sleep and never wake up.

Sylvestra stood weakly, and the lights went on. Sreet had imprisoned her in a bedroom, but where that bedroom was, she had no idea. She had free rein of the room and, thankfully, the adjoining refresher room. Sreet had magically sealed the rest of the home against everything but light and air, and the latter only worked one way, allowing her the air she needed to breathe and removing waste gasses but blocking sound.

She stumbled to the refresher, where she drank copiously from the bath. It was stale water, since the barrier also prevented water from flowing, but it felt wonderful in her dry mouth and gullet.

She caught a glance of herself in the refresher mirror and was surprised at how well she looked despite her intense hunger. Her face was not as flush, perhaps, and her feathers were a little disarrayed from her disordered sleeping, but that was all she had to show for two days of not eating. She knew, of course, the real toll was internal. Averians couldn't go much more than two days without food.

She walked back out into the bedroom, stretched her wings to their full length, and let out a primal cry. She refolded her wings and went back to the one thing that had kept her occupied for the past few days, reading the books that she had loaded on her chrono. She'd read them before, and the small screen on the chrono made reading anything like a book an exercise in frustration, but it had kept her mind active for the time being. Two days ago, she had walked around the room while she read, just to keep exercised. But yesterday she'd only been able to walk in intervals with long breaks in between. Today, she didn't feel like walking at all. But she forced herself to do it. She also read out loud to break the silence.

Suddenly, she stopped. *There's that sound again,* she thought. She'd heard the very faint sound a few times the day before. Each time she'd paused to listen for it, it hadn't repeated, so she had believed it to be her imagination.

This time it was much louder. In fact, it had sounded like the whine of an aircar. The magical barrier allowed light through the window but otherwise made it translucent, so Sylvestra could see nothing outside. Now that she was still, the sound seemed to come from that direction. Eyes closed and ears perked, she walked gingerly toward the window. She heard it again! She ran to the window, and her heart leaped. The translucency had thinned! It was late, and night had fallen, but she could see pinpoints of light from other trees, and the running lights from passing taxis. Those *were* the sounds she had heard, she realized as another aircar swept past twenty meters from the window.

Sylvestra rushed to the bedroom door and flung it open with a flourish. She pressed against the barrier with all the strength she had left. It sparked and sizzled furiously at her, but not at all with the ferocity it had when she had first tested its limits. Back in the refresher, she unscrewed the seat from the waste chute and returned with it to the doorway. Grunting with effort, she hammered the barrier with the seat. She nearly toppled over when the barrier flashed brilliantly and dissipated.

Panting, she stood there, incredulous, half-in and half-out of the bedroom. Part of her expected Sreet to suddenly appear and imprison her again, and she readied the waste chute seat, prepared to batter him with it if he did. But after a few minutes, she realized he was not returning. His spell had faded, for whatever reason, and she was free.

She dropped the seat and looked around, finding familiarity in the flat's style. It resembled her own. Then she spotted some photos and realized she was in her neighbor's apartment. *That sneaky bastard! I was right next door to my apartment the whole time!* She recalled that her neighbor was in To-Weetsa-Woo on holiday.

Without wasting another minute, she went to her apartment, gulped down half a liter of nutria, armed herself, drank the other half liter, then left for the precinct.

FREESEWEE sat at his desk, reviewing the statements provided by Lezàl's companions. He found their willingness to talk, and that their accounts both matched, very refreshing. Combined, their accounts tied up most of the loose ends surrounding the Terran boy, from his landing in the public bath, his recruitment by Sreet and the Hawk Sorcerers to his rampage at Freet-See. The one point that both girls were intentionally vague on was how they all got to Averia. Miss Lee had at least referred to some kind of device that caused the boy to end up on Averia, but Freesewee hadn't pressed her on that. In the end, that would've satisfied his curiosity, but not been relevant to the case.

Both girls had also confirmed that Terrans did not possess magical capabilities, a fact which had thrilled Freesewee. He'd heard that some Elmarians possessed the ability, however that entire species was reclusive. He could count on one hand the number of Elmarians that had ever registered at

Freet-See. And as far as he knew, not one of them had been a sorcerer.

All of that is irrelevant, of course, he thought. *Even if they don't have sorcerers, they clearly have the capacity for magic. That in itself is a problem. At least it's in the open now, and pressure can be put on the Berdians to never allow offworlders into their ranks. It's the only way I can see this ending without more chaos. Hopefully the politicians see it the same way.*

As if the man had overheard his thoughts, the comm chimed and the Mayor's image appeared beside the call indicator. Freesewee had left a message for him earlier.

He took the call and updated the Mayor.

||What about the Chief?|| asked the Mayor.

||I'm about to interview Lezàl.|| Freesewee glanced at the time and wondered what in the seven bowels of Sirteer was taking them so long to bring Lezàl. ||But I believe he won't have that answer either.||

||Then who does? The Terran boy?||

||I don't want to speculate without more facts, sir.||

||That's fair. I'm sure you're doing all you can to find her. I've kept this from the media so far, but the word is bound to get out sooner rather than later.|| Unsaid, but implied, was that the leak would come from someone in the precinct. Freesewee didn't like it, but he knew it was true.

||Understood. Then there's the matter of this Terran boy. We will do what we can, as you know, but after Freet-See… we're just law enforcement. I can set up a perimeter around the city in case he's spotted here, but we're not equipped to take on a rogue sorcerer.||

||That's understood, Captain. I've already reached out to the Grand Masters of Berdia and have an emergency conference with them and the Council of Mayors in two hours.||

Deliberations will last at least an hour, fretted Freesewee. *That means no decision for at least another three hours. Wonderful.*

The door to Captain Freesewee's office flew open and an officer stepped in.

||Sir,|| gasped the birdman, but stopped when Freesewee held up his hand.

||Mayor,|| sang Freesewee, letting the young officer know the call he'd interrupted in his haste, ||good luck at the conference. We'll keep the peace in the meantime.||

||Thanks, Captain.||

The call clicked off, and Freesewee looked up at the officer. ||What's up, Officer Troo-ee?"

||Kormèr Lezàl has escaped, sir.||

||He's what?|| Freesewee stood and paced behind his desk.

||Escaped, sir. And the female, Jeransy Bolsner, is also missing.||

||Missing! Are we a police precinct or port control?||

The officer knew better than to answer. Instead, he continued delivering his news. ||We found the three guards assigned to watch Lezàl locked inside his cell. They claim he vanished from the cell. Surveillance footage shows the same.||

||I see.|| *So Kormèr Lezàl has some surprises up his sleeve yet*, thought Freesewee. ||And did Miss Bolsner vanish as well?||

||No, sir. Surveillance shows someone in uniform interacting with her just before both vanished. We suspect the imposter was Lezàl.||

||What about Miss Lee?||

||She's still in her cell. The Sergeant has doubled the guard on watch.||

During his conversation with the Mayor, Freesewee had kept his concern for his officers at a professional level. What he'd actually wanted to tell the mayor was that he feared for their lives. He imagined that sorcerers weren't invulnerable to projectiles, but he'd never had to put that to the test before. No sorcerer had ever gone rogue like this in Averia's history. At least, not that he was aware of.

He brought up the surveillance footage and quickly found the segments containing Lezàl's escape and his helping Bolsner escape. *Damn! If I didn't know better, I wouldn't have known that was Lezàl in disguise. Could he be the first Elmarian sorcerer I've ever seen? If that's the case…*

||Bring Miss Lee here,|| he ordered.

||Yessir.|| With that, the officer was gone.

Freesewee considered how the next moments would go, or perhaps how he would like them to go. This time, he didn't have to wait long before the officer returned with Anndrew Lee in binders.

||Remove her bindings,|| chirped Freesewee.

||Are you sure, sir?||

||Yes, yes. And you can wait outside.||

||Yessir.|| The officer unlatched the bindings and returned them to the clip on his belt. He left the room, closing the door behind him.

"Hello again, Miss Lee. Please, have a seat."

"Hi," she replied, warily, sitting in a seat he'd placed in front of his desk. Freesewee sat behind his desk.

"I believe you've been honest with me so far, and I would like that to continue," he told her, and she seemed to relax. He had dealt with Terrans on Freet-See and felt he could read their body language well enough. "How long has Kormèr Lezàl been a sorcerer?"

He caught the flash of surprise cross her face, but was she surprised that he had figured it out or because she hadn't known? He hoped that would reveal itself in her answer.

"Is this part of the interrogation?" she asked.

"This is an interview. As I mentioned earlier, you're not under arrest."

"Yet," she reminded him. "Earlier, you had said 'yet'. So, if not, why the cuffs and the holding cells?"

"I don't understand… Cuffs?" She held up her hands, now freed. "Oh, the binders? That's our procedure once a civilian passes beyond the desk floor. The cell… well, that's because I hadn't made up my mind about you yet."

"And now you have?"

"Will you answer the question?"

She watched him, deliberation behind her gaze. "He wasn't a sorcerer until the Hovel was destroyed."

Oh! Was I wrong about Lezàl? thought Freesewee, surprised by the answer. *Could Tseeo have actually been on to something when he accused Lezàl of destroying the Hovel to steal magic?*

"Please elaborate," he said.

"We found Kormèr's sorcerer friend dying in the ruins. The last thing he did was to give us what he felt we needed to stop Cecil."

||He gave Kormèr his magic?|| The news so surprised Freesewee that he slipped back to Averian song. "I'm sorry. He gave Kormèr magic?"

She nodded. "He gave all of us magic." She held up her hand, and a small ball of flame hovered over her open palm. When she rotated her hand vertically, the ball split into five small flames that burned from the tips of her fingers.

Freesewee stared at the flames until she snuffed them out. Then his eyes slid up to meet hers. *Stormy skies! Another two Terran sorcerers.* "You could've escaped at any time."

She nodded. "But Kormèr asked us to trust you and to answer your questions truthfully."

"Well, I'd suspected that you and Miss Bolsner were being honest in your statements. But now… now I believe you."

Anndrew nodded, and any remaining tension seemed to flow out of her expression. "Well, I'm glad because it is the truth."

"Yes, well, be that as it may, we have a problem. Lezàl was interrogated by one of my subordinates, who overstepped his authority. And he may have given Lezàl the wrong impression about your… situation."

"I don't understand," she replied.

Freesewee sighed, realizing he'd been vague. "My primary concern has been finding out where my boss is, and the three of you were my only leads to her whereabouts. When Lezàl finally broke some actual laws, I jumped at the chance and had you brought in. I was going to interview the three of you. But one of my sergeants jumped the gun with Lezàl. And this sergeant has strong opinions of Lezàl from an incident three years ago."

Anndrew Lee nodded, and Freesewee assumed she knew about the heist. "Kormèr thinks most of you don't like him because of what happened."

Freesewee flashed a quick smile. "He's not exactly popular here, no. I wasn't connected to the case, but I've heard enough of the Sergeant's ranting. I don't condone his behavior, however, and I know when to put my feelings aside to do my job."

"But the Sergeant can't."

Freesewee frowned. "Correct, and he backed Lezàl into a corner." Anndrew peered at him, so he added, "Lezàl's escaped with Miss Bolsner."

Anndrew's surprise showed briefly before she suppressed it. "Good for him. You're right; he probably felt he had no choice."

"I agree. When he comes back for you, please let him know that… well, that there's someone here he can trust if he needs help. I mean, someone other than the Chief."

Anndrew smiled. "Thanks, Captain. I'm sure he'll appreciate it. He really loves Sylvestra, you know. He'd never hurt a hair… err, a feather on her head."

Freesewee inhaled deeply, held it, then exhaled. "I believe that." He straightened as she gave him a knowing glance. His affection for Sylvestra was probably plain on his face.

Mercifully, Anndrew made no comment and asked instead, "What are you going to do with me now?"

"I wish I could just release you. But since your companions escaped, I can't do that right away. Not without jeopardizing my career. I'll try to make your stay a comfortable one."

"I understand." She seemed resigned but confident.

Freesewee stared at her. "You believe he's coming back for you?"

She shrugged. "He's my ride home, and he knows it."

"Alright, then." He took another deep breath. "I'll just have to make things as simple for him as I can."

CHAPTER 29

CUTTING grooves through the mashed oats on her plate with a protein stalk, Anndrew wondered what was taking Kormèr so long. Her parley with the Captain had been over an hour ago, and she'd expected Kormèr to show up soon after. She hoped he hadn't gone after Cecil with only Jeransy at his side.

She stared at her food art, wishing she could go back to the Captain's office and give him her opinion. This food did not inspire any kind of desire to eat.

Anndrew surveyed the room, idly calculating her odds of success if she tried to escape. She wanted to be civil, especially given the Captain's effort to minimize the security around her cell, but she was going stir-crazy.

There had originally been four guards, but after her conversation with the Captain, two had been called away. Anndrew had also noticed that another two at the end of the corridor had been reduced to one.

"Hey." She smiled at the guards and waved when they looked her way. "Tell your Captain: no offense, but this food sucks."

One of the guards, a short brown-feathered fellow, didn't react. He whistled something to his taller companion, who watched Anndrew with amused curiosity. "You no eat that?" he asked in broken English, as he stepped closer to her cell. He pointed disdainfully at her food, wearing a mocking smile as he swiped his baton noisily against the bars.

"Why, are you hungry?" Before the guard could answer, Anndrew scooped the mashed oats with the protein stick and flicked it across the cell, splattering it across the guard's face. "Help yourself!" Hopefully, they'd revoke her meal privileges for the rest of the day—she *really* couldn't stand the stuff.

"This is the thanks I get," murmured the guard in a familiar, oddly accented English over the cackles of the other two guards.

Kormèr! Anndrew gasped. Then she joined the laughter as the guard swiped the mess off his face with his hand.

"Har, har. Very amusing," said Kormèr's voice in her head. He flicked some of the mash in his hand at short-brown as he twittered something. Short-brown laughed harder. *"Enough of this; time to go. Give me your hand."* He slipped his hand between the bars, and Anndrew put her hand in his. *"Deep breath, and…"*

SITTING in the cockpit, Jeransy kept her eyes on the foot traffic in the impound lot, and specifically around a sleek little ship sitting thirty meters off the port side. Kormèr didn't want to add kidnapping to any charges the police had against him, so he and Jeransy had risked carrying the unconscious officer over to the smaller ship and locking him inside. Then Kormèr had rushed off to collect Anndrew. That had been nearly two hours ago, and though no alarm had yet been raised, she knew better than to let that calm her worries.

Movement on the screen caught her eye; the hatch on the small ship opened, and the officer stumbled out holding his head. Double doors ahead flew open as Averian police swarmed into the lot and fanned out around the mini-yacht. A beeping filled the cabin, startling Jeransy with its suddenness. She remembered that passive sensors were still on and moved to shut off both the sensors and the alarm.

A *boop boop* sounded from the overhead panel.

Jeransy double-checked that she had shut down the sensors, then realized that the sound had come from the hatchway, and the face of an officer appeared on the screen. She left the audio off, but the birdwoman seemed to chirp adamantly.

"Hurry up, KL," mumbled Jeransy, her foot tapping nervously.

"You've only to ask."

Jeransy spun in her seat as Kormèr entered, followed by Anndrew. "Aces!"

Kormèr sat in the pilot's chair, checked his screens and nodded. "Nice! You ran the preflight check." The double-*boop* sounded from the hatchway again, so Kormèr retracted the boarding ramp. The Averian on the screen vanished with a flutter of her wings.

"Okay, ladies. Get ready; this might get rough."

As soon as the girls were safely in their seats, he lifted off, turned the ship around, and opened the throttle.

"What now?" asked Anndrew.

Kormèr didn't answer right away. Jeransy watched him as he simultaneously guided the ship and scrolled the menu on one of his screens. He tapped a selection and nodded at what he read there. "We're fugitives now. They're probably loading up that big ship of theirs again to come after us."

"Um, about that…" Anndrew recounted her conversation with Freesewee. "So they probably won't be coming after us."

"Hmm," said Kormèr. "With all due respect to the good Captain, he reports to the Mayor of Birshetland, and the Mayor reports to the Council of Mayors, all of which I think would give their flight feathers for the chance to apprehend me." He looked at Anndrew over his shoulder. "I'm sorry, but it's probably best if we assume they're going to give chase."

Anndrew nodded. "That's fair."

213

Kormèr turned back to his screens. "I don't know about you, but I'm exhausted."

"I'm bloody shattered," said Jeransy. "I even passed out waiting on the interrogation."

"Right," said Kormèr. "But we can't risk landing and having them catch us again. What I see here," he pointed at the screen, "is that we can set the autopilot to follow a random flight pattern. If I can set that up to avoid other ships and major population centers, we can get some rest."

"Can you make it avoid the police?" asked Jeransy. It wouldn't make sense to just fly around randomly; the police could surround them in the air as easily as on the ground.

Kormèr nodded, scrolling the options on the screen. "Good idea." He stopped and read the display. "It can be set to avoid specific objects. I'm sure I can adjust that to vehicles matching certain settings. Oh! That reminds me…" He resumed flipping through screens.

Jeransy smiled after a moment, amused at his loss of focus. "Reminds you of what? You can't just leave us hanging like that."

He chuckled. "Sorry. I was told that our transponder is disabled, but it looks like it's working just fine."

"Transponder," said Anndrew. "What's that?"

"It's a system that transmits ship information whenever it receives a signal from a satellite, ground control or another ship. It prevents collisions and helps with tracking air traffic. It's critically important, so it's supposed to be impossible to disable." He turned and looked at her again. "Why?"

Anndrew smiled sheepishly. "When I was connecting the radio, I tapped into a system labeled 'transponder receiver'. I didn't change anything about it, I just tapped the line."

Kormèr's grin widened into a smile. "Congratulations! You have earned the honorary title of 'pirate'."

Anndrew smiled. "Thanks, I think."

"Now go turn on that radio. It'll really make it hard for the police to track us."

As Anndrew left the cockpit, Kormèr glanced back at his screen, then he looked at Jeransy. "If we get the chance, I'll hook you up with flying lessons. But for now, while I fly us around, do you think you can poke around the auto-pilot menu and figure out how to make it do what we need?"

"I've been watching you and I was poking around the menus a bit." She nodded confidently. "I think I can do it."

"Great." He passed the screen to her side of the control board. "Have at it. Once we set that up, we can sleep."

"Now that's motivation!" Jeransy continued digging through the menus.

THE alarm went up around the station the moment Anndrew Lee vanished, along with one of the officers watching her cell. The second alarm came from Officer Rreeseer, who'd been assigned to the impounded mini-yacht. He'd woken up in a different ship with no recollection of having fallen asleep.

Not surprised in the least by the news, Freesewee arrived at the impound lot and found two squads of officers surrounding the mini-yacht, and one female officer on the boarding ramp trying to hack the hatch control. She jumped clear as the ramp suddenly retracted. Then the ship rose, spun around and shot away.

| |Requesting permission to pursue, sir,| | chirped one of his lieutenants.

Freesewee nodded. | |Permission granted.| | But he knew the effort would be fruitless.

He contemplated the situation as he walked back toward his office. It wasn't going to be easy to cover up this incident; too many officers had been involved, even two imposters that somehow no one had noticed weren't members of the precinct. When the questions came, Freesewee would have to answer truthfully. It wasn't his way to fabricate stories to cover up blunders. He would just have to soften the edges to protect his personnel. He would take the blame for it when the time came and hope that the magic involved would be enough to save his career.

As he approached his office, he saw the door to Sylvestra's office was open and the lights on. He frowned at first, wondering why someone would be in her office. Then he grinned. *Lezàl!* he thought, imagining the man had returned to her office, perhaps for some clue to help him find her. This would be Freesewee's chance to tell him—

Freesewee stopped at the door and his jaw dropped. | |Sylvestra?| |

The birdwoman turned away from her display and smiled. It was as if the sun had suddenly risen in the middle of the darkest night. She came and hugged him, and he found he had moved to meet her halfway without even realizing it. | |Thank the heavens you're alright,| | he chirped when she stepped back.

| |I'm sorry I couldn't contact you sooner,| | she sang between bites of fruit. | |I was being held captive by a Berdian—| | She stopped as information on Kormèr appeared on the display. She scanned it, manipulating the data windows swiftly. | |Kormèr is here? And you thought *he* had kidnapped me?| |

| |Yes. Well, not anymore… to both of those. He…| | She peered at him quizzically. He sighed, unable to find an easy way to tell her. | |He escaped, not ten minutes ago.| |

Sylvestra nodded. | |Okay. Are you pursuing?| |

| |I authorized a pursuit.| | He kept his opinion of their chances of success to himself. She didn't know yet that he knew magic, and he couldn't know how she would take that news.

| |Good. He's going to need all the backup he can get. I saw you'd

impounded his ship.||

||That's how he made his escape.|| He decided she needed to know. ||Also—||

Sylvestra dashed past him into the corridor. ||I'm sorry, Freesewee. I'm in a rush.||

||Chief.|| Sylvestra stopped. He only called her Chief when he was being respectful or demanding her respect. ||You should know that Lezàl has magic. I mean, they all do, him and his Terran friends.||

||I don't understand. Has magic how?||

||There's a lot you've missed in the past few days. The Terran boy that you sent Kormèr to Berdia after has become a tremendous menace to the planet.|| He'd present the highlights now and fill in the details later or if she asked for them.

||Cecil Murphy, yes, I know. What's that got to do with Kormèr and magic?||

||The Hovel was destroyed, allegedly by Murphy.|| Sylvestra gaped. Freesewee gave her a summarized version if the Terran girls' statements.

Sylvestra pressed her back to the corridor wall as she processed the information. ||Thank you for the update,|| she sang, at last. ||That's a lot to process, but perhaps it will help improve the situation.||

That wasn't the reaction he'd been expecting. ||It will? How?||

She pushed off from the wall. ||Without magic, Kormèr would've been walking right into a trap. Now he stands a chance. But I need to help him even the odds a bit more. You have the transponder code for his ship?||

||We do, but it's useless. The transponder is being jammed by a radio.||

||A radio? Never mind; not important.|| She crossed her arms and stared off into the distance. ||How can we track that ship?||

Freesewee spotted Rreeseer walking toward them. He immediately noticed the birdman's empty sash. ||Officer, you appear to be missing your badge.||

||Sir. In the commotion, I didn't notice that it was missing until a few minutes ago. It must've fallen off when I was being moved.||

Freesewee shot a quick glance at Sylvestra and saw her quizzical expression. ||Of course. You've traced it?||

||Yessir. It's not on the premises. I think it might be aboard Lezàl's ship.||

Sylvestra was suddenly alert. ||That's it! If it is aboard the ship, we can track them.||

Freesewee nodded slowly. ||Maybe. The badges don't generate a powerful signal, especially inside a ship. If he has the shields up, we'll get nothing.||

||I know, but it's the best we've got. Send me that trace, right away.||

Rreeseer hesitated. | |Chief, I've never—| |

| |Step into my office,| | Freesewee told him. | |I'll show you how to do that.| |

Sylvestra straightened her sash. | |Now that that's resolved, I have to make one more stop.| |

Freesewee breathed deeply and held it. | |How can I help?| |

| |Get me that badge trace. And if you can, get a message to Kormèr that I'm back.| |

| |Of course. That's it?| |

| |Join the chase,| | she sang, walking backwards. | |Even with magic, he'll need all the help he can get.| | She turned and dashed off again.

CHAPTER 30

AFTER sleeping a solid four hours, Kormèr woke up and then struggled to fall back asleep. He slipped into a light sleep twice, but only for thirty minutes at a time. After the second time, a restless tension enveloped him, and he gave up on sleeping and sat on the edge of the bed nook. Red night-lighting automatically came on, providing a dim illumination.

At least there haven't been any alarms, he thought. *Though I wonder what Cecil's up to.*

He's right, said another voice in his head. *We haven't heard from him since the Hovel.*

Hey! Srrcheel? I can hear you.

Well, thank the heavens for that! I've been trying to get back in touch with you since yesterday.

Great. This is much simpler than me having to do all that deep meditation. So what did you want to chat about?

Practice, said Srrcheel. *You and the girls need it. And I've teased out some of the spell knowledge, I think. It's really complicated in here.*

Thanks.

Take it as a compliment. But I have some new things for you to try.

"Hmm," said Kormèr, out loud. *We can't really practice inside the ship.*

No, definitely not, said Srrcheel, as Kormèr brought up the auto-pilot log and scanned the events of the past six hours. *Am I reading that right? No police run-ins?*

Kormèr nodded. *That's right. I guess I can risk landing for a bit. But the girls are still asleep.*

Then let's be productive and go through the collection of stuff you stole from the Hovel.

Kormèr considered arguing that, technically, he hadn't stolen them, but he let it drop as unimportant.

Kormèr emptied his pockets of artifacts and, with Srrcheel's help, quickly divided up them up into three categories: useless, moderately useful and potentially useful.

By the way, said Srrcheel when they'd finished, *are you going to try for the Tseerleeltrr Stone again?*

Honestly, the risk of capture is too high to chance returning for the stone.

Kormèr sensed relief from Srrcheel. *I think our link is getting stronger,* he said. *I felt your reaction there.*

A brief wave of embarrassment suddenly dissipated. *I'm sorry. I'm learning as I go along here. I didn't mean to flood you with my personal feelings.*

Not at all. The world... the galaxy might be a better place if we could all communicate at this level. Kormèr thought back to his early interactions with Srrcheel. *I might not have been so... obnoxious to you years ago.*

You weren't that obnoxious. No wait, I was thinking of someone else. You were.

I deserved that, thought Kormèr, with a chuckle, as Srrcheel broadcast some mirth of his own.

We're hungry, you know, said Srrcheel. And Kormèr suddenly realized that his stomach was churning emptily.

I'll make some breakfast. Kormèr stood and headed for the galley. *The girls will probably be up soon. Then we can make a stop for that practice session.*

THE complex sigils Cecil traced in the air were of his composition, as he cast a very special spell he had created. There was no art to his design; the Hawk Sorcerers would truly have been disappointed to see him work. But he'd gained his knowledge of magic through brute-force memorization. In the single day he'd spent learning, he couldn't possibly have picked up the artistry involved in what the sorcerers did. For that reason, he paid the price for his crude conjuration with his own wasted energy.

He stopped and sat heavily on the rock on which he had been standing, exhausted after being up for the last two days designing the spell. He removed his glasses and rubbed his weary eyes vigorously. *I don't even need these stupid things for this part of the spell,* he thought. Remarkably, he could see the filaments perfectly with or without his glasses. He tried hanging them on his collar, but it sat awkwardly and rubbed his neck constantly. He thought about putting them in his pocket, but that's how the bridge had broken to begin with. Finally, he gave up and put the glasses back on.

What a job! He sighed, looking up at the two moons in the darkening sky. They seemed extra bright tonight, as if glowing with a magic of their own. One of the books Sreet had given him to read had mentioned the names of each of the moons. He closed his eyes, and the words appeared straight from the page he'd read them on, as they always did: Seertsor and Thencarree. The book had gone on to talk about a celebration called Cheerretee which took place the night that Seertsor eclipsed Thencarree. The sorcerers also had some kind of celebration that night, but Cecil's focus had shifted to the spell books at that point, so he hadn't read that part. *I'm sure I have that book in my collection. Now that I'm seeing this event live, I'm kind of curious about how the sorcerers celebrate it.*

But that can wait until after I'm done with this spell. He stood. *Now what I need is some eleron.*

"Spot!" called Cecil, seeing that his pet was nowhere in sight. After learning that Lezàl could track his excavations of eleron, Cecil always brought Spot with him to the quarries. *"Spot,"* he called with his mind and received a mental stirring in response from the semi-telepathic creature. *"Spot, come."*

In moments, the creature's sleek black pelt slid up behind Cecil.

"Good boy." Cecil traced a pattern and transported himself and the beast to an eleron quarry.

"I'll need…" He paused to consider the amount, then shrugged. "Meh. A lot." He performed the excavation spell *srootee* then traced the length of the seam he wanted to extract. The height and depth seemed to be automatically set to roughly twelve by twelve centimeters. He triggered the spell, and the section of ore he'd selected vanished from the quarry surface, leaving behind the tailings from the automatic processing.

What if I need more? None of the spell tomes he'd read so far had described a consistent eleron to energy ratio. Instead, they merely indicated the requirement per spell. He felt sure that he must have missed the mention of the ratio, however, since later tomes didn't even list the need for eleron. Since he'd crafted this spell on his own, he had no basis from which to even extrapolate the required eleron.

And with Lezàl presumably monitoring eleron quarries, Cecil had to minimize his use of them. *Better to have too much than to have to make another trip,* he decided.

He repeated the excavation spell and processed another large section of the quarry wall.

"Away," he shouted theatrically, casting a teleport spell.

AROOO Arooo. Kormèr's chest vibrated as if the alarm were stabbing its way through him.

"What the bloody hell is that?!" cried Jeransy, dismissing the Gauntlet and covering her ears.

Anndrew hopped quickly toward the ship's boarding ramp from the rock where she'd been practicing her fire spells. "I guess that means practice is over." She ran inside.

"That's the alarm I set." Kormèr also ran for the ramp. "Something tripped the sensors. I guess it's getting late, anyway." The girls had slept until late morning. They'd eaten a quick brunch after which Kormèr had landed the ship for some spell practice

"Eleron hit," said Anndrew from her station as Kormèr followed Jeransy into the cockpit. "It's a big one."

"Keep a lock on it," said Kormèr, sliding into the pilot's seat. Out of the corner of his eye, he saw Jeransy powering up the engines from her station. "I don't want to lose it this time." Kormèr's fingers danced over the navigational controls, and the ready ship lifted off and lunged forward.

"It's gone!" cried Anndrew a moment later. "There are just traces now."

"That would be the freshly exposed lode at the quarry." Kormèr sighed. *Dammit! He's gone again.*

Go to the quarry anyway, said Srrcheel. *There's still a chance.*

They arrived in less than a minute. Kormèr directed the ship's lights at the quarry, and two fresh scars lit up brightly.

Cast this, directed Srrcheel. *Quick.*

Without standing, Kormèr moved his hands and right foot in the pattern that came to his mind. Immediately, he felt a tingle down his spine and throughout his extremities, and he just *knew.* "It *was* Cecil. He's teleported. How strange; I can actually sense it."

Track it, offered Srrcheel. *The same spell reveals the end point of the spell. Follow the traces of magic.*

Kormèr closed his eyes, focused on that tingling sensation as it faded... faded... and dissipated completely. But that contact was long enough.

"I know where he is." Kormèr throttled up the engines.

"What are we going to do once we catch up to him?" asked Anndrew.

"We stop him," said Kormèr, hearing apprehension in her voice. Or perhaps it was his own. But he didn't let it show as he looked at them each and added, "By any means necessary."

"Do we have enough power to stop him?" asked Jeransy.

Kormèr would've jumped at an opportunity to confront Cecil without endangering the girls. But if there was such a way, it eluded him. And now that he thought about it, he hadn't ever asked the girls if they were in for this.

"I believe so," he told her, honestly. "I strongly believe that if we work together and focus, we can do this. But if you—either of you—tell me now that you're not ready, I will turn this ship right around, and we'll think of something else."

He looked around at Anndrew. She was solemn but calm. She gave him a quick nod. "I'm with you."

He looked at Jeransy. "What? Of course, I am, too!"

"Alright," he said with a grin.

A double-*boop* alerted that something had triggered the sensors.

"Two organisms ahead," reported Anndrew. "One registers as a Terran and the big one... unknown."

"Huh. What could be unknown to the ship's computer?" Kormèr brought up the defense menu and tapped the shield control. "Shields up. No sense getting surprised."

DUE to the complexity of Cecil's spell project, he had broken it up into four stages. He had only recently discovered that he didn't have to trigger one spell before starting another, leaving a completed *srootee* in a suspended state until he was ready to trigger it.

He had completed the first two stages of his master spell over the past two days. These created the basic components and an access point to a unique region in space-time. An hour ago, Cecil had finished the third stage, a simple preparation for the next and final stage, which would connect the pieces and trigger them together as one massive spell. The stages became progressively simpler; the first stage had taken four hours to cast and left Cecil drained beyond exhaustion. The final stage comprised a single simple pattern that would take only seconds to cast.

Tense with anticipation, he prepared to cast the final spell.

And once it's done, he thought, closing his eyes and letting his arms hang loose at his sides, *everything will change.*

He opened his eyes and glanced up at the bright moons, his only source of light this night as he conserved energy for the spell. A dim speck caught his eye, like a firefly against the night sky, but low to the ground. He watched curiously as the tiny dot grew larger, clearly coming closer to him.

He reached out with his mind, his perception telescoping toward the dot. "It's Lezàl," he growled with repugnance, sensing the other's mind. Behind him, Spot's silky black pelt shuddered, the creature empathizing with its master's annoyance. "I should've been keeping a closer eye on him, but I've been too busy with this project." Cecil's eyes narrowed with suspicion. "What's he up to? He can't still be thinking of returning me to Earth." Before Cecil could probe more deeply, the ship's shield activated and ejected him.

"Damn shields. But how did Lezàl find me?" wondered Cecil. Then he shrugged. "You know what? I don't care. Let's end this now."

He traced a quick *srootee,* and a brilliant bolt of coruscating energy streaked toward the approaching craft. The deadly glow that raked the ship in the distance glistened gratifyingly in Cecil's eyes. But when the glow vanished and the craft was still coming, seemingly unharmed, fire replaced the delight. Again technology had countered magic, and despite that complying with the laws of physics, it made Cecil's blood boil.

But technology had its limits, and Cecil was certain that he could shatter them. He started a new *srootee,* but a torrent of annihilating energy rained down, tearing up the ground around him, pelting him with dirt and rock. Spot leaped into the line of fire, yowling at the barrage that pummeled his flank.

Mustering up all his anger and his power into a terrifying blend of destructive energy, Cecil thrust his hands after the passing ship. The toxic blend poured forth from his palms and slashed the craft's shields with blazing fury.

The rear of the ship exploded brilliantly, the hull peeling open like tin. It plunged to the ground, and with a grinding shriek, ripped through the loose, loamy upper layer of one of the huge floating rocks. A cloud of soil and debris ballooned into the air as the ship smashed into an outcrop of stone, splitting apart like an eggshell. There it remained, a smoking ruin of twisted metal.

"That's that," said Cecil, half to himself, watching as the wreckage exploded again in the distance. He took several deep breaths, realizing that he was out of breath. He stepped over to his beast and cast a healing spell, though the damage was not severe. "Good job protecting me, boy." He scratched Spot around the large horns. "You heal right up, now, while I finish my—"

Spot tensed, then jumped up and stared into the darkness to the right of the burning wreckage.

"What is it, boy?" asked Cecil. *Surely no one could have survived that.* Cecil reached out with his mind again, scanning the darkness for any sign of whatever Spot was sensing. In moments, he found one, then two more. *Lezàl!*

CHAPTER 31

LEGS splayed to keep his balance, Kormèr stared in shock at the flaming wreckage of the ship. *By the gods, we made it!*

"Wha— what happened?" asked Jeransy. Kormèr turned to see her drop squarely on her rump. Holding her head, she murmured, "So dizzy."

"I teleported us," mumbled Kormèr, and his stomach heaved. *It was too sudden,* he thought, afraid that he'd vomit if he tried to speak again so soon.

"Good timing," said Anndrew. She looked the least distressed, though she kneeled on the ground next to Jeransy. "Let's not cut it so close next time, okay?"

Kormèr nodded in complete agreement. The cockpit hatch had sealed as soon as the engine lost containment and exploded. But the raw energy from the reactor had hammered the hatch, and Kormèr knew that it would have overwhelmed the safeties and cooked him and the girls alive if he hadn't managed the teleport.

The hairs on the back of his neck prickled as the girls' faces were suddenly set aglow, as if by fire. Kormèr whirled, hands automatically weaving a quick spell. A wall of water formed in time to be vaporized by a fiery blast.

"How the *hell* did you…" Standing forty meters away, awash in the bright moonlight, Cecil lowered his hands. With a slight gesture, he caused the sky above them to glow, casting an unnatural bluish hue over the area. A large creature stepped lithely up behind Cecil and leered at Kormèr and the girls with crimson eyes. Kormèr had seen many different kinds of creatures in his travels, but he'd never seen anything as menacing as this creature looked. *Unknown organism!* he remembered from the ship's sensor readings.

"You know magic," said Cecil. "Or you've learned it as fast as I have, which I highly doubt. Did Sreet think he could use you to control me?"

Kormèr straightened up, his stomach still trying to settle. He glanced at the sky, and the proximity of the moons unsettled his stomach once again. "Does it matter?" He did his best to sound casual. Now was not the time to show weakness. "Sreet's dead; you've seen to that."

"He got off easy. I had planned much worse for him for betraying me."

Jeransy stepped up on Kormèr's right side, and Anndrew flanked Kormèr on the left.

Cecil looked at Anndrew. "Anndrew Lee. I never had any problems with you, Annde. In fact," he tapped his cheek thoughtfully, "you once helped me pick up my papers when someone pushed them out of my hands."

Anndrew nodded. "I remember that."

"Then why are you pestering me now?!" His hands clenched into fists at his sides.

"Because you've changed."

Cecil opened his mouth, looking as if he were ready to shout again. But then he closed it and grinned. "Yes, I have. I've become wiser and powerful."

Anndrew shook her head. "You're only half right. You were a victim then, but you're the bully now."

"You have *no* right to say that. *You* aren't the one whose books they knocked onto the floor. *You* aren't the one they shoved into lockers at least once a week, or who they shoved aside and into a wall because I was in their way. When I get back, that ends! I'll remake the world so that others like me can thrive."

"By hurting or killing everyone that's different from you?" asked Jeransy. "How's that not bullying?"

Cecil sneered at her. "You, of all people, should understand. You, who live under the thumb of anyone with a little more power than you."

It surprised Kormèr to find that Cecil knew that about Jeransy. He supposed that Cecil had read their minds or cast a new scrying eye at some point.

"We don't need them." Cecil swiped a hand through the air. "No one needs them. They contribute nothing to society, only slow progress by using fear and intimidation to keep people from reaching their potential."

Until now, Cecil had been an almost faceless shell of a person in Kormèr's mind's eye. Now, talking to the boy, Kormèr's resolve was weakening. Cecil was clearly an emboldened victim, his behavior shaped by abuse. Kormèr even sympathized with the boy; though he'd never experienced any abuse himself, the class structure on his homeworld of Elmar did, occasionally, border on the powerful subjugating the powerless. Yunzen had become a politician and thief, and had raised Kormèr as a thief, to do their part to fight that injustice. They used their power to try to remake their small corner of the world into a better place.

But Yunzen had drawn a very bold line at hurting others to achieve his goals. Kormèr had always refused to cross that line as well. Which was why, despite all that Cecil had done, Kormèr really didn't want to have to hurt the boy if he could avoid it.

"I want to help you." Kormèr hoped to prolong this avenue of discussion, to buy time. *Srrcheel, is there anything else I can do with him, anything other than kill him?*

"You... You what?"

"I agree with you. There are people on my world like that, too: they want to stop progress, keep things the way they are just because that's the way it's always been, and they think it should always be."

Cecil peered at him, and Kormèr sensed him probing, trying to reach his mind, but finding only a magical block.

Kormèr shrugged. "So I know how you feel." *Srrcheel!*

The answer is no, Kormèr. And into Kormèr's mind came an image of Cecil's hand making small motions just out of Kormèr's line of sight. Kormèr's eyes shifted to Cecil's pet; apparently the beast's mind was not shielded against probing, and it had a clear view of Cecil's subterfuge. *He's preparing a spell, something with wind, I think.*

"You do?" The fire in Cecil's eyes seemed to waver, but his hands continued tracing the small pattern.

"Yes. It's not easy being a thief, you know." Alert now, Kormèr felt Cecil's power gathering. "Everyone always after you for one thing or another." With a sad emptiness inside him, Kormèr telepathed to Anndrew and Jeransy: *"He's getting ready to attack. I can't reason with him; I tried. Get ready to strike."*

To kill? Anndrew wondered silently, but loud enough in her own head that Kormèr picked it up.

"Let's just see if we can stop him from casting, knock him out, whatever. We'll figure out how to deal with him after that. Ready?" When the girls acknowledged, he added, *"Go!"*

"You don't say—" With a sneer, Cecil raised his hands to unleash his spell, then he vanished momentarily behind the radiance of their combined attacks. A ball of flame from Anndrew's hand, needles of energy from Jeransy's gauntlet and a crackling bolt of lightning converged on him. The radiance dissipated, lingering for just a moment on a hemisphere of magical shielding that seemed rooted to the stone, immobile. The last of the glow faded, revealing Cecil, down on one knee and casting.

Jeransy pressed the attack, hammering Cecil's shield with flashes of energy from her silver glove. Before Kormèr could join her, a vortex of rushing air forced him to defend. Following Cecil's lead, he rooted a shield to the stone where it blocked the barrage of stones and debris. But he noticed with disappointment that it also blocked attacks from both girls.

Cecil pressed his momentary advantage and rapid-fired a random mix of energy bolts at the trio, all while the vortex continued whipping detritus at them.

Completely in a defensive position, Kormèr knew they wouldn't last against this kind of persistent barrage. The shield absorbed a portion of the energy hitting it, using that energy to power itself. But it was a lossy exchange, and the drain on the filaments increased with each passing second. Somehow, they had to coordinate their attacks and defense.

Try this, said Srrcheel, pushing several images into Kormèr's consciousness. Kormèr relayed the idea to the girls telepathically.

On his mark, Kormèr dropped the generic shield while Jeransy and

Anndrew switched to defense against the debris storm. Kormèr then focused on individually blocking the different energies hurling their way. But he was completely unprepared for the intensity of Cecil's casting and the randomness of the energies. Several flashed brilliantly, blinding him momentarily. A sonic blast shook him to the core and broke his concentration, and his shield dropped. Rocks slashed his cheeks and forehead as fire needles rained around him, singing his hair and setting his pants on fire. *Buomp! That was an utter failure. He's too damn fast.*

Anndrew dropped to her knees beside him as lightning bolts crackled past her. The air warped and blurred as she formed a plasma bubble around the three of them. It blocked sound and adjusted instantly to changes in brilliance, but it wasn't impervious.

"Are you okay?" she asked Kormèr.

"I'll be better when this is over," he told her, perhaps too truthfully. He didn't want to lie, but he hadn't expected this fight to go anything like this. "Nice job with the shield."

"Thanks, but I think it's fading. Are we ready?"

"Ready," said Kormèr.

"Yeah," said Jeransy.

Anndrew re-focused the shield into a shimmering wall of blue-hot flame and shoved it toward Cecil. It vaporized the hail of debris in its path, but the air vortex was too much for it, and the two forces canceled each other. When the air cleared, Cecil had vanished.

"Where'd he go?" Jeransy spun around, her gauntlet arm extended and searching for a target.

Kormèr snapped up as general a shield as he could find just in time, as white lances of plasma slammed into it from his right. *Srrcheel, can I coordinate the shield to drop with each of our attacks? It's pretty useless the way it is.*

It wasn't meant for this use, but I'll see what I can do.

Kormèr turned in the direction from which the plasma bolts had come and saw Cecil vanish again. "He's teleporting."

The shield flared and roared like a thunderclap as a massive force slammed into it. But Kormèr had imitated Cecil's shield and rooted it to the rock. Still, the impact cracked the stone underfoot and reverberated inside the shield deafeningly.

"Ugh!" cried Jeransy, her gauntlet vanishing as she pressed her palms over her ears. Kormèr heard her as if from a distance, over the ringing in his own ears.

Lightning crackled over the shield from behind them, but when Kormèr turned, Cecil had already gone. *This guerilla tactic of his is going to wear us down without our even getting a shot in.*

Use this, offered Srrcheel.

A *srootee* came to mind for a teleport blocker spell, though Kormèr struggled with it, as if he had to tug it out from under a great weight.

He pirouetted on his heel until he spotted Cecil casting off to the left. He quickly traced the pattern and dropped the shield just long enough to trigger the spell. A violet wave briefly sparkled over Cecil's shield. Unperturbed by this, Cecil finished his spell, and again, a massive force slammed Kormèr's shield. Kormèr grimaced as again his body vibrated with the shock of the impact. *What the hell?!* he cried silently as he watched Cecil teleport away again.

Cast it around him, not on him, said Srrcheel. *I've found a shield spell that should do what you want.*

Cecil slipped in two more attacks before Kormèr caught him popping into his new destination, only a few meters away. Once again, Kormèr cast the teleport blocker, and this time, nothing at all happened. Cecil cast the force slam again. But through the distress of the impact, Kormèr grinned as he watched Cecil cast a teleport and fail.

"That's the end of that," he murmured as he took advantage of Cecil's brief pause to drop the shield and cast the new one that Srrcheel had provided. Once again, drawing on the memory of the *srootee* felt sluggish, and he only finished it just as Cecil resumed his attacks. "Attack now," he said. "It should work."

The three of them launched a simultaneous barrage, with the shield flickering perfectly to allow the spells to pass. *Nice job, dude!* thought Kormèr at Srrcheel. And suddenly a thought occurred to him. He cast the old shield spell around Cecil. They wouldn't be able to wear him down, but it would also give them a short breather, as he wouldn't be able to attack them through it. Sure enough, Cecil cast what looked like the force spell, and he instantly crumpled to the ground, hands over his ears as it triggered within the shield.

Kormèr managed a smile, despite his insides empathizing with Cecil at that moment. *Hah! Gods, I hate that spell.*

Kormèr said to the girls: "We have a moment to catch our—"

A blood-chilling roar split the air. *Buomp! Cecil's pet!* Kormèr turned and stared into the soulless crimson eyes of the hideous creature, amazed at how stealthily it had snuck around behind them despite its size. With a hiss, it bared its shark-like grimace, row upon row of serrated needle-like teeth, which looked shockingly white against its black gums and tongue. With a last flick of its spiked, mace-like tail, the creature charged, evading Jeransy's beams and Anndrew's fireballs with unnatural agility. It leaped toward the trio, razor claws extended, and landed atop Kormèr's shield. The shield flared and crackled as the beast slashed and clawed it. Jeransy fired a red bolt up at it, and when the shield yielded to allow her shot through, the claws raked through. Jeransy yelped as they slashed her arm, but when Kormèr saw her checking the gauntlet, he realized the glove had saved her arm.

Behind them, Cecil cried, "Yeah, get her!" his voice distorted by the double shielding.

"Don't attack it," said Kormèr.

"Got that," said Jeransy. "How do we get it off?"

"Working on it." *Srrcheel?*

Something's wrong, said Srrcheel. *The spells are getting harder to push to you.*

Worried about Cecil at their backs, Kormèr looked toward the boy and saw him discharging a tight hot beam at the inside of the shield. The effort would slowly weaken the shield until it dissolved completely.

I need options quickly, said Kormèr, the effort of keeping both shields going quickly draining him. *Can I electrify the shield to get this creature to jump off?*

I have something for that, but I can only get part of the srootee *free from the tangle of spells.*

"It's getting through," said Anndrew.

If Kormèr let the shield around Cecil drop to power this one, then Cecil would be free to combine his attacks with his beast's.

Roll the shield! shouted Srrcheel.

What do you mean?

It's a sphere. Spin it.

Kormèr released the rooting to the stone and spun the shield along a horizontal axis. With frustrating ease, the creature scampered quickly and managed to stay atop. With an annoyed grunt, Kormèr added a vertical direction to the spin. The beast howled as it lost its footing and tumbled off the shield. Immediately, Jeransy and Anndrew attacked it.

Seeing they had the beast under control, Kormèr turned his focus back to Cecil just as a flash of silver-white swooped gracefully through the glow in the sky. He looked up, and his heart leaped and sank at the same time at seeing Sylvestra stop to hover above and behind Cecil. *No! She can't be here. She's got no chance against— What's she doing?* Sylvestra had something in her hand that looked a lot like the Tseerleeltrr stone. She swung her arm back, then hurled the jewel at Cecil.

With a *ping,* the jewel ricocheted harmlessly off Cecil's shield. Peppered with smoking and blistering patches of burned flesh, Cecil's beast leaped away. Jewel and creature collided in a burst of golden light. Kormèr squinted against the brightness, and when he opened his eyes, both beast and jewel were gone. But a small hairy bundle wrapped in what looked like burlap wriggled on the next rock.

"Spot?" Cecil stood with his hands against the shield, a forlorn look visible on his face even across the short distance.

"SPOT!" cried Cecil in anguish, blindly flailing his arms, hoping to find that his pet wasn't really gone.

Sylvestra swooped down and landed beside the bundle, instinctively spreading her wings in what Kormèr recognized as a defensive posture. Kormèr dropped the shield around Cecil and recast it around Sylvestra as she bent, scooped up the bundle and lifted off again, with visible effort.

"You did this!" Cecil launched a fireball at Sylvestra.

The fireball washed harmlessly over the shield as Sylvestra soared overhead. Kormèr heard her land behind him and spared her a glance.

Crouched over the bundle, Sylvestra looked up at him, her eyes brilliant and clear. ||No time to explain.||

Kormèr staggered as the ground shook, the rock beneath them cracking thunderously. Anndrew and Jeransy leaned on each other to keep from falling, while Sylvestra spread her wings to keep her balance. The indirect attack surprised Kormèr. Thinking quickly, he pulled a new spell from the jumble in his mind and traced the patterns rapidly. Though he didn't have enough energy remaining to fully counter the attack, he held the ground together long enough to teleport everyone to another rock a few meters away. Their old perch crumbled and disappeared into the dark abyss below.

I can't keep this up forever, thought Kormèr. The surrounding filaments had already lost their brilliant sheen.

Anndrew and Jeransy each discharged another round of fireballs and projectiles, all of which missed and struck the stone supporting Cecil's shield. Cecil tottered, arms flailing to maintain his balance, leaving him unable to retaliate. If that had been their intent, Kormèr was impressed.

I don't think Cecil can either, said Srrcheel. *I've been analyzing his attacks; other than that disintegration spell he just used, his spells have all been low energy casts.*

So he's conserving energy?

That's my guess. At least until the moons overlap.

"Stop attacking," Kormèr called to the girls and Sylvestra. To Srrcheel, *Keep an eye on his hands again, please.*

I will, came the reply.

"Cecil," he called in the few seconds of silence that followed, "let's talk."

Breathing heavily, Cecil seemed to consider the request. "About what?"

Kormèr wiggled his fingers. "No tricks."

Cecil threw up his hands. "Talk or fight, Lezàl. Which is it?"

"Fine. Look, you've got skill, without a doubt. We've got numbers." Kormèr flicked his index finger between them. "Fighting is pointless; we're too evenly matched."

Cecil crossed his arms. "What are you proposing?"

Kormèr heard a groan behind him, but couldn't chance turning and giving Cecil his back. This was more than a simple battle of strength. It was like a game of strategy, and he had to play his pieces just right. He only hoped Cecil was as disoriented as he was, because he suspected the boy could easily out-think him.

"How about a truce?" Kormèr replied, half-distracted by whispers behind him. He wished they'd shut up and let him focus. "I'm sure we can work something out, something mutually beneficial." He knew that was redundant, but he was so tired.

Cecil peered at him. "I don't trust you."

Kormèr thrust his arm toward the smoldering wreck of the mini-yacht. "Seriously? *I* didn't attack *you* first."

Cecil chuckled. "That's true. I guess I've become a little impulsive."

"Yeah. But we can work on that, right?"

Cecil shook his head. "I can, but not with you. As much as I'd love to negotiate with you, I've made other plans."

"So, back to fighting?" Kormèr glanced nervously at the nearly overlapping moons.

You too can draw from that power, said Srrcheel's voice in his head. *I only wish you could use all the powers at your disposal. But things seem to be getting worse in here.*

Kormèr continued: "Come on. You're smarter than this."

"You're right about that. I'm done with fighting you, too. That's not my way. But I have another means of conveyance, something *you* are very familiar with."

Kormèr's mind raced. If he didn't know what to expect, how could he protect the group? The filaments around him were recharging, but much too slowly. He tried reaching out to whatever minute essence of power the nearly overlapping moons could be producing, but found nothing. Either there wasn't enough there yet, or he was completely unattuned to it. *I can't do this, dammit!* The most disturbing thought in his mind was that he'd be letting Sylvestra, Jeransy and Anndrew down if he failed, not just himself. And he couldn't let that happen.

Kormèr heard an unfamiliar voice behind him mumble, "I'm ready."

"What is it, a spaceship?" asked Kormèr, that being the only other mode of transport he could think of that Cecil might be contemplating. "I think we can work that out. I know a fellow—"

"Not a spaceship." Cecil made wide circling motions with his arms. "Something much more practical."

Damn it all, thought Kormèr, anticipating a resumption of combat. *He's casting.*

Cecil swept his hands out then back and cupped them together, fine rays of light briefly flaring through the gaps between his fingers. He held out his hand, and on his palm rested a crystal cube with a single black face. "A portal cube."

Chapter 32

EVERYTHING other than the cube seemed to vanish, as Kormèr stared at it in horror. *He stole my cube!* he thought, as his hand instinctively reached into his coat pocket. He breathed a sigh of relief when it closed around the familiar smoothness of his cube. *Thank the gods!* he proclaimed quietly. *But then... how can that be?*

Srrcheel answered, *It's a conjuration of his own. He's made a copy of yours.* *How do we block it? Stop it? Anything!*

Srrcheel had no ready answer.

Cecil snickered. "Your expression is priceless!"

"Is that yours?" asked Jeransy in a low voice.

Kormèr shook his head. "No. He's made his own."

"Bloody hell."

Cecil stared at the cube. "Such a small thing, and yet so much potential." He looked toward Kormèr. "If only—" His eyes widened as they slid up over Kormèr's head, his mouth forming a silent "O".

Kormèr craned his neck around. Sylvestra stood behind him, and past her stood a large winged dragon. Kormèr rolled his eyes up toward the dragon's head, and as he did, it bent its head to glance down at him and rumbled, "Helloo." With a fantastic rush of air, the creature flapped its wings and took to the air.

Sylvestra turned, and Kormèr gave her a shocked stare. ||I don't know how you manage it,|| she warbled, shaking her head, ||but you have the most amazing luck.||

Kormèr had no idea what she meant. Had the bundle been a dragon egg? Impossible! He spun back around as the dragon circled behind Cecil, then swooped down toward him. Cecil launched some magical projectiles at it, but the beast met the projectiles with a blast of white incandescent breath. Cecil dodged reflexively as the dragon raked his shield with its lethal claws.

The creature arced graciously and landed on an adjacent rock where it squatted and roared at Cecil. With renewed conviction, the girls drew in closer to Kormèr and prepared their next attack. Sylvestra kneeled on one knee to Jeransy's left, her needlegun ready.

Looking frazzled, Cecil scanned the battleground.

"Now *your* expression is priceless," mumbled Kormèr. *At least he's still teleport-locked to that rock. But I can't let him open that portal.*

I have an idea, said Srrcheel. *But we need to get his shield down.*

Then what?

He might be drained enough... I think we can put him to sleep.

Kormèr telepathed the plan to his companions, including the dragon. Then he added, *"Attack on my mark... Now!"*

The full force of the combined attacks that assailed Cecil dislodged his shield from the rock. Shield and boy tumbled back a few meters. On his hands and knees, Cecil groaned. He raised his head, but his hair hung over his eyes.

The moons were almost overlapping; only a sliver of the furthest moon was visible. *I could really use some of that power right now,* thought Kormèr, realizing too late that the girls' casting also had to be using filament energy. *Why can't I feel it?*

"Again," he telepathed. As the others attacked, however, he held back. He closed his eyes and focused on the energy around Cecil, sensed the drain of the shield as it absorbed, deflected... failed.

"Stop!" he telepathed as the shield dissolved and the last vestiges of the onslaught racked Cecil. The blast hurled him back and across to another rock. There he lay, face down in the dirt, his clothes singed and smoking.

"Is he..." began Anndrew, but didn't finish the difficult question.

"No," said Kormèr, still sensing the power of Cecil's mind.

The body moved, and Kormèr looked up at the moons.

They had overlapped!

Quickly! urged Srrcheel. *Cast this spell.*

Kormèr waited for the usual flash of memory. *What spell?*

The same spell you used on the guards in your cell. Why won't it...

Srrcheel? I don't remember the motions from yesterday. Why can't I remember the srootee?

Cecil vanished.

"NO!" Kormèr gathered the last of his energy and teleported after Cecil. While teleporting used only a small amount of energy, Kormèr had only enough for himself. He appeared right on top of Cecil, the boy back on his hands and knees. He grabbed at the collar of Cecil's robe, but his hand came up empty as Cecil ported again. Kormèr followed him through two more teleports before Cecil finally stopped fleeing.

Dizzy and unfocused from exhaustion, Kormèr appeared a few meters short of Cecil. He took a step toward the boy, but his left foot was stuck. He looked down and realized that the heel of his left boot had materialized in the rock. And Cecil was on the next rock this time, out of reach. Kormèr struggled to extract his foot from the boot, but the leather had pinched tightly around his foot. He drew his adamantine dagger from his pocket, but when he bent to cut the boot, the world swam, the rock sliding out from under his feet. He teetered, overbalanced, and fell flat on his back. The world continued spinning as he prodded the boot with the dagger, tearing whenever the point stuck.

Cecil groaned, and Kormèr turned his head toward the boy. Cecil stood slowly, methodically. Blisters pocked his left cheek and ear, his hair singed short and melted into clumps. The leg of his glasses had sagged in the heat, and now the left side drooped. He turned twice, limping on his right foot. Then he stopped and faced Kormèr.

He croaked something and coughed noisily. "Power… from the moons?" he rasped.

He's reading my mind, Kormèr knew, but there was nothing he could do about it.

"Cheerretee!" Cecil's voice sounded steadier. "I remember reading about it, but I never realized…" He sneered. "You can't sense it, can you?"

Without another word, he cast a spell that ripped Kormèr free of the rock. Kormèr had just about cut through his boot, and only that saved his ankle from breaking. Kormèr flipped over and watched the ground slide away until he dangled over a large gap between the rocks. He moved his hands, a desperate attempt to cast a final teleport. But his arms flailed instinctively, the spell broken, as he dropped into the dark void.

I've failed you, old friend, he thought.

You did the best you could, said Srrcheel.

Kormèr thought about Jeransy and Anndrew, now stuck in this time forever.

Srrcheel consoled him, saying, *Sylvestra will help them adjust, I'm sure.*

Sylvestra… At least she hadn't seen him fall to his death. He would simply have disappeared from her life once again.

Unless that Terran monster goes back for them, he thought, the very idea tearing at his heart. *If I could only…* He moved his arms to try again to cast a teleport, then frowned. *Are we still falling?*

What do you mean? asked Srrcheel.

There's no wind on my face, no resistance when I move my arms.

Suddenly, he found himself staring at the gap between the rocks once again. *What kind of sick game is this kid playing?* he wondered. Then he hovered over a rock and settled gently onto it.

"Oh, my god! What do I have to do to get rid of you?!"

Kormèr propped himself up on his elbows and looked in the direction of Cecil's voice. Confused and helpless, he squinted against the brightness as Cecil hurled an incandescent pulse of heat at him. The bright pulse dissipated meters away from Kormèr, leaving colorful spots in his eyes. Cecil tried another, but this flash of intense heat didn't come anywhere near Kormèr before it too dissipated.

Cecil staggered, splaying his legs and tottering as if about to fall over. He looked up at the moons, thrust his arms up toward them, and bared his teeth. Then his arms flopped to his sides. "What have you done?" he spat at

Kormèr. Then he shook his head and peered into the surrounding darkness, searching. "No. It's not you. Something else is interfering."

The air shimmered, and a dark figure suddenly appeared between Cecil and Kormèr. Four more appeared, two at each side of the original, each on its own rock. Another four appeared, completing a semi-circle around Cecil. Then another eight completed the circle.

"What trick is this, Lezàl?" asked Cecil.

Kormèr stared at the dark figures. Were they members of the other Berdian sects? Had they finally joined the fight? He couldn't make out their plumage colors in the dim light; they all looked black.

They are black! said Srrcheel, his voice full of surprise.

Fitzbew's black sorcerers?!

Cecil backed away, turning slowly and discovering that he was surrounded. He traced a simple *srootee*, and unleashed a concussive pulse that warped the air away from him in all directions. The pulse immediately reversed itself and slammed into him. Kormèr grimaced, hearing bones crack as Cecil flipped upside-down into the air. His clenched fist glowed a soft blue as he fell. Then his fingers popped open as a portal opened under Cecil's body. He plummeted through, and the portal snapped shut.

Kormèr watched impassively as several of the dark figures dashed to where the portal had closed. He shook his head, closed his eyes and plopped backward into darkness.

CHAPTER 33

"KORMÈR. Hey! Hello. Averia to Kormèr Lezàl. Please respond. Come on, old friend; it's getting lonely in here."

"Srrcheel." The word conveyed feelings of weakness, like the croak of a tired voice.

"There you are."

"How'd I get here? I don't remember going into a trance."

"You're not in a trance. You passed out."

"Oh. So much for energy from the moons. Any idea why that didn't work for me?"

"I don't, sorry."

"Could that whole thing be a myth? A placebo, as the Terrans say."

Srrcheel was quiet for a moment. *"I honestly don't know, KL. I'm trying to remember my raisings to see if there was any true sign of an effect. But I was so wrapped up in each of the events that I can't say for sure."*

"That makes sense; you were caught up in the moment. You know what is a myth? That Berdia's suicide-effect only affects you the first time you visit the city." Kormèr unconsciously gave off feelings of disappointment and frustration. *"All that worrying about Cheerretee for nothing."*

"Either way, the boy needed to be dealt with before he hurt more people," said Srrcheel.

"Yeah, but another day of preparation would've given us an advantage. It doesn't matter much now, anyway; he's gone."

"I've been thinking about that…"

"Knock yourself out. I've got to go meet Fitzbew's black birds, if they're still around."

"This should be interesting."

Kormèr silently agreed as he eased back into his aching body.

He opened his eyes, squinting against the brightness of lights. As his eyes adjusted, he found himself lying on a pallet in a large circular room with gray walls and a granite floor. A diagnostic screen on the wall above his head displayed his vitals. Several other diagnostic pallets sat empty along the perimeter of the room, their uniformity interrupted by two doorways and a desk. Both doorways were closed.

Huh. I didn't expect to be indoors, he thought. *I wonder where this is.*

At the desk were two of the darkest Averians Kormèr had ever seen. Even Srrcheel's surprise filtered down into Kormèr's consciousness. One was seated and pointing to a large screen while warbling quietly to the other, who was standing behind him. Neither noticed Kormèr had awakened.

Kormèr spotted his coat draped over the back of a chair to the right of his pallet. Half-tucked under the chair, he saw a new pair of black boots.

A sharp pain near his shoulder blade suddenly faded, followed by the pain in his left ankle. As several of his other aches ebbed gradually, he became more aware of a gentle, soothing hum coming from the pallet through his back. Under other circumstances, Kormèr would've given in to the gentle vibrations. Instead, he sat up slowly, pivoting on his rear to make as little noise as possible, and swinging his legs over the side of the pallet. He listened intently to the conversation between the two birdmen, catching only fragments. The one that was standing was completely turned away from Kormèr, and his song was completely muffled.

||...checked it three times,|| warbled the seated one. ||...directly related... most two generations.||

The screen displayed various windows, most of which made no sense to Kormèr. One contained a photo of him which appeared to have been taken during the incident with the police, just a day ago. However, Kormèr didn't remember anyone taking his photo. In fact, he realized now that the photo was taken in the interrogation room prior to Tseeo's entrance. He hadn't been alone at the time, but he didn't remember anyone standing at the angle from which the image had been taken.

One of the other windows contained a photo of a young man with black hair, brown eyes. Kormèr recognized the man immediately, though he had never met the man in person. In other photos, Kormèr had seen, the man had sported a mustache and goatee, but here he was clean-shaven. In fact, he looked much younger than in any photo Kormèr had ever seen. Regardless, the man was unmistakably Seirojj Lezàl, Kormèr's adopted grandfather. And no one had taken this photo surreptitiously; he had clearly posed for it. Kormèr squinted, trying to make out the background of the photo. Seirojj had been standing in front of a bright structure, though Kormèr couldn't quite make it out. It had been taken outdoors on a clear, sunny day. Kormèr refocused on the structure, finding it familiar in some— Kormèr's eyes went wide. *But it can't be. That looks like a pseudo-tree!*

Kormèr jumped off the pallet, landing silently on his feet. Then he cursed quietly as the diagnostic board at the head of the pallet beeped successively a few times, then powered down.

The two birdmen spun, clearly startled.

||He's awake,|| twittered the sitting one.

||You said he would not awaken,|| warbled the other.

||Should not. I said *should not* awaken. You knew there was a risk bringing him here.||

Kormèr slid slowly toward his coat. These birdmen appeared unarmed, but Kormèr would feel much more secure having the cube within reach.

||But if he is related to Seirojj,|| continued the sitting birdman, clearly

237

not knowing or not caring if Kormèr understood Averian, | | he is entitled to know, isn't he? | |

Kormèr tried not to let his confusion show on his face. *These guys think I'm related to Seirojj?* Which, of course, was not possible. Yunzen Lezàl had adopted Kormèr after the latter's parents died in a fire. Yunzen Lezàl was the son of Seirojj Lezàl. Kormèr was technically his adopted grandson, though he had never met the man. Seirojj had disappeared mysteriously years before Kormèr's birth.

| | He's entitled to nothing. Seirojj has been gone a long time, Whoortee. This young man doesn't know us, and we don't know him. | |

So Seirojj *had* been to Averia! But how was that possible? Elmar had no extra-planetary capability. Three years ago, Kormèr had researched Elmar and found that the planet was in a remote corner of the galaxy. It would be years after Kormèr's own time before anyone would stumble across it.

| | What's he doing? | |

| | Going for his coat, I suspect. | |

Kormèr hesitated. The birdman didn't seem to care if Kormèr reached for his coat. That meant one of two things: either they had removed anything dangerous from its pockets, or they didn't think anything in its pockets posed a danger to them.

<<Go ahead,>> said the standing birdman in unaccented Elmarian. <<Take your coat if you wish.>>

Kormèr took the coat and rummaged through its pockets.

<<We've taken nothing,>> said Whoortee, the seated birdman.

<<I don't know you,>> said Kormèr with a smirk. Let them wonder if he had understood their conversation in Song. While it would take time to find out if all the contents of the coat's pockets were there, Kormèr felt it safe to assume that they would be. After all, the laser pistol and many of his gems were there, even his adamantine dagger. Most importantly, the cube was there as well. He considered putting on the coat, but decided against it for now. The room was warm enough that he didn't really need it. He palmed the cube and draped the coat back over the chair. Then he sat and slipped into the most comfortable pair of boots he'd ever worn.

The standing birdman approached him then. <<I am Cheetoo Rees. I am the head of this facility.>> Whoortee stood and shuffled up beside him.

Kormèr also stood. <<You already know who I am.>> He glanced at the display, then back at them. <<While it's nice to know who you are, the more pertinent question is *what* you are.>>

| | He certainly speaks like Seirojj, | | warbled Whoortee.

<<Then we are both on the same branch,>> said Cheetoo. <<I know who you are, but I don't understand *what* you are.>>

<<I'm surprised.>> Kormèr once again glanced at the display. <<You seem to have a good deal of information already.>>

<<It would appear that way. But knowing that you are Kormèr Lezàl does not explain the fact that you are here, on Averia, nearly five hundred years after your date of birth.>>

Kormèr nodded. <<I can see how that would be confusing. I propose an information exchange. As I am your... guest, I'll let you begin.>>

Cheetoo gave him a knowing look. <<It is only because you are the grandson of Seirojj that I haven't had you put back under sedation.>> Before Kormèr could say anything, he continued, <<Now, how much do you know about us?>>

<<Next to nothing. The Grand Master of the Hawk Sorcerers believed you could be called on to help resolve problems with magic. We had in fact been planning to contact you to help with Cecil Murphy... with the Terran boy.>>

<<Seirojj told you nothing of us?>>

<<I never met him. He disappeared before I was born.>> Kormèr was still judging how much to reveal to these Averians. He was not ready to burst their bubble just yet about his parentage. *Let them keep thinking I'm Seirojj's actual grandson for a little longer.*

<<I see.>> Cheetoo mulled this over for a minute, and Kormèr let him. These birdfolk were some kind of secret group, and secrets do not remain secrets if the wrong people know about them. Finally, Cheetoo came to a decision. <<Follow me, Kormèr.>>

Kormèr grabbed his coat and followed his enigmatic hosts out of the room and down a long, wide corridor with doors roughly every thirty meters on each side. The *click-click* of the Averians' talons on the granite floor echoed along the otherwise silent corridor. Kormèr found the large quiet space eerie, the stillness echoing of a time long past when crowds bustled busily along its length, in and out of the doorways. He figured it had to be his imagination at work; after all, there wasn't anything to hint that such a time had existed. The concrete walls lacked images or decoration of any kind.

I have the same feeling, said Srrcheel. *I'd say the place is haunted, if I believed in that nonsense.*

Their brief journey ended when his escorts led him through one doorway into a small rectangular office. A brushed-metal table nearly bisected the room with a perch bolted to the floor on one side and a few movable perches on the other side. A six-drawer cabinet stood against the wall to Kormèr's right, beside which was a waist-high shelf bolted to the wall. Both were of the same brushed metal.

On the table was a large display, similar to the one in the first room. Cheetoo and Whoortee each took a perch on the far side of the table. Kormèr tried his best to sit on the fixed perch, but finally gave up and simply sat on the table. He'd never gotten used to the rounded perches.

Cheetoo collected his thoughts, then began, <<We are The Guard. We

are an elite group of specially trained Averians appointed long ago by Seirojj Lezàl as the keepers of normality.>>

<<Normality?>> Kormèr wondered how such a word and Seirojj could be used in the same sentence without causing the universe to implode.

<<Averia, as you see it today. It is devoid of turmoil: a paradise. It does not remain this way on its own. We don't meddle in day-to-day operations, only when a deviation has a significant chance of disrupting our delicate society.>>

<<Like when Cecil came along.>>

<<An interesting choice of words,>> said Whoortee, not without a touch of annoyance.

<<Had he come to the planet via normal means,>> continued Cheetoo, <<our tracking mechanisms would have alerted us to his deviation. We only noticed him after Freet-See. We've been scrambling to catch up ever since.>>

<<Freet-See was before the Hovel,>> said Kormèr, slightly accusingly. If they'd known about Cecil then, why hadn't they stopped him before he destroyed the Hovel.

<<Yes. The Hovel was a terrible loss. Not only did we lose a monument to our past, and an entire sorcerer sect, but we also lost three agents that had been stationed there.>>

<<Stationed?>> Kormèr's eyes lit up. <<The corridors behind the walls!>>

<<Well, yes, those were our first headquarters. But that outpost proved to be too close to civilians. However, the agents I spoke of were sorcerers. One was on Fitzbew's council of masters. They were working to correct some of the loose ends that had resulted from Fitzbew's overly long tenure. They had noted Cecil's presence at the Hovel, but were unprepared for his level of information absorption.

<<You and your Terran companions are also here via extraordinary means, and this is not your first time either. So we come full circle back to you, Kormèr Lezàl. How did you get here, to Averia?>>

Kormèr hesitated, but finally decided that enough people already knew about the portal. Ultimately, it was because of the portal that Cecil had bypassed The Guard's tracking mechanisms. So Kormèr reached into the pocket of his coat and set the cube down on the tabletop. <<This is how. This device opens a portal crossing time and space. I have no idea how it works or who built it. But it came from Elmar, as far as I know.>> Kormèr was now wondering if Seirojj himself had once owned the device. It would certainly explain how he'd been to Averia.

<<Excuse me a moment.>> Cheetoo turned to Whoortee. ||Did you scan that?||

||Yes. It was completely inert. If it does what he claims, it's beyond our tech.||

Cheetoo turned back to Kormèr. <<So you used this device to come to Averia, bringing the three Terrans with you.>>

Kormèr shook his head and briefly told them of the accident in the classroom.

<<Ah!>> Understanding dawned on Cheetoo's face. <<This same device is the one Cecil used to escape.>>

Kormèr nodded. <<Unfortunately, yes. He could be anywhere now, in any time, and there's no way to track him.>>

Cheetoo's crest feathers fluffed. <<You said the portal will open to anyplace you could think of. Can't you simply open it to wherever Cecil is?>>

<<That's a possibility, although I've found that doing so is unreliable. People move a lot more than places, and time adds another wrinkle. But it might get me to the immediate vicinity. I'll try that once we're done here.>> Whoortee coughed. Kormèr's right eyebrow rose in curious response. *What now?*

<<We have a dilemma on our hands,>> said Cheetoo. <<Seirojj's mandate stipulates that we not allow Averian magic to leave the planet. Unfortunately, we couldn't stop Cecil from leaving with his knowledge intact.

<<And now we have you. While you are the grandson of Seirojj, our mandate leaves no room for interpretation.>>

<<I can't leave the planet because I know magic?>> This idea did not bother Kormèr as much as he had expected it to. *That's almost serendipitous.*

Cheetoo nodded. <<Correct. Yet, Cecil must be stopped, and *we* cannot leave the planet.>>

Kormèr sighed. *So much for serendipity.* <<But I can.>> He longed to ask why The Guard could not. Was it simply Seirojj's stipulation, or something more? But his question would have to wait. <<And not only that, but I possess the means of actually locating him.>>

<<Precisely. We witnessed the end of your battle with Cecil; we saw your dedication to stopping him. Are you willing to see that cause to its end?>>

When Kormèr had seen Cecil vanish through the portal, he'd surrendered to the fact that Cecil was gone, out of his reach for the time being, if not forever. Kormèr dreaded the thought of Cecil returning to Earth to wreak havoc, but wasn't Jeransy proof that Earth would survive Cecil Murphy? Kormèr wasn't sure if time worked that way, but he certainly hoped so. The boy would do his worst for a while, then either stop, get himself killed, or grow old and die. Either way, his reign would end.

Kormèr would take the girls home, and with nothing to drag him away this time, he would come back and stay on Averia. He'd rebuild his relationship with Sylvestra, perhaps permanently, even without marriage. They'd make it work, the way it should have worked three years ago.

In those seconds before he'd passed out on the rock, that was how he had imagined the future would come to pass.

All that came crashing down with Cheetoo's one question. The birdman had appealed to the deep-rooted sense of duty that Kormèr's adopted father had so instilled in him. Cheetoo had opened an avenue to finding Cecil that would forever haunt Kormèr if he didn't follow it. Kormèr answered the only way he could.

<<I… I am willing.>>

||A true Lezàl,|| warbled Whoortee, so low that Kormèr almost missed it.

<<I see the burden of this in your eyes,>> said Cheetoo. <<We all feel we failed Seirojj by allowing Cecil to escape. Having to ask you to set things right for us is… difficult. I appreciate your effort in ways words cannot express.>>

<<If there is anyone to blame, it's me,>> said Kormèr, picking up the cube and replacing it in his pocket. <<But let's not revisit an old topic. I'll do what needs to be done, and that's all there is to it.>>

<<Very well.>> Cheetoo stood and held out his left hand. A small gray box appeared in it. Cheetoo approached Kormèr and offered him the device. <<We can at least give you this to help against the boy.>>

Kormèr took the box. <<Magic?>> He saw it had five positions where humanoid fingers could grip it.

<<There is no real magic, Kormèr,>> said Cheetoo. <<There is merely technology.>>

The offhand comment took a moment to sink in. *Did you hear that, old ghost?* asked Kormèr of Srrcheel.

I don't know what he's talking about, replied Srrcheel. *Magic is… just magic. You either have the spark or you don't.*

Hmm. It seems to me there are a good number of things about which you sorcerers are not aware, whether intentionally or not.

That's becoming clearer by the moment, said Srrcheel with feelings of bewilderment.

Cheetoo changed the topic in the meantime. <<That device will permanently disable the mechanism in an attuned being. When you encounter Cecil, place your fingers on the five contact points and he will be a mere Terran boy once again.>>

<<I could've used this an hour ago,>> mumbled Kormèr. Cheetoo either didn't hear or pretended he didn't. Kormèr studied the device's exterior. <<There is no specific orientation to the device?>>

<<No.>> Cheetoo watched him closely.

<<I see.>> In his words was the understanding that, when the device triggered, Cecil wouldn't be the only 'attuned being' to lose his powers permanently. Kormèr and any attuned near him up to some unknown range would also fall victim to the device. Kormèr sighed. It wasn't like he would

need magic after Cecil was gone, anyway. <<Fair enough.>>

<<In that case, I think our business here is ended,>> said Cheetoo.

Kormèr disagreed; he had many questions he wanted answered. But this meeting had been a business transaction, not a question-and-answer session for Kormèr's edification. Kormèr stood. <<Yes. My companions are probably very worried about me by now.>>

<<They are never to know of this meeting, you understand. Word must never get out of our existence.>>

<<I'll tell no one of you or this meeting.>> They seemed to accept that. <<One question, before I go.>>

<<Ask.>>

<<Why was Seirojj here, on Averia?>>

Whoortee shook his head. <<We can't—>>

Cheetoo held up a hand. <<He was here to right a wrong. Beyond that, we can say no more.>>

Kormèr nodded slowly, the answer spawning more questions. <<I see. Very well, then. I am ready to go.>>

<<High sky, Kormèr Lezàl. And good luck.>>

<<High sky, Cheetoo Rees.>>

Chapter 34

THE small bonfires that Anndrew had set around their location when Kormèr vanished had dimmed to embers after the first half-hour, but they still provided a warm, welcoming glow. Anndrew hopped from rock to rock, searching for something else to burn, anything remotely flammable, but she had exhausted the scant supply of dry grass and twigs nearby. Though, if she were being honest with herself, her searching had more to do with staying away from the others than of actually finding any kindling. Together they might try to talk about other things, but inevitably they'd end up speculating about... things she didn't want to speculate on.

Anndrew watched as Jeransy's lithe figure settled on a boulder not too far away from the rest of the group, in front of one of the dimming fires. The girl looked off into the darkness, then up at the moons. *I guess she feels the same way,* thought Anndrew.

Sylvestra squatted near another fire, having a quiet, solemn conversation with the tiny, dark man who called himself "Klurt", or "Klaatu" or something like that. He was talking a mile a minute, in a small voice that reminded Anndrew of a leprechaun. Sylvestra furtively glanced at Anndrew with stricken eyes, beseeching her silently to save her, or maybe to share in her misery.

Anndrew looked over once again at Jeransy's seated figure and gestured to Sylvestra that she would be there momentarily. It had been a hard battle, and Anndrew didn't begrudge anyone the need for some solitude, but one glimpse at Jeransy's slumped, trembling shoulders told her something was amiss. She approached silently, but shuffled her feet on the rough, dry ground to give Jeransy a moment to compose herself, if she so chose.

Jeransy squared her shoulders and wiped her eyes hastily before she turned her head towards Anndrew. "Any sign of 'im?"

"Not yet." Anndrew took a seat at the other end of Jeransy's boulder. "I'm sure he won't be much longer."

Jeransy wrapped her arms around herself. "I wish we knew where he was. I hate just sitting here, doing nothing."

"I don't mind getting a moment to catch my breath." Anndrew shrugged. "It gives me a chance to count my blessings."

Jeransy snorted. "Back home, there aren't many moments like these, at least not outside of prison or death."

"You sound like you've lived through a lot. This fight with Cecil must have seemed like a mere scuffle to you."

"Well, I wouldn't go so far. Without his magic, though, Cecil Murphy's just like any other punk."

"Before magic," Anndrew said soberly, "he used to be an honor-roll student whose mom made him soy-butter sandwiches on gluten-free bread with the crusts cut off." She only remembered because Todd had teased Cecil about his diet restrictions in the cafeteria one day, just before one of Todd's cohorts knocked Cecil's binder out of his hands. Before that incident, Anndrew had accepted the existence of school bullies as one of those unavoidable unpleasantries of life, like mosquitoes and acne. She had been content just to not be singled out for attention.

Something about that encounter with Todd had irked her, however, and before she could think better of it, she had left her friends at the lunch table to help Cecil pick up his papers. "Hey! Annde, why are you helping out this dipshit?" Todd had asked, laughing.

Anndrew had frozen in place, realizing too late that she had effectively painted a bull's-eye on herself by coming to Cecil's aid. Too late to back out gracefully, she had decided to brazen it out. She had stood and faced Todd, whose eyes automatically focused elsewhere on her. "Because, unlike some other guys," she had said acidly, "he actually knows to look at a girl's face when he talks to her."

Anndrew snapped out of her reverie and noticed Jeransy watching her. "This is hard for me," she confessed. "I've never been in a situation where someone that I know tried to kill me, or where I need to find a way to… to stop him first. Is that how your life is back home, just fighting and death?"

Jeransy shook her head slowly. "There are good days and bad days. I've never killed anyone, but I've had to maim a few." She sighed. "This is very different for me, too. I've never had so many people depend on me. It's very… daunting."

"But unfortunately, very necessary."

"Is it? Do you really think Cecil's capable of widespread mayhem?"

"After all he's done? Without a doubt." Anndrew shook her head. "This is all so crazy! If he had never left Earth, he might have channeled his intellect constructively like other sociopaths, and gotten a CEO position or a high-ranking government job. If only I hadn't left the portal by the door…"

"Oy! It wasn't your fault. It wasn't like you shoved him through the portal against his will. I could just as well say that I should've been more careful. I knew as well as Kormèr how dangerous that thing could be. If only KL hadn't gotten distracted by those bleedin' trees of yours!"

Anndrew smiled mischievously. "Are we saying now that it's Kormèr's fault?"

The girls looked at one another for a moment, then burst into nervous giggles. After the stresses of the day, it felt good to release it all, and the girls leaned against one another for support. Anndrew looked up and saw Sylvestra and the Tiny Brown Man—Kirk, Klute, Kookaburra?—approaching, no doubt curious about what they were finding so damn funny about their situation.

What a bedraggled bunch we are, Anndrew mused. Jeransy looked especially weary, shivering in the fading firelight. Anndrew concentrated on the dying flames in front of them and clapped, turning the stones beneath the bonfire into a glowing pool of lava. It warmed the air at once, and Anndrew was relieved that the pool didn't reek of sulfur or anything else as noxious.

Sylvestra and the little man settled close by. "I've wanted to ask you," began Sylvestra, "how you do that?" She pointed to the molten rock. "You didn't have magic before."

Anndrew glanced down at her hands. Of course, Sylvestra didn't know. "Have a seat. Jeransy and I have a story to tell you. And perhaps," she said, nodding her head to the strange little man, "you'll have one for us, too?"

KORMÈR stood in near-darkness, his eyes adjusting gradually to the soft glow of moonlight on the rock beneath his feet. An instant before, he had been standing in the room with Cheetoo Rees. Unfortunately, it was at the instant of his transport here that he thought of one last question that he would have liked answered above all others: How could Seirojj Lezàl have been present at the time of the Hovel's construction to put The Guard in place?

Kormèr felt a chuckle from Srrcheel. *It seems that your grandfather has some interesting history.*

That's a fact. That man is more of an enigma than I ever realized.

Kormèr spotted a red-orange glow in the darkness. Now able to see the breaks between the rocks, he headed in that direction. As he got closer, he saw Sylvestra and the girls huddled around it, talking animatedly and laughing. Suddenly, he felt the urge to run, their voices like a siren's song calling to him, promising a warm welcome home.

Careful, came Srrcheel's stern warning. *It wouldn't do for you to go plunging to your death now, after everything you've been through today.*

Of course, you're right. He cast a minor spell that lightened gravity's effect on him, allowing him to cross the rocks with ease. As he approached the group, he noticed Jeransy and Anndrew leaning against a large, furry black bear-like creature. *First a dragon, now a bear? Oh! A shape shifter, I'll bet!*

I've read about them. From the planet Halgarin?

Kormèr nodded, then realized that Srrcheel couldn't see the gesture. *That's right.*

You've been there, too? Why am I still surprised by the things you've seen?

Don't poke around those memories, please. That was… not a great time in my life.

I try not to poke around any of your memories. But when you think about them, and

246

they carry such potent emotions, it's very hard for me to ignore them.

Gotcha. Thanks for the privacy.

Sylvestra noticed him first. ||KL!|| she twittered with a wide smile, standing so quickly that she nearly launched herself into flight.

Jeransy and Anndrew jumped up, relief on their faces. Jeransy reached him first. "We were so worried!" she said, hugging him in a stranglehold. Then she stepped back and punched his shoulder. "You're a right nump, you are, for charging off after him alone."

"What she said!" chastised Anndrew, who gave him a kiss on the cheek, anyway. "Welcome back."

"Oh my! What man could ask for a warmer welcome than that?" asked a peculiarly accented voice.

Kormèr followed the voice to the "bear", which morphed before his eyes into a little man, whose height barely skimmed Sylvestra's hip. The tiny man's dark, deep-set eyes looked up at Kormèr from a light brown, wrinkled face draped with long black hair that flowed over his shoulders and down to his waist. He was clean-shaven, but a fine black hair coated his exposed muscular arms.

Kormèr spread his arms. "I'm Kormèr Lezàl," he said to the small man. "Thank you for your help earlier."

"'Twas a pleasure," the man replied. "Kloort's me name."

Before he could say more, Jeransy asked, "Intros later, please. What happened with Cecil?"

"Alright, alright. But…" Kormèr looked around, from the shaded faces around him to the distant, smoldering wreckage of the mini-yacht. "Anyone against moving to more comfortable surroundings?"

Jeransy simpered. Then she crossed her arms. "Fine."

"I can't just leave scene of a crime," said Sylvestra. "Is there a body out there?"

Kormèr couldn't help but let his shoulders sag. "There's no body."

The relief was clear on Sylvestra's face. "Oh. I have a team on the way. We are quite far from any city, but they should be here soon."

"Are we waiting for them?" asked Kormèr. "I'd rather not go back to the precinct right now."

Sylvestra stared off into the distance, then made up her mind. She tapped the badge on her sash to start the built-in recording device. ||Identify Chief Chreel,|| she sang. ||I am at the scene of a battle between Terran suspect Cecil Murphy and a group of offworlders including Elmarian Kormèr Lezàl, Terrans Jeransy Bolsner and Anndrew Lee, and a Halgarin named Kloort. In evidence is the wreckage of a mini-yacht of Freet-See registry. I am returning to Birshetland with all parties for questioning.|| She tapped the badge again. ||That should do.||

"Clever." Kormèr opened the portal, and Kloort gasped. "Oh, sorry," said Kormèr. "This is… a doorway. My room is on the other side."

"You don't say!" said the short man, his surprise replaced by curiosity, as he approached the portal.

"Hold it," said Sylvestra. "Can't use that. I…" She shook her head. "Sorry. Song is easier." Switching to Averian Song, she twittered, ||I'd have to explain the time discrepancy in the debrief recording.|| She tapped something into her chrono.

"Oh," said Kormèr. "So how do we get back?"

||I came in a skiff.|| She pointed, and Kormèr turned to see a bright light approaching. ||When I saw your ship explode, I left it parked a kilometer away and flew over. It's a four-seater, so it'll be a little cramped.||

"I can always use the portal and meet you—"

||No. You'd show up on surveillance. We have to return this way.||

The skiff stopped, opened a side door, and lowered a set of deep steps. Sylvestra climbed in, taking the pilot's seat. Kormèr stood aside while Jeransy and Anndrew chose their seats. Then he looked at Kloort.

"Looks like there's enough room for me to stand," said Kloort. "But I can shift if I have to."

"However you feel comfortable," said Kormèr.

"Alright, then." Kloort climbed the two steps, then positioned himself in the space between the seats, his hands gripping the back of Jeransy's seat. "This should be fine, so long as we don't juke about."

"Juke?" repeated Anndrew. "Where did you say you learned English?"

"From my gran," said Kloort. "Why d'ya ask?"

"That's an unusual word. Did she like hockey?"

"That's a game, isn't it? It's played on ice?"

Kormèr grinned, intrigued by the odd conversation and unexpected common ground between the two strangers. He took one last look around, his eyes lingering with melancholy on the ship's wreckage. Then he stepped up into the skiff and took the last seat. The door closed, and they sailed off.

SYLVESTRA spotted a patrol car with three officers parked at the front entrance of the Hotel Cheerees as she guided the skiff down. The exchange with Kloort had dwindled quickly after takeoff. When Sylvestra glanced back at her quiet passengers, she found the girls asleep and Kormèr staring out at the twilit landscape with hooded eyes. She had welcomed the quiet, as it had afforded her a chance to gather her thoughts and plan how she would handle her team.

"We are here," she said, as she landed the skiff and triggered the door to open. Kloort stepped out first, clearing the way for her to scoot out ahead of the others. With two big glide-hops, she approached the trio of officers.

||Good morning,|| she sang.

||Chief!|| they all cried, nearly at once. Then they sang happily over each other for a moment before one of them spotted Kormèr over her shoulder.

||It's Lezàl,|| chirped the officer, pointing.

Sylvestra flicked her wings open, then relaxed them again. ||Yes, I have Kormèr Lezàl and his companions with me. Are there any others inside?||

||Four watching the ground entrances. We were... um... supposed to be in the lobby. But we had just come out here to trade places.||

Sylvestra heard the guilt in the officer's tone; she'd caught them, maybe doing what she had said or maybe goofing off. Sylvestra peered at her but didn't press the issue. ||Comm the others and let them know you can all return to your regular duties as of now. I will take this case from here.||

They seemed hesitant, and she thought they might actually question her. But then they all acknowledged her order and flew off with the patrol car.

"Everything okay?" asked Kormèr, when Sylvestra returned to the group.

||Yes, just clearing our way.|| Kormèr nodded, then led the way inside, almost running into Theeseeo who appeared to be on his way out.

||Kormèr! Oh, it is so good to see you!|| He looked over at Sylvestra. ||Good morning, Chief Chrreel.|| He had never called Sylvestra anything other than her title and last name. ||When the police came looking for you,|| he sang to Kormèr, ||and waiting... well, we feared the worst.||

Before Kormèr could say anything, Sylvestra sang, ||I will conduct some preliminary interviews with this group. Until then, they should say nothing.||

Theeseeo nodded. ||Understood, Chief. I'd offer you a conference room, but you all look like you need something more comfortable. I can offer you the presidential suite; it just became available today and would fit a group this size more comfortably.||

Sylvestra smiled. ||I would appreciate that, Mister Whoorreea. We should only need a couple of hours.||

||Take as much time as you need,|| sang Theeseeo, returning to the front desk. ||Go right on up. I will have some refreshments sent up as well.||

Kormèr explained to the others what had transpired as they walked to the lifts. Once there, his biometrics unlocked the suite, and the lift carried them up. Under the lift's bright lights, Kormèr's pallor and bleary eyes stood out. *The poor dear.*

Sylvestra had never been in such a large hotel room before, neither as a guest nor as part of her work. The sitting room alone seemed to be half the size of her flat. Six doorways led to the left and right, presumably to four bedrooms, a bathroom and a kitchen. *That's if each bedroom doesn't already have its own bathroom,* she mused. *Some people really have money to burn.* She watched

Kormèr flop into a gray leather wing-chair. *And some do, but decide to do better things with it.*

Kloort, too, seemed in awe of his new surroundings; she could imagine the expansive room might be very overwhelming for the little man. He made several gestures that Sylvestra found curious. She had never met a Halgarin before, but she had read of their shape-shifting abilities. She'd also read they supplemented verbal communication with hand gestures. Like emojis or simple body language, the gestures conveyed emotion and intent.

Jeransy sat on a plush burgundy settee, staring blankly at nothing, her luminous hazel eyes heavy-lidded with exhaustion. Sylvestra estimated that the young Terran would last another fifteen minutes, at most.

Anndrew sat at the opposite end of the settee, looking tired but alert. She didn't seem to be as physically demonstrative as Jeransy, but the quick flicker of her almond-shaped eyes around the room and her straight posture spoke volumes.

The door buzzed and Sylvestra opened it. A bellhop came in with a cart carrying three pitchers, cups, an ice bucket, and a tray of assorted snacks. Sylvestra tipped the bellhop and grabbed an oat bar. As she took a bite, she glanced around the gathering.

What an odd assortment of creatures, Sylvestra mused. They were all humanoid, albeit of different sizes and colors, all from different corners of time and space. And though he sat off to their left, Kormèr was central to them all, the unwitting catalyst that managed to gather just the right people around him at just the right time. She remembered thinking that he had to be a master manipulator of people, somehow orchestrating their movements to have them be where they needed to be, or say what he needed them to say. But as she spent more time with him, she'd found that he just naturally engendered friendship and trust from others.

Kormèr ran a hand through his hair and sighed heavily. "What a night!"

"Quite exciting," said Kloort.

"Kloort, is it?" asked Kormèr, looking at the little man curiously.

"At your service." Kloort made a gesture with his hand, and Kormèr flinched reflexively. "Oh! I'm sorry," Kloort said, clenching his hands into fists at his sides.

Kormèr repeated the gesture. "Forgive me, please. It's been a long time since I was on Halgarin."

Kloort nodded. "Quite understandable, Mister Lezàl."

"Call me Kormèr, please. Or KL, if you prefer."

"I am honored," said Kloort, gesturing. This one gesture Sylvestra knew meant respect. "I remember people talking aboot ya froom the last time ya passed through Halgarin."

"Halgarin is in a neighboring solar system," Kormèr explained, looking between Anndrew and Jeransy. "The Halgarin are known for their exceptional shape-shifting…" He paused, probably tipped off by something in the girls' expressions. "You've heard this already, haven't you?"

"You were gone for over an hour," said Jeransy, her eyes closing.

"He's from the Dootrin tribe," Anndrew said.

Kormèr nodded. "So, this gathering is mostly for my benefit, then."

"Yes," said Sylvestra. "Excuse me one moment," she said, glancing at the others, before looking at Kormèr. ||KL, Kloort speaks Terran English but so fast and heavily accented that I have trouble following him sometimes. Can you translate for me?||

"Of course. Hmm. Actually, I have an idea," said Kormèr, smiling. He moved his hands in a graceful pattern in the air before him. Sylvestra watched his eyes focus on that space, as if they were seeing something that she could not. She had seen that look before, in the eyes of the Berdian sorcerers. He flicked his right wrist and smiled. <<I've cast a translation spell,>> he said. <<Now we should be able to speak our native languages and understand each other just fine.>>

||Wow!|| Sylvestra sang. ||That was Elmarian, wasn't it?|| It was one thing to hear Freesewee explain that Kormèr and the girls had had magical abilities given to them, and then to hear Jeransy and Anndrew relate the first-hand details, but it was quite another thing to observe Kormèr using it to such effect.

Kormèr nodded smugly. <<This is Elmarian.>>

She missed hearing the melodic tones of Kormèr's native language. Perhaps later she'd ask him to do away with the spell so she could hear him speak it again. For now, Jeransy's unanswered question remained like an ungroomed pin feather. ||Let's have the story then: what happened with Cecil?||

"Right. He teleported, and I chased him down," Kormèr said. "Srrcheel had taught me how to follow a teleport. Then we fought for a while… or for a few minutes, anyway. We were both so exhausted, it felt like hours." Something about his response piqued Sylvestra's interrogator instincts. *Is he hiding something?* she wondered. "We got to where we just didn't have the energy to cast anymore," continued Kormèr. "And honestly, when you get to that point, you don't have much energy for anything. I watched helplessly as he opened the portal he had created and tumbled through. I can't say for certain if he was conscious when he did, or where he ended up." Kormèr shrugged. "I don't really know whether his portal even works."

"When you didn't come back right away, we worried," Anndrew said.

"And for that, I'm sorry," Kormèr replied, seeming genuinely contrite. "I was so tapped by the fight that I needed to recover my strength before I could return. Nothing less would have kept me away," he said, his eyes resting on Sylvestra. In that look, she saw that he was not being entirely truthful. The others might not see it, but despite all their years apart, Sylvestra knew him

251

too well. "I couldn't wait to get back," he concluded.

||Well… Sreet was a manipulative little worm,|| sang Sylvestra, ||but he wasn't a brute. He kidnapped me, but he knew not to hurt me. I got the sense that he didn't enjoy getting his own feathers dirty.||

"Did the girls tell you what happened at the Hovel?" asked Kormèr.

||My Captain did,|| sang Sylvestra. ||The girls filled in the details while we waited for you. I'm very sorry about Srrcheel… and the others. Sreet had it all planned out; he even laid it out for me. But he severely underestimated Cecil's ambition and power.||

Kloort helped himself to the cart, and Sylvestra poured a glass of nutria for Kormèr.

"Sounds like you two became fast friends," Kormèr quipped, taking the glass from her.

Sylvestra shrugged as she poured another glass for herself. ||Sreet was an egomaniac. He liked to talk about how brilliant he was. He said he planned to hold me hostage until either you caught Cecil, or Cecil caught you. If you succeeded, then Sreet would be lauded and perhaps even promoted for having ensured your cooperation. He didn't have to tell the elders that he pressured you into helping, or that he was the one who set Cecil loose in the first place.||

"And if Cecil prevailed?" Kormèr asked, setting the nearly empty glass down on the table.

||Oh, well, Sreet knew how to play both sides. He made a deal with Cecil: Cecil was free to return to the Hovel and destroy Fitzbew and the other masters. Sreet and his followers would stay out of Cecil's way, provided that Cecil spared them. He didn't count on Cecil destroying everyone and everything.||

Kormèr frowned. "I don't understand. He underestimated Cecil, yet he went so far as to kidnap Anndrew and Jeransy, and later you, to force my cooperation."

Sylvestra looked over at the girls and found them both fast asleep. ||I can't speak for the girls, but he told me that I was extra insurance to guarantee your cooperation. I suspect he planned to use me to bargain for your continued cooperation, even after the Cecil matter was resolved. If you'd lost to Cecil, I'd hate to think what would have happened.||

Sylvestra saw Kormèr's jaw tense and his brow furrow. It pleased Sylvestra to see that time had not diminished his abundant empathy. "I freed the girls as soon as I could. But I couldn't get to you; I didn't know where you were, and Sreet blocked my portal. I figured my best option… my *only* option, was to do what he wanted until I dealt with Cecil or figured out a way to get to you." She could hardly imagine the burden Kormèr had bared, worrying about her and about confronting Cecil. But it was all there in his countenance.

252

||I know, KL,|| she warbled, knowing the words would do little to placate him. Regardless, she added, ||You made the right choice. I knew you were going to need all the help you could get, so as soon as I got free, I rushed over to the museum to get back the Tseerleeltrr stone you gave me and tracked you down.||

Kormèr looked so adorably befuddled that Sylvestra had to smile. "How did you get away from Sreet?" he asked her. "How did you know what the stone was going to do, and how did you find us?"

Sylvestra first briefed Kormèr on her cramped but cozy accommodations, care of Sreet. ||I can only assume that when Sreet died, his spell gradually lost strength, so all I had to do was walk out the door.||

^Fascinating,^ said Kloort. ^You were quite lucky the boy was so impulsive.^

||All those lives lost just to save mine?|| Sylvestra shook her head. ||I might be lucky, but the price was too high.||

Kloort seemed to shrink into himself. ^I... I didn't mean it like that.^

"We know," said Kormèr, then added a gesture that Sylvestra did not know. His gazed lingered on Kloort, then he turned his eyes back to Sylvestra. He looked ready to pass out. "And the... other questions?" he said.

||Sreet said he'd found out about the Tseerleeltrr stone from Srrcheel. Then he bragged to me about the stone's mythology and all its secrets that he knew. He really was very scholarly, you know.||

"A great loss to Averia, I'm sure," quipped Kormèr. "And what about finding us?"

||Oh, that's simple. Did you remove one of my officers from your ship?||

Kormèr nodded. "Yeah."

||You knocked off his badge. All our badges have locators. I just followed the signal. It took me all day to track you down. I almost lost you until I saw the ship burning in the distance.||

"Ugh, the ship," Kormèr groaned. "Jeremy is going to be pissed when I tell him it's wrecked."

||I could petition to have it reported as being destroyed during official police business, and try to get your friend reimbursed for the cost,|| Sylvestra offered with a coy smile.

"Could you, really?" Kormèr said, with as much excitement as he could muster. "Sylvee, I could kiss you!"

^Shall I find another room, then?^ Kloort asked mildly.

||No, that's not necessary,|| twittered Sylvestra. Then she laughed at Kormèr's disappointed frown. ||I doubt Kormèr could get out of that chair even if he wanted to.||

^I don't mind, really,^ Kloort said.

"But nothing," Kormèr interceded gently. "If not for you, we might not even be alive. I'll ask the hotel manager, and I'm sure he'll have no problem finding you a room. Or maybe you can do that, love? You're right: I'm too tired to get up."

Kloort grinned. ^I appreciate and accept your offer,^ he said, adding a gesture. ^I've never… never left my world. I didn't even know there were other worlds.^

Sylvestra frowned, confused by Kloort's comment. *How can he not know there are other worlds? Halgarin has been part of the union for years. Not to mention that he speaks Terran English.*

"Ask of us anything you want," continued Kormèr. "We're in your debt."

^That is kind of you to say, but the credit is all Sylvestra's. I was imprisoned in the… well, the jewel that you call a stone, during a mission of mine on Halgarin. When I came out, I just did what the pretty lady asked me to do, that is all.^

||I had to try a few languages before I realized what you speak,|| Sylvestra admitted, seeing an opportunity to probe into his comment. ||You're the first Halgarin on Averia, that I'm aware of. Thank the gods you spoke Terran English.||

^Thank my dear Grandma Hally for that,^ said Kloort, adding a gesture that rose from his forehead into the air.

||Had she been offworld?|| asked Sylvestra.

^Oh, no. Not that she ever mentioned. But I doubt she would've told such a story, lest everyone think she was stoned.^

Sylvestra imaged that the translator spell had to be mistranslating again. For now, she let the matter drop. She'd look into the little man later.

"Do you remember anything from your time in the stone?" asked Kormèr.

^I wish I did. I'd give anything to know how I ended up on Averia.^

||According to Sreet,|| Sylvestra chirped, ||the Tseerleeltrr stone is like a traveling circus, or maybe more like a prison barge. When it comes into hard contact with objects, it consumes them… or carries them inside it somehow. I had intended to capture Cecil with it, but it hit Cecil's monster and consumed it instead.||

^And dumped me out at the same time? Is that what happened?^

||That's right. Sreet never mentioned that it would do that. But I'm glad it did.||

^So am I,^ said Kloort, with a smile. ^Perhaps it was too full to hold any more, or perhaps some kindly ancestor of mine wished me well from beyond. Either way, it was a fair exchange. if you ask me.^

"Did Sreet mention how it got from Halgarin to Averia?" asked Kormèr.

||No. I don't think he had any idea it had done that. But the stone is not a recent development; as you know, it is legendary here.||

"Hmm," said Kormèr, his eyes closed and his head lolling.

^I guess we'll never know,^ said Kloort. ^But I'm not one to question good fortune. I'm free of the stone, and I'm alive. And I helped you folk along the way.^

Sylvestra gave him a smile that she didn't truly feel. She appreciated his personal relief, but too much had happened that Kloort didn't know about.

"I'd love to hear more of your story," said Kormèr. "But I can no longer be held responsible for anything I say."

||Why don't we get some rest,|| she suggested, now noticing the glow of morning light through the translucent blinds. ||We can continue this after we've slept.||

"Good idea," said Kormèr. "Let's get Jeransy and Anndrew to bed first." He gestured with his fingers, raising the sleeping girls from the settee. They gradually stretched out flat, as if lying on an invisible plane in the air. He leaned forward as if to stand, then thought better of it. "Would you kindly just… delicately guide them toward the bed? I'll release the spell when they're there."

||Umm… sure,|| warbled Sylvestra. It was strange to be pushing two grown females around in mid-air; in fact, she would say that this qualified as one of the strangest things she'd ever had to do. Once they were over the bed, she wondered how to set them down on it. But they slowly dropped onto the sheets on their own. Sylvestra returned to the sitting room to let Kormèr know. She smiled wistfully when she found Kormèr fast asleep.

^He was asleep a minute after you left the room,^ said Kloort, in a low voice as he stopped beside Sylvestra.

||I'm amazed he stayed awake as long as he did.|| Sylvestra's gizzard rumbled, despite the oat bar and nutria. Her sense of duty demanded that she return to the precinct, but she decided this once to borrow a page from Kormèr's book. ||Kloort, I'm tired but also hungry. You are welcome to stay here; Kormèr wouldn't mind. Or you can join me for some food downstairs. We can get you a room at the same time.||

^I have been asleep long enough, if you get my meaning. I would be glad to join you for a bite, but I am worried that your food might not agree with me.^

||I'll help you select. I've never heard of Averian fare disagreeing with any species.||

^Well, then, lead the way.^

CHAPTER 35

KORMÈR'S eyes fluttered open. Head wedged against the inside wing of the chair, he stared through the room service tray of drinks and oat bars, fragments of memories from the night before flitting around his head. Gradually, his head cleared, and he noticed the lights were off. Dappled sunlight splashed across the marble floor, taking the shape of the window through which it shone.

Kormèr straightened and stretched, wincing at the many aches all over his body. *Always worse the day after,* he thought. *Even with The Guard's healing-pallet treatment. I wonder how long I slept.*

It felt like more than you've slept over the past few days, said Srrcheel.

Ah, good morning!

Good morning, KL.

A question popped into Kormèr's head. He tried to suppress it, immediately thinking it awkward and even rude. But with Srrcheel wired directly into his brain, the question could not be suppressed. *What do you do while I'm sleeping?* He immediately added, *I'm sorry. That was insensitive.*

Nonsense, said Srrcheel. *I know it's awkward right now, but we're both going to have to get used to this sharing of thoughts. At least for now.*

For now?

Yes. Until I find a way to unlink us.

Oh, I see. Of course.

And it's mostly quiet, by the way.

What is?

When you're asleep. It's quiet when you're between dreams. Those are stormy, so I stay away from them.

Kormèr considered that phrasing. *Stormy, huh?. Funny, I barely remember my dreams.*

Kormèr turned to his right where a rustling noise caught his attention and found Sylvestra sitting there reviewing a flimsy.

||Good morning, love,|| he sang.

Her smile energized him like no stim in the universe could. *If only I could wake up every morning to that smile once again.*

||How do you feel?|| she asked.

||I'm hungry, achy, but otherwise not too bad.|| He grabbed an oat bar. ||I don't even remember falling asleep. How long have I been out?||

||Six hours.||

||That's more than I expected,|| he sang, between bites of the oat bar. ||Ooh! These have chocolate chips!||

Sylvestra nodded enthusiastically. ||They're good, right? Must be a new recipe.||

||Did you get any rest?||

||A little. But I needed to eat more than I needed rest.|| She related the details of her last two days in Sreet's custody.

Kormèr was horrified. ||By the gods! That was too close. I'm so sorry, Sylvee. I should have come looking for you first.||

||No. You did the right thing. You put the safety of Averia over mine, and there's absolutely nothing wrong with that. It's what I would have done in your position.||

Kormèr sighed, not feeling any better for her words. He thought about the events of the past few days, wondering where he could have taken some time to look for Sylvestra.

||Hey, sweetie,|| called Sylvestra, ||snap out of it. I don't want you to pluck yourself bald over this.||

||Fine, fine.|| Kormèr waved his hand, as if pushing away his thoughts on the matter. But they were too fresh. He knew they would haunt the back of his mind for at least the rest of the day. ||Where are the others?||

||Jeransy and Anndrew are still asleep in the bedroom. I talked to Theeseeo and got Kloort his own room, on the precinct's tab.||

Kormèr nodded. ||Thanks. What do you make of Kloort?||

||I had a chance to talk with him at length this morning after you fell asleep.|| She held up a flimsy. ||I was just doing a little research, but I'd need to request confirmation from Halgarin by courier.||

||That'll take weeks,|| sang Kormèr, remembering the small robotic ships that carried messages across space at breakneck speeds. But with Halgarin located in a remote corner of the galaxy; even the high-speed couriers took time to make the round trip. ||But I can understand that… umm… the law enforcement database—||

||AvoNet.||

Kormèr snapped his fingers. ||That's it. AvoNet wouldn't have that info handy. Halgarin wouldn't share the names of its agents unless they were here on official business.||

||True. But that's not the reason. We just wouldn't keep such deep-history data cluttering AvoNet.||

Kormèr frowned ||Deep history?||

||Yes. It seems our guest is over two hundred years old.||

Kormèr leaned forward and rested his elbows on his knees. ||What? Halgarin don't live that long.||

Sylvestra tapped the flimsy and held it out to him. ||It's a list of missing persons from the year the Galactic Federation made first contact with

Halgarin.||

||Well, look at that. Kloort Shalespur.|| Kormèr met Sylvestra's eyes.

It has to be the Tseerleeltrr stone, suggested Srrcheel. *The poor guy was trapped in there, unaging, for a long time.*

Kormèr repeated this to Sylvestra.

||Oh, how horrible!||

||He doesn't know yet, I assume,|| sang Kormèr.

||I only just found out. I showed him how to browse the net, but he wouldn't find this there.||

Kormèr nodded. ||That's good, though he might figure it out if he looks up the latest news from Halgarin. We should break it to him slowly.||

||Speaking of which, do you want to take a trip down to the precinct?|| asked Sylvestra with a smirk.

||Willingly? I don't think so.||

Sylvestra stood up. ||Come on; you'll be with me. They'll be glad to see you.||

Kormèr raised an eyebrow at her in disbelief, but he stood anyway.

Sylvestra took his hand and gave him a playful kiss before tugging him toward the door.

||Wait,|| chirped Kormèr, using the screen to record a quick message for the girls. He set the message to play whenever someone used the door.

He looked at Sylvestra, who was holding the door open, and twittered, ||This way at least someone will know where I've gone when I disappear mysteriously.||

Sylvestra gave him a withering look, and Kormèr laughed as they left the room and made their way back to the skiff.

Kormèr watched Sylvestra as she guided the skiff up and looped around toward the precinct. She smiled when she caught him looking at her, and he smiled back.

||This brings back memories,|| she sang.

||It sure does,|| he sang, remembering the many mornings he'd ride with her to work in Feestoo's taxi. She could have flown, of course, and she did occasionally. But the trip had become a fun part of their routine. ||Can I stay in the skiff like I used to with the taxis? And just... you know... circle back to the diner for breakfast.||

||It's a little late for breakfast. And no, not this time.||

||Alright.|| He shrugged and grunted at a sharp pain in his neck.

||Are you alright?||

||Yeah. Just achy.||

||Did you take anything for the pain?||

||I haven't left your side since I woke up.||

A minor heal spell will take care of those pains, suggested Srrcheel.

Oh! I didn't even think of that. ||But this should help,|| he sang as he traced a small pattern and triggered the spell. He sighed as near-immediate relief washed over him.

Sylvestra's eyes widened. | |That was quite the reaction. I assume it worked.| |

Kormèr raised his arms, shrugged his shoulders and bent to touch the tips of his boots, all with no pain. | |It sure did.| |

| |Can you cast it on someone else?| |

| |Are you in pain?| | he asked quickly. | |I'm sorry, I didn't realize—| |

She waved her hand. | |I flew a lot more than usual, that's all. So it's just a case of sore muscles.| |

She gasped when Kormèr recast the spell on her. | |Wow!| | she chirped. | |That is impressive. Thank you.| |

Kormèr grinned | |So now can I just—| |

| |Will you stop that!| | she chirped, laughing.

Kormèr smiled. | |They know you're back, right?| |

| |Yes. I had gone into the precinct before getting the Tseerleeltrr stone. You had everyone running around in a frenzy, so I ran into a few officers and my captain. I updated him this morning, so he knows I'm coming in... with you.| |

| |Just me? Not the girls.| |

She touched her badge. | |I have enough here that there's no need for them to come in.| |

Kormèr sensed an implied "for now", but he let it go. There would be time to deal with that if it came up. | |Alright. So... We haven't had much of a chance to catch up.| |

| |I was just thinking the same. I'm sorry I ran out on you that first day.| |

| |Let's not start apologizing for the past, because I would be at a great disadvantage there.| |

| |I won't argue with that. In that case, how have you been these past six years?| |

Kormèr winced. | |That's fair. I'll be honest, I was a disaster when I left here. I couldn't go home, didn't want to see friends and family... or anyone. I jumped from place to place, and I don't remember a single one.| |

| |Oh, my. And with the portal, that could've been dangerous.| |

Kormèr shrugged. | |Probably not. I'm sure I was somewhat careful, even in my randomness.| | He paused, wondering how much he should tell her. But their relationship had thrived on their open communication. She was the one living being in the entire universe that he could be completely open and honest with. He couldn't break that now. | |It was the portal that eventually took me right where I needed to be. I ended up on Halgarin.| |

| |That's quite a coincidence!| |

| |Saved by the Halgarin twice,| | he sang, nodding. | |I spent a year

there, I think. I wasn't really keeping track, and they weren't part of the galactic community yet.||

||So you got over me, when you were there. Then what?||

Kormèr frowned at her. ||I did not 'get over you', love. Not there, not anywhere.||

||I'm sorry,|| she warbled. ||I was trying to make light of it, but that came out wrong.||

Kormèr watched her skirt around a pseudo-tree and easily avoid several Averians flying past. He'd been afraid to pilot a vehicle himself years ago, and felt the same now. The vehicles had alert and avoidance systems to deal with potential collisions, but he knew he'd still be a nervous wreck the whole time.

||So, after Halgarin, I stayed home for a while, until the wanderlust hit me again. And I've been hopping around the galaxy... possibly even further, since then.||

||Further? As in other galaxies?||

Kormèr shrugged, though with her eyes ahead, Sylvestra didn't see it. ||I suspect so. It's hard to tell since a planet's a planet. And if there's no one there to tell you where you are, or they're too primitive to know— Like Halgarin. I had no idea I was still in this galaxy at the time.||

||You'd never explained it like that before.||

Kormèr cringed as an Averian swooped past, directly in their flight path. ||I didn't have that kind of experience then.||

||That's... a bit scary, I have to say.||

He turned sideways in his seat so he could watch Sylvestra instead of the path ahead. ||How so?||

||How do you know you'll get back?||

He smiled. ||The portal is pretty smart. It mostly follows my commands, as long as I'm clear with them. So, if I want to return to Elmar from another galaxy, it gets me back there. It's very specific moments in time that it has trouble locking in on. Which I guess makes sense.|| He stopped as the precinct building came into view. It wasn't part of a pseudo-tree, though it looked like a tall stump of a tree. A wide platform protruded from nearly the top and branched out to two promenades. The building above the platform housed the operations and admin offices, while below were the prison cells, motor pool, and storage. It surprised Kormèr to realize that he'd now been to nearly all of those locations in this building that he disliked the most of all on Averia.

||Should I do anything, say anything when we get out?|| he asked, turning to face forward again.

She maneuvered the skiff down toward the small parking area on the platform. ||Nothing out of the ordinary... from when we used to do this, I mean. I'm landing in the plaza, so we can walk in together.||

Other than a few turned heads, no one paid much attention to Sylvestra and Kormèr as they exited the skiff and made their way toward the precinct entrance. But when the door opened and Sylvestra entered, a crowd of precinct staff awaited inside. They gave a great cheer that left Kormèr's ears ringing.

Despite his trepidation over being there, Kormèr felt very proud of Sylvestra. When he'd first come to Averia years before, Sylvestra had only recently become the Chief of Police. She'd been very young, unsure of herself and trying hard to prove herself to her subordinates, several of which resented her for her age and position. Now, almost three years later, she had become their revered leader. Kormèr couldn't be happier for her.

The cheer morphed into a quiet murmur as they noticed Kormèr standing beside Sylvestra. From left to right, Kormèr looked across the assembly of Averian faces. But no one made a move until Freesewee stepped out of the crowd. He walked up to Sylvestra and chirped, ||Welcome back, Chief.|| Then he turned to Kormèr and clasped his shoulder. ||My apologies, Citizen Lezàl.||

Kormèr returned the clasp. ||No harm done, Captain. The important thing is that your Chief is safe and Cecil Murphy is gone from Averia.|| *I hope,* he thought to himself. There was always the possibility that Cecil had simply portaled to another part of Averia to recover, a possibility that hadn't occurred to Kormèr until now.

||That is wonderful news!|| chirped Freesewee. ||Is this a good time to bring me up to date, Chief? I would greatly appreciate it.||

Sylvestra grinned. ||This is a perfect time, Captain. Let's go to my office. We'll talk over lunch.||

Freesewee turned and chirped loudly, ||Everyone, back to work!||

Sylvestra corroborated the interviews to Captain Freesewee and made certain that the records for Kormèr and the girls were clear. Kormèr filled in as many details as he could.

||I wish you hadn't flown off,|| twittered Captain Freesewee to Kormèr. ||I was prepared to let you all go, had it not been for Tseeo's zeal.||

||Like I said earlier, Captain,|| cheeped Kormèr, ||no harm done.||

Freesewee stood. ||Well, then I'll go make my final notes and close the case.||

Kormèr stood to face Freesewee. ||Captain, you're an asset to the precinct. I'm glad I got to meet you.||

Freesewee stared at Kormèr for a moment, then nodded. ||So am I. High sky, Kormèr Lezàl.||

||High sky, Captain.||

Kormèr sat as the door closed. ||Well, that went much better than I had expected.||

||Of course it did, you silly man,|| twittered Sylvestra, tossing the

remains of lunch into the recycler. | |They're police officers, not vigilantes.| |

Kormèr waved a hand dismissively. | |Yes, yes. So you've said. Then there's Tseeo...| |

| |I've been looking for an excuse to suspend him for a long time,| | chirped Sylvestra. | |He's finally given me one. And with this...| | She held up a flimsy which activated to show the interrogation room with Kormèr, Tseeo and his thug. | |I'll have him doing filing by the end of the day.| |

| |Aha! Room surveillance. I didn't even think of that.| |

| |Actually, the recording isn't ours. The cams in that room were disabled. There's no proof that it was Tseeo that disabled them, although I might persuade him to admit to it.| |

| |Then how...| | He didn't know how to finish the question. Who had made the recording? How was there even a recording?

| |I found this in the case file when I got here and reviewed it while you were in the restroom. I'm sorry you had to go through that.| |

| |As the Terrans say, it's water under the bridge.| |

| |What does that mean?| |

| |I'm not sure, but they use it to mean that what's past is past. Back to the recording; if the recorders were disabled—| | Kormèr stopped, remembering the mysterious photo of himself that The Guard had. They had infiltrated the precinct that day and not only taken his picture, but also recorded his interrogation. He glanced around, wondering if one of them was present even now.

Sylvestra must've interpreted his trailing off as a prompt. | |I'm not sure. I'll need to validate it if I'm going to use it against Tseeo, but it is otherwise a mystery. I'd say someone, somewhere, is watching out for you.| |

| |Yes, well. If that isn't a disturbing thought, I don't know what is.| |

Boop.

| |That's me,| | chirped Kormèr, glancing at his wrist comm. He relaxed. | |It's Theeeseeo letting me know that Almp went out with the girls.| |

| |You'll make a great father someday, you know,| | warbled Sylvestra.

Kormèr shifted in his seat in mock-discomfort. | |That's a... um... long way off.| |

Sylvestra chuckled. | |You've got to settle down first, of course.| |

| |Settle-what? I can hear you singing, but the words don't make sense.| |

| |Cute.| |

Kormèr sighed. | |You know what really irks me is that, on top of everything, we missed the Cheerretee celebrations, again.| | It disappointed him that the group had returned to Birshetland too late to enjoy the festivities, not that they had been in any physical condition to do so anyway. But he'd missed the event during his last visit and had hoped they'd all enjoyed it together this time around.

||How *do* you get yourself into these messes?||

||Believe me, I wish I didn't. Now I'm stuck with this magic ability, I've got Srrcheel in my head and Cecil… who-knows-where, out there.||

Sylvestra furrowed her brow quizzically. ||The girls tried to explain about Srrcheel, but I'm still not sure I understand.||

||There isn't much to tell,|| Kormèr warbled. ||My friend was so intent on transferring all his knowledge and power to me that he transferred his consciousness into me as well. Figures that the gods would decide to give me another conscience, and make him Averian, too.||

||So Srrcheel isn't exactly dead.||

||Only physically. He's been helping me understand all this magical knowledge he gave me. It's thanks to him that I was able to stand up to Cecil at all.||

||He can hear and see everything you do?||

||I'm not sure. We've been too focused on Cecil to think about those details. Anything to chime in, old spook?||

I am a consciousness, separate from you, said Srrcheel. *We can't both exist in the same brainspace, so I am not technically 'in your head'. I never even knew this was possible, KL, so I'm figuring this out as I go along too. The answer to her question is: I have to actively connect to your mind to experience what you experience.*

||In short, he can't always hear and see what I do,|| Kormèr chirped, shortly. ||He has to 'tune in', I guess you could say.||

Sylvestra stood. ||Tell him I want to talk to him.||

||Okay.|| *Sylvee wants to speak with you,* he told Srrcheel. As he too stood, Kormèr imagined he felt a change in his head, but it had to be his imagination. It wasn't as though Srrcheel were really moving around inside his skull. He nodded when Srrcheel confirmed his connection to Kormèr's senses.

Sylvestra came around the desk and gave Kormèr a kiss. ||Thank you, Srrcheel. For putting your trust in KL, and for your sacrifice, I am indebted. I'll do what I can to make sure the Council of Mayors knows of your name and deeds.||

Thank her for me. That really means a lot.

||Thank you, Sylvee, from both of us.||

||It's the least I can do.|| She leaned back on the edge of her desk. ||So, what now?||

||Now,|| repeated Kormèr, his mind drifting off to his deal with the Guard. ||Now, I have a promise to keep,|| Kormèr continued. ||I have to go after Cecil, wherever he's gone, and take the magic away from him.||

||Oh.||

Pained by her bleak expression, Kormèr continued in a rush, ||I had rationalized that the universe would outlive Cecil, that I could stay here and grow old with you without giving Cecil another thought. I was ready to do that, and if you ask me to, I will. I'll say that I can't do it.||

||I won't do that,|| warbled Sylvestra, shaking her head as she returned to her feet. ||And it's not fair of you to ask me to make that decision for you, even if you're asking with good intentions.|| She brought her hand up to caress his cheek. ||I know you too well, KL. Well, enough to see that you'd never stop thinking about Cecil.||

He held her hand to his cheek. ||You know, I am a fool.||

||I know you are honorable, loyal... and a bit of a fool, perhaps, yes.||

Kormèr turned his face towards her hand and kissed her tenderly on each finger. ||But there isn't any immediate rush. And the girls will probably be gone all afternoon.||

That's my cue to go, said Srrcheel. *I'll be somewhere... else.*

Sylvestra's smile broadened. ||Well in that case...|| She leaned in and kissed him.

Continued in *Trials of Halgarin*

Did Cecil survive his encounter with The Guard?
Is he now free to go wherever and whenever he wants with no one
to stop him?
Will Jeransy and Anndrew return home?

All this and more is revealed in the next story:
The Trouble With Thieves, Book 2:
Trials of Halgarin

Read on for an exciting sneak peek.

by Maurice X. Alvarez & Ande Li
Available from Room 808 Press!

THE door to the hotel staff's maintenance elevator slid open. Dressed in gray trousers and a fitted white dress shirt with the sleeves rolled up above his elbows, Kormèr Lezàl stepped out. ||This is my floor,|| he chirped to the handyman that had escorted him up. ||Thanks for the lift, and take care of those hatchlings; they'll be grown before you know it.||

||I will, Mister Lezàl. You have a good evening.||

With a spring in his step and a content smile adorning his face, he strolled to his room. A passing couple watched him with intent curiosity, so he gave them a warm smile. ||High sky,|| the female blurted.

||High sky to you both,|| he replied. They whispered excitedly in his wake. But he hardly noticed as he palmed his door control and entered his room.

The hotel room door clicked shut, and the lights came up to his default preset, medium bright. With a sigh he leaned back against the door. It felt like he hadn't been in his room in weeks. In all his portal travels, he had rarely found accommodations as luxurious as those provided by Cheerees, so he relished and appreciated the familiar, quiet coziness.

His eye was drawn to the dresser-top where he found a chilled bottle of Averia's finest nectar. The accompanying card identified it as a gift from Theeseeo's son, Almp. ||*Sorry I missed you for Cheerretee,*|| said the note, referring to last night's festivities celebrating the annual overlapping of Averia's moons. ||*Maybe we can catch up and land a club or two before you go.*|| Kormèr would have liked to catch up with Almp, but Cecil Murphy's descent into his darker desires had ruined what should have been a very pleasant week for Kormèr.

Kormèr closed his eyes, pictured the love of his life, Sylvestra Chrreel, and sighed at her breathtaking smiling visage. <<No,>> he said in his native Elmarian tongue. <<I've just had a wonderful day with Sylvee; I will not ruin it with thoughts of Cecil.>> And that was all he needed. Immediately, memories of his day made him smile, as only thoughts of the woman he loved could. And he truly loved her with every fiber of his being. Leaving her the first time had been the most difficult thing he had ever done, then and since. It had taken him months to recover; he'd drowned himself in a slew of forgettable ventures through the portal.

Until Halgarin, he realized, his right eyebrow rising in curiosity at the coincidence that it was once again a Halgarin that came to his aid after an adventure on Averia. He had been a depressed wreck when he'd stumbled onto Halgarin. But there, he'd met a very special woman who had reintroduced joyous color onto the darkened canvas his life had become. While it would still be several more months before he'd at least come to terms with reality—not accept it; no, no, never that—she had set him on the right road.

Kormèr stretched, grunting at the aches and pains from the battle and from other more pleasant recent activities. He decided it was time to visit Kloort to see if the fellow needed someone to talk to about his situation. Kloort had tipped the scales in the battle with Cecil, and Kormèr felt he owed him a bit more than the Theeseeo's hospitality.

But first things first; while he'd washed up at Sylvee's, he was still wearing the same clothes from the night before, and it showed in the ground-in dirt, scuffs and burns. Kormèr stripped and dumped his clothes into the recycler. He changed into some of the new clothes he'd bought that first night in Birshetland. He reveled in the crispness of new shirt fabric, the silkiness of new trousers and socks and the faint lavender smell that was a staple of new Averian clothes.

His coat was another matter. This he liked just the way it was, worn and soft, beaten and broken in by the elements of countless worlds. He pulled a fabric brush from one of its pockets and gently brushed away dirt and dust from the previous evening's scuffle. An electronic feature of the brush also zapped any microbes and bacteria that might produce disagreeable odors. Slipping the brush back into the pocket, Kormèr carefully and lovingly hung the coat in the closet.

Kormèr called Kloort's room to invite him over. While he waited, he thought about Jeremy. He'd sent Jeremy an e-mail apologizing for the destruction of the ship and deposited extra funds in his account. *If I get a chance, I'll see him personally later. He'll grumble about the paperwork he'll have to fill out once the wreckage is found, but the credits I transferred to his name are much more than the ship's worth, so hopefully he won't be too put out.*

Kloort didn't answer, and Kormèr wondered if perhaps he didn't know how to use the communication system. It would certainly make sense, after all the poor fellow had been locked in a prison-gem for over two-hundred years. Kormèr recalled that the technology he had seen on Halgarin was quite different from that of Averia, more mechanical in nature. Of course, Kormèr had reached Halgarin via the portal, so he had no idea *when* his visit was relative to Kloort's time. On top of that, Kloort was a Dootrin, one of two groups that kept to a low-tech lifestyle. So the little man would have even more issue with Averian tech than the average Halgarin.

Kormèr clicked off the comm. He'd just have to stop by Kloort's room in person.

A presence touched the back of his mind. Kormèr cringed. Three days had passed since his old friend's entire consciousness had been effectively downloaded into Kormèr's brain. And he was still not used to the feeling. He very much doubted he'd ever get used to sharing his brain with another entire being.

"Oh, you tormented soul, what is it now?" Kormèr muttered aloud.

Ah, good! proclaimed Srrcheel, his words coming as if they were Kormèr's own thoughts, except in a different voice. *You're back at the hotel.*

Kormèr was glad of the fact that Srrcheel could ensconce himself away and remain unaware of Kormèr's activities. Otherwise Kormèr would never again be able to have a private moment.

I want a couple of moments of thought with you, continued Srrcheel. *Is now a good time?*

"Yes, fine, if you promise to leave me alone afterwards," Kormèr replied. He dropped onto the bed and slipped into a trance-like state, as Srrcheel had taught him. In this state he and Srrcheel could both manifest mental avatars and have a "face-to-face" conversation.

"How are you feeling?" asked Srrcheel, making no such promise. "Are you resting?"

"Well… not really." Kormèr tried not to think about his afternoon with Sylvestra.

Srrcheel retreated a little, and Kormèr hoped it was to make himself less receptive to Kormèr's stray thoughts. "You're regaining your strength, I assume," Srrcheel added with a mixture of mirth and embarrassment.

"I guess. How can I tell without trying to run a kilometer?"

"By probing the filaments. Their brightness tells you how much power they have recovered. Considering you drained them battling Cecil, I'm surprised you were able… to… that is…"

"Yes, yes." Kormèr grunted. Life was going to be very awkward indeed, he realized. "Let me check the filaments."

Kormèr came out of the trance and focused his mind. It was as if he had slipped on augmented reality goggles; the golden gossamer strands that powered magic gradually came into view, superimposed over the physical reality of his hotel room. Kormèr was still wrapping his head around the fact that what he thought of as magic was actually some kind of technology. He wished fervently that more explanation had come with that tidbit of information. Whatever magic was, he believed it might be his only means of finding Cecil.

He dropped back into a trance. "Is it just me, or do they seem a little dim?"

He sensed worry from Srrcheel with regards to precious time being wasted. "That bad, huh?"

"They are recovered… more than I'd expected but…" Srrcheel gave the equivalent of a sigh. "It's not like it really matters at this point anyway; I've been running through the catalog of spells in here, and… things are worse now than before the battle."

"Huh? How can that be?"

"I don't know yet. But we can't go looking for Cecil with your spells scrambled like this."

"Well, that's good and bad. At least the girls will get a chance to relax and enjoy Averia until we sort things out. Gotta keep morale up."

"You're enough of a morale boost to the ladies as it is," said Srrcheel, projecting amusement. "What about the Halgarin?"

"I'll be going to chat with him as soon as we're done here. Sylvestra had a good chat with him, and she says he's one of the good guys. That's good enough for me. He apparently vanished from Halgarin around two hundred years ago."

"And Sylvestra knows this because…"

"She accessed the official records from Halgarin. Now he's got to adjust to modern life and a modern Halgarin." Kormèr sensed Srrcheel's feigned indifference. But he knew it was just a cover. Berdians didn't get out much from their stony island, and as a result, they were somewhat xenophobic. After what Srrcheel had been through, Kormèr didn't blame his lack of trust. "I know what you're thinking, but the Halgarin are good people," Kormèr defended.

"So are Terrans, in general. Yet, there is Cecil."

"And Anndrew and Jeransy, mind you." He paused. "So how long to sort things out?" Kormèr asked to change the subject.

"Well, much of the knowledge I gave you is tangled up waiting for your brain to process it, but it looks like your brain is ignoring it."

"So…"

"So, we're going to have to do something about it. I wish I could do it myself, but like I said earlier, I'm not really in control of your brain. What I can do is tease apart the pieces and feed the reconstructions to your brain to catalog, but that's a slow and tedious process. It would be better if I could teach you how to view and manipulate data in your brain. Then we can work on building your magical stamina."

"I see. It sounds like fun, but let's leave it for later, shall we?"

"Oh, fine! Here's a little incentive: there may be another way to find Cecil if portaling doesn't work."

"Sounds great, old spook, but I must work on my own morale."

Srrcheel squawked in disbelief.

"Arrivederci," said Kormèr, ignoring him and surfacing from the trance. He grabbed the bottle of nectar and left for Kloort's room.

THE door to Kloort's room stood open when Kormèr arrived, but Kloort was not in sight. Kormèr heard clipped conversation coming from the refresher, but the voice was muffled. He rapped on the doorframe. "Kloort?"

The conversation ceased immediately, but it took nearly a minute before Kloort stepped out of the refresher, his hair wet and disheveled. ^Hello, Kormèr. I was… the controls are different. Come in, please.^

Kormèr stepped in and closed the door. He discarded his "How are you adjusting?" path of conversation. "I had similar issues when I was first here," he said, instead. He offered Kloort the bottle of nectar. "This will help ease your mind for a while. It's an excellent local beverage."

^Thank you. Would you be kind enough to serve it? I don't exactly know where… anything is."

Kormèr touched the sensor on the corner of the bar top. It slid open revealing packaged food and beverages along with ice and cups. Kormèr removed two cups and opened the bottle while Kloort added, ^Averia is very different from Halgarin.^

"Yes, I've always thought so," Kormèr answered, pouring nectar for the two of them. "But that's true of most planets that haven't yet become part of the galactic community."

^Unfortunately, at this time, Halgarin is part of the galactic community.^

"Ah. Sylvestra told me you've been catching up on news from back home."

^Well, yes,^ Kloort said, taking the offered glass with a gesture of thanks. ^Two hundred years is a lot of catching up.^ He tugged on the kinky ends of his long hair, his eyes distant. ^I… it…^ He shook his head. ^Halgarin is not my planet anymore, not my home.^

Kormèr nodded. "I can understand."

Kloort stared at him intently. ^Can you?^ he spat. ^Have you lost everything, everyone?^

Kormèr wasn't surprised by Kloort's burst of anger. He had expected this kind of reaction to the news. The first time Kormèr realized he had traveled through time, it was very strange to think that at that moment, everything he knew was gone. That while Elmar was still there, it was a different place than the Elmar he knew. He had experienced panic, melancholy, homesickness, all in varying degrees. It had taken days to get used to the idea.

The difference between him and Kloort was that, with the portal, Kormèr always had a gateway back "home". With that thought came the question of whether or not he should offer Kloort passage back to his own time. He had never done such a thing before; as he had explained to Srrcheel, he didn't believe in changing the natural flow of events. Had Kloort come to Averia by way of the portal, Kormèr would have had nothing to consider; he would have made the offer already. But that was not the case. While Kloort's two-hundred year transit from Halgarin to Averia was unexplained, it was an event that was meant to occur.

Standing there, faced with Kloort's tortured expression, Kormèr didn't feel any better for his ideals.

"No," he replied, gesturing respect. "I have not."

Kloort kept his gaze locked on Kormèr for a moment longer, then he turned away and climbed into a seat. He emptied his glass in one long drink.

Kormèr frowned. "Tell me about it, friend." He sipped nectar from his glass and sat back, ready to absorb what Kloort was about to tell him.

Kloort didn't look up. ^What's to tell? Everyone I knew and loved is gone.^ He shook his head slowly and muttered, ^So much death.^

Death? "I'm afraid I haven't kept up with Halgarin history. What exactly happened?"

Kloort looked shocked. ^You don't know?^ he asked, accusingly, as if Kormèr should have been aware. ^But you were—^ He peered at Kormèr. ^The pandemic... it killed more than half of the population!^

"By the gods! Kloort, I'm sorry." Kormèr was too shocked to remember to make any gestures. "I had no idea."

Kloort's head lolled. ^All indications are that it began in the Stone Forest. The population there was decimated, and not just the Dootrin, but the Zantrlin too.^

"Was it from first contact?"

^No. That didn't occur until eighty years ago. The pandemic happened over two hundred years ago, sometime soon after I... left.^

Kormèr thought that was an odd coincidence. At the same time, he felt some relief that he had not yet offered Kloort a trip back in time. While Kloort was now displaced, he was at least alive. Alive he could move on; dead limited the possibilities.

Kloort continued, ^The population is only now getting back to the numbers we'd had before. But the Stone Forest... it hasn't recovered.^ He shook his head. ^If I'd only been there.^

"Not to be insensitive," began Kormèr, making a gesture of respect, "but you do realize you probably would have died too."

^Of course I know that. But what is life? Life is surrounding yourself with people and places that make you happy. I no longer have either.^

"Now *that* is something I *do* know about. I visit new places and meet new people all the time. Some make me happy and some don't, but the point is that while things look bleak now, there are many places and many people in this great galaxy. And you've got to be ready to realize when they are making you feel happiness once again."

^How long am I supposed to wait? A month? A year? A decade?^ Kloort shook his head. ^I can't imagine that I'll ever be happy knowing what befell my world.^

Kormèr said nothing. He knew that there was nothing he could say to diminish Kloort's pain at that moment. Ironically, only time would heal that wound. Kormèr felt his best option was to change the topic.

"Would you mind my asking how you ended up in the stone?"

Kloort snorted. ^It all seems so petty in hindsight. Petty disagreements, petty fanaticism...^ Kloort peered at Kormèr again. Kormèr was getting the feeling that Kloort wanted to say something but just wasn't comfortable enough to say it.

"What is it, friend? You can ask me anything."

^You said you had been to Halgarin; did you visit the Stone Forest?^

Kormèr nodded. "I was there, briefly, mostly on the Dootrin side of the border. But I did learn a little about Zantrlin culture from a Zantrlin I met."

^Does the name Jarrek sound familiar?^

Kormèr's thoughts turned inward as he thought about the people he'd met, but the name wasn't familiar. "I'm afraid not. Is that who imprisoned you?"

^Huh. You could say that. So you didn't meet any members of the Prophets?^

"No, I would remember that. I never heard of any such group."

Kloort swept his hand through the air as if wiping it clean. ^I'm confused. You appear so young, but to not have heard of the Prophets, you must be from before my time.^

"Ah!" Kormèr cringed. He hadn't wanted to get into this with the Halgarin, but he had no other way of explaining it. "My portal allows travel across space *and* time. I must have been in Halgarin's past, relative to your time, that is."

Kloort's eyes went wide in their deep sockets. ^That's... very interesting,^ he said slowly, as if his mind was elsewhere. Kormèr had a pretty good idea just where it might be. Kloort focused on Kormèr again. ^I'm sorry, you asked if I knew how I got into the stone, and I went off on a tangent. The short answer is yes; I trapped myself.^

Kormèr raised a curious eyebrow. "Wow! That's not at all what I'd expected."

^It wasn't what I'd expected either, believe me. But it was necessary... or at least I thought it was. Now it seems it was all for nothing.^

"Can you talk about it or is it 'classified'?" Kormèr made quotes with his fingers when he said the last.

Kloort harrumphed. ^It's two hundred year old information; I doubt anyone cares if I talk about it.^ He sighed. ^I mentioned that I was on a mission.^ Kormèr nodded. ^I was an agent assigned to Zantrlin to infiltrate a radical fundamentalist group called The Prophets. If you know our culture, then you know that the Dootrin and Zantrlin only differ in their interpretation of the written laws of the Ancients.^ He made a sign of reverence over his head, as demanded of all Forest dwellers when speaking of their Ancients.

Kormèr nodded again. "Yes. That's the way it was explained to me." Kormèr knew the Ancients to be the first Halgarin to rebel from the strict authority of the provinces and settle the Stone Forest.

Kloort continued, ^We've occasionally had trouble along the borders of our territories, idealists getting into scuffles, preachers getting 'forcibly' turned back, and such. But never anything serious.^ Kloort paused, holding out his cup as Kormèr refilled it with nectar.

Kormèr said, "I remember an almost brotherly camaraderie between the Forest factions."

^That changed, around three years ago… well, three years for me.^ Kloort's voice trailed to a whisper at the last. Then he shook his head and continued. ^Anyway, this group calling themselves 'The Prophets' suddenly sprang up and began a propaganda campaign against the Dootrin way. They were led by a charismatic Zantrlin named Jarrek. At first they seemed like any other peaceful, non-threatening group, if perhaps more organized.^

Kloort paused to drink. ^Two years ago, we began finding some of our Dootrin kin murdered. No connection was made at first between the murders and the demonstrators; no one could conceive of the idea of that level of hostility between our tribes. But when it was discovered that these were shift-kills, there was only one answer.^

"I'm sorry," interrupted Kormèr. "What are shift-kills? I never heard of that when I was there."

^With good reason. We can shape shift into almost any shape, as you know. But have you ever wondered why we do not assume the shape of other Halgarin?^

"I asked once, and received quite a reprimand. But I was simply told it was forbidden."

Kloort snorted. ^Whoever it was no doubt thought you daft and let you off easy. It is the worst imaginable crime; to even speak of it is a high crime.^

Kormèr was shocked. "Are you saying that if you assume the shape of another Halgarin, you kill them?"

^Precisely. We do not merely 'assume a shape', as you say, we become the thing that we are mimicking. It is possible to introduce differences so as to not become exactly the person you are mimicking, but you can never know if there isn't someone with exactly those differences.^

"Of course."

^This is what we discovered, and we demanded justice. But without concrete proof, the Zantrlin leaders refused to take action against Jarrek and his Prophets.

^The matter became very political very quickly. The Dootrin had no choice but to send an agent to infiltrate The Prophets.^ Kloort took another drink and settled back into his chair. Kormèr was glad to see that, whether from the nectar or the distraction of talking, Kloort was gradually becoming his old self. When Kloort felt comfortable, he continued.

^It took me three months to work my way in. I reported on their habits, methods and ties to many of the Zantrlin leaders, which hardly proved surprising. Once a month I relayed all I had learned to a contact that would wait for me on the border between our lands.^

"Did you ever find evidence that they were connected to the shift-kills?"

Kloort seemed to struggle with his next words. Kormèr took a sip of his nectar as he waited out the awkward moment. Finally Kloort said, ^No.^

Kormèr waited for more, but when nothing more came, he prompted, "So you met your contact each month…"

Kloort shivered, sipped his nectar and continued. ^Yes. One evening, when I was scheduled to meet my contact, a Zantrlin border patrol caught me. I was bound, gagged and practically dragged back to a cell under Prophet Headquarters.

^Jarrek met me there and told me that he had discovered my forged documents a few days earlier and had me followed. He mocked the Dootrin leaders saying there was nothing that could stop the Prophets, as they were everywhere and protected by the Ancients. I must've made some kind of gesture of disbelief; I don't really remember. Maybe he just wanted to gloat more. Whatever the case may be, he told me he had proof. Jarrek said the Ancients had graced him by delivering the Rootlar Jewel to him.^

Kormèr felt caught up now. ||The Tseerleeltrr Stone,|| Kormèr twittered.

Kloort nodded. ^Exactly.^

^But your people know it as the Rootlar Jewel?^ asked Kormèr, switching to Halgarin to pronounce the name properly.

^It's the stuff of legends, though until that day, I'd never actually seen it. I didn't even believe it was real.^

Kormèr was fascinated that two planets that were so disconnected from each other could both have legends about the same enigmatic gem. But Kloort wouldn't have any answers about that, so Kormèr filed the thought away for now.

^Jarrek said its secrets had been revealed to him,^ Kloort continued, ^that it was an artifact of the Ancients. Of course, I didn't believe he had *the* jewel. But if he did have something that was potentially dangerous to my people, I had to find out. So I talked him into taking me to see it. It was hours before dawn, so the lab was empty when we entered it. But more than half of the lab was alive with machine activity. I'd never seen so many machines in one place, and all of them seemed to be there for one purpose, to work on the jewel. I was… well, I was truly astounded when I saw that jewel. As Jarrek gloated, I watched the screens, absorbing whatever information I could. I knew that if I managed to escape, I'd have an amazing report to deliver.

^I had my eyes off Jarrek, and when I looked at him, he was loading an injector with a vial of clear liquid. By the Ancients! It was so long ago, and yet my memory of that moment is so clear in my mind.^

Kormèr finished his nectar and set his cup down. "Go on," he prompted as Kloort was lost in his memories.

^Ah, sorry. Jarrek rushed me and injected me before I could react.^ He shook his head and pounded a fist on the arm of his chair. ^I should have been prepared, but I was so caught up with all that machinery… He told me he had injected me with a variation on a centuries-old plague that had nearly decimated Halgarin. He had modified the plague to attack the Dootrin, and I would be the carrier.

^That changed everything, of course. I knew I couldn't go back home now. The best I could do was take down Jarrek, destroy the jewel and deal The Prophets as much of a blow as possible.

^Any other Halgarin bound the way I was would not have been able to shift. But I'd trained for that and easily shifted free. Jarrek was caught by surprise, and I hit him hard and fast. But he was no stranger to fighting; he recovered quickly. We struggled and the sound must've drawn attention; several others came into the room. Seeing I was outnumbered, I decided I'd take myself out of the equation. I grabbed the jewel and stabbed myself with it. That's the last thing I remember before waking up on Averia.

^In the end, my fate didn't matter. Less than a year later, there was no one left in the Stone Forest to purge.^ Kloort drained his glass again.

"Untrue," said Kormèr. "It was a valiant effort on your part despite the outcome. You might have succeeded, and with the information you had, you believed you would. The only unfortunate thing is that no one knew of your sacrifice."

Kloort waved that away. ^That never matters.^

"Hmm," said Kormèr, pensively. "Have you exhibited any symptoms yet?"

^Symptoms? Of wha— By the Ancients! I've been so caught up… No, I have no symptoms at all. By now I should be showing some signs of illness, if Jarrek's information was accurate.^

Kormèr nodded with a grin. "You must've received the standard Averian inoculation by now."

^Yes. But this is a Halgarin plague.^

"But Halgarin is now part of the galactic community, so I'm sure they've incorporated the vaccine into the standard regimen that everyone gets here."

Kloort was staring off slightly to Kormèr's left, his yellowish eyes wide. His lips moved slightly, but if he was speaking, Kormèr couldn't hear it. Suddenly he looked Kormèr right in the eyes and said, ^I need to go back. I want you to take me back to Halgarin, to my time.^

AFTERWORD

Thank you for reading *The Trouble With Thieves: Return to Averia*. We hope you enjoyed the novel.

Want to know more about us and keep up with our latest writing projects or extracurricular activities?

* Maurice on Twitter: twitter.com/mauricexalvarez
* Maurice on Amazon: amazon.com/author/maurice-x-alvarez
* Maurice on BookBub: bookbub.com/profile/maurice-x-alvarez
* Maurice on GoodReads:
goodreads.com/author/show/4709660.Maurice_Alvarez

* Ande on Twitter: twitter.com/andeliauthor
* Ande on Amazon: amazon.com/author/andeli

* Find us on Facebook: facebook.com/Room808Press/

And if you have a moment, please review *The Trouble With Thieves: Return to Averia* on Amazon and/or Goodreads. It helps us and it helps other scifi-fantasy fans by telling them why you enjoyed reading it.

ABOUT THE AUTHORS

Maurice X. Alvarez is the author of *The Trouble With Thieves* series (available through Amazon.com). Born and raised in Queens, N.Y., he now lives with his wife and co-author, Ande Li, their two children and pets in New Jersey. When he's not writing, Maurice enjoys cycling, science fiction in various media formats, and plotting the next exploits of Kormèr Lezàl and the multiverse.

Ande spent her childhood in Hong Kong, China, and the various boroughs of NYC, and has settled in the NJ suburbs with her husband and co-conspirator Maurice X. Alvarez, their children, their free-range budgie and exquisitely patient mix-breed dog.

OTHER BOOKS FROM THE AUTHORS

by Maurice X. Alvarez
co-written with Ande Li

The Trouble With Thieves Series
Book 1: Return to Averia
Book 2: Trials of Halgarin
Book 3: Elmar of Tranquility

The Trouble With Love : A Kormèr Lezàl Story

by Ande Li

The Xonen Archives
Book One: The Healer's Girl
Book Two: The Children of Xon
Book Three: The Second Life of Cyrus Ex
Book Four: The Trickster's Game

The Gideon Files
Book One: Red Lotus
Book Two: White Jade
Book Three: Gold Peony

FROM THE DELETE KEY BUFFER
(AKA: THE CUTTING ROOM FLOOR)

Movies on DVD and Blu-Ray often have a section dedicated to bloopers, outtakes and/or deleted scenes. This section is the latter. It's not at all relevant to the overall story, so you won't have missed out on anything if you skip it. But if you enjoy watching deleted scenes, you might enjoy the three "clips" that follow, complete with a brief explanation of what they're about and why they were cut.

[ORIGINAL COLD OPEN]

[The earliest version of this story opened with Kormèr and Jeransy on the bug planet running frantically from the swarm of locusts. Much of what today forms the prologue and first two chapters was told in quirky flashbacks and exposition, all of which obviously needed to go. The scene is now only told from Anndrew's point of view when the portal first appears in the classroom. Note that the portal was originally referred to as "plane".]

"Hurry!" cried Jeransy, her lengthy brown hair whipping wildly in her wake.

Running beside her, Kormèr Lezàl restrained himself from tossing her into the maelstrom behind them, if only to get her to stop repeating 'Hurry'. She was too cute to waste, he decided as he fumbled through the deep pockets of his long black overcoat.

"I'm hurrying, *okay*." He was less than his usual charming self, but at that moment, Jeransy could not have cared less for his charm. She glimpsed back over her shoulder, and her pace quickened that much more.

A huge swarm engulfed the fertile green land behind them, leaving in its wake a barren savanna. Jeransy thought she could almost make out the large locusts that made up the roiling, buzzing cloud. Those in front stopped to devour then rejoined the swarm from behind making it look like a hurricane laid on its side, rolling ever closer toward them.

"Got it!" shouted Kormèr, his fingers locking around the object of his search. From his pocket he extracted a clear crystal cube, one of its six sides colored black. Without stopping, he pressed the black face with his thumb and tossed the cube several meters ahead. The airborne cube glowed softly, expanding into a sky-blue rectangular plane. An eight-buttoned tab protruded from the top. The plane hovered several centimeters off the ground directly in Jeransy and Kormèr's path.

Kormèr looked back over his shoulder. *It's gonna be a close one,* he thought. With two meters to spare, he leaped at the plane. He bounced against the surface and tumbled forward as the plane drifted away, propelled by the impact. Jeransy tripped over him and ended up sprawled on the ground beside him.

"Bbmp!" cursed Kormèr in his own language. "Not now! Don't do this now." He stood and scrambled to catch the plane as Jeransy glanced nervously at the advancing swarm. She turned back wondering what stupid primal instinct kept making her look. The swarm wasn't going to go away, after all. Neither was her anxiety. She stood and watched as Kormèr stopped the plane from drifting away.

"Kormèr," said Jeransy, impatiently. Through gritted teeth, "Hurry."

"I know." Kormèr shook a loose strand of brown hair off his face with a quick twist of his head. *If she says it one more time, just one more time... But she's so damn cute.* "I know."

Kormèr ran a hand over the surface of the plane. It was solid! He prodded it again, with no success. He took a deep breath, trying to control his anger and randomly punched buttons on the tab. *There's no time for this now!* His first frustrated instinct was to smash the damn thing into the ground a few times. Regardless of whether or not doing that would help, it sure would make him feel better. At least for the brief instant before he was eaten alive by the locust cloud. He punched buttons and prodded the surface in rapid succession. Button. Solid. Button. Solid.

"Grr!" He slammed his fist on the tab. His hand passed through the surface!

"Go," he told her immediately. Then added, "Hurry!"

The cloud was almost on top of them as Kormèr let Jeransy through first, then twisted the tab as he lunged through after her. The plane collapsed behind them, vanishing, just as the swarm passed and continued on its destructive way.

[KORMÈR'S PRANK GETAWAY]

[Kormèr's original rescue of Anndrew from the Birshetland prison had taken the form of a prank. During editing, it ended up being silly, confusing and frankly out of place considering the urgency of the moment. So it was cut and altered.]

The scene begins when additional guards are sent to keep watch over Anndrew's cell in anticipation of a rescue attempt by Kormèr. Unbeknownst to anyone, one of the guards is Kormèr in disguise. He's just let Anndrew know that it is him.]

Suddenly Kormèr-guard pointed at the third guard and chirped in surprise. Anndrew followed his gaze, and her mind reeled. The guard posted at the end of the corridor now looked exactly like Kormèr!

Short-brown squawked and drew a weapon, aiming it at the Kormèr-doppelganger as he . Startled to see a guard charging toward him with weapon drawn, Kormèr looked around quickly, back up at the guard, then bolted through the double doors with short-brown in pursuit.

Anndrew watched as Kormèr-guard whistled a lazy tune while swiping a badge on the cell door's reader.

"Kormèr?" said Anndrew, uncertainly.

"Yes." He did not look up, merely finished unlocking the door.

"Where'd you get the badge?"

"One of the other guards gave it to me while he wasn't looking." The door swung open. "Come on. That little trick will last only as long as Kormèr keeps running."

"You're confusing me again."

"Fine, as long as the guard that looks like Kormèr keeps running."

She punched his downy shoulder. "That doesn't help."

| |Move aside,| | ordered Freesewee. | |What's all the commotion?| | Several guards stood at the door to a closet. Many other officers were gathered around, attracted by the running around that had taken place moments before.

One of the guards spoke up. | |We've trapped Kormèr Lezàl in the closet, sir.| |

| |What?| | The news was too incredible to believe.

| |We caught him trying to sneak up on us while we were guarding the Terran female's cell. We gave chase and he locked himself in here.| |

| |Well, let's open it,| | twittered Freesewee, somewhat disheartened. Now it would be more difficult to release Lezàl.

Weapons drawn and ready for a charge, the guards blew the lock on the door and flung it open. Huddled in a corner was a trembling officer. The other officers gaped.

| |What's this?| | asked Freesewee. He extended a hand to the young officer, and warbled, | |Tell me what happened, son.| |

| |They all came after me,| | cried the trembling youth, | |like they were crazy!| |

Freesewee smiled, as he realized immediately what must've happened.

| |Sir,| | began one of the officers, | |the female prisoner! This was a distraction. Lezàl must be aiding her escape at this moment!| |

Freesewee bit the inside of his cheek to hold back his laughter and waved his men back. | |Don't bother checking,| | he managed at last. | |She's gone already, no doubt.| |

| |Sir,| | chirped an officer who had come running from the prison block, | |Anndrew Lee has escaped.| |

The officer beside Freesewee made a strangled noise. ||They're probably making for the impounded ship. Should we intercept, sir?||

||Yes, good idea.|| It was a futile effort, he knew. Freesewee felt something like admiration for Lezàl and understood why his colleagues disliked the Elmarian so. Even if his men did manage to detain Lezàl again, Freesewee would arrange for his release, somehow. As much as Freesewee would've preferred to have met the man in person, there was little time for that now. Perhaps when Cecil Murphy was gone for good, and when Sylvestra was safe. *Good luck, Lezàl.*

||I'm so sorry, sir,|| said the officer that had been in the closet. He continued to bumble on in apology until Freesewee clasped his shoulder.

||It's okay,|| Freesewee told him. ||Lezàl is a tricky guy. It won't be held against you; he outwitted us all.||

||Thank you, sir.||

Freesewee shook his head and walked slowly toward the impound platform exit. He was sure there was no need to rush, not that he doubted the capabilities of his team. Lezàl just seemed to be particularly crafty. Freesewee decided he'd have to do some catching up on his knowledge of Elmarians and their culture. If they were all like this, perhaps some protocol changes were in order.